"Pardon me," Billy said, "but let me get this straight. You bought the painting from somebody, some sort of criminal, who thought he had a fake, but it was actually authentic and the only one who can attest to that fact is this fella Raymond Pearson, who's probably dead."

"In a nutshell, Billy, that's correct."

Zoe saw the color rising in Billy's face. He leaned forward, his two hands clenched into a large fist. "What kind of money are we talking here, anyway, if you don't mind me asking?" He turned to Zoe. "You're the expert, ma'am. What's the value of an original Van Gogh painting in today's market?"

It took an effort for her to summon the energy to answer. "One from the sunflower series could be worth seventy to a hundred million dollars."

Billy looked back and forth between Simon and Mayte. "I may be a hick cowboy, folks, but I'd say that's enough to justify looking a mite deeper than the words of a dead man. But since we're asking questions, there's something else bothering me. Van Gogh's a pretty famous guy, right? So, why is it nobody's ever heard about this deal with Pearson until now?"

R. J. KAISER

HOODWINKED

MIRA

ISBN 1-55166-820-3

HOODWINKED

Visit us at www.mirabooks.com

Printed in U.S.A.

For
Jaws on her fiftieth birthday

Thursday
July 20th

The old mambo led Poppy along the dusty road. Marie Vincente de la Croix had promised the girl that she'd be pregnant by spring, and Marie was determined to use all her power to see that it happened—not only for the girl's sake, but also for her own. Her reputation was riding on it.

"There is nothing to fear, *ma petite*," Marie said, firmly holding Poppy's hand. "Erzulie is the spirit who loves us all. *Toutes les femmes.* She will give to you babies. You will see. *Beaucoup d'enfants.*"

Poppy stared at her with round, desperate eyes. She'd told Marie how badly she wanted a child, but admitted she was uncertain about using white magic. Once the doctors had given up, though, voodoo was her only hope. For Marie, Poppy's misfortune was a golden opportunity—she badly needed something that would make people of the island take notice. Since coming from Haiti, she hadn't gotten much of a following other than a few old women who wanted their fortunes told. It was not easy being a voodoo priestess on an island where the Anglican Church still reigned supreme.

So Poppy was a godsend—not that Marie wished ill on her. But if she were to help someone, it was just as well that it be a person with status—a girl like Poppy who was the wife of an aide to the president, Mr. Jerome Hurst. But there was much work to be done. Marie knew better than anyone that the spirits weren't easily coaxed.

For two Sunday nights in a row Marie had done the rituals with Poppy, contacting the spirits of Baron and Erzulie to gain favor. Marie had made the cornmeal veve on the floor; she'd used the candles and oils; she'd poured the libations and made the blood sacrifice. "Good fortune is coming," she'd told Poppy. "It is certain." But after much reflection, Marie had decided to take Poppy on a ritual visit to the sea for cleansing. "You must draw from the strength of Yemalla," she told the girl, "the mother of love and ancient wisdom. Her secrets are in the sea."

Poppy had confessed to a fear of the waters and Marie concluded that was the problem, which meant that only an appeal to the spirit world could dislodge the impediment. The place Marie selected was a quiet cove on the leeward side of the island. Until the whites had built the polo club with its tennis courts and polo field, the area had been deserted. But the beach remained undeveloped and little used. Marie felt the calm waters of the cove would be the perfect spot for the immersion.

Dusk fell as they left the road and crossed the last few yards to the beach. Poppy, clad as Marie had instructed in a loose skirt and overblouse with nothing underneath, remained silent as they struck out across the sand. When they came to the water's edge, Marie stopped and faced her charge, firmly holding both her hands.

"We walk into the sea together," Marie told her. "*Tous les deux.* Slowly we will go until the water rises to our chin."

Poppy seemed anxious. "Is it necessary to go so far, Bon Mambo Marie?"

"Yes, little one. You must give up your body to Yemalla's strength. She is both powerful and loving."

Poppy was clearly frightened, but she did as she was told, wading slowly into the sea at Marie's side. She didn't make a sound until the gentle waves began lapping against her private parts, making her gasp.

"Relax, *ma petite,*" Marie said reassuringly. "Allow the spirit to take you."

They continued until at last the warm waters covered their breasts and neared their chins. Marie took both of the girl's hands again. "Give yourself to Yemalla," she said.

There were deep furrows on Poppy's brow and Marie told her to close her eyes and to think of her husband. The girl did as she was told, appearing to relax after a couple of minutes. Then Marie began a soft rhythmic chant.

"Ko lo jee mo!" she sang. "Ko lo jee mo!" Over and over.

They had been thus for several minutes, Marie chanting, the two communing with the spirits, when a sudden loud shout came from the shore. Marie, whose back was to the sea, saw a white man emerge from the undergrowth at the edge of the beach nearest the country club and begin running along the water's edge.

Poppy turned and, seeing the man, was as startled as Marie. He was a hardy-looking fellow, clad in a white suit and tie. Most significantly, he ran with an air of desperation. There were more shouts. Then three black men, two bare-chested, emerged from the undergrowth at the same spot. They waved machetes and clubs as they pursued the white man.

Poppy gasped and Marie, knowing a bad omen when she saw one, took the girl's face and made her look at her. "Yemalla is vanquishing the evil spirits," she said firmly. "This is a sign. Close your eyes and leave it in her hands."

Poppy did as she was told. Marie, chanting louder than before, saw a horse and rider come out of the vegetation. The horseman, a white man, wore a helmet and pink polo shirt and carried a mallet, which rested on his shoulder like a lance. At his urging, the horse, a powerful beast with black and white markings on his head, broke into a gallop. The horseman very quickly passed the black men and closed rapidly on the white man.

They were just about opposite the place where Marie and Poppy had entered the water when the rider swung his mallet off his shoulder, striking the runner's legs and knocking him to the ground. Then, quickly pulling up his mount, the horseman turned and dashed back toward his victim. Just as the man regained his feet, the rider struck again. This time the man lay in the sand not thirty yards from Marie and Poppy.

As the horse spun and reared, the horseman struck his victim twice more. Marie, horrified, could see blood spilling onto the man's white suit. By now the men on foot had arrived.

Her chanting just a whisper now, Marie urged Poppy to sink still lower into the water. On shore the horseman shouted orders and the men picked up the limp body of their victim and began carrying it back along the beach. As the man on horseback took off his helmet and watched the procession, he wiped his sweaty forehead on his sleeve. Only then did Marie recognize Charles Van Biers, son of the owner of the big plantation house on the south end of the island. She had never spoken to him, but she'd seen him in town. He had a reputation among the natives as an arrogant, harsh young man. From what Marie had just seen he was cruel, a killer, as well.

Darkness was rapidly falling, but when Marie saw Van Biers rise in his saddle and peer up and down the beach, she realized he was looking for witnesses. Would he gaze out to sea? Deciding to take no chance, she drew her face close to Poppy and whispered to her.

"Now it is time to give your body to the sea spirits, *ma petite*," she said. "Take a deep breath and we will go under the water together. Stay until your lungs can take no more. Do you understand?"

Poppy nodded and they both took deep breaths, lowering themselves beneath the surface. Marie's old lungs were not what they once had been, but she fought the impulse to rise for air as long as possible. At last she and Poppy came to the surface, gasping.

Marie wiped her eyes and peered toward the beach. Charles Van Biers had gone fifty yards up the shore, galloping into the gloom. Marie took Poppy's face in her hands and wouldn't let her turn around.

"What is it, Bon Mambo Marie? What's happened?"

"Nothing, little dove. Yemalla has vanquished the evil spirits. You will have good fortune now."

"Is it true?"

Marie Vincente de la Croix nodded and smiled, but she had not been truthful. This was an omen of the worst possible sort. She feared for Poppy. And herself.

She had witnessed the whole thing from the mountaintop while standing on the deck outside her glass-enclosed office. Charles had said it would happen in the barn and stables, so Mayte Van Biers had trained the telescope on the structure eight hundred feet below. She had seen Raymond Pearson walk across the carefully manicured lawn from the clubhouse and through the gate. She had seen Charles exercising his horse on the field as he'd knocked the ball from one end to the other. Then Pearson had gone inside the barn.

Mayte had not expected to see him again—at least not alive—but within moments he'd charged out the back door and into the undergrowth with Charles's minions in hot pursuit. Something had gone wrong. Charles must have reached the same conclusion because he'd taken off after the whole bunch.

Once her stepson had caught up with Pearson on the beach, Mayte had seen him pummel the man with his polo mallet. She was certain that Charles had enjoyed every minute of it. Though he was twenty-seven and old enough to know better, he had a cruel streak as wide as her native Rhode Island. He was also arrogant, which made him vulnerable and prone to mistakes.

Charles most certainly was oblivious to the two women

who'd watched his every move, so she'd have to tell him there had been witnesses. Everything they had worked for was now in jeopardy. Mayte flinched. As if they didn't have enough problems already without this.

She had known from the start that by joining forces with Charles she was playing with fire. But who had ever built a fortune from nothing without taking risks? The trick, of course, was playing it smart. Careful calculation separated those who succeeded from those who failed. Continuing to stand on the deck, watching the twinkling lights of a cruise ship in the distance, Mayte heard the roar of the engine of Charles's Porsche as it raced up the mountainside. He was coming to report to her. And to gloat.

Mayte went inside. Turning on her desk lamp, she caught a glimpse of herself in the dark window glass—the huge diamond stud earrings, the cheekbones and eyes. "My exotic beauty," as Simon called her. To her classmates at Harvard she'd been the Ebony Empress, the Pawtucket Panther. At least her husband recognized her genius, and had the good sense to turn the day-to-day operation of Victoria International over to her. "Smartest move I ever made," he said.

Simon Van Biers was deceptively clever, Mayte had decided. He didn't have her quick mind, her education, her analytical ability or her administrative skills, but he did have native intelligence and an uncanny ability to sell. Simon was the most disarming, pleasant, likable fellow you could ever hope to meet. Of course, he was also a con. Right down to his toenails.

Looking through the glass wall separating her office from his, she could see his prize Van Gogh—a huge vase of drooping sunflowers—in the illuminated case on the far wall. That painted chunk of canvas had proven to be both a bane and a blessing. It had given Simon the seed money to establish Victoria International and put them on the road to fabulous wealth—his sunflower seed, as he laughingly called it. Though that first loan had long since been paid off, the painting still figured prominently in their operation; giving rise to scheming, extortion and murder.

Since they couldn't allow everything they'd worked for to go down the drain, they'd had little choice but to deal with Pearson. The appraiser obviously hadn't counted on their willingness to do whatever it took to defend themselves, or he wouldn't have come to St. Margaret in the first place.

"I knew I was taking a risk bribing the bastard," Simon had said to her recently, "but that seemed the lesser of evils at the time."

If Simon had made a mistake, it wasn't in doing business with Pearson, it was putting Charles in charge of silencing him. "The more deeply the boy's involved, the more loyal he will be," her husband had argued. Of course, the same could be said of her. And that could explain why Simon had so readily taken her into his confidence right from the beginning—the family that commits crimes together stays together. But he hadn't anticipated his wife and son joining forces against him.

The problem was that in Charles, Mayte could very well have put her money on the wrong horse, especially after what she had just witnessed. She heard her stepson in the outer office. A moment later Charles walked in without knocking.

"The deed is done," he said, an arrogant grin spreading across his face.

"It went well?"

"Our problem is solved and that's all that matters. Pearson won't be shaking us down."

Charles was still in his polo attire—boots and jodhpurs, polo shirt. He was broad-shouldered, his chest and arms muscular—a sturdy chap, as the locals would say when being charitable. He wore his black hair slicked back, but it was slightly mussed at the moment, his posthomicidal toilette evidently having been cursory.

Almost exactly ten years her junior, and utterly without regard for the fact that she was married to his father, Charles grinned suggestively. He always behaved as though it was inevitable that one of them would eventually proposition the other—though to this point he'd done nothing overt.

"Did you have enough confidence in me to put some champagne on ice, Mother dear?" he asked, sliding into the leather visitors' chair across the desk from her.

"I watched the whole thing from the deck," she said, arching an eyebrow. "You don't deserve champagne, Charles."

"A minor glitch, which I resolved with dispatch," he said, his confidence unbroken.

"In front of an audience."

"You hardly count."

"I'm referring to the two women in the sea, the two who waded ashore after you went galloping off from the scene of the crime."

He frowned. "What women?"

"The ones who undoubtedly saw everything. I was half a mile away, and it was hard to tell how they reacted, but I can't imagine they missed a thing."

Charles sat upright. "What women, Mayte?"

"I have no idea who they were. I have a powerful telescope, but it was dusk and they were difficult to see. They were female, that's about as specific as I can be."

"Are you shitting me?"

Mayte indulged him with a smile. "Hardly. It's no joking matter."

"Well, what did they do? Where did they go?" The concern in his voice was palpable.

"As I say, it was very dark. They went to the road. Beyond that, I don't know."

"Shit," he said, rubbing his jaw.

"Assuming the police don't come for you first, I'd try to track those two down, if I were you, Charles."

He thought for a long moment. "That won't be easy without arousing suspicion. And you're not much help. You can't even tell me what they looked like."

"You're lucky I saw them at all," she snapped.

Charles stood abruptly and walked over to the window. He

seemed to be peering down at the beach, though given the darkness it was unlikely he could make out anything. "Two women, huh?"

"Yes."

"Natives, I take it."

"Most likely."

He slammed his fist into his palm. "Damn it to hell."

"Your men were witnesses, too, Charles. They won't be sparing you if their own necks go on the line."

"Don't worry about that. None of my men would cross me. Earl's completely trustworthy and he controls the other two with an iron fist."

"Yes, I know, their allegiance is like that of a son to his father."

He turned and stared at her, his eyes narrowing. "Is that supposed to be a joke?"

She shrugged. "Never assume you can trust anyone, Charles. That's the best advice you'll ever get."

"Does that include you?"

"A great deal is riding on what we're doing, you know. I'll handle my end. You'd better handle yours, and that means finding out who those women are."

"Damn," he said. "I had plans for the evening."

"Think about tomorrow, not tonight."

He nodded. "So, what are you doing? Going home to watch the old man snore in his chair?"

"With all due respect, it's none of your business, Charles."

He gave her a dour look, then strode from the room. Mayte heard the outer door slam and several seconds later the engine of his Porsche roared to life. She stared down at the open file on her desk. She'd intended to work for an hour or two before going home, but had no heart for it now. She closed the file and turned off her desk light. Then she went to the door that led to the deck, intending to lock it. Instead she stepped out for a breath of air.

It was much darker now. There was only a faint glow on the horizon off to the west. She could barely make out the beach. She wondered what this would do to her plans, fully aware it would only be a day or two before she knew whether Charles was with her, or if she'd have to contend with Simon on her own.

Stepping back inside, she locked the door, then fetched her purse from the desk. As she turned the key to lock the drawers, she glanced up at Simon's sunflowers. Ah, the storied history of that painting—so much of it murky, even in Simon's mind. He'd never told her where he'd gotten the original, except to say, "from some poor fool who's best left in the dark."

Raymond Pearson's part of the story, though, her husband had shared in detail. How else was he to explain why some art dealer was at their door demanding twenty-five percent of Victoria International?

"If I had it to do over again, I'd have done the same thing," Simon told her and Charles when they'd had their strategy meeting. "Believe me, the other dangers we face are far graver. Pearson's bill of sale could be the difference between glory and oblivion."

"You aren't going to tell us what to look out for?" Charles had asked.

"Let me put it this way, the problem has been solved," Simon replied. "And I see nothing to worry about once Pearson has been silenced. We definitely can't have him running around flapping his lips, though."

Mayte stared at the painting, which was illuminated day and night. Around the case, the lights of the electronic security system that made it virtually impregnable glowed dimly. Even so, nothing was left to chance. Three guards remained on the premises at all times and the security system was wired directly to the police station in town. Not even the Mosad could snatch Simon's sunflowers and make it off the island without getting caught.

She was about to leave when the phone rang. She picked up the receiver.

"Yes?"

"Can you meet me tonight?" he asked, the familiar rumble of his voice striking a chord deep within her.

"No," she said after a moment's hesitation. "I'm afraid I can't."

"You're sure?"

"Yes, Jerome, I'm sure."

"I know I'm calling at the last moment. I only now got freed up and I thought…"

"I wish I could."

"Saturday, then, as we planned?" he asked.

"Yes, Saturday." Mayte dropped the receiver back in the cradle.

She stood at her desk, pondering the call for a moment. She had a strong sense of the power of her sexuality and that gave her pleasure. She'd never understood why some of her sisters were offended by the notion that sex should be a factor in a woman's climb to the top. After all, wasn't it the result that counted? Taking satisfaction in the clarity of her understanding, Mayte Van Biers picked up her purse and left the office.

Cheyenne, Wyoming

Billy Blue preferred married women. He rarely had anything to do with the single types—not that he meant the husbands any harm. Every woman he was with seduced him as much as he seduced her. In fact he had a rule—he always made the woman ask first.

In his thirty-four years of life—fifteen of which he'd spent on the rodeo circuit—Billy had learned that being a cowboy was a big reason for his success. Women loved a man on horseback whether or not they knew the difference between a steer and a bull, a reata and a grass rope. Then, too, maybe he was lucky. He seemed to have a natural, God-given talent with the ladies. Charming Billy. Sometimes it seemed they just fell right into his lap.

There was a certain danger associated with cavorting with

the married variety of female, of course. Most gals had to see him on the sly. And Billy had to be careful not to get himself killed by an irate husband. The danger didn't bother him, though; danger was part of his professional life. He lived with it, cheek and jowl, every day.

Ironically, what he liked best about a woman who already had a man was that she always had someone else to go home to. Which meant he had no responsibility after he kissed her goodbye.

The trick, he'd learned, was avoiding the gals whose intent was to make their old man jealous. Better a woman whose husband was decent—a good provider but deficient in the sack. All a gal like that needed was a little excitement and a good time. Enter Billy Blue.

But Billy had his frustrations. Like now, as he stood at the bar of the Salty Dog in Frontier Park, sippin' beer and listening to Luther Meeks regale the boys about the competition the next day. Ike, Tommy, Buzz and Cotton listened to the old dude going on and on, nodding in turn to each thing he said, even though Billy knew damned well that, to the man, they were off somewhere else in thought, wishin' Luther would get drunk and pass out.

Billy, who'd mostly been staring at the foam in his beer, glanced up at Luther, who happened just then to look right at him. "We need to do better, boys," he said, "or I'm going to be out of business and you all are going to be looking for a new daddy. Not a one of you's won a competition since Arizona. Anybody noticed that? Damn if I can afford to feed you when you don't seem to give a hang about bringing in the bacon." Luther jabbed his finger Billy's direction. "Do I look like a goddamn welfare office to you, son?"

The way Luther, his face florid from booze and anger, kept starin' at him, Billy knew he was expectin' a reply. "Hell no, Luther," he said after a moment. "You look about as much like a welfare office as you do a pregnant rattlesnake."

The laughter did not please Luther Meeks. Billy was sort of sorry he'd poked fun at him. It was, after all, Luther's wife,

Connie, who Billy'd been screwing the past three months. And it was Connie who was waitin' for him now over by the amphitheater, in a trailer that stars like Randy Travis, Garth Brooks or Tim McGraw would be using as a dressing room once the concerts started. Connie had a friend who was a big muckety-muck with the Cheyenne Frontier Days, an old pal willing to make a trailer available for a few hours on a Friday evening.

"Can you believe it, Billy," she'd said when she told him the news. "You and me getting it on in Randy Travis's dressing room?"

He hadn't told her that the thought of Randy Travis didn't do a whole lot for him, though Trisha Yearwood might be a different story. He was glad, though, she'd found a place they could meet, considering Cheyenne was packed to the gills with tourists.

Normally Billy's relationships were brief, lasting about as long as they'd be in town—a week or two at most, which made this fling with Connie unique. The downside to cheating with your boss's wife was obvious, but there were advantages, not the least of which was that Connie was readily available. By all rights he should have ended it, though. They both knew time was working against them. But as Connie said, "It's hard to turn your back on something that feels so good."

She'd said that two weeks earlier in a motel out in California, lying on his bare chest with those big marshmallowy breasts of hers melting into him like sweet butter on a hot biscuit. Connie had a point. But it had Billy wondering if maybe he was getting soft in his old age.

Luther, meanwhile, had slowed down enough to pause for a couple of draws on his beer. Then he took a stogie out of his shirt pocket, resting his hand on his ample stomach as he savored the smoke ahead. Billy figured he wouldn't have to stick around more than another ten or fifteen minutes before he'd be free to hotfoot it over to the trailer.

Luther lit his cigar, holding the smoke in his lungs a few seconds before exhaling through fat, pursed lips. "Just to show you boys my heart's in the right place," he said, "I'm going to treat you all to a nice steak dinner."

"Hey, all right," a couple of them said.

"Let's get us a table."

Billy's gut sank right down to his knees. Shit. How was he going to duck a steak dinner without looking suspicious? He saw no alternative but to level—only partially, of course. Getting laid was about the only worthwhile excuse a guy could have.

Luther, despite having downed three or four beers, immediately sensed Billy's hesitation. "You don't look too thrilled, Billy," he said, rolling his cigar between his fingers.

Luther Meeks had plenty of blind spots when it came to his own wife, but the man was nobody's fool. He was a sharp businessman. He'd set up a rodeo-cowboy cooperative that averaged out the risks of rodeo life by sharing expenses and profits. "Economy of scale" was the way Luther had explained it. A lot of the savings went into Luther's pocket, of course, but Billy and the others considered it a form of insurance that benefited them almost as much as Luther.

"A steak sounds pretty sweet," Billy told him, "but not as sweet as a piece of ass."

"You sayin' you got a date? That's fast work, son. We've only been in town a day and a half."

"She's an old friend."

Luther Meeks nodded with understanding, then ran his hand over his thin brush of blondish-gray hair. "Well, I won't keep you from your pleasure. Just remember to save a little strength for tomorrow. Too much heifer the night before makes the steer you gotta wrestle the next day all the stronger, you know."

"I'll pace myself." Giving Luther a nod and his friends a wave, he headed for the door. So far as he knew, none of the guys was aware he and Connie were getting it on, though there had to be some suspicion. Billy had a reputation.

Once out the door, he set his straw hat lower on his forehead, took a deep breath of the evening air, hitched up his pants and plunged into the throng of tourists. It was only about a five-minute walk to the trailers. He was eager to see Connie, having thought about that soft womanly scent of hers all afternoon. First, though, he had to get Luther out of his mind.

Billy's theory was he'd saved more marriages than he'd ruined, if only because an affair gave a couple a break from each other, and the wife something to feel guilty about. He believed the marriages that fell apart were doomed long before he happened on the scene. Maybe it was a rationalization, but it was one he could live with—provided some old boy didn't take exception to his benevolence and blow his fool head off.

But to live like Billy Blue, it helped to be wise. He was no braggart, but he did share his convictions with his closest friends. Of the guys on the circuit he had probably been closest to Cy Krebs, an old bulldogger who Billy had known since he was a fuzzy-cheeked teenager. Cy was retired now, but they'd had many a conversation about life. Never having known his old man, Billy regarded Cy as a kind of father figure. Their last conversation, in a saloon up in Boise, the two had gotten pretty deep into their cups and waxed beer profound. Cy had asked if Billy ever had regrets screwing other men's wives.

"Yeah, once," Billy had replied. "Down in Arizona two years ago. I spent three days and nights with this absolutely incredible woman. She was eight or ten years older than me, but the most beautiful thing I'd ever seen. And no draggletail, either. Classy lady, smart, drove a Mercedes. I'd run out of gas on the interstate north of Tucson and she gave me a lift. We talked friendly like, just chitchat on our way to a service station. Nothing special. Mainly I was amazed she'd risked stopping for a stranger. Well, to make a long story short, she pulls into the first motel we come to and asks me if I'd like to get a room and take a bath with her."

"No way. Just like that?"

"Yep, right from talk of riding horses in the desert heat to strippin' buck-ass naked and getting it on."

"She was married, of course."

"Yep."

"So, what's to regret?"

He shook his head sadly. "Her goddamn husband was an invalid, Cy. Had a stroke or something a couple of years earlier. I didn't find out until we said goodbye."

"Billy, I'd say you was doing the lady a favor. She didn't have no alternative if she wanted sex. If it wasn't you, it was going to be somebody."

"That's not the point. Her husband didn't do anything wrong, Cy. When a guy's wife screws around behind his back, normally he's got nobody to blame but himself—either for marrying her in the first place or not satisfying her. But this guy was innocent. And the worst part was she loved him. Cried when she told me about him."

"Billy, what's your point? That since he wasn't to blame, it had to be your fault?"

Cy had hit the nail on the head. Billy didn't know the woman's husband, of course, had never even seen him at a distance, but he had dreams about him just the same. And he still got shivers of regret thinking about the poor bastard.

The sun having set, the lights of the carnival off to the north were starting to take hold. The huge Ferris wheel reminded Billy of his youth, the times his grandparents had taken him to any carnival that came within a three-hour drive of Elko, Nevada. The thought made him think of the way his grandmother, Sophie Blue Bear, thrilled at the sights and sounds of a carnival. She especially loved fortune-tellers—palm readers, tarot-card readers, to Sophie it didn't matter which kind they were.

When Billy was little, his grandmother would pay to have his fortune told, as well. It was almost always the same—that he'd grow up to be rich and famous.

By the time he was twelve, Billy pretty well had the con figured out. There were basically four fortunes—girls and young women would find love; boys and young men would find wealth and fame; old people would find health or religion and everybody in between would travel. All a person had to do to figure this out, Billy realized, was listen to people talk about their dreams.

From age six on mostly what he cared about was getting a cow horse of his own. Each visit to a fortune-teller prompted the same question—"When will I get my horse?" The answer was invariably vague and usually ended with a reference to fame and fortune. On a recent visit to see his grandmother, Billy had reminisced with her about their trips to fortune-tellers.

"You *are* famous, Billy," she'd said.

"More like infamous, Granny."

She'd frowned and pursed her lips. "What do you mean by that?"

"Nothing, really." Certain things a fella didn't discuss with his grandmother.

"Well, you finally did get your horse."

"One out of three's not so bad, I guess."

"You'd be rich, too, if I hadn't given that painting to your father so cheap."

Sophie was referring to the time she'd given away a fortune to save his hide. It wasn't something he liked to think about much, because when he did, he got upset. "No reason for you to feel bad," his grandmother had said early on. "I'm the one who did it, not you."

"But only because of me."

They'd scarcely spoken of the incident since. And he sure as hell didn't need to think about it now. Brushing it from his mind, Billy shouldered his way through the crowd, the carnival music in one ear, the giddy laughter of some teenage girls in the other. A threesome had been following him for some time—teenyboppers with big hair, short skirts and a stick of cotton candy in their fists. Local kids out ogling the cowboys. Jailbait.

Billy and most of the guys stayed as far clear of the tender stuff as possible. Nor did he have an interest even after the girls reached the age of consent. Billy was a good-time Joe with enough conquests under his belt to blacken a map with the X's marking the spot, but he never messed with kids, drunks or head cases. They were too vulnerable to look out for themselves.

Getting a little tired of playing Pied Piper, Billy decided that if the girls didn't go on their merry way soon, he'd have to give them the what-for. A glance back and a frown had no effect and so, coming to the spot where he'd have to leave the mall for the trailers, Billy stopped abruptly. He turned on his heel, bringing them up short.

"You ladies lost?" he said.

"No," one of them managed. "Why?"

"If I wanted to be followed around, I'd have brought my dog."

"We aren't following you," the most mature-looking and brazen of the three said. "We were checking out your caboose."

The comment incited a cascade of giggles. Billy gave them one of his more stern looks, which only made them laugh.

"Aren't you going to offer us any candy?" the ringleader ventured. She was a bottle blonde and bosomy for her age.

Billy wagged his finger at her. "You're developing a bad habit, young lady. Not every fella you encounter is going to be as gentlemanly as me."

"Who wants a gentleman when you can have a cowboy?" she replied.

The other two covered their mouths and squeaked with laughter. The blonde cocked her hip and licked her cotton candy provocatively. Billy spotted a couple of city cops strolling on the other side of the mall. He whistled, catching their attention and signaling for them to come over.

"Hey, why're you doing that?" the leader of the trio said.

Billy didn't answer, waiting until the cops arrived.

"Officers," he said, "these young ladies are lost. Being a stranger in these parts, I can't help them. Would you mind showing them the way home?" Then, tapping the brim of his hat, he said, "Evenin', ladies," and went on his way.

"Jerk!" the little tart called after him.

He chuckled to himself. "Jerk" he could live with.

By the time he found the trailer, Billy had forgotten all about the girls and was focused on Connie. It had been the better part of two weeks since they'd gotten it on and he was more than ready. Sometimes it was a real disadvantage to be around a gal, and not be able to do anything about it. When they were on the road Connie traveled with Luther, of course, but when they'd stop to eat, they'd go into a coffee shop and she'd give him one of those I'm-thinking-about-fucking-you looks. Once, when she sat across from him in a Denny's, she slipped off her shoe and put her foot in his crotch, all the while talking to her husband. Connie Meeks was a real test of his mettle.

The window shades were drawn. No light coming from inside the trailer. Billy wondered if maybe something had come up and she couldn't make it. But then he heard faint music. Most likely there'd be a couple candles burning and Connie'd have on some skimpy little negligee. The woman had a hell of a naughty streak.

Billy rapped on the door. After a moment he heard the lock turn and the door open a crack. But no sign of her.

"Connie?"

There was no reply, so he pushed the door open a bit wider. It was dark as pitch inside, not even a flicker of candlelight. He could hear Dolly Parton's sweet tones, but not Connie's. What game was she playing?

"Connie?"

He got a whiff of the cool, perfumed air coming from inside the trailer, but no response. Billy felt a stirring in his loins. Connie Meeks wasn't what you'd call a classy woman, but she did have imagination. She'd obviously prepared some little surprise.

As he stepped across the threshold, the scent of Connie's perfume was even stronger. But there was still no other sign of her.

"You here, Connie? What are you up to?"

He stood square in the doorway now, the ambient light il-

luminating the interior of the trailer enough that he began to
pick up images—the outlines of furniture, walls, then a faint,
gauzy figure in the corner. As his eyes adjusted, he realized it
was Connie, sitting in a straight chair, buck naked. She was
bound and gagged, her eyes round with horror. Billy took a
step toward her. It hit him an instant too late that it couldn't
have been Connie who'd unlatched the door.

They jumped him simultaneously from both sides. Hands
on him, blows to the head, knocking him to the floor as more
booted feet came rushing into the trailer behind him, the door
slamming shut and a light coming on.

Billy, squinting up at the circle of faces hovering over him,
picked out the florid face of Luther Meeks. Only then did he
realize what was happening.

"Looks like your old friend is my wife," Luther said.
"Isn't that a coincidence, though?"

Luther kicked him in the stomach, putting all two hundred
and fifty pounds of his girth into the blow. Billy doubled up
in agony. Wincing with pain, he glanced at the half-dozen
faces above him, recognizing none but Luther's. Local toughs,
probably. At least they weren't his friends.

"Fucking scumbag," Luther seethed, kicking him again.

Billy felt a rib crack and the kicks and blows started coming
in profusion. The agony didn't stop until he lost consciousness. But there was a final image that clicked in his brain
before everything went black. Through the forest of jean-clad
legs and muddy boots, he had a glimpse of Connie sobbing.
Billy, choking on his own blood, realized then somebody had
made a terrible, terrible mistake. There was no question about
it. It was him.

Sunday
July 23rd

Cheyenne, Wyoming

He'd regained consciousness sometime during the night, relieved to find himself in a hospital bed instead of a ditch. The doctor, a little bald man with lots of chins and no neck, told Billy he'd damned near died, which hardly came as a surprise. His injuries were the equivalent of what he might expect over the course of ten years of bull riding—broken shoulder, six broken ribs, concussion and broken nose, ruptured spleen, bruised kidney and a shattered vertebra. The last, while not life-threatening, probably meant the end of his rodeo career. As the doctor put it, "You'll be lucky if you can sit on a horse long enough to ride in a parade."

At the end of their conversation the doctor told him they'd notified the police, and a detective would be coming over to discuss the circumstances of his injuries. That, of course, posed a moral dilemma. Billy had practically been beaten to death, but some folks would say he had nobody to blame but himself. Normally he'd get up, dust himself off and move on. Luther had gotten his revenge and Billy his comeuppance.

That was the way the game was played. End of story. But in this instance, he'd probably lost his means of livelihood—the worst thing that could happen other than getting killed.

After the doctor left, Billy did something he hardly ever did—he thought about the future. He'd known, of course, that his rodeo days would end eventually, but it never occurred to him that it would come this soon. Mostly he'd push such thoughts to the back of his mind and concentrate on his next competition—or his next lay. Tomorrow or the day after was about as far ahead as he liked to plan. But now he was suddenly faced with the vast void of a thousand tomorrows.

It was difficult to picture life without his buddies, without the hustle, the competition, the celebrity and the endless string of towns, arenas and crowds. Rodeo could be a bit like the circus in that regard—a whole culture, a way of life. *His* way of life. But now, because of his injuries, all of that had gotten turned on its head, so much so that nothing would be the same anymore. Nothing.

Billy hadn't had the courage to ask the doctor if his sex life was over. But he did think of that invalid down in Arizona whose wife he'd screwed. Maybe it would be like that for him. Maybe he'd only be half a man from here on out. Maybe this was a case of what goes around comes around.

At about ten o'clock Billy had a visitor. It was Connie with a little bouquet of flowers in hand and two black eyes. She was all puffed up, looking like a prizefighter the day after a bout.

"Jesus," Billy said. "He did it to you, too?"

Connie, wearing a western shirt and jeans that showed off her tidy figure and ample breasts, moved slowly to the side of the bed. "Yeah," she said in a hoarse whisper.

Billy shook his head, though he couldn't turn it very far because of the pain. He felt dreadful, thinking of the trouble he'd caused. "God, I'm sorry," he said, closing his eyes. "Guess we never should have done it."

Connie sighed. "Probably not."

They looked at each other, seeing the consequences of their

lust. Billy couldn't call it love—he didn't know much about that. The only time he'd felt what he thought was love was when he was seventeen. Her name was Shelly and she, too, had been party to what until now had been the defining tragedy of his life. Apart from that experience, sex was the beginning and the end of his knowledge of women.

"I'm surprised Luther let you come," Billy said to her.

"He told me to. He's downstairs waiting for me, as a matter of fact. Paid for the flowers." She put them on the bedstand.

Now he understood what the visit was about. Luther wanted to know if he was going to honor the code.

"I know you're hurt bad," Connie said. "Everybody feels real sorry about that. Nobody intended permanent injuries."

"It wasn't a picnic for you either."

She looked away. "No, and he's expecting me to make up for it."

"What do you mean?"

"Get your cooperation."

"By saying whatever's necessary?"

"I've got to think of my future, Billy," she said, tearing up. "Before I met Luther, I waited tables and hated every minute of it. I'm going to be forty before long and I don't want to go back to that. I may not have an ideal life, but I like the traveling and…well…Luther's been good to me… better than I've been to him, I suppose. But he's willing to give me another chance, if…"

He studied her. "Are you sure Luther's the solution to your problems?"

She blinked back her tears. "You plan on taking me with you, Billy?"

He lowered his eyes. She knew his interest in her pretty much began and ended with getting laid. The fact that he liked her, thought she was a nice person, hardly mattered.

"That's what I thought."

"It's got nothing to do with you, Connie. You know me."

"Yeah, I do," she said stoically. "And I feel sorry for you."

"I'll heal."

"That's not what I'm talking about. I'm talking about your fear."

"Fear? Me?"

"Oh, I know there's not a man nor beast alive that scares you, Billy. But sure as I'm standing here, there was a time when things were different. Some girl hurt you a long time ago, and you ain't never been the same."

"You're jumping to conclusions, Connie."

"I don't think so. You never said nothing, but I've sensed it all along. And I never asked you about it, because we're just friends—friends that have sex...or used to. But I like you, Billy, and it makes me sad to see you running from love."

"Jesus, Connie."

"Am I wrong?"

Billy closed his eyes. He didn't need this. Connie might mean well, but this didn't help. It was bad enough that he felt guilty and his body was all broken up. He didn't need reminders of the past on top of everything else. "All due respect, but this isn't a subject I'm eager to discuss."

She lowered her head. "I'm sorry. Maybe I'm feeling as guilty about you as Luther."

"Thanks, Connie, but save your feelings for your husband."

She shifted uneasily. "Do you know what you're going to do?"

"I guess maybe go back to Elko and see how I heal up."

It was obvious they had nothing left to discuss except what he was going to do about Luther. Billy decided there was no point in dragging it out.

"Why don't we get down to brass tacks," he said. "What's Luther offering for me to forget this?"

"He'll forgive me and take care of any of your medical expenses that the insurance won't cover."

"That's it?"

"A thousand dollars cash. Buzz would like your horse, if

you want to sell. One or another of the boys will take every-thing else. Luther's willing to front the cash.''

"A thousand's not much of a retirement,'' he said.

"I convinced him to throw that in.''

"And all I have to do is tell the cops I didn't get a good look at the boys who jumped me.''

"Yes.''

"This what you want, Connie?''

She drew a long, slow breath. "I think it's best.''

"All right,'' he said. "It's a deal.''

Connie looked relieved. Then she sighed. "I'm afraid I've got some bad news. There was a call from Elko last night. Your grandmother's in the hospital, Billy. She's very sick. Probably cancer.''

His heart stuttered. "Christ. When did this happen?''

"She's been ill for a long time, they said. But it's critical now. I didn't talk to her, but they said she wanted to see you because she had something important to discuss.''

Billy was numb. It was so unexpected. Worse than what had happened to him. "Did they say how long she had?''

"Her doctor said a few weeks, maybe a month. He said she'd probably wait for you. People do, when there's some-thing that's important to them.''

Billy could feel the blood pounding in his head. A vivid image of Sophie Blue Bear came to mind. Usually he visual-ized her in her rocker in the cramped little front room of her house, amid her knickknacks. She'd sat in that chair, holding him on her lap when he was small, humming to him over the squeaking wooden joints. And when he had visited her as an adult, she'd sit in it, contemplating him as he sat opposite her in his grandfather's leather chair, proud of him as could be, though Billy never saw cause for it.

"I guess I'd better get myself out of this bed,'' he said.

"You won't be going anywhere for a while,'' Connie said. "Look at you, Billy. You'd be lucky if you could stand up. Though I suppose you're a fella who does things his own way.''

Billy smiled weakly. "And look where it's got me."

"You deserve better, I swear you do."

"Well, you can tell Luther you accomplished your mission."

Connie stepped a little closer and, taking a check from her shirt pocket, put it on his chest. Then she touched his hand, letting her fingers rest on it for several moments. "I'm sorry, Billy. About everything."

Everything, he realized, covered a whole lot. There was his grandmother, his back, his career, his life. He didn't feel like Billy Blue, rodeo champion and cowboy hero to the ladies anymore. He wasn't even sure who Billy Blue was, assuming he'd ever known. For a fella to know himself took deep thought, and he hadn't done much of that over the years. Seemed like something he'd have to learn to do, though. He'd definitely have the time. Boy, would he ever.

Monday
July 24th

Poppy waited until Basil was settled in his chair and involved in his football match on TV before telling him she was stepping out for a breath of air.

"Righto," he said absently.

"Can I bring you anything before I go, then?"

"No, I'm fine, love," he said, dismissing her offer with a wave.

Poppy slipped away, taking Basil's bicycle from the front hall with her into the street. Dusk was approaching, just as it had been that evening the previous week when she had gone with the Bon Mambo Marie Vincente de la Croix for her immersion. The parallel made her shiver uncomfortably.

The days since had been unsettling. First, Marie had told her that she was not to have sexual relations for at least five days. That had been difficult to justify because, as a matter of course, she and Basil had sex nearly every day.

Second, the island had been in an uproar over the disap-

pearance of the American tourist, Mr. Pearson. He'd vanished
and with the passing of each day the level of tension in the
president's office had increased. For three days Basil had spoken of nothing else.

Mr. Pearson had been last seen at the country club and there
was speculation he may have gone for a swim and drowned.
In accordance with Bon Mambo Marie's instructions, Poppy
had said nothing about having been to the beach near the country club the evening Pearson had disappeared. But that hadn't
kept her from thinking about the man in the white suit—the
one who'd been pursued. After the immersion, as she and Bon
Mambo Marie had walked along the road together, Poppy had
asked about the incident.

"It is nothing to think about, *ma petite*," Marie had said in
her heavy French accent. "The spirits are always sending
signs."

"But what does it mean if a group of men chase a man
alone?" she'd asked.

"It is a sign of purification," Marie had replied.

"And what did they do while I was not looking?"

"They left. That is all you need to know." Then they'd
stopped in the road and the Bon Mambo Marie Vincente de
la Croix had looked deep into Poppy's eyes and said, "The
spirits must not be questioned, little one. Accept this and keep
your silence. Only then will you have your baby."

Poppy had accepted Marie's instruction. But that was before
she'd learned of the disappearance of Mr. Pearson. From what
Basil had said at the dinner table, there was a possibility the
incident she'd witnessed was somehow connected with the
missing tourist. Of course, she hadn't really gotten a good look
at the white man who'd emerged from the bushes, so there
was no way to know if he was the same man whose picture
had been in the newspaper. But with the mystery deepening
and tensions on the island growing, Poppy felt she needed to
speak with Bon Mambo Marie.

Pulling up her skirts, she mounted Basil's bicycle and began pedaling along the quiet street where she and her husband had lived since their marriage. She passed the seamless row of whitewashed houses, greeting neighbors lounging on their stoops or sitting on wooden chairs by their doors. Since their house was near the edge of the town, it wasn't long before Poppy was in the countryside.

There was very little vehicular traffic on the island and not much chance of being struck. Still, she turned on the small headlamp mounted on the handlebars. With darkness rapidly falling, she was soon able to see the pale spot of light from the headlamp swinging back and forth on the roadway. She pedaled steadily, but not with great speed, her heartbeat rising moderately from the exertion.

Poppy had been to Bon Mambo Marie's cottage twice before, but never after dark. She'd passed one entire afternoon with the mambo doing fertility rituals. Poppy was not an educated woman but she had a natural skepticism about voodoo. Yet, the Bon Mambo Marie Vincente de la Croix was her last hope, if Poppy were to have the baby she so badly wanted. "It can only work," Marie had told her, "if you surrender to the spirits."

There was also the law and Poppy worried that in obeying the spirits they might be withholding information that could bear on the disappearance of Mr. Pearson. Basil would be unhappy with her if he learned that his own wife was somehow involved. But Poppy wanted a baby so badly. Dare she risk dashing her last hope by making a fuss over something she didn't understand?

Poppy had ridden a mile from town when she heard the sound of a vehicle behind her. The car was coming fast—she could tell by the roar of the engine. Chancing a glance over her shoulder, Poppy saw the flash of headlights. Filled with a sudden fear, she moved close to the edge of the roadway, the bicycle wobbling beneath her.

Just then the car whooshed past, close enough that the draft nearly pushed her over. The wind did catch her skirts, causing her to lose concentration. Swerving, she caught her wheel in the rut at the edge of the road and was pitched off the bike, into the tall grass. Dazed but unhurt, Poppy stared up the road in the direction the car had gone, its taillights disappearing around a curve.

She got to her feet then, brushing herself off. She had scarcely seen the car but there weren't any others like it on the island. It was the Porsche that belonged to the arrogant, mean-spirited son of the island's banker, Simon Van Biers, the wealthy man who Basil said had brought prosperity to St. Margaret.

"Perhaps he will make us richer," Poppy told her husband when they'd discussed the matter, "but the son is trouble." She'd heard stories of his boorish attitude toward the girls of the island, his cavalier treatment and sexual demands. He spent money on them like it was water, but he expected favors in return. At least one girl had left the island for an abortion.

Climbing back onto the bicycle, Poppy continued on. She passed the St. Margaret Polo Club, the playground of the Van Biers family and their friends. Beyond the club was mostly land that had once been part of the old Queen's Head Plantation, which Simon Van Biers, the current owner, had re-named Biloxi Plantation. The only other dwelling at this end of the island was the little house occupied by the Bon Mambo Marie, which, back in the nineteenth century, had belonged to the mulatto mistress of the original founder of the Queen's Head Plantation, Sir Horace Bastable.

The cottage, which had been in shambles when Marie moved in, was down a little-used track, a quarter of a mile off the main road. Between the gravel surface of the road and the darkness, it was difficult to ride, so she got off the bike and pushed it along in the still, lush air.

Nearing Marie's little cottage, Poppy heard the sound of

drums. This was not a familiar sound on St. Margaret where, except perhaps among the teenagers, the music tended to be subdued, the Caribbean rhythms more sedate than on some of the other islands. She was aware that drumming was an important part of voodoo ritual, but that Bon Mambo Marie, having too few adherents for a congregation, was unable to hold a full voodoo ceremony. So where had she found the drummers? Poppy wondered. Or was it a recording?

When she neared the cottage, she could see light coming through the trees. Drawing closer still, she realized that the light was coming from torches behind the cottage where Marie had built a small temple—her hounfour, as she called it. The structure consisted of a corrugated metal roof supported by several poles, the principal one at the center—what Marie called the *poteau-mitan,* where the spirits communicated with the people. It was on the ground at the base of the pole where Bon Mambo Marie had created the veve with cornmeal in the ceremony for Poppy. The mambo had implored the help of the spirits Erzulie and Baron. Marie had promised to commune with the spirits nightly on Poppy's behalf.

Poppy could hardly criticize Marie for a lack of sincerity because the mambo had asked for nothing in advance for her services, saying there would be no payment required until Poppy's belly was large with child. This made it easier as Basil could hardly complain about the expense. The doctors had made no such deal.

Poppy was only a hundred feet or so from Marie's cottage. She could see the torches burning brightly in a ring around the hounfour. Then she spotted Marie. The aged mambo was in the middle of the temple, dancing to the rhythm of the drums, her skirts swaying with the swing of her hips. Poppy wondered if the ritual could be for her.

Leaning Basil's bike against a tree, Poppy crept closer, winding her way through the bushes and palms. When she came to the edge of the clearing, she stopped to watch. The mambo danced to the beat of the drums, recorded music coming from an old boom box that sat in the dust by the *poteau-mitan*. Poppy could see that Marie was sweating profusely, her ebony eyebrows shimmering in the torchlight, her brightly colored blouse soaked with perspiration. Marie chanted as she danced, her eyes rolling back in her head.

The rhythm of the drums quickened, as did the pace of the mambo's dance. Soon, Marie seemed to have worked herself into a frenzy. Stopping suddenly, she dropped to her knees, raised her shining face to the heavens and cried out, "Erzulie!"

As if on cue, the drums stopped and there was a sudden silence. Marie sagged forward until her head touched the dusty ground. She lay like that, the only movement of her body the heave of her shoulders as she breathed.

Then something very strange happened. The Bon Mambo Marie Vincente de la Croix sat up and turned her head directly toward the place where Poppy stood hidden in the shadows. Marie rose to her feet.

"Poppy?" she called. "Poppy, are you there?"

Poppy was dumbfounded. She didn't know what to say. Marie, her forehead coated with dust, took a step in Poppy's direction, her eyes round as though she'd seen a ghost.

"Poppy, I feel your presence," she called. "Come out of the darkness."

Not knowing what else to do, Poppy stepped out into the clearing and the light of the torches. Marie, who'd moved out from under the roof of the hounfour, lifted her face to the starry sky. "Thank you, Erzulie," she cried. Then to Poppy she said, "*Venez, ma petite.* Come."

Poppy moved tentatively toward the wizened old woman whose eyes shone like flames. When she was finally before her, Marie took her by the shoulders and beamed.

"I was doing a ceremony for you, little one. My prayers are answered. The spirit has brought you to me."

"I came to speak with you, Bon Mambo Marie," Poppy said. "I am frightened."

"Yes, Erzulie wanted you to come for comfort. This is a very good sign, Poppy. Erzulie told me that tonight is the night you will take your husband's seed."

Poppy's mouth dropped open. "I will become pregnant tonight?"

"This is what the spirit told me."

Poppy wanted to ask if she was certain, but she didn't want to show skepticism. She wasn't even sure now that she wanted to ask about the men on the beach and the police investigation into the disappearance of Mr. Pearson.

Seeing Poppy's uncertainty, Marie said, "You haven't lain with your husband, have you, Poppy?"

"Oh, no," she assured her. "I did as you said."

"Then he will be ready for you and he will give you your baby."

Poppy stopped to calculate. She was still a week from the best time of the month. "Really tonight?"

"Erzulie told me. I worried how to let you know and look what happened, the spirit brought you here to me. You must go to your husband, little one. Now."

Poppy was prepared to hurry home, but her conscience also tugged at her. "First, I must ask you, Bon Mambo Marie, have you heard about the man who disappeared?"

"Yes."

"That day on the beach..."

Marie reached up and touched Poppy's lips with her finger. "Everything happens for a reason, *ma petite*. We must not question the wisdom of the spirits. Erzulie has made your body ready to take the seed."

"But shouldn't we say something?"

Marie's eyes narrowed. "There is nothing to say, Poppy. Not until the loa tell us to speak. You must leave this to the spirits. Birth and death must never be confused. Now, if you want your baby, go to your husband."

Poppy hesitated before she turned for the road. As she entered the darkness of the vegetation, Marie called after her.

"Give your husband much pleasure, little one. And find pleasure yourself. Hurry home!"

Poppy found Basil's bicycle and trotted along the track with it. She pictured Marie's shining eyes, still feeling energized by her certainty. If the mambo was to be believed, she would awaken in the morning with a child in her womb.

Wednesday
August 2nd

Elko, Nevada

The last fifty miles on the bus were sheer torture. Billy stood in the aisle most of the way from Salt Lake, sitting whenever his legs got so fatigued that back pain seemed preferable. The doctor had told him not to make the trip, but Billy knew he had to see Granny before she died, no matter what. He'd spoken on the phone with Ed Carlsen a couple of times. Ed was his grandmother's friend and banker, and had looked after her financial affairs since Billy's grandfather had died. "Don't think she'll be hanging on much longer," Ed had said. "Come as soon as you can. She said she had important business to discuss with you."

"What sort of business?"

"I don't know."

So the next day Billy checked himself out of the hospital in Cheyenne and hopped a bus. Buzz had bought Billy's horse and, as a courtesy, shipped his personal effects to Elko for him. He did drop a small case with a couple of changes of clothes by the hospital before the crew left town. "We'll miss you, partner," Buzz said.

Billy saluted him. "I'll miss you fellas, too. Give my best to everybody."

He had no idea he could feel so nostalgic about a bunch of roughneck rodeo cowboys, but he did. Hell, the circuit had been his life.

If the first week of his recovery was any indication, Billy thought he'd almost be better off dead. His grandfather, Willard Blue Bear, had gone through a similar ordeal when he'd lost the ranch and they'd been forced to move into town. "This is no way to live," he'd said. "Cooped up like this, I feel like a bird in a cage." And so he'd checked out, dying within a year. Granny had said it was her husband's Indian blood. Billy had only been fourteen at the time, but he'd allowed that the same blood ran in his own veins. It probably explained the feelings he had now.

As the big old Greyhound lumbered off the interstate on the outskirts of Elko, Billy stared toward the southeast at the snowcapped peaks of the Ruby Mountains where he and his granddad had roamed when he was a kid. He couldn't help but feel a twinge of nostalgia at the sight, which made this particular homecoming all the more poignant.

Willard and Sophie Blue Bear were the only family Billy had ever known, considering his mother had died of a blood virus when he was just a toddler. He'd never so much as laid eyes on his old man, who, according to Sophie, was a gambler and ne'er-do-well. Billy knew his dad's name, Irwin Pettigrew, and the fact that he'd once owned some sort of small business in Vegas, but that was it. His grandparents had rarely mentioned Irwin and considered him a scoundrel—which explained why Billy had been given his mother's family name.

At long last the bus rolled up to the Greyhound station on Commercial Street. Billy was dying to lie down, but the first order of business was to get his butt over to Elko General. It was up on College Avenue, which made it a good six or eight blocks from the bus station. When he'd left the hospital in

Cheyenne, they'd given him a cane, which made it easier to get around, but till now he'd only gone short distances. After the long bus trip, Billy figured he'd be lucky to get as far as the corner. He had little choice but to call a taxi.

The bus driver, an affable black man, helped Billy down the steps. The last long one to the ground was agony.

"You goin' to be all right?" the driver asked, handing him his case.

"I'll be fine, thanks." Billy turned to go inside when he heard a woman's voice.

"That you, Billy Blue Bear?"

He stiffly turned his body. She was chunky, the face older but still familiar. He couldn't come up with the name, though. She'd been Shelly's best friend in high school, that's the best he could do.

"It's me, Cookie," she said. "Don't you remember?"

It all came back in a rush. "Sure I remember. Cookie Calso. How could I forget?"

She had short chopped-off hair, a plain cotton blouse and big loose-fitting pants that made him think of a circus tent. About the only jewelry she wore was a gold chain and a sports watch. No makeup. Her skin was splotchy, but she looked healthy enough.

"So," he said, "how's it going?"

"It's going great. I'm a lesbian."

He was momentarily taken aback. He couldn't recall anyone having made an announcement like that before. At least, not on the heels of hello. "Is that right?"

"It's very right." She beamed like the happiest chick on the planet.

"Congratulations, I guess."

"No need for congratulations. I'm up front about it nowadays, that's all."

Billy didn't know what to say so he nodded and smiled as politely as he could.

Cookie glanced down at his cane. "What happened to you, Billy?"

"Got kicked by a bull in Cheyenne."

"Oh, yeah? Were you hurt bad?"

"I've got a pretty good kink in my back, but they tell me I'll live."

"We read about you in the *Free Press* all the time, the championships you win and all. Billy Blue, one of Elko's heroes."

"Hardly."

He found himself wanting to ask about Shelly, but figured he dare not. He hadn't discussed her with a soul since he'd left Elko, fifteen years ago. Granny hadn't mentioned her and nobody else would have had the nerve—not that he'd seen all that many folks over the years, his trips home being infrequent and brief.

"So, you in town for long?" Cookie asked.

"I'm not rightly sure," he said, setting down his case and tipping his hat back off his forehead. "Looks like this back will keep me from the circuit. I'm more or less retired."

"What a shame."

"Yeah, that's the breaks, I guess...no pun intended." He shifted uncomfortably, his back screaming at him.

"Sounds like you'll be around for a while, then," Cookie said.

"I'm here mainly to see my grandmother."

"Yeah, I heard she was in the hospital. Shelly told me. People say it's pretty serious. I'm sorry."

Billy didn't hear much after the mention of Shelly's name. "Shelly told you?"

"Yeah, she works at the hospital."

"That a fact? I thought she'd probably be long gone from Elko by now."

"Her and Todd just moved back last year. They've been living all over the state, getting transferred every few years. He's with the highway department."

"Oh?" Billy knew little about his former girlfriend's life. He'd heard she'd gotten married, though he didn't know when or to whom. Funny how the mention of her husband's name made it seem so much more real. In his mind Shelly would always be the sixteen-year-old he'd once thought he loved.

"She's got two kids," Cookie added. "A boy and a girl."

"Oh, yeah? That's nice…. Nice for her, I mean…uh…" He glanced around, hating the pain in his back, though not as much as his embarrassment. "Well, I've got to get going, find a pay phone so I can call a cab."

"Where you headed? To the hospital?"

"Yeah."

"I can give you a lift, Billy. My car's just around the corner."

"I wouldn't want to impose."

"It's no trouble. I'm headed that way."

Cookie picked up his case and they started up the sidewalk, Billy leaning heavily on his cane. He was in serious pain and would gladly take another of the pills the doctor had given him, except he'd already had his quota for the day. He'd known guys who got hooked on painkillers after a serious injury and he had no desire to go that route.

He considered what Cookie had said about Shelly working at the hospital. Since her name had already been mentioned, he figured he could safely bring her up again.

"So, what does Shelly do for a living?"

"Lab technician. She's doing really well."

"I'm not surprised. She was always smart."

They went around the corner, Billy feeling every step. Neither of them were saying what was on their minds—at least he wasn't—but then a man could scarcely ask after a woman whose father he'd killed, even if it was in self-defense.

The incident had messed up his life, and Shelly's. The way Billy had dealt with it was by leaving town and making the rodeo his life. He hadn't been sure what all had happened to Shelly. She hadn't attended the trial—her mother wouldn't let her. And for a while the two of them had gone to stay with relatives in Oregon.

"Since she moved back, we've gotten to be good friends

again,'' Cookie said. "Todd doesn't much like the fact that I'm a lesbian, but screw him.''

Billy chuckled. "I can't see why he'd care. It's got nothing to do with him.''

"He doesn't like the way it looks, Shelly running around with me. You know men.''

He poked his tongue in his cheek. "Yeah, Cookie, I reckon I do.''

"Well, what do you think about it? Not that it really matters, but I'm sort of curious, you being so macho and all.''

"Hell, I got too many problems of my own to worry about what other folks do. I guess I believe in live and let live. Beyond that, I haven't given it much thought, to be honest, not having run into all that many lesbians in my line of work.''

"You have, Billy, you just didn't know it.''

He glanced over at her, feeling a little like they were talking religion or politics, subjects he tended to avoid. "So, what do you do to keep busy?'' he asked.

"County social services caseworker.''

"That a fact?''

"Keeps me hopping.''

They came to Cookie's car. She opened the passenger door for him. Billy slipped into the seat, relieved to get off his feet, but accomplishing little more than trading one kind of pain for another. Cookie handed him his case, then went around to the driver's side and got in.

He glanced over at her, seeing a different person than the unhappy little girl who'd been Shelly Richards's best friend— the friend who'd given Shelly cover so that she could secretly be with him. Billy had a vivid recollection of the night Shelly had given him her virginity. It was a July evening up in Lamoille Canyon, on a mattress in the back of his grandfather's old pickup truck. Afterward they'd gone to Cookie's, where Shelly was supposedly spending the night. Billy had had to put a ladder up against the side of the Calsos' house so Shelly could climb in the second-story window without Cookie's parents knowing. It seemed so long ago it could have been a different lifetime.

Cookie started the car and they headed for the hospital. "Shelly knows you're coming to town," she said, as though it was information he needed to have.

"Then it won't be a surprise if I happen to run into her."

"No."

They rode in silence for a while. He saw no point in playing adolescent games and he wouldn't have a better chance than now to ask.

"How does she feel about me, anyway?" he asked. "We never had a chance to talk after they arrested me."

"It's all long in the past, Billy."

"I understand that. I guess what I'm wondering is if she's bitter or anything."

"She doesn't talk about it," Cookie said. "At least not with me. Besides, why bother with something that happened when we were kids? We've got grown-up problems and grown-up lives to worry about."

Grown-up lives. That was an interesting idea. Billy wasn't so sure his had been all that grown-up—some would say it had been anything but. Still, sometimes late at night when he was alone in some motel room, staring at the shadows on the ceiling, he'd think back on that life-and-death fight with Kyle Richards and get a sick feeling in his gut—the sick feeling of regret. That had been the day he'd lost his innocence.

"Some things are best forgotten, maybe," he agreed.

Billy gazed out at the town where he'd been born and raised and had pretty much come to a bad end. That he should be back now, and that Shelly should be living here, too, seemed bizarre. All the towns and women and countless miles of road he'd seen since leaving Elko seemed a meaningless interlude when he thought of her now.

They arrived at the hospital, a flat-roofed two-story structure of stucco, glass and steel that Billy had always thought of as extremely modern, probably because he'd been born in the old brick structure that had been Elko General before they'd torn it down. He noticed new construction on the building was under way.

"They adding on?" he asked.

"Yes."

"You go away for a few years and everything changes," he said.

"Shelly said the same thing."

Billy nodded, wondering if all this talk of Shelly—her return to town and all—wasn't some kind of omen. But she was a married woman now, and after Connie, he figured another problem like that was the last thing he needed.

He reached for the door handle. Twisting was painful. "I appreciate the lift, Cookie."

"No problem. Have a good visit with your grandmother."

"Thanks." He slipped out of the seat with difficulty, standing upright with the help of his cane. He clutched his case.

"Billy?"

He bent down to peer into the car. "Yeah?"

"You didn't ask for my advice, but I'm going to give it to you anyway. Stay away from the lab."

He pondered the warning. "I wasn't planning on going there. But out of curiosity, why do you say that?"

"Shelly doesn't need the complications of seeing an old beau."

"Especially not one who killed her old man?"

"She doesn't hate you, if that's what you're getting at. But it's best to let sleeping dogs lie."

"I reckon."

"A word to the wise."

"Thanks again for the ride."

She nodded and he closed the door. Then he limped to the entrance and went inside, ruminating on Cookie's comment, wondering if the message was really coming from Shelly. The elderly woman at the reception desk asked if she could help him.

"I'm here to see Sophie Blue Bear," he said.

"You must be her grandson, the rodeo cowboy. Thought I recognized you."

Billy smiled uncertainly.

"She'll be glad to see you, young man. Second floor, patient room 208." She pointed toward the elevator.

"Thank you, ma'am."

He went over and pushed the button, leaning on his cane while he waited. Finally the door slid open. There was a woman alone inside, ready to step out. She was in a white uniform dress, her blond hair brushing her shoulders, her large brown eyes weary and so terribly familiar—the eyes that had haunted him in thousands of dreams over the past fifteen years. It was Shelly.

"Billy..."

"Hi," he said soberly, not knowing what else to say.

She was frozen. They stared at each other across a chasm of a million uncertainties.

When the door began to slide closed, he reached out and stopped it. Then he moved to the side to allow her to pass. Shelly stepped past him and turned, hesitating for a moment as though pondering what to say.

"I'm h-here to see my grandmother," he stammered, hoping to reassure her.

She nodded, looking pained. "I'm sorry she's ill."

"Yeah, it's rough."

Shelly lowered her eyes, as though looking at him would bring back the past with all the pain and regret and longing.

"I ran into Cookie," he said. "She gave me a lift from the bus station." He indicated his case. "Just hit town."

"Are you staying?"

He didn't know whether to read hope or fear in her voice. "I don't know."

A very long silence lapsed, then Shelly said, "Billy, I've got to go."

Without waiting for a reply, she hurried off down the hallway.

"See you," he called after her, though probably not loud

enough for her to hear. Still, she glanced over her shoulder before going around a corner and disappearing from sight. Seeing him had upset her, he could tell that. But he wasn't sure why, or what she was thinking.

Billy stepped into the elevator car and pushed the button for the second floor. He let his case drop and leaned against the back wall. As he stared up at the floor indicator, his eyes filled and the sorrows of the past choked him up a little. Seeing Shelly was like seeing a person who'd risen from the dead.

Billy sat next to the hospital bed, watching his grandmother sleep. She seemed so frail, and the fact that she'd kept her illness from him was troubling. But it was also like her, not wanting to burden him. He could hear her explanation—"Why should I bother you with something you can do nothing about?"

Sophie Blue Bear hadn't had an easy life, though she wasn't one to complain. She'd been orphaned when she was small and then been adopted by a Presbyterian minister and his nervous and sickly wife. Finding the household stifling and her adoptive mother's devotion as much a curse as a blessing, Sophie left home right after high school to attend teachers college. But her academic career was short-lived because she soon married a refugee from the Elko Indian Reservation. Willard Blue Bear was a Native American rancher with an independent streak that matched Sophie's. Their daughter, Janine, was born the next year.

"Maybe your mama had a little too much of my blood in her," his grandmother had told him once. "Janine had a wild, defiant side, same as me, and wouldn't listen to either me or your granddaddy." Billy hadn't needed to know much more than that his mother had gotten involved with Irwin Pettigrew in order to understand what Granny was saying.

He drew a deep breath, fatigued by all the physical and emotional pain. Having sat about as long as he could, he got to his feet and hobbled to the window. Billy stared out at his hometown for a couple of minutes before he heard his grand-mother's voice behind him.

"Billy? Is that you, son?"

He turned. Sophie Blue Bear smiled at him from her bed with all the radiance of an angel. Billy went to her bedside. Leaning over, despite the pain, he kissed her cheek.

"What's this I hear about you being under the weather, Granny?"

She laughed. "So far under the weather, I'm about sunk."

"Not my granny," he said with a grin, though he was a lot closer to crying than laughing.

Sophie put her bony arms around his neck. "I can't tell you how good it is to have you here, son. But I just hate having you see me like this."

"Granny, you're a sight for sore eyes, no matter what."

She stroked his cheek with dry, brittle fingers, her once lovely blue eyes sunken and gray. "How's your own health, Billy?"

"I'm hobbling a bit, Granny, but a few more days and I'll be right as rain."

"Surely you aren't going back to the rodeo, are you?"

"They tell me I can't," he said, his voice quavering slightly. "So, I guess those days are behind me for good." He sighed. "It's hard, because it's all I've ever known."

"I understand. Your granddaddy was the same way when we had to give up the ranch. Being out in the wide-open spaces, riding from morning to night, was his life—his only life apart from me."

"I remember."

Sophie drew a long, slow, painful breath. "There's some-thing we need to talk about, son, something you probably won't find so pleasant, but it needs to be discussed just the same."

Billy gingerly lowered himself into the chair next to the bed. "What's that, Granny?"

"Remember when they were going to put you away for what you did to Kyle Richards? Remember how I had to sell my Van Gogh to your…to that bastard Pettigrew in order to afford that fancy defense lawyer from Reno?''

"I remember."

"Well, I never did quite tell you the entire story," she said, extending her hand to him.

Billy scooted his chair a bit closer and took his grandmother's hand in both of his. "I'm listening, Granny."

"Most of what I told you was the truth—me calling Pettigrew in Las Vegas and begging him to come help save the life of his own flesh and blood."

"He came," Billy said, "but he wanted something for his money and you sold him the painting."

"That's the part that's not exactly right. Pettigrew loaned me the money, Billy. In exchange, he took my Van Gogh sunflowers for security. We had legal papers drawn up. They're in the safe-deposit box at the bank. I gave him a note due and payable in twenty years or sooner. My intention was to save the money to pay him back, principle and interest. Before coming to the hospital I had Ed calculate what I owe. It comes to nearly fifty-five thousand. I've finally saved up enough to pay back the loan and get my sunflowers."

Billy was shocked. "How come you never told me this before?"

"I didn't want you worrying about there being any unfinished business with that man. Maybe it was wrong, but I wanted you thinking about him as little as possible."

"I never have cared about him. You know that, Granny."

"Well, maybe the time has come to care about him, son…or at least deal with him."

"What do you mean?"

"I've only got weeks to live. And I don't want Pettigrew to steal my dreams along with everything else. When I got my painting in that estate sale, I thought God had truly blessed me. I had big plans for the money I was going to get for it."

"I thought it wasn't a hundred percent certain that it was a genuine Van Gogh. Weren't you just hoping it was?"

"When I heard how ol' Bob Halloway got it in Germany

during the war, I figured the chances were good it was genuine, an item that had been in a private collection and unknown to the art world."

"He stole it, was that it?"

"His unit ambushed a German convoy transporting booty back from France. Bob had no idea what he had. As far as he was concerned, he was taking a pretty picture of flowers home to Mary Lee. I didn't know what I had myself until I got everything in the shop. I thought I was getting Bob's collection of western art, and lo and behold there's this little still life signed 'Vincent' in the crate along with everything else."

"But you had it appraised, right?"

"One dealer in Salt Lake who knew French Impressionism told me he thought there was a good chance the painting was genuine, but admitted it might be a fake. He took photos and sent them off to an expert on Van Gogh in London. That was maybe six months before your troubles began. So, when it came down to choosing between hiring a top-notch lawyer or allowing them to put you away for twenty years, I was desperate enough to call Pettigrew and ask for help."

"But now you're telling me you didn't actually sell him the painting."

"That's right. I told him I couldn't part with it, but I would offer it as security against a loan. He wasn't too keen on the idea, but he finally agreed."

"Did he think it was a genuine Van Gogh?" Billy asked.

"I was honest with him. I told him I wasn't sure. But I was clear about wanting the painting back. It wasn't a month after he gave me a check for twenty-five thousand and left with my sunflowers that I got a letter from the Van Gogh expert. He told me that he needed to examine the canvas to be certain, but that it fit the description of a painting that had been rumored to be in a private collection in France and stolen during the war.

"What I should have done was take a partner, paid Pettigrew off and gotten the painting back, but I was preoccupied just trying to hold things together. And I figured the papers would secure my rights to the painting whether Pettigrew was trustworthy or not. I was lucky to hang on to The Blue Bear. That shop was my only means of putting food on the table. Thirty thousand at that point was a fortune.''

"And all because of me.''

"We've been over that, son. It wasn't your fault. A man comes at you with an ax handle, you've got to protect yourself. You being with his daughter gave him no right to try to beat you to death. But all that was settled in court. No need to hash it over again here. It's Pettigrew and the painting I want to talk about.''

"After he left with it, did you talk to him again?''

"We spoke a couple of times. He said he'd had the painting examined and that it was confirmed to be a fake, though an excellent copy of Van Gogh's style. He admitted it could be worth as much as fifty thousand and offered me twenty more to buy it outright. I declined and he offered me thirty. When I refused, he cut off communication, but not before saying he'd be keeping it until he was paid back in full, plus interest.''

"You think what he said was true about it being a fake?''

"Knowing the man, I'd lay odds that whatever he says, the opposite is most likely true.''

"Since you had the legal right to it, why didn't you borrow what you needed to get it out of hock?''

"I tried, Billy. Ed at the bank said they'd consider making a loan, but not until I'd gotten an appraisal from a certified expert—that letter I'd received from the man in London wasn't good enough because he hadn't actually seen the painting. I called Pettigrew again and told him I wanted to get my sunflowers appraised. He refused, saying if I wanted to see the painting, I'd have to pay him off. Ed talked to the bank's lawyer and was told I could probably force the issue in court, but that would be expensive. And there was also the expense of the appraisal. I decided the best thing to do was pull in my horns, save my money and get my Van Gogh out of hock as soon as I could.''

"You're convinced it's the real McCoy?"

"It's got to be, son. God wouldn't be that cruel to lead me on all these years. Besides, there are two things I've wanted more than anything else in life. One was to establish a trade school on the reservation in honor of your granddaddy. I told Willard I would do that before I was gone and he thought that was the finest tribute a man with no education could have. That's been my first dream, Billy. The second was to buy back the ranch and make that your inheritance so you'd have someplace to call home when your rodeo days were over."

"Granny, you don't need to fret over me. I'll be just fine."

"Listen to me, Billy. I'm an old woman and I'm dying. I've got two dreams. I want them fulfilled. I want your grandfather to have his school and I want you to have his ranch. The Van Gogh can make both dreams come true."

Billy stroked her hand. "I have a feeling this is leading someplace specific."

"I want you to do what I can't, son. I've told Ed to pull together fifty-five thousand and put it in your hands so you can redeem the Van Gogh. Once you've got it, I want you to sell it, build your granddaddy's school and buy the ranch. It'll cost five or six times what we got for it, but in today's market a Van Gogh is worth a king's ransom. My estate consists of that painting, Billy.... You've got to get it back. I'm putting my dreams in your hands."

Billy Blue didn't relish the thought of that sort of responsibility. Granny was talking about sending him on a crusade and he didn't much consider himself the type.

"You know I'd do just about anything to make you happy," he told her, "but I'm not so sure sending me to deal with my old man is a very smart move. I'm a cowboy, not a bounty hunter."

"If not you, Billy, then who?"

He didn't have a ready answer for that. He either stepped up to the plate or her dreams crumbled and she died leaving no legacy. Sure, he could promise her one thing and do another, but that wasn't his style. Billy Blue Bear was a lot of things, but he wasn't a liar and he never broke a promise. Never. "You know damned well I wouldn't say no to you, Granny," he said. "I just wish I was better suited for this."

"You sell yourself short, Billy. You always have."

"I'll discuss the matter with Mr. Carlsen," he told her.

"No, Billy, that's not good enough. I want you to get the painting back, whatever the cost. Swear you'll do that for me. Please."

He looked into Sophie Blue Bear's eyes. They were filled with pain and longing. She'd given up hope for herself, but she still clung to her dream. How could he deny her? "Okay, Granny," he said. "You've got my word. I'll get your painting back. I promise."

Thursday
August 3rd

Queenstown, St. Margaret

Simon Van Biers rode to the presidential palace in his Mercedes limousine—one of two on the island—the other belonged to the government and was for the use of the Honorable Jerome Hurst, president of the republic. Simon, a man of prudent benevolence, had in fact purchased both vehicles, making one a gift to the people of St. Margaret. But it was Jerome Hurst's gratitude he'd inspired, and it was Jerome Hurst's gratitude he'd sought.

Technically, Hurst was in command, which was why Simon had to curry favor. The moment he lost his leverage, or his usefulness to Hurst, Simon knew he would be the one with hat in hand. For that reason he was always wary when the president summoned him, as he had that morning, without so much of a hint as to what was up. "We've got a problem, Simon," was all Hurst would say. "Please come by around four so we can discuss the matter."

As he rode through the streets of Queenstown, Simon Van Biers told himself there was nothing to fear. Whatever problem had developed, he could take care of it. It was, after all, his genius and his guts that had put them all into this privileged position, and his genius and guts would keep them there. The situation was clear. St. Margaret needed Victoria International as much or more than Victoria International needed St. Margaret.

Having given himself a pep talk, Simon felt better. Funny how easily a person's confidence could slip. One day a guy could feel invincible, the next he could be certain he was doomed. At the moment Simon was somewhere in between, capable of toppling in either direction, depending on what awaited him at the presidential palace.

Looking out at the town, he reminded himself how in a few short years he gone from being a perfect stranger to the power behind the throne. Queenstown—a mere village even by the standards of his own native Biloxi—was little more than a scenic curiosity, with its whitewashed houses occupied by black-faced people who lived at a pace that could only be described as tropical urgency. And yet, thanks to him, St. Margaret was on the map. The financial world was buzzing about them.

The island was not only a sleepy little place with a bank that produced money and jobs, though. St. Margaret, previously just a novelty to some of the more adventurous travelers, had begun attracting both Americans and Europeans in greater numbers. Even in the off season, like now, pasty-skinned tourists, equipped with cameras and dollars, could be seen wandering the streets of the town or lounging on nearly deserted beaches. It would be some time before the cruise ships made St. Margaret a port of call and big hotels lined its shores, but one moderate size resort was already operating and there were a dozen new shops in town that catered to tourists.

Simon took great pride in the fact that his presence on the island was a major factor in its development. The locals both admired and reviled him for his contribution. But none could deny that most of the change was attributable to him and Victoria International.

Officially a citizen, Simon had begun to feel the sort of attachment he'd once felt to Biloxi—never mind the fact he hadn't set foot in Mississippi for the better part of four decades or that he himself bore little resemblance to Irwin Pettigrew, the boy he'd been. His goal that day long ago when he'd boarded a bus for New Orleans had been to conquer the world.

Simon had not exactly met his goal, but he'd come as close as a man from humble origins could reasonably expect. Geographically, his domain was modest. The island, occupying less than five square miles, claimed a population the fraction of his native Harrison County. But Victoria International had tentacles that already extended to the far reaches of the globe. St. Margaret was his personal fortress against both scrutiny and adversity. Still, there was no certainty in life, which was why Jerome Hurst's call that morning had given him pause.

Simon had learned how mercurial life in the business world could be by watching his father, Maximilian Pettigrew, a man with a keen sense of survival though only modest achievement. During the Great Depression the elder Pettigrew sold insurance to blacks in rural Southern Mississippi, an undertaking some wags likened to squeezing blood from a turnip. But Max Pettigrew saw it as a business opportunity. His clients were like untilled soil and the field of play totally devoid of competition. Nor did he see any reason to be embarrassed by virtue of working among poor, ignorant black folk. "The nigras," as he was wont to say to Simon, "are not to be scorned, son. They put the food on our table. Remember that and you'll never be without business to conduct."

Simon's father had been dead for nearly fifty years now and, at seventy-one, Simon was no spring chicken himself, but the lessons he'd learned at his father's knee still applied, even if he had put his own spin on things to account for changes in the times. Among other adjustments, Simon had learned to reinvent himself when circumstances required. When he'd hit upon his international investment banking scheme, he'd found it convenient to expunge his past altogether, laying Irwin Pettigrew to rest. Only the most acute observer could discern the

Dixie origins in Simon's speech, though from time to time he'd drawl a little and let slip a "y'all" or two. Even Mayte had only a vague understanding of his background. He rarely discussed his life before Las Vegas, finding enigma a valuable tool.

Having passed through the tiny complex of government buildings, Simon's chauffeur, Andrew, a gray-headed man with mahogany skin, guided the limo up a curving road lined on either side by rustic stone walls smothered in bougainvillea. At the top of the hill overlooking the town sat the presidential palace, formerly the residence of Her Majesty's colonial governor before St. Margaret attained its independence in the mid-seventies. Jerome Hurst, the fifth president of the country, had been elected by fifty-four percent of his compatriots the first time he ran for the office. In his reelection bid he'd garnered eighty-two percent of the vote. The difference was attributable to Simon Van Biers and the largesse of Victoria International Bank.

The next election was in October when Jerome would be trying for an unprecedented third term. Simon had jokingly suggested that Jerome's goal should be a hundred percent of the vote. "No," Jerome had said. "Those are Fidel-like numbers. I'll settle for eighty."

"Maybe I should throw a little money to the opposition," Simon had teased. "Can't have the president thinking he's invincible."

"I think this time around a low profile will serve everybody's needs."

Simon had been picking up little indications of that sort—that Jerome was getting a little nervous about their relationship. And he was calling on the president today with the knowledge that there was trouble in the air. Was it regarding Raymond Pearson? Or had the fragile financial condition of the bank finally come to Hurst's attention? Until now, Simon had successfully maintained an aura of financial stability, but to continue on meant bringing in more and more money at an ever-increasing rate. Eventually someone was going to catch on, he knew that, but so long as he kept a step ahead of the game, he could continue to skim and salt away his ill-gotten gains before the house of cards he'd so carefully constructed came tumbling down.

There was no question that the key to everything was his relationship with Hurst. Again, it was a lesson Simon had learned from his father. During the Great Depression, Maximilian Pettigrew had made it a practice to sell insurance to every black minister he could find at rates of thirty or forty cents on the dollar. The trick, of course, was to befriend and win the gratitude of the right people.

Thinking about his father, Simon smiled. Wouldn't the old man be shocked to learn that his son not only understood the commercial value of the black man, but had taken the concept a step further by marrying a gorgeous young black woman with a Harvard education. Old Maximilian might be even more surprised to learn Simon had put her in charge of his empire. Mayte was a far cry from the "nigra gal" who worked out of the steamy back room of the Shipyard Tavern over in D'Iberville, the girl old Max "called on" all those years Simon's mother lay in her sick bed, dying. A far cry, indeed. Yes, Simon had learned a thing or two.

When the limousine rolled to a stop at the portico in front of the palace, Andrew got out and opened the rear door. Simon stepped out of the back seat, allowing the chauffeur to take his arm and help him. "Thank you, Andrew," he said. Simon Van Biers was polite to a fault.

Glancing up at the aging stucco facade faintly tinged pink, he slowly mounted the steps, his heartbeat rising from the exertion, but also in anticipation. The Hursts' butler, Rogers, greeted Simon at the door, but Elise Hurst, the nation's first lady, was not far behind. She was in a white-and-blue-flowered silk dress, her hair slicked back and shiny. The first lady was tall, slender, but heavy-bosomed. Her skin tone was a rich cocoa. She wasn't an elegant woman, but she had a cool serenity, a presence. In her mid-forties like her husband, Elise was always the gracious hostess, but with reservation. Simon knew people well enough to know the woman continued to reserve judgment about him.

"Simon," she said with seeming warmth, the gracious fullness of her lips blending smoothly into a smile, "how good to see you."

"Elise, you look lovely as always," he said, kissing her hand.

Simon, even his detractors were quick to admit, was a charmer. The reason was easily explained—he liked people, he liked to rub shoulders with them and win their allegiance. Their gratitude, as well, if he could. But most of all Simon liked seeing the world dance to his tune. The image of his father moving among the "nigras" of Southern Mississippi like a potentate was something he'd never forget.

"Jerome will be with you shortly," Elise said. "Let me fix you a drink while you wait."

"That would be delightful."

Simon, willing himself into an upbeat state of mind, savored the familiar clean, woody smell of the place. Following Elise Hurst into the sitting room, he stole a glance in the direction of her husband's office, seeing that the door was closed. The room they entered was a successful blend of comfort and formality. Elise and her predecessors had managed to maintain the colonial stateliness of the original mansion while infusing it with local art and artifacts, giving it warmth and charm.

"Vodka tonic?" Elise said, going to the bar.

"Perfect."

"Isn't this terrible business about poor Mr. Pearson just dreadful?"

Simon hardly expected those to be the first words out of her mouth, wondering if it was an omen. "Distressing beyond words," he said, shaking his head as he dropped into a wicker armchair. "I continue to hope he'll turn up alive, but I'm beginning to think it's not likely."

"He'd come to St. Margaret to do business with you, didn't he, Simon?"

Again, he wondered at her tact. "Yes," he replied easily.

"I've known Ray for years. He's done appraisals for me, found some wonderful paintings, including my Van Gogh sunflowers."

"Mr. Pearson was the one who found that Van Gogh for you?"

"He was indeed. Ray did some quality work for me over the years. I considered him a prime resource."

Elise, who made it a point to recall how he liked his drink, poured a splash of tonic into the glass and added a twist of lime, seeming to accept his comments with equanimity. Simon anticipated the bite of the vodka as she carried the drink over to him.

"Aren't you having one?" he asked.

"It's a little early in the day for me."

"It's a trifle early in the day for me, as well," Simon replied, "but I never let that stop me."

She chuckled appreciatively.

"To good company," he said, saluting her before taking a healthy sip.

Elise eased onto the sofa across from him, crossing her legs. "So, what do you think happened to Mr. Pearson?"

She was being persistent. Why? he wondered. Out of curiosity? Or did she know something? "I've pondered that," he said thoughtfully, "but I haven't come up with an explanation. Must be one of those chance things."

"You think a swimming accident, like some people are saying?"

"Possibly, though I didn't know Raymond to be a swimmer. I suppose foul play is a possibility, as well."

"But we have so little crime on St. Margaret."

"There's always the exceptional circumstance," he said, taking another sip of his drink. Simon suspected that Elise knew a good deal more than she was letting on, but beyond that he wasn't reading her. There was no question her mind was a good deal more subtle than her husband's. Mayte had made that same observation.

Chief Inspector Reginald Goodson, the head of the police,

and the only high-ranking white official on the island, had personally questioned Simon about Raymond Pearson's disappearance. Jerome Hurst undoubtedly knew what was said in the interview, which meant Elise did, as well. St. Margaret being so small, everybody's business seemed connected to everybody else's. The whole sordid affair reminded Simon of the time during his youth when the black mistress of the mayor of Biloxi was murdered. The gossip had everyone who was anyone somehow involved, but no one was ever arrested, which most people considered just as well, given what a mess it was.

"It's unfortunate he was American," Elise observed. "We've heard his disappearance was reported in many of the newspapers in the States. Negative press is the last thing we need, not that I mean to trivialize the poor man's misfortune."

"Yes, and it came at a bad time for me, too," Simon replied.

"How so?"

"I just hired a curator and I would have liked to get Ray's input. He was very knowledgeable and understood the way I do business."

"A tragedy all around."

"Indeed." Simon took another big slug of the vodka tonic, savoring the flavor, liking it a bit too much. Drink had always been a weakness.

"So, you've hired a curator, Simon? Would that be to handle your personal collection?"

"Yes, and to help with the collections we intend to syndicate. There's big money in major works of art, Elise. And a potential for profit."

"That's what you're in business for, I suppose."

He smiled, swirling the ice cubes in his nearly empty glass. "It's not just for the fun of it, though I've always enjoyed the game."

"Is your curator American?"

"Yes, Charles and I were in New York and we found her at Sotheby's. Zoe Marton is her name. Bright, charming young lady. Not surprisingly, my son found her charm to be the more persuasive factor.''

"The young man does have an eye for the ladies," Elise Hurst said, arching a brow.

She hadn't said it unkindly, but Simon read her disapproval. Charles had proven to be something of a liability because of his errant ways. On several occasions he'd been an embarrassment. But he was Simon's only family and his heir. Their relationship fell well short of the one Simon had had with his own father, but Charles did have his qualities, if only a willingness to take on troublesome and messy tasks.

Having entered his seventh decade of life, Simon Van Biers, the Silver Fox, as he'd been known in Las Vegas some years ago, had no stomach for blood and gore. He much preferred to leave the dirty work to others, as had his father. Max Pettigrew had employed a man named Amos Tull, the "meanest nigra" in Mississippi, to take care of slow-paying customers. Amos, who was willing to smash heads with impunity, had been so valuable that one summer night Simon's father had put his own neck on the line to save him from a rampaging mob of Klansmen. Amos never forgot the kindness. Simon, for his part, had learned to indulge his son in a similar fashion.

"Sorry to keep you waiting, Simon." It was Jerome Hurst at the door, crisply dressed, as always, in shirtsleeves and a tie.

Hurst was a large, athletically built man, handsome, distinguished-looking, with a graying mustache and flecks of white at the temples. He was bright, but not so clever as his Oxford education suggested. Hurst had political skills, yet lacked the killer instinct essential for the major leagues. To Simon, politics was war without bloodshed—or so it had been in his native South, though some politicians there were so firmly entrenched that they behaved more like monarchs than public servants.

"Not a problem, Jerome," Simon said, struggling to his feet. "Your lovely wife and I have been gossiping about affairs of state, once she loosened my tongue with a delightful vodka tonic."

"Let me fix you another," Elise volunteered.

"No, dear lady. I thank you, but your husband won't be so gentle in conversation as you. I must keep my wits about me." He gave her a wink.

Both the Hursts chuckled.

"I'll leave you two to discuss business, then," Elise said. "Give my regards to your beautiful wife, Simon," she said graciously.

"I'll do just that," he replied.

Elise went to the door. "Shall I close this, dear?" she asked her husband.

"Please."

The doors closed, Jerome Hurst's expression changed to stern sobriety. The two men regarded each other for a long moment, Simon uncertain what was coming, though he was now positive it was ominous.

"I'm having trouble with your countrymen," Hurst finally said.

"Trouble?"

"Yes, the American government, the Securities and Exchange Commission in particular, is hounding me, insisting we investigate the bank."

Simon sat down without waiting to be invited, but he did so casually, maintaining an untroubled demeanor. The president hesitated, then sat on the sofa where his wife had been moments earlier. But unlike Elise, he was at the edge of the cushion, his hands clasped together, concern on his face.

"Simon, is there something I should know that I don't?"

Simon fought to keep the color from rising in his face. "About what?"

"The bank."

"No, of course not."

"What are you doing that has them on edge?"

Simon sighed impatiently, as though the question bored him.

"I don't tell them what I'm doing, Jerome, and they hate it. You know how bureaucrats are. You have a few of your own."

"This is more than bureaucratic nonsense. The American ambassador flew in with two SEC officials this morning. They spent an hour hassling me."

"Well, what did they say? They must have given some indication as to what they wanted."

"They complained about a lack of oversight and regulation on our part."

"Sounds to me like they're a darned sight more frustrated by your government than my banking operation," Simon said a bit too gleefully.

"I suppose that, too, was the implication, but something you're doing at Victoria International has them concerned."

"I can't imagine what. If you want my opinion, they're fishing. I'm pulling in large sums of money from the States and it makes them nervous because they do not have a single piece of paper in their files to help them understand why. Not so much as a prospectus."

"Maybe that's the problem then," Hurst said. "What's the harm giving them a little paperwork? I mean, you do run an honest business."

Simon tried to decide between brushing aside Hurst's concern with disdain or showing annoyance at being questioned. He chose the latter approach, knowing if his friend had damning knowledge, he could probably force him to reveal it. "You know damn well I run an honest business, Jerome. And I happen to run it in St. Margaret where you and your compatriots can enjoy the benefits. I trust that little detail hasn't been forgotten along the way."

"No, of course not, Simon. I'm not being critical, I'm simply trying to understand."

"I think I've made clear from the beginning that the more freedom I enjoy, the more money there'll be for everyone," Simon said. "If I'm going to pay to have government officials looking over my shoulder, second-guessing my every move, I might as well be in New York paying a battalion of lawyers and accountants to cover my backside. Instead, I've chosen to plow my money into your economy, Mr. President.'' Simon hesitated. ''And, dare I say, into your private accounts.''

''Though not illegally,'' Hurst quickly replied.

''True, but still not the sort of information you want coming out in an election year, Mr. President.''

''You needn't remind me,'' Hurst replied. ''But as to the Americans, I'm searching for a solution, a way to buy the bloody bastards off cheaply.''

Simon was starting to see that Hurst was simply nervous and was in need of reassurance. ''Fear not, Jerome, the U.S. Marines won't be invading St. Margaret. There's no reason, I assure you.''

''Well, it's not exactly unprecedented,'' Hurst said, his mouth twisting wryly.

Simon laughed. ''Communism has already been vanquished, my friend. The only things the American government has to fear now are terrorists and rogue states and I'm afraid you don't qualify on either score. If you want my advice, tell the American ambassador to stuff it. St. Margaret is a sovereign state.''

''But we must live with the giant. And you aren't the only bone of contention.''

''They want something besides my head on a platter?''

''They're concerned about the disappearance of this chap Pearson. Apparently his family has ties to an influential U.S. senator and they're all raising a ruckus, questioning whether enough's being done to find him or, in the event of foul play, to determine what happened and to punish the offenders.''

''Is the ambassador claiming that Goodson is not doing his job?''

''He offered us resources, let me put it that way.''

For the first time in the conversation, Simon Van Biers sensed serious danger. He cleared his throat. ''That's hardly ominous,'' he said, maintaining his calm demeanor. ''Nobody approves of violent crime, not even free-wheeling bankers such as myself.''

''No, I came to the same conclusion. Reginald and I discussed the matter and we've decided to take the Americans up on their offer. They'll be sending a couple of FBI agents to help with the investigation.''

"Good. I don't like having to lock my doors at night any more than any other honest citizen." Simon reflected a moment before forging ahead with the thought forming in his mind. "But take care that investigating a disappearance is all the bastards are interested in doing, Mr. President.''

"Meaning?"

"I don't have to tell you, of all people, how open and informal government is on this island."

Hurst nodded. "I understand your concern, but everything truly sensitive remains under lock and key. And I have the key.''

Simon smiled faintly. "Well, a word to the wise." He consulted his watch. "I'm afraid I've got to get rolling. I'm going to try and see if I can get that wife of mine to tear herself away from the office long enough for me to take her to dinner.''

Hurst smiled stiffly. "Sounds like a pleasant prospect."

"In so many respects it is, Jerome."

"I hear qualification in your voice."

"A word of advice—think carefully before marrying a woman thirty-five years your junior. It can take a toll."

"I don't think my condolences are required," Jerome Hurst said.

Simon grinned. "Ever the politician."

Both men got to their feet. They shook hands. Simon left the presidential palace. He didn't take out his handkerchief to mop his brow until they'd gone through the gate and were headed down the road.

Manhattan

Zoe Marton had heard the phone ringing while she was in the shower and, as she dried herself off in the cramped little bath in the cramped little apartment on the West Side, it rang again. She did not answer the phone. She was afraid it was Ahmed.

With the date on which their divorce would be final drawing near, her husband, Ahmed Cherif, had grown more and more frenetic. By day he haunted the building where she worked and by night he haunted the building where she lived. The week before, she'd called the police three times to report she was being stalked. They'd come and politely urged her husband to leave, but even the involvement of the cops hadn't deterred him for long. The next day he was back.

"Look, lady," the older cop who'd come last time said to her, "there's not much we can do so long as he isn't violent or threatening. Your best bet is to get a restraining order. Then when he comes around, the judge slaps him with a contempt citation."

Zoe had talked to Winifred Kern, her divorce lawyer, about it, but decided in the end it wasn't worth the trouble. "If you're going to the Caribbean in a couple of weeks anyway," Win had said, "then he can stand in the street weeping till hell freezes over. If he gets violent, though, it's another story."

Zoe did not expect her husband to go that far. She'd seen flashes of temper on several occasions but, for the most part, Ahmed had been tender, sensitive, affectionate. And yet, even after three years of marriage, Zoe sensed she didn't truly know the man. Whether it was his Arab blood or the fact that he was a man and she a woman, she wasn't sure. Cultural differences had played a role in their eventual alienation, though. Stupid as it sounded, they were simply from two different worlds.

Ostensibly Zoe had left because Ahmed had had an affair with one of his models, a Brazilian girl, Cha or Che or something like that—the details were unimportant. It was enough that her husband was unfaithful. But truth be known, the infidelity was the excuse she'd been seeking, almost from the outset. Not that she hadn't had deep feelings for Ahmed, or had found him unappealing. If anything, he was too attractive, the most beautiful man she'd ever laid eyes on, in fact.

A fabulous photographer, he enjoyed a certain degree of fame, especially in the fashion world. His success had brought in a lot of money; they'd lived extremely well. But Ahmed's success, and their glitzy life, had distracted her from focusing on what truly mattered—the man her husband was at heart.

Ahmed had put on an act, but in his heart he wasn't as liberal and westernized as he'd led her to believe. His expectations were conditioned more by his Middle Eastern origins than the enlightened philosophy he'd espoused during their engagement. In short, Zoe had made a mistake.

Her husband had refused to accept the fact, however. He was certain the whole problem was his "slip" with the Brazilian girl, and nothing she could say made him understand. Weeping, he'd begged her to reconsider the divorce. At one time the ploy might have worked, but Zoe had grown up.

"Never assume you know the man you're married to," Winifred had counseled, "because women almost never do. There's something about legal papers that brings out their true colors." Deepening Zoe's concern was the fact that Winifred had dealt with Arabs before, and not with a happy result. "At this stage, no man is Prince Charming," she'd said, "but something about these devils makes them especially unpredictable, and therefore dangerous."

Zoe hadn't thought of Ahmed as unpredictable or dangerous, though he had surprised her on several occasions. Once, he'd read her a letter from his family in Jordan with news that his cousin had been arrested briefly for raping his estranged wife. Zoe was horrified when Ahmed defended his cousin. "So what if she was his wife!" she'd exclaimed. "Your cousin didn't own her!" Ahmed hadn't argued the point insistently but his comment had given her pause. And the incident had come to mind more than once during their separation.

Zoe had dried herself and was combing through her wet hair when she heard a knock at the door. Oh, God, she thought, please, not Ahmed. Slipping on her robe, she went to her triple-locked front door and, rising to her toes, looked out the peephole. It wasn't her husband, though. It was a man she'd never seen before.

"Yes?" she said through the door.

"Ms. Marton?"

"Yes, what do you want?"

"I'm Special Agent Mark Harris with the Federal Bureau of Investigation. Could I have a word with you?"

Zoe couldn't have been more surprised. The FBI? Could it have something to do with Ahmed? She was at a complete loss.

Ever cautious, she unfastened the locks, though she left on the chain, opening the door a crack and peering out. The man reached in his breast pocket and flipped open a badge case.

Zoe scrutinized it carefully. "You've caught me at a bad time," she said. "I just got out of the shower."

"I won't need but a few minutes, Ms. Marton."

She could see he wasn't the type who'd care whether her hair was wet and she had on no makeup. He doubtlessly interviewed people in far more distressed states than she was in now. She decided to let him in and unchained the door.

He was in his early forties with thinning blond hair. Medium build, though fairly broad-shouldered. He had a no-nonsense manner that was typical of law enforcement. "I apologize for dropping in like this," he said, scarcely looking at her, "but we understand you're leaving the country soon and we felt it was important to speak with you before you left."

"How did you know I was leaving the country?"

"We've been looking into your background and getting up to speed on your present situation, Ms. Marton."

"I don't know whether to feel reassured or alarmed," she said. "What's going on?"

They were standing at the door. Harris looked as though he wanted to sit down, so Zoe gestured toward the small sofa. The agent went over, dropping onto the cushion with the sigh of a man who'd had a long day. She sat in the small armchair that had been her mother's, the only piece of furniture she'd brought with her from the penthouse she'd shared with Ahmed.

"We understand you've taken a position with Victoria International Bank down in St. Margaret."

"Well, you've certainly done your homework. Why would that be of interest to the FBI?"

"Do you mind if I ask you a few questions before I answer that?"

"I guess not."

"What are your proposed duties?"

"I'll be the curator of Mr. Van Biers's art collection—his personal collection as well as collections the bank will be syndicating for investors. I'll be doing appraisals and some acquisition work, as well."

"To what degree will you be involved with the investment operation?"

"If by that you're asking if I will be working with investors, the answer is no."

"Did Van Biers discuss the nature of his operation with you?"

"Only in general terms. I'll be concerned with the art side, not the financial side."

Harris considered that, not looking very happy.

"Why?" she asked. "Is there a problem?"

"Let me be frank, Ms. Marton, the SEC has concerns about the way Mr. Van Biers conducts his business, but because the U.S. government has no jurisdiction, we are at something of a disadvantage to press an investigation. Simply put, Victoria International enjoys the protection of the government of St. Margaret. Even so, we wish to learn as much as we can because most of the funds flowing into the bank come from the U.S."

"What, exactly, are you accusing the bank of doing?"

"We're not making accusations. We're at an information-gathering stage."

"And you suspect them of illegal activity?"

"We don't know for sure," Harris said, "but if the bank

was under U.S. jurisdiction, there may very well have been violations of U.S. laws.''

"What does all this have to do with me?'' Zoe asked.

"Victoria is privately owned and most of the employees are citizens of St. Margaret and other Caribbean countries, which makes it difficult for us to obtain information necessary to our investigation.''

Zoe was beginning to get the picture. "You're asking me to spy for you.''

"I don't know if I would put it quite that way.''

"Let's not mince words.''

"It does seem you'll be in a unique position to evaluate what's going on.''

"As I said, Special Agent Harris, my work involves the art and there's not a lot of potential for crime there…or do you have other suspicions you haven't shared?''

"The problem is we just don't know enough about what's happening on the inside,'' he replied. "But there's another matter of concern, as well. Do you know Raymond Pearson?''

Zoe had wondered if Pearson's name might come up in the conversation.

"I don't know Mr. Pearson personally, but I do know of him.''

"You're aware that he disappeared recently while visiting St. Margaret.''

"I've seen the news stories,'' she replied, "and it's been mentioned at work. Some of the people at Sotheby's knew him.''

"Did you know Pearson was in St. Margaret because he was doing business with Victoria International?''

"I suspected it,'' Zoe said. She studied the man. "Are you suggesting that the Van Biers or the bank are somehow responsible for his disappearance?'' That possibility did concern her.

"No, ma'am. We don't speculate about such things, not publicly. But you might like to know that we have an agent

on the way to St. Margaret at the request of the local government to assist in the investigation.''

"And you're telling me this, why? To scare me?"

"Not at all. We wanted to apprise you of the situation."

"Well, you aren't inspiring a lot of confidence in my new
employer, Special Agent Harris. I mean, what am I supposed
to think? That I'm about to fall in with a band of thieves?''

"Frankly I was hoping to inspire enough concern that you'd
be sensitive to the issues and...well, be willing to share any
information you happen across, whether concerning the banking operation or Mr. Pearson's disappearance."

"You do want me to spy."

"I trust you don't intend to become a party to any questionable or illegal activities that may be going on down there."

"I get your drift. So, what, specifically, are you asking me
to do?"

"Obviously we're taking a chance in contacting you, Ms.
Marton. I hope you appreciate that. We'd rather not compromise our investigation. On the other hand, sometimes risk is
necessary. This is one situation where we have very few options. Simon Van Biers has done a good job of insulating
himself."

"And you need a Trojan horse."

"We'd like to be informed of any questionable activity the
bank or its employees might be engaged in. Like fraud, for
example."

Mention of the term "fraud" gave her pause. Zoe had not
said anything, though she had her own suspicions about Simon
Van Biers. She could see no point in telling Harris about those
concerns though, because they had nothing to do with either
Victoria International or Raymond Pearson, as far as she could
tell. But the fact was, she and Simon had some history that
even he didn't know about. Of course, that was another matter.

Zoe could see that it wouldn't be a bad idea to have the
FBI on her side, though that didn't mean she necessarily had
to tell them everything now. She could always do that down

the road. For the time being, there was no harm in playing her cards close to her vest.

"The other advantage, Ms. Marton," Harris continued, "is that by working with us you won't be suspected of complicity in a criminal enterprise."

"That almost sounds like a threat, Special Agent Harris."

"No, not at all. We'd like to be able to say your heart's in the right place, that's all."

"What do you want me to do, then—phone you if I spot something suspicious?"

"Yes. I'd like to give you the name of our agent in St. Margaret and a number where you can reach her. If something develops that we should know about, all you have to do is let her know."

"Simple as that."

"That's it."

Zoe thought for a moment. The last thing she wanted to do was jeopardize her chance of recovering the Van Gogh. But so long as her cooperation with the FBI would be at her option, not theirs, she saw no danger. It could even be useful to have someone she might turn to in case of an emergency.

"Okay, Special Agent Harris," she said. "I'll keep my eyes and ears open. If anything comes up I feel you should know about, I'll contact your agent."

"Excellent," he said, smiling for the first time. He took a slip of paper from his pocket and handed it to her. "Special Agent Joyce Tsu will be your contact. She'll be working with the national police in Queenstown."

Zoe examined the paper for a moment, then nodded. "Okay. I hope I won't need to call her."

"Personally, I hope you do. But that's a law enforcement perspective." Harris got to his feet. "I'm sorry for the intrusion and I appreciate your time."

She went with him to the door. They shook hands and he left. Zoe turned all the locks, then leaned heavily against the door. Maybe Simon Van Biers was the arch villain she thought him to be. Whatever his crimes, past or present, she hoped and prayed that bringing him to justice wouldn't interfere with the crusade she'd been working on for years—her promise to herself that she would retrieve the Van Gogh sunflowers, if she accomplished nothing else of consequence in life. After all, the painting was rightfully hers.

Monday
August 7th

The day of Sophie Blue Bear's funeral, Billy felt more alone than at any other time in his life. He had healed enough that he could drive himself to the funeral home in his grandmother's car. There were twenty-five people in the small chapel, mostly merchant friends of Sophie's. The only relative besides Billy was Sophie's adoptive cousin, Ernest Willoughby, and his wife, who'd driven up from Sparks. Billy had seen them maybe two or three times in his life.

The service was brief. Despite her Presbyterian upbringing, Sophie wasn't much into organized religion. She did like the local minister and had arranged in advance for him to say a few words. The only other person to speak was Ben Hawks, a Native American holy man who'd been a friend of Willard's and Sophie's. Billy saved his own words for private communion with his grandmother at her grave site.

They buried Sophie Blue Bear next to her husband in a cemetery at the edge of the prairie with the Ruby Mountains rising majestically beyond the rolling sea of sagebrush. Billy stared at the mountains during the ceremony, the dry, high desert wind parching his eyes before the tears could trickle down his cheeks. Now he was alone.

After the final words were said, the mourners drifted away. A couple of old ladies who'd been Sophie's friends touched Billy's arm and expressed their condolences. When they were gone, he retreated to a nearby bench where he sat down to say goodbye to his grandmother.

Billy knew there was no way he could have prepared himself for this. Sophie Blue Bear was the only mother he'd ever known, his only family. This was the woman who'd treated wounds—both physical and emotional—who'd pointed the way down the path of life. And now she was gone. Worse, in a sense, he was her only legacy, meaning he had to bear a hell of a burden.

"I'll do my best for you, Granny," he muttered as he stared at her grave. "And I hope I can come through. I already asked Gary to check up on Pettigrew and see if he can get an address for him in Vegas. So I'm trying." Billy wiped his eyes. "Bet you didn't know how hard this was going to be for me, jumping off a horse to play avenging angel. But then, maybe you planned it this way, knowing that if it was up to me, I'd walk away.

"All I can say, Granny, is you're getting your way. But I suppose that's the least I can do, considering all the trouble I caused. Maybe in some small way, this'll make up for my screw-ups along the way." Billy wiped his eyes again. "You knew I loved you, even if I didn't say it enough. So, if my best efforts don't pan out, you'll always have that." He took out his handkerchief and blew his nose. "Guess I best be getting along, then. Bye, Granny," he said, touching the brim of his hat in salute. "I'll be back to see you. Hopefully, it'll be with good news. Take care…,I love you. And I always will."

Billy got to his feet and headed back to Sophie's old Ford. A woman was waiting by the car. It was Shelly.

For a moment Billy couldn't believe his own eyes. He hadn't really expected to see her again, but he was glad she had come, if only because she was the last remaining constant in his life—constant in memory, if not reality. Since running into her at the hospital, he'd thought about her a great deal, but always with a poignant sense of how things had changed since the days when she was the most special person in his life.

"Billy," she said as he approached her, still limping, though not as badly as before. "I wanted to tell you how sorry I am about your grandmother."

He stopped ten feet from where she stood. He didn't want to be closer because there was an unreal quality about Shelly, and a danger—not so much because of her, but rather a danger that was centered in his own feelings. "Thank you," he said.

Shelly, her blond hair tossed by the wind, seemed a bit embarrassed. She lowered her eyes. "I'm sorry about the other day at the hospital. I didn't mean to be impolite."

"You weren't impolite."

"Yes, I was." She fiddled with her fingers, not engaging his eyes.

Out of habit, Billy took her in, his eyes skimming the lines of her body before settling on her pretty mouth. Shelly was more voluptuous than she'd been at seventeen. The sleeveless cotton navy dress was a bit snug and a little shorter than he might have expected. She managed to look respectable, considering the occasion, but still sexy. A part of him wanted to think it was for him, yet another part, a bigger part, was afraid that it was.

Shelly glanced up, squinting at him in the bright sunshine. When the wind blew a strand of hair across her cheek and mouth, she pulled it away. "So, how you doing, Billy? I know you were awfully close to your grandmother."

"I'm okay."

"You need anything?"

"Naw," he said. "I'm fine." He wasn't sure what this was about, but something was happening, Shelly had something in mind.

She tossed her head and let the wind carry her hair back off her face. He recalled her doing that as a girl, remembered her shy smile, her innocent way of flirting that made his heart ache so.

"Well," she said, "I made a casserole anyway. Figured you probably aren't doing much cooking. If it's okay, I'll bring it by later."

Billy knew then she had definite intentions. This was more than just a neighborly gesture.

"Sure," he said, uncertainly. "Much obliged."

Shelly seemed pleased. "See you later, then." She walked to her car, an Oldsmobile that was two or three years old, got in and drove off.

Billy watched until she was gone from sight. Then he leaned on the roof of his grandmother's car and stared at the Rubys, thinking how they'd been witness to his first go-around with Shelly and that now they were witness to this go-around. But the funny thing was, Billy wasn't so sure he wanted them to get together again. He liked it that in his mind she was still an innocent girl. And besides, there'd already been enough women like Connie Meeks in his life—too many, probably. If Shelly reduced herself to that, all it would mean was that she was bored or wanted to have a little fun. The thought that she might be no different from so many other women he'd known would kill him. It truly would.

By the time Billy got back to his grandmother's little bungalow, his back was killing him. But his aching back disappeared from his consciousness the moment he noticed a police car out front. To most cowboys, city cops meant trouble, and Billy was instantly wary. Pulling in the driveway, he was relieved to see Gary Blackman get out of the patrol car. Blackman was one of the few cops on the Elko force that Billy had any regard for. Back when Billy was having trouble over Kyle Richards, Gary had been the only one who'd been inclined to believe him, having had problems with Kyle himself.

Gary, a big guy with a gut hanging over his belt, sauntered across the parched lawn toward where Billy waited by Sophie's car. He gestured toward the grass. "You might want to put a sprinkler on that before it's completely dead."

Billy glanced at the lawn. "Yeah, I've been meaning to get around to doing that. Seems like I never remember at the right time."

"How you doing, Billy?" Gary said, sounding as if he genuinely cared. "Funeral go okay?"

"I guess as funerals go, it was fine."

"I'm on duty or I would have come. My condolences."

"Thanks."

"I wouldn't bother you now, seeing as you're probably preoccupied, but I'm going to be off for four days' fishin' with my boys and thought I'd better let you know what I found out about your old man before I go."

"Oh, yeah," Billy said, leaning against the car. "Great. The sonovabitch still in Vegas?"

"No, that's the thing. From what I was told, Pettigrew took off a number of years ago. Sold his business and left Nevada. There's no point in you going down there."

"I got to find the bastard, Gary, so maybe I'll head down anyway, see if I can pick up his trail."

"Suit yourself, but it might save a lot of time and energy to hire a P.I. The fellas that specialize in tracking people can be pretty efficient, turning up leads that could take you weeks to develop. That's what I'd do, anyway."

"Maybe I'll consider that. You didn't get a feel for where Pettigrew might have gone, did you?"

"No. I talked to a guy in the department down there, somebody I met at a training program. He knew your old man, all right, but had no idea where he is now. People like that have a tendency to keep moving on."

Billy stroked his chin. "What'd he say about Pettigrew, out of curiosity?"

"Basically, that he's a con. Vegas knew him as the Silver Fox. Has an arrest record, though nothing real serious. Seems to specialize in taking people's money without delivering what he promises."

"Flimflam man fits what I know about him," Billy said with a glance up at the hot sun. "Want to come inside for a soft drink or something?"

"No, thanks. I would, but I'm supposed to be patrolling the mean streets of Elko. I'll be running along."

"Much obliged for your help."

"Don't mention it," Gary Blackman said, waving him off. Then, touching the brim of his hat, he went back to his car.

Billy went inside the house, tossed his hat on the sofa, then limped into the kitchen to get a beer. After opening the bottle and taking a couple of swigs, he got the Southern Nevada phone book out of the cupboard where he'd spotted it while looking for the coffeepot. It was a few years old, but Billy figured any P.I. that had been in business for a while was more likely to be reliable. He found one in the Yellow Pages specializing in missing persons. Curtis Feeney.

Billy dialed the number of Finders for Hire, an outfit with a slogan that seemed to sum things up pretty well—"You lose 'em, we find 'em." A man answered. "Finders for Hire, this is Feeney," he said.

"Mr. Feeney, my name's Billy Blue, up in Elko. I'm interested in tracking down a businessman who left Las Vegas a number of years ago. What would you charge to get me an address?"

"How long's he been gone?"

"I don't know for sure, but probably ten years minimum."

"Ten years. That's a long time."

"Yes, I know. How much will it cost me?"

"That depends," Feeney said. "Who you looking for, anyway? Maybe I know him."

"Irwin Pettigrew. Older fella, late sixties, early seventies by now. His handle was the Silver Fox. Don't know what business he was in, but most likely some kind of fraud was involved. From what I understand, he's a con man."

"Pettigrew, huh? The Silver Fox. Now, why does that name sound familiar?"

"Could you have tried to locate him before?"

"Maybe. Hold on, let me check my files."

Billy waited, wishing his grandmother hadn't given him thi charge, but feeling duty-bound to fulfill his promise. Billy drew on his bottle of beer. After a minute or so Feeney came back on the line.

"Yeah, I've got the gentleman in my files, all right," he said.

"How come, if you don't mind me asking?"

"He was the subject of an investigation. Minor matter. Long time ago."

"Can you tell me where I can find him?"

"What's the nature of your business with him, Mr. Blue, if you don't mind me asking?"

"Sorry to say, but Pettigrew's my old man. Never so much as laid eyes on the sonovabitch, but I need to track him down now."

"You're his son?"

"Technically speaking."

"Hmm. That's unexpected."

"It doesn't please me none too much to have to admit it. But the facts are the facts."

"Tell you what, I normally expect a fee, even for infor- mation already in my files, but what I've got is dated, and frankly, I don't have time to take on another case right now. You're welcome to what I've got, which isn't much."

"I'm listening."

"As of about eight or nine years ago, the subject was living in New York City."

"No kidding? You got an address?"

"I have the name of a lawyer who represented him. That's probably better. They don't move around so much. The fel- low's name is Bergman. Joel Bergman."

Billy got a piece of paper and jotted down the name and number Curtis Feeney gave him. "Much obliged, Mr. Fee- ney."

"There's one other thing you ought to know. Your father's

no longer Irwin Pettigrew. Legally changed his name to Simon Van Biers.''

''Van Biers?''

''Yeah, for a long time he used both names. Finally dumped Pettigrew altogether.''

''Must have got inconvenient,'' Billy said.

''That or he wanted to completely change his image. You work the Big Apple, I guess, you got to sound like you belong. What can I say?''

''You've been very helpful, Mr. Feeney.''

''Good luck.''

Billy hung up the phone and stared at the climbing rose on the side of the house next door. He'd been hating Irwin Pettigrew for so long, only to discover that the bastard no longer answered to the name. Lord, what else was he going to learn about his daddy before this was over?

Manhattan

Zoe met Winifred at a crowded bar off Fifth Avenue. It wasn't the best place for a drink and a little conversation, but they needed to talk. Simon Van Biers, the FBI and Victoria International Bank were the topics du jour. They also needed to discuss Ahmed, though he was almost secondary now. ''Funny how quickly we forget them,'' Win said. ''You're lucky, Zoe. It's the women who cling that are to be pitied. The key is learning to wash them right out of your hair.''

Zoe laughed. ''For a second there I thought you were going to break into song.''

''Main thing is you don't let your guard down,'' Win replied, giving her drink a swirl with the swizzle stick before taking a sip. ''The buggers can surprise you. Just when you think it's over and that part of your life is behind you...zap!''

''Okay, I promise to stay vigilant. But let's change the subject.'' Zoe sipped her Chardonnay, ignoring the leers of a desperate-looking little man at the bar, concentrating instead on her friend.

Winifred, a woman who could only be described as zaftig, was big in every respect—big red hair, big head, big lips, big breasts, big hips, big thighs. But small feet. "I love my feet," she'd once confessed to Zoe in a moment of candor. Win also had a big heart and a big brain. Zoe had come to rely on her heavily, both professionally and personally. The relationship was mutual, though. Win used Zoe as a sounding board in dealing with her self-destructive impulses vis-a-vis men.

"The question, of course, is whether by going to work for Simon Van Biers, you're jumping out of the frying pan and into the fire," Winifred said.

"I'm just going to have to take my chances. I've been working for this for years, you know. I mean, here I am struggling, knocking my head against the wall, trying to figure out how to get my painting back, and what happens? Van Biers comes walking right into Sotheby's, saying he's looking for a specialist on Van Gogh. If that's not destiny, what do you call it?"

"But that was before the FBI came into the picture."

"Well, I can't let their problems with the bastard get in the way of what I'm trying to do."

Win swizzled some more, then lifted her glass to her lips, pausing there. "This painting must be awfully important for you to give up a wonderful job and run off to an island inhabited by a den of thieves on the off chance you might get it back."

"Two things. First, it rightfully belongs to me, and second, we're talking about a previously undocumented Van Gogh from the Arles sunflower series worth zillions of dollars. How can I not go after it?"

"I'll give you one good reason—that guy Pearson. And the FBI. And the SEC. And the creepy son. What was his name?"

"Charles."

"From the way you described him, that alone might stop me," Win said. "But even if you can prove that the painting once belonged to your mother, Van Biers could be a purchaser in good faith and is thereby protected against your claim."

"I know, Win, we've been through all that. I'm sure Simon Van Biers knew he was buying a painting that was obtained illicitly. It's a Van Gogh original, for heaven's sake."

"Knowing it and proving it are two entirely different things."

"We know he's a con man."

"Past criminal behavior is not evidence of a crime. That's a long-established principle of the law."

"Oh, Win, do you always have to talk like a lawyer?" Her friend groaned, rolling her eyes. "What would you have me talk like? A hairdresser?"

"Well, at least a hairdresser usually agrees with anything you say."

"If you're looking for a yes-man, honey, you've come to the wrong place. I didn't go to Columbia to get these brass balls and not use them."

Zoe laughed. "Okay, okay."

"Excuse me, miss, but haven't we met?" It was the little man from the bar, standing over her, grinning in his Brooks Brothers suit. He was even less appealing up close.

"I don't believe so," she replied.

"But you do work for Coopers & Lybrand, don't you?"

"No, I'm afraid you've got the wrong person."

"I would have sworn it was at a conference a couple of months ago."

"Look, Jack," Win interjected, "the lady said she doesn't know you, so beat it so we can talk, okay?"

The little man's mouth dropped open and he turned on his heel and made a hasty retreat. Zoe shook her head, feeling badly but also relieved.

"You've probably destroyed his confidence for a month," she said.

"He's lucky I let him live. I step on most cockroaches."

Zoe laughed. "I guess I'm going to have to adjust to the single life again."

"Trust me on this. After you've shot down a few, you don't even feel it," Win said with a sly smile. "Sort of like being a professional killer. It's a jungle out there, kid."

Elko, Nevada

Billy lay on the bed in the guest room where he'd been sleeping since his return, measuring the pain in his back against the pain in his heart. His life had been turned on its head, he was at a crossroads, feeling helpless as hell—and all because he'd screwed the wrong gal. If there wasn't a lesson to be learned in that, he was beyond hope.

Two things above all others were eating at him. One was the promise he'd made to his grandmother, and the other was Shelly. It was hard to say which tore at him more. Billy sure as hell wasn't a crusader. If he felt comfortable fighting anything it was an ornery bull. Even at that, the fight only lasted a few seconds. The mere thought of having to go after the father he'd never known to demand the return of his grandmother's painting made him sick with dread.

And Shelly...well, she was his soft underbelly, the tragic love of his life. It was Shelly who defined all women and Shelly who determined how much or little he could feel. Seeing her again was bittersweet, maybe more bitter than sweet, if only because, as Cy Krebs used to say, "You can't take the same drink of water twice."

When there was a knock at the front door, Billy knew it was Shelly and his heart did a slow roll. Struggling to get off the bed and back onto his feet, he padded into the front room in his stocking feet. When he opened the door he found that it was her, all right. She stood on the porch with a casserole dish in her hands.

"You had supper yet?"

He shook his head. "No."

"Then here it is."

Billy hesitated before he stepped aside to let her in. Shelly moved past him and he savored the familiar scent of vanilla and honeysuckle. He found himself wanting—but knowing he couldn't have—the same drink of water again.

Billy followed her as far as the kitchen door, watching her as she put the dish on the stove top. Her body was riper than before, the face fuller, but it was Shelly. He remembered lying in the sun with her, stringing his fingers through her golden hair.

"It's still a bit warm," she said of the casserole. "All you have to do is heat it up. Medium oven."

"You wear the same perfume," he said.

The color rose in her cheeks. "You remember."

"I do."

Shelly seemed a bit self-conscious. "Actually, I don't wear the same perfume. I went and bought a bottle this afternoon."

It was a brave statement. Aggressively frank. "For me?" he asked.

"Yes, for you."

Billy appraised her, though not as kindly as she might have liked. Shelly picked up a tea towel from the counter and wiped her hands. "This ought to be good for a couple of meals, anyway."

He nodded. "What about your husband and your kids?" he asked.

Shelly thought a moment, then took it as an innocent question. "The children are visiting Todd's folks for a few days."

"Where's he?"

"Carson City."

"Is that why you're here?"

The remark hurt and surprised her, he could tell by the way she frowned. She tossed the towel on the counter. "Why did you say that?"

"I wanted to be clear."

She sighed with disgust. "Maybe I'm being too subtle."

Billy watched her tuck her blond hair behind her ear. He said nothing.

"Or maybe it doesn't please you."

"I didn't say that," he replied.

"Do you want me to leave, Billy? Is that what you're trying to say?"

"I'm wondering what you're really thinking. When you look at me, Shelly, who do you see? The boy I was when we made love for the first time?"

"No."

"Then who? Some guy who just got off the bus?"

Her eyes flashed. "Of course not." She regarded him with disbelief. "I can see this was a bad mistake." She shifted uneasily, looking very uncomfortable. "And you know what? I really don't know what I was thinking, coming here."

He continued to stare at her, his gaze unrelenting.

"I think I should leave now." She came toward the door, but Billy didn't cede the way. She stopped in front of him. "What?"

Billy reached out and touched her cheek, drawing his fingertip across her flesh. "I really, really loved you," he said.

Shelly's big blue eyes flooded. She didn't wait for the tears to overflow. She pushed past him and ran to the front door. Yanking it open, she flew out without stopping to close it. Hearing her car start, he sagged against the doorjamb, his own eyes glistening.

After a minute he went over and closed the front door. Then, for the sake of his back, he returned to the guest room and lay down. Billy supposed he'd done what he'd set out to do. Why, he still wasn't sure. For the sake of the past? Out of fear of the future? The only thing he felt fairly certain of was that she hadn't come out of love. Maybe that hurt more than anything.

It wasn't unfamiliar territory, though. All his relationships since Shelly had been for other reasons. And that wasn't because she had been his first—she wasn't. He'd been initiated into manhood by a divorcée over in Battle Mountain, a cowgirl and part-time insurance agent by the name of Lyn Peterson. She was his first woman if you excluded the hooker who'd actually got his cherry. Lyn, at thirty-one, was fourteen years

Billy's senior, a divorcée with eight- and twelve-year-old sons, three dogs, a dozen horses and a few hundred head of cattle. For six months or so he'd driven over to Battle Mountain once a week—more often when he was able to scrape up the gas money—to get his education in sexuality. Lyn was a fabulous teacher. Mainly, though, she was a milepost on the road to maturity. He'd considered Shelly the destination.

But then, disaster struck and their lives had gone awry.

It really saddened him to think that the only reason she'd wanted him now was because her husband was out of town. Or maybe it was that a little walk down memory lane would have been good enough for her. But that wasn't good enough for him. Not now. Not ever.

Tuesday
August 8th

Biloxi Plantation, St. Margaret

Mayte Van Biers heard Simon snort and she glanced up over her reading glasses to see him asleep in his chair, his chin sagging to his chest, the open file folder on his lap in danger of slipping to the floor. She started to call out to him to be careful, but decided what the hell. If a man on the brink of financial disaster could fall asleep reading about it, more power to him. Anyway, there wasn't much he could do unless he was willing to tap into the money he'd salted away. Keeping the balls in the air and the cash flowing was primarily her job.

Simon had said, though, that if their cash-flow crunch got severe enough he could always use his Van Gogh again as collateral against a larger loan. They'd tapped out their operating line of credit with their New York bank, and Simon was reluctant to try to restructure their debt just when they were about to put out a new offering—their first art syndication. "Everything in this business is perception," her husband had said. "The very last thing we need is to appear strapped for cash. If the guy with a checkbook in hand figures his money is going for salaries and toilet paper, I guarantee you he'll want no part of it.''

"Yes, Simon, but our existing investors and our creditors also can sink the ship. Once they start complaining, we're in the same mess as if we refinance.''

"Oh, I agree, sugar. That's why I'm always preachin' that we pay back the investor first. Keep our early investors happy and they'll sell our offerings for us.''

"But we pay them with a bad check and the word they give their friends won't be 'Go with these guys.'''

Simon had stroked his chin pensively then said, "Maybe I should fly to New York and see about a personal loan, using the sunflowers, and keep Victoria International out of the loop for now. Perhaps I can make a case for using the extra capital to enlarge my personal collection. I can then make a loan to the company and you can reimburse me out of the first round of investment money coming in on the new syndications.''

Simon knew perfectly well what he was proposing was illegal—at least in the States and most other countries—but he'd told her it was something he'd routinely done when he operated his string of pawnshops back in his "Las Vegas days." "What's more," he'd said, "our friends here in St. Margaret are incapable of policing a banking operation, even if they wanted to.'' They both knew the plan was dangerous, but Simon was adamant. "Victoria International never failed to make a scheduled payment to its investors, and won't until the day we decide to close up shop.''

"True," she'd said, "but at the rate we're going, that day is fast approaching. We aren't taking in new money fast enough.''

"All we need is a temporary infusion of capital...until we get the art syndications going. I say we turn the problem over to Van Gogh.''

Mayte couldn't help admiring her husband's optimism. But Simon was quick to point out that a positive attitude was essential to success in business. "In many ways, you are what you seem, sugar," he'd say. "That's a lesson always to keep in mind."

She hoped her own motives were somewhat better disguised because Mayte was, above all, an opportunist. Even her affair with Jerome Hurst was opportunistic—not that she didn't find him attractive. Jerome was a rare combination of brute and swordsman—an animal in bed, but an animal with finesse. Mainly, though, their relationship was a form of insurance. If Simon went down, Jerome Hurst could help her survive. And, if she played her cards right, she could end up holding all the broken pieces, but with a mandate to put them back together. Of course, there was Charles to contend with, as well, but she could almost count on him shooting himself in the foot. The important thing was to keep her own foot well clear.

Sighing, Mayte got up and left her husband snoozing under the ceiling fan of the huge salon, his silver head bowed. She moved with catlike grace across the hardwood floor, her filmy caftan swirling about her long legs. Wanting a breath of the balmy night air, she stepped out onto the veranda.

Mayte was greeted with the loveliest of sights—the silvery light of the moon shining on the Caribbean. The plantation house sat on a point atop a pleasant rise, offering a two-hundred-and-forty-degree view of the water. The lawn, gray-green in the moonlight, sloped down to the cliff above the white sandy beach a hundred yards from where she stood. Both the mansion and the grounds had been completely renovated.

Part of the reason for the company's cash-flow problems was the enormous sums Simon had either salted away in his private accounts or poured into the plantation. She considered the estate a monument to his ego, but Simon insisted it was essential to doing business. Of course, she enjoyed the benefits of his self-indulgence, but she couldn't help wondering if it wouldn't have been wiser to be more discreet. Simon wouldn't have it. "That MBA mentality of yours is useful in many respects, sugar," he'd say, "but they didn't teach you one thing at Harvard about the importance of perception. Nothing could be more important than showing your wealth. You don't show it, people assume you either don't have it, or you're hiding it because you dare not let people see.''

Mayte savored the breeze coming off the water. It made her think of that afternoon with Jerome in their love nest on Bristol Beach. With the island so small, and everyone aware of everyone else's business, they had to be extremely careful. Thus far, there hadn't been a problem. Mayte usually left her car in the public car park at the far end of the beach and walked to the villa. Jerome would have his driver drop him off on the road, then he'd walk the hundred yards through the palm grove to get to their rendezvous spot, the vegetation keeping him safely out of sight of snoopy neighbors.

Sometimes she'd arrive first, sometimes Jerome. Considering they were both busy, coordinating a secret rendezvous wasn't easy. They had a rule, though, which rewarded the more punctual partner. First one to arrive got to name the game they would play. That afternoon Mayte had walked in the door at the appointed hour but Jerome had already been there for fifteen minutes.

"You bastard," she'd said, genuinely annoyed. "I was in the mood for oral sex."

"I have something a little different in mind," he'd said, his handsome grin spreading under his mustache. "I think you'll like it."

Jerome, for all his sexual energy, did not often stray into the kinky realm, but when he took ropes and a blindfold out of a briefcase he'd brought, she knew she was in for something a bit outré.

"I don't know if I like this idea," she'd told him.

"You have no choice, my love," he'd replied. "We have an agreement." Then he tweaked her nose. "You may undress now."

She'd watched him arrange his paraphernalia on the bed as she slipped out of her clothes, laying them carefully on the chair in the corner. "Do you do this with your wife, Jerome?" she'd asked.

"No."

"So, I'm the lucky girl."

He laughed. "Have I ever failed to please you?"

She had to admit he'd been among the best lovers she'd had. Clearly he reserved his creative energies for her, though they met seldom enough that he must be able to keep his wife satisfied, too. And, surprisingly, Mayte usually managed to be receptive to Simon. In spite of his age, her husband was not without an interest in sex, though their relations were sporadic and infrequent at best. Simon, she had to admit, approached their encounters with a certain amount of vigor—she suspected, without being absolutely sure, that his fantasies turned on some sort of racial theme. She had to admit that early in their relationship thoughts of the white slave owner had entered her mind, as well—a theme which, if not a source of pleasure to her, did imbue Simon with an aura of sexual power not fully deserved.

More than once she'd heard him utter something that sounded an awful lot like "black bitch" at the magic moment. Mostly she found it amusing. Simon, she suspected, was perfectly aware that she tolerated his illusions of virility by letting him pretend. And he had to suspect she'd had lovers.

Jerome Hurst was a fortunate conquest in many respects. His ropes had turned out to provide a more erotically satisfying experience than she'd have thought. After tying her to the bed, he'd blindfolded her, then told her he'd engaged a young man to "warm her up." At first, she'd been amused, but then Jerome had gone through all the sound effects of letting someone in the room. There'd been whispering—the same voice or two? Then this mystery "apprentice" had gone down on her. Mayte had to admit it was terribly exciting, if somewhat frightening. She'd felt vulnerable and helpless, not knowing if it was really Jerome or not. That, of course, was the whole point.

Afterward he'd refused to tell her what had in fact happened, which infuriated her. "You've had your fun, Jerome,

ow tell me if it was you.'' Grinning, he shook his head. ''Half
he pleasure is in confounding you, my dear.''

''I won't come back,'' she'd warned.

But that only brought a smile. He knew as well as she it
vas an idle threat. Their relationship, after all, was about a
;ood deal more than sex.

Mayte heard a sound behind her on the veranda, but before
he could turn around, two strong arms enveloped her. She
mmediately recognized the spicy scent of Charles's cologne
nd, at about the same time, saw his white arms clamped
round her midriff.

''Charles! What are you doing? Let go of me!''

His mouth close to her ear, he chuckled. ''I've been watch-
ng you, Mummy dearest. You were thinking naughty
houghts. I could see it on your face.''

''Charles, I said let go of me!'' She could smell the alcohol
n his breath, too. ''You're drunk.''

''Not so drunk I couldn't tell you were twitching. And don't
ell me you were fantasizing about the old man, because I
/ouldn't believe it to save my soul.''

Jamming her elbow into his stomach, Mayte finally got her
•oorish son-in-law to loosen his grip and she squirmed free.
'urning, she glared. ''You have no idea how offensive that is.
don't find it amusing at all.''

''Don't get your tit in a wringer, Mayte. We both know you
lon't get what you need in your marital bed.''

''You know nothing!'' she seethed. ''Nothing!''

Charles, broad-shouldered and muscular in his polo shirt,
hrew back his head and laughed. ''The lady doth protest too
nuch.''

''Fuck you!''

''Okay, fine. When? Now? Here on the veranda? Or would
ou rather do it in the salon? We won't disturb Pops from his
•eauty sleep.''

''You're disgusting, Charles, you truly are. Why don't you
o annoy one of your whores?''

"Oh, don't put on airs, Mayte. You like it when I tease you. As much as any other woman."

"You're oblivious, totally delusional, so full of yourself you can't see the truth in front of your nose."

He sighed wearily. "All right, maybe I went a little too far. I apologize."

She gave him a disgusted look, but said nothing further. Instead, she turned toward the sea, folding her arms under her breasts. Charles stepped up beside her, brushing his shoulder against hers. She moved away. Charles sighed again.

"You're aware that an FBI agent has arrived from the States," she said after a while.

"Yeah, I heard."

"I don't suppose you're any closer to finding out who those witnesses were. By now you could have interrogated every woman on the island."

"Nobody knows a damned thing. Whoever they were, they haven't been gossiping with their friends. That's assuming they actually exist."

She turned her head sharply. "What do you mean by that?"

"It was pretty late. Are you sure you weren't imagining a couple of women coming out of the water?"

"Charles, I saw them. And there's nothing to be gained by making up stories. You're not the only one with something to lose."

"Well, I'm increasing the pressure," he said, "because discreet inquiries haven't produced a thing. Now I've got a couple of men going door to door in search of potential witnesses. And I've authorized a reward for anyone with information about Pearson's location."

"How are you justifying this? Surely people won't believe you're being a good Samaritan."

"Pearson was doing business with Victoria International and we have reason to be concerned when he disappears while visiting us. Shit, I'd do anything within my power to find the poor bastard." He grinned. "I think people buy that."

"There are at least two women on this island, besides me, who wouldn't. They know you're a murderer."

"Don't make it sound like I'm some kind of monster. The sonovabitch took the first shot when he tried to rip us off. I was just trying to protect the bank and everybody involved, including the people of this island."

"Well, the witnesses don't know that. Besides, the less said about what Pearson was doing, the better."

"Fear not, Mayte. I'm on top of this. It's going to take a little more time than I thought, that's all."

Mayte glanced over at him. "I hope your men understand discretion."

"Don't worry, everything's under control."

She scoffed to herself. The day Charles Van Biers was under control was the day she could retire to a life of leisure and leave Simon, the bank and the whole weary business behind.

They stood there for a while, neither speaking. Mayte wasn't sure what bizarre thought could be running through her stepson's mind, but it was certainly something.

"So," he said diffidently, "feel like going for a walk on the beach?"

"With you, Charles? No, thank you very much. Actually, I'm going inside. I've had a rough day." She turned to go.

"Yeah, I noticed."

Mayte, who was halfway through the French doors, stopped dead in her tracks. "What do you mean by that?"

Charles Van Biers smiled his evil smile. "If I'm not mistaken, Mummy dear, those are whisker burns on your chin. Good thing the old man is half-blind, isn't it?"

Mayte turned on her heel and went inside, her cheeks burning. She heard him laugh, which infuriated her even more. When she got back to the salon, Simon, who'd been snoozing, opened his eyes, apparently awakened by the sound of her footsteps.

"Ah, there you are. Where've you been?"

"I stepped outside for a breath of air," she said, picking up the files and documents she'd left.

"Are you going to work some more?" her husband asked.

"No, I'm going to bed."

Simon grinned a smile reminiscent of his son's. "Perhaps I'll join you."

"Fine," she said. But her fervent hope was that all he had in mind was sleep.

Wednesday
August 9th

Though he'd grown up in a town of thirty thousand, and had never been farther east than Omaha, Billy Blue didn't consider himself a hick. He'd been to L.A. and San Francisco and Seattle and Dallas and Denver, and along the way he'd rubbed shoulders with a few folks with money and class. Billy knew enough about the outside world to carry on a conversation and order a meal in a fancy restaurant. He read newspapers and magazines and books, and he liked to think he understood people pretty well, especially women. But he had this thing about being true to himself and not putting on airs.

Billy didn't consider it strange that he should look like who he was, so he arrived at JFK wearing boots, a hat and jeans. He had put on one of his better western shirts, but he didn't bother to pack his only suit, which was designated for funerals and weddings and court appearances. Nor had he packed chinos, a polo shirt and loafers—hell, he didn't own any.

New York was much like it looked in the movies—a swirl of humanity that wasn't half so orderly as a cattle stampede.

From the time he hit the terminal building until he left the bus station in Manhattan, Billy could tell people saw him as an oddity. But then, half the folks he encountered looked pretty strange to him, too.

Billy had used the thousand he'd gotten from Luther for the plane ticket. To cover his expenses, Ed Carlsen at the bank had advanced him two thousand dollars against the money he'd be inheriting from his grandmother, and he had the fifty-five-thousand-dollar cashier's check made out to Irwin Pettigrew for the painting. He hoped to transact his business and be back in Elko by the weekend.

The irony was, his feelings were as mixed about returning to Nevada as they were about coming to New York. With his grandmother gone, if Elko represented anything, it was Shelly. And after their last conversation, she was as good as dead and buried, too. In the two days since she'd tearfully run from Granny's house, Billy had thought of little else but her. Shelly was all he knew about love, yet he'd spurned her. Why? The only thing he'd come up with was that she hadn't offered him what he really wanted.

But he was in New York now and he had business to transact. That's what he had to focus on. Shelly was where she belonged—consigned to memory. And he was on his own.

The travel agent in Elko suggested he take a taxi from the bus terminal to the hotel, which was only six blocks, but after all the sitting, he felt like stretching his legs. His back was getting better and a stroll seemed more interesting than daunting, whether it meant lugging his case several blocks or not.

Even knowing he was in a city of several million people, Billy Blue studied the faces he encountered, wondering if old Pettigrew would in any way look familiar. His grandparent had never said if Billy favored his old man or not. When he first looked into Pettigrew's eyes, would he see bits and pieces of himself? The notion was an uncomfortable one. Having lost his mother and grandparents, Billy tended to think of himself as the lone survivor. He didn't much like the idea of being family to Pettigrew.

The hotel the travel agent had booked was on a side street, a small, shabby place that carried a price tag he would have expected at a place like a Hilton. Thin as his wallet was, Billy wasn't pleased, but he took comfort in the fact it would only be for a few days. If for some reason Pettigrew wasn't cooperative, Billy planned to hire a lawyer and let him slug it out with the old boy. Mostly he had to find some time to reflect and figure out what to do with his life. Initially that meant getting his butt back to Elko. What happened then remained to be seen.

Billy registered at the front desk and found he couldn't go to his room without being escorted by the bellhop, a youngish man of foreign origin. Billy gave him two bucks for opening the door, putting his case on the stand, pulling back the drapes and turning on the bathroom light. Service like that didn't exist in Bozeman, Montana. Even if you asked the motel maid for extra towels, she'd be shocked if you handed her a buck.

"Know a good place to eat?" Billy asked when he handed over the greenbacks.

"Downstairs," the guy replied.

Billy thanked him.

It was too late to hotfoot it over to Joel Bergman's law office, but Billy figured if he called he might catch him before closing time. Bergman wasn't in. His secretary told Billy he would be on vacation until the following week. That didn't bode well. Billy could see his big adventure was off to an ominous beginning.

"Maybe you can help me then," he said. "I'm trying to track down one of Mr. Bergman's clients. All I need is an address and a phone number."

"We don't give out that kind of information," she replied, her tone nasal and impatient.

"How about you point me in a direction where I could find him?"

"Who you looking for?"

"A man named Simon Van Biers. Also goes by the name

Pettigrew, Irwin Pettigrew. Came to New York from Las Ve
gas some years ago.''

There was a long silence on the line, then the woman sai
''Mr. Bergman no longer represents Mr. Van Biers.''

''That doesn't matter, I just want to contact the man.''

''Well, Mr. Van Biers isn't living in New York anymore.
can tell you that.''

Billy groaned. ''Great. I flew all the way from Nevada
talk to him.''

''Sorry about that. Anything else?''

''If you were in my shoes, and you wanted to find this guy
where would you go next?''

''Maybe I'd go talk to somebody at the *Wall Street Jou
nal*.''

''Seriously?''

''Mr. Van Biers is a big-shot banker now. They probabl
know all about him. Look, mister, it's closing time. I've g
to go, all right?''

With that, the phone went dead in his ear. Billy hung u
the receiver and lay back on the bed. Irwin Pettigrew a big
shot banker? That he didn't expect. Could Bergman's secretar
have been putting him on? Billy wondered if he'd just gotte
his first taste of New York humor. Or had his old man mac
it to the big leagues? If Pettigrew was a big-shot now, ho
would that affect their business dealings? He didn't kno
whether to expect his father to treat him better or worse. Th
unexpected news left Billy more wary than ever.

Queenstown, St. Margaret

Poppy lay on her bed, beaming with joy. Twice the test ha
come up positive. She'd promised herself if it came up positi
the third time, she'd tell Basil. Maybe the doctor would deci
the test result had been wrong—that she wasn't really pre
nant. That's why she hadn't said anything after the first te
or the second. But three positives couldn't be wrong. Surel

She was going to have a baby! And it was all thanks to Bon Mambo Marie Vincente de la Croix.

The trouble was there were rumors going around that the white man, Raymond Pearson, had been killed and that there were unknown witnesses to his murder. Basil had been talking about the case more and more, which made Poppy anxious. Bon Mambo Marie hadn't said the commotion on the beach had anything to do with Mr. Pearson, but Poppy had wondered and worried. Several times she'd considered ignoring Marie's admonition to leave the matter to the spirits, and she'd very nearly told Basil what had happened, but then she thought of the baby she so badly wanted. Now she was glad she had held her tongue. The spirits, with the help of Bon Mambo Marie, had blessed her. She could not defy them now.

Hearing someone at the front door, Poppy got up from her bed and went to the front room, where she found her husband looking tired and hot as he so often did after a day of work at the presidential palace. Basil, a tall, sturdy young man with broad shoulders and a gentle demeanor, smiled at the sight of her.

"There's my little flower," he said, wearily slumping into his chair.

Poppy went over and, kneeling beside him, took his hand and pressed it to her cheek. He was so dear to her with his smoothly handsome features and soft brown eyes. "Basil, I've got wonderful news."

"I do, too."

She was disappointed. "Oh? What's your news?"

"No, you first," he said.

She shook her head. "No, I want to hear yours."

Basil scratched the mutton-chop sideburn on his jaw. "Well, you know the old Haitian woman who lives around the far side of the island, the one who does the witchcraft?"

Poppy's heart skipped a beat. "Yes...what about her?"

"Chief Inspector Goodson thinks she may have information about the disappearance of the American, Raymond Pearson."

She was shocked. "Truly, Basil?"

"Yes, when one of his officers dropped by to question her, she became most agitated and tried to run away. It was a very suspicious reaction to routine questioning. So she was arrested. And now she won't say a thing. Even pretends not to understand English."

"Basil, the poor old woman is probably frightened."

"What does she have to be afraid of?"

"I don't know, but she is all alone in a strange country."

"You're overdramatizing, Poppy. Chief Inspector Goodson said her behavior is most suspicious and he believes she knows something, but won't say."

"He doesn't believe she's responsible for whatever happened to Mr. Pearson, does he?"

"No, but he's convinced she's hiding something."

The news was very upsetting. Poor Bon Mambo Marie. Poppy could picture the old woman's wizened face and her intense, dark eyes, knowing how frightened she must have been when confronted by the police. Poppy wondered what she should do. After all, she needed the blessing of the spirits if she was to have a healthy baby. Bon Mambo Marie Vincente de la Croix was her spiritual guide. Poppy needed her as much as ever.

"Well then," Basil said, "what's your news, love?"

Poppy was so distressed by what her husband had told her that she could hardly bring herself to tell him the news. She made a long face.

"Poppy?"

She pressed his hand to her cheek again. "I have very good news, but I want to keep it until after you've had your supper."

"Why, Poppy? Why not tell me now?"

"Because I want the mood to be right and I want you to recover from your hard day."

"You're sure?"

"Yes," she said, smiling into his eyes, even though she was churning inside with worry.

"As you wish, my little pet."

Poppy rose to her feet. "I'll start your supper now, Basil. You read your papers."

He smiled appreciatively and she went off to the kitchen. Her anxiety was so great, though, that she couldn't start work without first stepping out back for a breath of air to calm her racing heart. Her wonderful news had been ruined. What could it mean that they'd arrested Bon Mambo Marie? The man the two of them had seen being pursued on the beach that day—could it have been Mr. Raymond Pearson? And, if so, what did Marie know that Poppy didn't? And most important of all, what did this mean to the spirits? If they were angry, surely they wouldn't take vengeance on her and her baby. Poppy needed to speak to the Bon Mambo Marie Vincente de la Croix as soon as possible.

Thursday
August 10th

Charles Van Biers hadn't ridden much of late and he felt badly about that—not so much for his own sake as for his three ponies, which he dearly loved. Much as he liked women, he had never found one he cared for half so much as his polo ponies. Sure, he was always up for a piece of ass, but nothing was as good as being on horseback, riding hard and being as one with a big powerful animal.

Charles had spent a fortune on his ponies, starting when he hired the finest trainer in the Caribbean, Tommy Epps. "You've got one job, Tommy," Charles said, "and that's to take care of my babies."

Tommy Epps, a Brit and onetime steeplechase jockey, had been in the Caribbean for years, mostly breeding and training polo ponies. He was in his sixties and had just been swindled out of his retirement when Charles hired him to oversee the St. Margaret Polo Club, of which he was president, as well as look after his own personal stock. But it wasn't exactly benevolence on Charles's part. Because of his reputation for being heavy-handed with his employees, finding qualified help to work for him wasn't easy. Charles and Tommy were in the odd position of needing each other.

"Here, lass," Tommy called to a slender mulatto girl standing in the shade by the barn. "Walk this pony until he's cooled down."

The girl, probably in her middle teens, came to take Charles's horse. She was slender, coltish, but with huge gray eyes and pleasing curves. She did not look at Charles, obediently taking the reins from Tommy and walking off with the horse toward the paddock. Charles stared after her.

"Never seen her before," he said. "Who is she?"

"Sister of one of the stable boys. He's in hospital with a bad appendix and she's filling in for him so the family doesn't lose any income."

"She's got a nice little ass," Charles said, still looking after her. "Maybe we ought to keep her and get rid of the brother."

"She's just a kid, Mr. Van Biers. Still in school. Only available because of summer holiday."

"Summer's a great time for fun, Tommy." He turned and headed for the locker room to have a quick shower before his meeting. After going half a dozen steps he had an idea and stopped. "Oh, by the way," he said to the trainer, "I noticed we're getting short of towels. Send the girl up to the club to bring a couple of stacks, will you?"

"I'll get them, Mr. Van Biers."

"No, Tommy. You aren't listening. I said send the girl."

"To bring towels to the men's locker room?"

"That's right."

"It wouldn't be proper, sir."

"Why not?"

"She's but a youngster."

"Tommy, do I look like a rapist? I'm a gentleman. Send the girl. And do it now. I'll be needing a towel soon."

Epps lowered his eyes. "Right you are, sir."

Charles started to turn away, but stopped. "What's her name, anyway?"

"CeCe."

"CeCe, huh?"

"Yes, sir."

Charles, feeling that familiar hunger for tender flesh, went inside the building to the locker room. He had the place to himself as he usually did midday, during the week. Most members rode evenings and weekends, which was why he enjoyed coming when he did.

He sat on the bench and removed his boots. Tired from his workout, he struggled to remove his shirt. He didn't take off his breeches, lying on the bench instead to catch his breath. Staring at the ceiling, Charles thought about the girl, CeCe's, tight little ass, wondering if there was any chance of enticing her. Tommy was right, she was awfully young. But she could be willing, given sufficient encouragement.

Of course, even a little too much familiarity could blow up in his face. Early in his stay on St. Margaret, he'd pushed a bit too hard with a couple of young local girls and there had been complaints. His father had warned him about the dangers of alienating the islanders. "It's better you fly in a party girl for the weekend," his old man had said. Charles had done that but, considering the size of his sexual appetite, it hadn't been sufficient. So he'd cultivated a few friendships on the island, as well. It was his nature, though, to go after fresh meat.

It took ten minutes before there was finally a knock on the locker-room door.

"Come in!" Charles called out. He still lay on the bench, wearing only his jodhpurs.

Lifting his head, Charles saw the door open a crack.

"Your towels, sir," came a girlish voice from outside. "I'll just leave them here by the door."

"No, bring them in, CeCe."

"Are you sure?"

He couldn't help smiling at the innocence. "Yes, I'm decent."

The door opened a bit wider and Charles could see her pretty oval face and round, distrustful eyes.

"Come in!" he commanded. Then, pointing to the adjacent bench, he said, "Put them there."

Struggling with the bundle of towels, CeCe carried them to the bench, scarcely glancing his way. Charles lifted himself to his elbow and admired the girl's slender curves.

When she started to leave, he said, "Hold on."

"Sir?" For the first time she seemed aware of his broad, downy chest, but didn't stare for long.

"Mr. Epps tells me you're replacing your brother."

"Only for a few days, Mr. Van Biers."

"You like horses, CeCe?"

She shrugged. "Yes."

"Maybe you'd like to take care of my horses for me."

"I do what Mr. Epps asks."

"The question, sweetheart, is will you do what I ask?"

She blinked with uncertainty. "I don't understand."

Charles grinned with amusement. "How old are you, CeCe?"

She looked at him warily, perhaps sensing the conversation was leading somewhere dangerous. "Fifteen."

"You're practically a grown-up young lady, then."

CeCe began to look worried. Charles swung his legs off the bench. Standing, he sauntered to the door and locked it. Then he leaned against it, folding his muscular arms over his chest. The girl became very anxious.

"Why are you doing that?" she asked, trying to sound indignant but falling short.

"I thought maybe we could talk, CeCe, get better acquainted. You don't have a problem with that, do you?"

"I don't want to talk, Mr. Van Biers. I want to do my work."

Charles drew a breath, expanding his chest. "You mean you wouldn't want to be my friend?"

"No," she replied, shaking her head. "Not as you mean."

"Just how do I mean?" he asked, grinning.

"Please, I want to go," she said, looking as though she might cry.

Charles could see he'd overplayed his hand, or that the girl was too immature to appreciate what was happening. He slowly nodded. "Okay, CeCe, but you're missing a great opportunity. Not many guys like me come along in a girl's life, you know." He unlocked the door and opened it halfway. Then he bowed with mock obsequiousness, indicating she could go. CeCe quickly slithered through the opening, but not before he reached out and gave her a slap on the behind. The girl went running down the hall and Charles Van Biers threw back his head and laughed. What a sweet little piece of ass, he thought.

Checking his watch, Charles could see he was already late for his meeting. From everything he'd heard, Mooky Blade was not a patient man. It was probably just as well the stable girl wasn't in the mood to hop in the shower with him. Charles had to focus his attention on the task at hand. He'd save the grab-ass for later.

New York

Billy Blue had been waiting in the reception area for the better part of half an hour. For the third time he got up to stretch his back, making a slow circle about the room. The girl at the switchboard half watched and half ignored him, but every time their eyes met, a quirky smile bent the corner of her mouth. She was sort of cute in a bouncy, round-faced way. Billy hadn't said much to her, but he was beginning to see he could use a friend if he was ever going to get past the palace gate.

So, finally he went over to her desk and leaned over it and gazed into her perky blue eyes. "You sure they know I'm out here waiting, Teresa?" he asked, having noted the nameplate on her desktop.

"I told them what you wanted and they said someone would be out to speak with you as soon as they were free."

"I heard you should spend each day as though it were your last. I sure would hate to think I blew my last day like this."

The girl laughed in spite of herself. The inside door opened just then and a woman of thirty or so with a confident, professional demeanor appeared. She was short and not particularly pretty but she had an attractive intensity about her. And, like most everybody else in New York, she seemed in a hurry.

"Mr. Blue?" she said, approaching the man who'd been seated in the corner, reading a paper.

"No, ma'am, that would be me," Billy said.

The woman turned on her heel and came toward him almost without breaking stride. She sized him up, drawing her conclusions as she extended her hand. "Natalie Stern," she said. "I'm a staff writer here at the *Journal*. I understand you want to talk about Simon Van Biers."

"To be perfectly honest, I wanted to get some information about him. The folks at his former lawyer's office suggested I come here."

She looked perplexed. "A lawyer sent you here?"

"His assistant did."

Natalie Stern frowned, shaking her head as though he was making no sense. "What kind of information are you looking for?"

"Basic stuff, like where I might find the old coot."

She gave a little laugh. "What do you know about Simon Van Biers, Mr. Blue?"

"Damned little."

"That's what I'm beginning to see."

She absently scratched her scalp through her short-cropped brown hair. He noticed she wore no rings.

"I understand he's a big-shot banker now," Billy said. "Back when I knew him...or, I guess I should say, knew of him, he ran a string of pawnshops in Vegas and was known as the Silver Fox. I understand he's no longer in New York, but I'm having trouble finding out where he is."

Natalie gave Billy an appraising look, one that signaled more than either impatience or curiosity. It was the look a gal

had before she asked a man to dance. "Van Biers's operatio
is headquartered in the Caribbean," she said. "On St. Ma
garet."

"The Caribbean?" he groaned. "Damn, I was hoping you'
say Philadelphia or Washington, or someplace close."

She laughed. "No such luck. The good news is the island'
small, so Victoria International Bank will be easy to find.
haven't been there, but I imagine if there's a building mor
than two stories high, it belongs to Van Biers."

Billy hated the thought of having to go to the Caribbean
He wasn't even sure he had enough money for an airlin
ticket. "I suppose it's not cheap getting down there, is it?"

"It is the off-season so you won't be paying premium rate
for a hotel."

Natalie looked him over again with a demeanor that Bill
could only describe as cocky self-assurance. There was some
thing blunt and no-nonsense about these New York girls. C
maybe she found him amusing. Or attractive. Whatever it wa
he had her attention and decided to press ahead with his que
tions.

"Do you know Van Biers very well?" Billy asked.

"I've interviewed him."

"Could you tell me a little about him?"

She checked her watch. "I'd like to help, but I've got
staff meeting in a few minutes." Her smile was almost apo
ogetic. "You know how it is."

"This is really pretty important to me, Miss Stern. Woul
you let me pick your brain if I buy you dinner?"

She chuckled appreciatively, but hesitated before she spok
Billy could tell she was tempted. Her expression turned ser
ous. "What's your business with him?"

"It's actually a long story."

"You're going to have to do better than that."

Billy saw no reason not to throw out a little bait. "Va
Biers is my old man, though I'm sure he'd as soon forget
existed. And he's got something very valuable that belongs
me. I want it back."

"What is it?"

"Dinner?" Billy said.

She smiled appreciatively. "I might bring along my note-book."

"I might just do the same," he replied.

"Okay, Billy. Dinner."

Newquay Bay, St. Margaret

Charles bumped along the dirt road in his Porsche. Some-times he hated this fucking island. There wasn't more than two hundred yards of straight level pavement where he could open her up—not unless he wanted to land in the drink or a brier patch.

As he took a sharp corner, his tires spun in the dirt and gravel, sending up a cloud of dust. Muttering under his breath, he fishtailed his way up the road. Finally he came to the drive-way of the house where the Blades were staying. It was a tidy, whitewashed villa nestled in a grove of palms a hundred yards from the beach. Charles pulled in and stopped behind the SUV that sat next to the house. Earl's motorbike was next to it, leaning against the palm.

Earl Gridley, Charles's chief lieutenant in matters of secu-rity, who had leased the place on Charles's instructions, came out of the house to greet him. Earl was sharper and better educated than the rest of the crew, which was why Charles put him in charge. He was in a white dress shirt, shorts and sandals, his usual attire. "Glad you're here, boss," he said. "Blade's getting impatient."

"Fuck him," Charles said. "I'm paying the bills, I do ev-erything in my own good time."

"Blade's a mean sonovabitch," Earl said under his breath. "I don't think who's paying the bills matters to him all that much. Says he only works on his terms."

Charles cast a dark look toward the house. "He's not the

only badass black sonovabitch in the Caribbean, is he? W
could find somebody else.''

Earl, looking uncomfortable, said, ''I had a deuce of a tin
finding him and getting him here, boss. Besides, the bloke
the best there is. And we're running out of time.''

''Don't talk to me about time, boy. My neck's in the noo:
right along with yours.'' He tossed his head. ''Come on, let
go inside.''

Charles marched to the door, determined to set this Jama
can nigger straight. He'd found that unless you let 'em kno
who's boss right from the get-go, you have nothing but tro
ble.

He pulled the door open, but the interior of the house w.
so dark that, after the bright sunshine, he could scarcely see
thing.

''You're lettin' the flies in, man,'' came a rumbling voi
from the interior. ''Close the fucking door.''

His ire roused, Charles stepped inside. He was in a moc
to kick ass. ''Listen, asshole, nobody tells me to…'' Charles
voice trailed off at the sight before him.

In the middle of the tile floor, a naked mass of gleamir
black muscle was stretched out, steel-rod rigid, doing pus'
ups at a lightning pace. But more remarkable still, sittir
cross-legged, square in the middle of his back, was a whi
woman in a bikini, as lean and hard-looking as the behemo
under her, except that she was a third his size. But for the fa
they were in motion, they might have been ebony and ivo
statuary.

The man, his shaved head gleaming with perspiration, co
tinued his exercise while the woman glared, catlike. ''You'
late, man,'' he said, looking up for the first time, the whit
of his eyes glowing eerily in the obscurity.

''I had business.''

''Maybe, but you had business with me.'' The two arr
kept firing like pistons. Charles watched in awe at the r
markable display of strength.

"Well, I'm here," he grumbled, not quite so brazenly as before.

After another ten push-ups, Blade stopped pumping. "That's enough, Dani."

The woman sprang off him, her movement as well as her looks evocative of a cat. She had straight black hair, cut short in a Dutch-boy style. Her skin was very white. She circled back and forth in front of Charles, all but hissing. Blade, meanwhile, began pumping out one-arm push-ups.

Her voice low, the woman said, "If I were you, mister, I wouldn't call Mooky 'asshole' again. His hearing's bad because of an explosion he was in, so he missed what you said. You're lucky."

Charles was speechless. People didn't talk to him this way. And yet, his sense of danger compelled him not to object. "He does know I write the checks around here," he finally muttered.

"You pay Mooky for results. It doesn't give you the right to treat him any way you want. He demands respect and he gets it." She spoke English with an American accent, though there was a tinge of something else. It wasn't Jamaican or British.

Blade finished his push-ups and sprung to his feet, his ebony skin gleaming with perspiration. He was a monster of a man— six and a half feet tall, two hundred and fifty or sixty pounds of solid muscle in black thong trunks. Charles couldn't help staring.

"What's up, babe?" Blade said to the woman.

"Mr. Van Biers was just apologizing for keeping us waiting," she said, elevating her voice half again louder than normal conversation.

Mooky Blade nodded. He did not smile, his heavy features even and strong, both pleasing and fearful to look at. Two gold hoop earrings hung from his attenuated lobes. His countenance alone was mesmerizing. "Probably won't happen again, will it, Mr. Van Biers?"

Charles shook his head.

Blade took the towel that the woman, Dani, handed him.
He wiped his face, his shaved head, his neck, shoulders and
arms. "You're probably busy, too, man," he said to Charles.
"Shall we talk now, or do you want to wait until after I've
had my shower?"

"Let's talk now." Charles noticed Blade was reading his
lips.

"That be fine," the huge black man said. "How about outside in the nice balmy air?"

"Okay."

Dani handed Blade a pair of baggy white terry shorts, which
he slipped on over the black thong. He then led the way out
of the house, followed by the woman, Charles and Earl Gridley, who'd maintained a cautious silence. There were two
wooden lawn chairs facing each other under the palms. Blade
sat in one, Charles in the other. Dani went behind Blade's
chair. Charles checked her out until he caught Blade's eye and
felt compelled to look away. Positioning herself behind Blade,
Dani began massaging the big man's shoulders. Earl went over
and leaned against a palm.

"So, man, you've got two women on this island who could
be an embarrassment to you," Blade said. "You don't know
who they are, but you want them found and…silenced. Do
understand your intentions?"

Charles nodded. "Yeah, that's it." He could not take his
eyes off the man's arms, chest and shoulders. Never had he
seen a more perfectly sculpted specimen. Even the comely fox
standing behind him, ample cleavage and all, hardly drew his
attention from Blade, who looked for all the world like some
sort of African potentate.

"I need all the details if I'm going to help, man."

Charles recounted what had happened, staying ambiguous
about what he and his men were doing on the beach. "Our
hands have been tied trying to find the pair," he said, "because it draws attention to us. We may have a break, though.
A couple of days ago, the police arrested an old Haitian
woman, some kind of witch doctor or something. She was

acting nervous and suspicious. The last thing I heard they released her from custody, but told her not to go anywhere. I guess she wouldn't tell them anything, but they're suspicious she's hiding something."

"Hmm," Blade said, pursing his thick lips. "Why, exactly, are the police involved in this matter?"

Charles could see there were limits to how obscure he could be. "They're investigating the disappearance of an American art appraiser, a guy named Raymond Pearson."

"I thought maybe it be something like that. And what's your connection to Pearson?" Blade asked.

"Connection?"

"Come on, man, how can I help if you keep me in the dark? It's not a coincidence the police are talking to this woman about a man's disappearance and you think she may be one of the women you're looking for. Did you kill this bloke, Pearson?"

"M-m-me?" Charles stammered.

Blade gave him a "Well, of course, who else?" look.

"My men did," Charles said with half a glance at Earl. Realizing it was a losing cause, he added, "On my orders, admittedly. The sonovabitch was blackmailing me."

"So, in the eyes of the law, you killed him. Now you want, what? The witnesses eliminated?"

Charles shrugged, trying to act cool but feeling helpless in the face of Blade's overpowering persona.

"This Haitian woman. You think she's one of the women involved?" Blade asked.

"Probably," Charles muttered.

"What say, man? Speak up so I can hear you?"

"Probably."

"If so, maybe she be more of a friend than an enemy."

Charles was perplexed. "Why do you say that?"

"Isn't it obvious? She didn't tell the police what she saw, did she? They arrest her for questioning and she doesn't point a finger at you."

"I can't be sure she won't, though. And what about th
other woman? I don't know who she is."

Blade focused on Charles's lips. "So, what is it you wan
man? I break her arm and find out what she knows?"

"Find out if she was there that evening, if she saw anythin
And if so, I also want to know who the other woman is."

"Seems to me that one's not saying anything, either."

"Yeah, but I don't want it hanging over my head that the
might. I just want to be sure what the fuck's going on. Rig
now I'm completely in the dark, at their mercy, and I don
like it."

"Okay, Mr. Van Biers. Dani and I will find out what yo
want to know. And when we do, then you tell me what yo
want done."

"Perfect."

"What's the name of the Haitian witch?"

"Bon Mambo Marie Vincente de la Croix."

"Ah, a mambo, eh?"

"What does that mean?"

"She's a priestess."

"So?"

Mooky Blade smiled. "You know voodoo, Mr. Va
Biers?"

Charles shrugged. "I know a little."

"Well, you better hope this Bon Mambo Marie don't g
stickin' a pin in the heart of a doll with your name on it."

Dani giggled. Blade, grinning, ran his hand up her arm.

"I'm not worried," Charles said disdainfully.

Blade's smile was so broad his large white teeth shone li
piano keys. Charles knew they were playing with him and
didn't like it.

"Well, she won't be sticking pins anywhere if she's dead,
he said.

"This is true, man. And I could off every woman on th
whole damned island and nobody would be talkin', but th
just might be overkill, don't you think?" He chuckled. "I'
be asking questions before I go killing anybody," Blade sai

"I assume you don't want innocent people dying any more than me."

"Handle it any way you want," Charles replied. "Just get the job done." He got to his feet. "Is there anything else we need to discuss?"

"Just my advance fee."

"Oh, yeah." He turned to Earl. "My case is in the car, behind the driver's seat. Get it, will you?"

Earl went to the Porsche and returned a short time later with the case. Charles motioned for him to give it to Blade, who in turn indicated Dani. She took the case and put it on the ground. Squatting beside it, she popped open the lid. Inside was twenty-five thousand dollars in bills. The woman fanned through several bundles, then nodded to Blade.

"Everything seems to be in order," he said. "Now, Mr. Van Biers, your job is to stay out of my way."

"You get the results and we won't have any trouble."

"Say again," Blade said, cupping his ear.

"Fine," Charles said, elevating his voice. "Just do your thing."

Mooky Blade did not shake Charles's hand. He returned to the house with Dani, carrying the case with him. Charles checked out her bikini bottom and toned legs, watching until they were inside. Then he turned to Earl.

"What's with the broad? Blade feel he needs an entourage?"

"She's his wife."

"Yeah?"

"That's right. French-Canadian, but grew up mostly in the States."

Charles's brows rose. "Pretty classy for a masseuse."

"She's more than that, boss. She's his right hand. Killed men with her bare hands, according to Blade."

Charles considered that, finding the woman's comely image, the cleavage, at odds with the notion of a killer for hire. "Well, I guess that means she won't have trouble with some old voodoo witch then, will she?'' He turned and headed for his Porsche.

Earl got his motorbike and pushed it to where Charles stood waiting by his car. Charles was horny. A well-filled bikini could do that to him. He leaned on the roof of the car and stared at the house where Blade and his woman were staying. ''I need a piece of ass, Earl. Go by Gloria's place and bring her to my room at the club, will you?''

''Okay, boss.''

''And if you can't find her, get the one with the huge ta-tas, what's her name?''

''Cynthia?''

''Yeah. Whoever. Just bring me a woman.'' Charles Van Biers got in the Porsche and drove off, leaving a cloud of dust in his wake.

Friday
August 11th

"**Y**ou're my first cowboy," she said. "Did I mention that last night?"

Billy looked at her in the dresser mirror as he buttoned his cuffs. She had the bedsheet pulled up discreetly under her chin, though fifteen minutes earlier, when he'd gone into the bath for his shower, she'd been lying there buck-ass naked, a sleepy grin on her face. "I believe you did," he said.

"You probably hear that a lot, don't you?"

"Not so much. In my country I'm not the curiosity I am here in New York City."

"Your country..." Natalie Stern said dreamily. "That might as well be the moon."

"I wouldn't go that far, ma'am," he said, turning to face her.

"Ma'am? Do you say ma'am to every woman you fuck?"

"No," he replied with a grin. "Not if I've known a lady more than twenty-four hours."

"You must think I'm a tart. A big-city girl who'll hop in bed with any cowboy with an adorable grin."

"That's not what I think and I'm sure it's not true."

"Don't try to make me feel better, Billy. Though I appreciate the gesture."

He sat in the small straight chair to put on his boots. The sun broke through the window just then, falling across the woman's face. She shielded her eyes against the rays.

"If last night is any indication," she said, "you socialize with a lot more than just the cows and the sheep."

"You tryin' to flatter me?"

"In my way, yes."

"Did I, by any chance, mention you're my first reporter?"

"No, I don't believe you did."

"Well, you are," he said, "so that about makes us even."

Natalie Stern was not beautiful, but she had a nice sensuous smile and big, white teeth, which she was prone to use on a fella's neck or shoulder when she came. He had two monkey bites to prove it. "I bet I'm your first Jew, too," she said.

"Now, I couldn't rightly say," Billy replied, his tone serious. "Folks out West don't run around with little signs around their necks."

"I'm your first," Natalie said with certainty.

"What makes you so sure?"

"Jewish intuition."

He chuckled. "Is that anything like feminine intuition?"

"More than you might think."

Billy stood, straightening his belt buckle. He gave her a wink.

Natalie sighed. "The greatest pleasures in life seem the briefest, don't they?"

There was a time when Billy might have agreed wholeheartedly, and thought if his greatest pleasures had been brief, it was because he wanted it that way. It was the melancholy, the bittersweet, that seemed to last forever. Like Shelly.

Billy knew she was the reason he'd gone to bed with Natalie Stern. He had to do something to get her out of his mind.

Natalie was a nice diversion. She was single and sexy. She was also smart and quite funny. They'd had a good time.

Natalie told him lots about Simon Van Biers. "He's taking in money hand over fist," she'd said, "but a lot of people think a bunch of it is going into his own pocket. Nobody says it publicly, of course, but privately he's called a con man."

"That sounds like my old man. He screwed my family over, too." Billy had told her about the painting he was retrieving on behalf of his grandmother.

"You're kidding," she'd said. "It's not his?"

"Nope."

Natalie admitted she'd heard stories about the Van Gogh. "Nobody ever suggested it might not be his, though," she'd said. "In fact, Van Biers has kind of considered the Van Gogh his trademark, from what I've heard. Owning a famous painting makes people feel special and important, I guess."

"Well, he doesn't own it. I do."

"Billy," Natalie had said, "are you telling me this on or off the record?"

"You're asking if you can put it in the paper."

"Essentially."

"Could you wait until I get the painting back? I wouldn't want to screw up my chances."

"On the condition that you give me an exclusive."

"You're pretty safe there, Natalie. I don't know any other reporters."

"You have a knack for getting acquainted, however. But as far as getting the painting away from Van Biers, it might not be as easy as you think."

"But I've got the papers proving it's mine."

"Not to rain on your parade or anything, but this isn't Montana."

"Nevada."

"Whatever. My point is, you're in lawyer heaven now. They can tie up the air supply here if they want, so that you're forced to negotiate just to breathe. In these parts, honey, the rich and powerful call the shots. You left frontier justice back home on the frontier.''

''We'll see.''

The entire conversation had taken place at the restaurant where two little pasta dishes cost him the equivalent of, say, six slabs of prime rib in Cheyenne. They hadn't talked about Simon Van Biers after that. Natalie had been real interested in hearing about the life of a rodeo cowboy and she'd invited him back to her apartment to hear more. She'd fixed them each a tall drink and then she'd attacked him. Billy hadn't resisted. He considered it therapy.

''When do you plan on going down to the Caribbean?'' she asked, still hidden under the covers.

''Just as soon as I can,'' Billy replied. He took his hat from the dresser. ''My first problem, I guess, is getting a passport.''

''That's not going to be quick, Billy. But you might not need one. Some of those countries will let you in with a driver's license and a birth certificate.''

''Well, I've got the birth certificate with me. I figured that since Pettigrew doesn't know me from Adam, I ought to have some proof of who I am. The birth certificate has his name on it as my father, big as life.''

''Check with the airlines, but that may be good enough.''

''If it isn't, I guess I'll have to go back home and save up enough for a trip to the Caribbean.''

''If you do, be sure and come through New York.''

Billy went over and sat next to her on the edge of the bed. Natalie reached out and took his hand.

''It's been special,'' he said.

''Yes, I'd agree with that. It has.''

''It sure was a pleasure meeting you.''

She gave a little laugh. ''Trust me, honey, the pleasure was all mine.''

''I'm much obliged for the lowdown on my old man.''

''I'm happy to accommodate.''

She reached up and put the palm of her hand against his cheek. Billy leaned over and kissed her softly on the lips.

"Good luck," she said.

"And I hope you figure out what you're going to do about Aaron."

His remark was inspired by a conversation they'd had in the afterglow of sex. Natalie had told him about her boyfriend.

"Oy vey!" she said, rolling her eyes. "Riding lessons are at the top of the list, I can tell you that."

Billy gave her a grin. "I'll be going then."

"Goodbye, cowboy."

He put on his hat and headed for the door.

"Oh, Billy..."

"Ma'am?"

"If you need anything while you're down there, give me a call. You still have my card?"

"In my wallet."

"I'll remember you."

Billy nodded and left the bedroom. He made his way through the cramped front room cluttered with books, newspapers and Natalie Stern's underthings. As he walked along the musty hallway, the words she'd uttered just before she'd fallen asleep the night before went through his head. "Now I can die a happy old lady."

He'd heard words like that before, and they never ceased to appeal to his manly pride. Even so, he was coming to realize it was not enough. Turn a woman on, have a little fun. Maybe there were worse ways to live, but sometimes when all was said and done, his life was a bit like the ponies at the carnival—at the end of the day, once the kids were gone and the laughter had ceased, there was nothing to look forward to but another ride, another day.

The Countryside, St. Margaret

The Bon Mambo Marie Vincente de la Croix had not slept since they'd released her. There was much evil on the island now and she was afraid that when her ti bon ange left her body it might be damaged by the evil spirits. So she'd spent nearly every moment serving the loa, beseeching the spirits for protection. She'd sacrificed a chicken, drinking its blood in the name of Ayza, the protector god. She'd performed ritual after ritual, chanting incessantly, "Ko lo jee mo, Ko lo jee mo, Ko lo jee mo, Ko lo jee mo," until she was practically in a stupor.

Marie had had visions, as well. She'd dreamed of a great black bull ridden by a woman. In her vision, the bull, who Marie was convinced was the evil Baka, entered her hounfour and tried to destroy it so Marie could no longer communicate with the spirits. The message was clear—keep maximum distance from the evil. With too few followers for there to be protection in numbers, Marie had no choice but to follow her instincts and the guidance of the loa. To tell the police what she'd seen would bring her into the circle of the evil. And more importantly, it would involve Poppy, as well.

"Why are you afraid to talk to us?" the policemen had asked over and over. "What are you hiding?"

Marie had refused to answer, except to say, "Nothing. I know nothing."

The spirits confirmed her wisdom when they sent Poppy to visit her at the jail with the good news of her baby. The blessing came because Marie had shielded her from the evil at the beach. Poppy was so happy, she'd paid Marie triple the fee. Now it was her duty to protect the baby, as well as the mother. The mambo knew the forces of evil were not sleeping, they were gathering force. The bull was lurking and Marie had to be very cautious, especially at night.

So, as darkness fell, she let it gather around her like a womb, sitting in the corner of her front room with a single candle on the table beside her and an asson in her hand. "Ko lo jee mo, Ko lo jee mo, Ko lo jee mo," she chanted, lightly shaking the rattle.

Sometime later—Marie had lost all track of time—a sound from the outside world brought her back. It was a vehicle coming down the little-used road. A sense of danger rising, she opened her eyes and peered about the small shadowed room, seeking answers. The sound grew louder.

Ayza whispered, "Danger!" so fervently that Marie blew out the candle and got to her feet. She felt her way through the darkness to the back door. The vehicle stopped in the road, which passed some distance from the cottage, just as Marie entered the small hounfour.

Knowing exactly what she had to do, she went to the altar, quickly removed the relics and articles and placed them on the ground. Then she tilted back the altar, raising the hinged door beneath it, which led to her underground hiding place. After crawling in the hole, she lowered the door, struggling with the weight until it rested on a small block, which left an inch-wide gap for her to see out. To make the crack less obvious, the edge of the door had been lined with fringe, which hung down to the ground. That way she could see without being seen.

Secreted in her hiding place, Marie listened and watched, her little heart beating like a bird's. *"A l'Esprit partout,"* she prayed under her breath. *"Royaume de Bon Dieu. Aidez-moi."*

There was a deep silence outside, then Marie heard voices. One was a man's deep voice, the other a woman's. Both were talking quite loud. They were speaking English. Marie could not understand all the words.

Poking her fingers through the fringe, Marie saw flashes of light coming from her little house. The intruders had gone inside. A gross violation. Soon the light appeared at the back door of the house, the beam sweeping across the yard, finally coming to rest on the hounfour.

"What's that?" the woman asked, her voice carrying clearly in the light air.

"That be the old mambo's temple," the man replied.

The light and two shadowy figures came toward the hounfour. Marie closed her eyes. "Ko lo jee mo. Ko lo jee mo."

"Man, does this take me back," the man's voice boomed in the night. "I seen my mama cook up the best food in the house and bring it to a shanty temple like this to feed the gods.''

"Mooky, feed the gods?''

"That's it, babe. Humans feed the spirits, give them food and gifts and, in return, the spirits grant their protection, good health and good fortune.''

The woman laughed. "The mambos must have figured that one out.''

Marie, rigid with fear, stared out through the fringe as the couple drew closer and closer. Then she saw his face in the dim light—a black bull, his eyes glaring eerily, his nostrils flaring—and beside him a woman who was pale as a ghost. So shocked by the sight was Marie that she fell back against the dirt wall.

"What was that?'' the woman said.

"I didn't hear nothing.''

"Of course you didn't, Mooky, but there was a sound.''

"Maybe it was the loa, babe. Or a rat!''

The bull's deep, throbbing laughter nearly brought Marie's heart to a stop. *"A l'Esprit partout. Royaume de Bon Dieu. Aidez-moi,''* she silently implored.

The beam of light swept over Marie's secret hiding place, cutting through the fringe and into her eyes. The old mambo gasped, certain she'd been discovered. She cringed, but when the door didn't fly open, she opened her eyes. Through the crack she saw four legs, two large black tree trunks and two more graceful ones, white as a dove.

"What's this?'' the woman said.

The couple bent over, not five or six feet from where Marie crouched, sweat running down her face and back. The bull grunted.

"This is stuff for ritual,'' he said. "What's it doing on the ground? Should be on the altar.''

"What's it for, Mooky?''

Marie could see him poking through the relics, gifts and other items.

"See these pieces of pink and blue ribbon, and the crumbs

of rice cake, the flowers and this little vial of perfume? These are women things, gifts for Erzulie.''

''Who's Erzulie?''

''Sort of like the Virgin Mary of voodoo. Somebody's wantin' to get married, is my guess.''

''Huh?''

''The devotees come to the priest, a houngan or a mambo, like our girl, if they want to find a husband. Or could be they invokin' the spirit Yemalla or Baron for fertility purposes, if it's a baby they want.''

''How do you know all this shit, Mooky?''

''My mama, babe. In my house we didn't take a crap without consulting the loa.''

''So, where's Bon Mambo Marie?''

Marie cringed at the sound on her name on the white witch's lips.

''How I suppose to know? I look like a bokor to you?''

''A what?''

''Sorcerer. You know, black magic.''

''Come on, Mooky,'' the woman said, standing, ''that's enough mumbo jumbo. All this talk is giving me the creeps. Seems to me our girl's not home. Let's go.''

''Could be she's hidin' out in the bushes.''

''Well, if so, she can't hide forever.''

Marie could see the bull fingering the pieces of ribbon as he squatted so close she could smell his heavy scent.

''So, we leaving or what?'' the woman said.

''This stuff's got me thinkin', Dani.''

''Thinking what?''

''We know the old mambo ain't got but a few devotees, mostly old women who can hardly walk, right?''

''So?''

''Why she tryin' to marry somebody off...or get her pregnant?''

''What's your point?''

''We be lookin' for two ladies, right? Could be the other one's tryin' to get engaged or pregnant.''

"That's probably true of half the girls on the island."

"It's a small island, babe. This bears askin' around."

Marie could feel the spike going right into her heart. She beseeched the spirit Ayza, praying so hard she could taste the blood of the chicken in her throat. *"A l'Esprit partout. Royaume de Bon Dieu. Aidez-moi,"* she silently prayed. Spare Poppy and her baby!

The bull stood then. Through the crack Marie could see his incredible animal body. He flashed around the light, sweeping the beam over her hiding place and to the corners of the temple.

"We going now, Mooky?"

"Yeah, babe, we goin'. But I'm thinkin' that maybe we need to call in a consultant."

"What are you talking about?"

"This Bon Mambo Marie knows the spirits. To handle that we just might need us a bokor."

"A sorcerer? Mooky, are you crazy?"

"No, babe, I know the power of black magic."

Marie did not breathe—could not breathe—even as the two sauntered out of the hounfour and into the night. It wasn't until she heard the engine of the vehicle start that she felt her lifeblood return. Shaking with fear, she resolved not to come out of her hiding place until the sun returned.

Mooky Blade flipped on the headlights, put the vehicle in gear and did a U-turn, heading back the way they'd come. Dani sat silently beside him. He reached over and grasped her knee with his large hand, giving it a squeeze.

"So, what you think?"

"I'm wondering if you aren't as crazy as everybody else on this island."

Blade threw back his head and laughed.

"I'm serious," she said. "Black magic? Give me a break."

"I said that for the mambo's benefit."

"What are you talking about?"

"I wanted her to hear, scare the piss out of her."

Dani gave him a look of incredulity. "Have you flipped out?"

"Didn't you see her, babe? The old bitch was hidin' under the altar."

"Huh?"

"She was. I could see her eyes. And smell her."

"Are you serious?"

"Do I ever lie to you?"

"Well, why didn't you grab her?"

"Because I had a better idea. I want her to know what we're up to. That way maybe she'll lead us to her client, the lonely heart or childless broad, whichever she is. Why break the mambo's brittle old arms if we don't have to? Besides," he said with a laugh, "I like fucking with the spirits."

Dani reached over and put her hand on his crotch. "Speaking of fucking…"

Blade grinned. "Funny thing, babe. I was thinking the very same thing. Now, why do you suppose that be?"

"We think alike, Mooky. What can I say?"

Manhattan

While her fellow workers at Sotheby's Appraisal Company chatted in the lounge where they were having a little going-away party for her, Zoe sipped her wine and pondered her coming adventure. Her flight was at ten the next morning. She was excited and a little scared.

Going head to head with Simon Van Biers didn't bother her so much as her fear that she might fail. Ever since college she hadn't be able to look at a fine piece of art without thinking of the Van Gogh that had slipped through her family's collective fingers. And now, with her marriage essentially over, a crusade for something she truly cared about seemed exactly what the doctor ordered.

"We're going to miss you, Zoe," her boss, Edmund Grey,

said, sidling up next to her and draping an arm around her shoulder.

"I'm already homesick," she said, only half kidding.

"Well, if and when you decide to return, I'll make a place for you if I can," he said.

It was a *pro forma* comment, but Zoe appreciated it.

"Maybe with your new job we'll be able to do business," Grey said. "That's the sole advantage to developing people, then losing them—you tend to have lots of contacts. In this business one cherishes one's friends and former colleagues."

"I'm sure you'll be hearing from me," Zoe said.

Grey, a tall, slender, aristocratic man of fifty with a neatly trimmed goatee and slicked-back silvery hair, grinned with amusement. "Simon will keep you busy, I'm sure. He called me just the other day and says he expects me to keep you informed about every major piece that comes to my attention."

Zoe wasn't surprised. Simon Van Biers had talked to Edmund about her even before she'd met the old banker herself. Edmund had told her about the conversation. "Naturally I sang your praises. I told him you've been one of my favorites, that he'd be a fool not to hire you and that when he did he'd better treat you well."

Zoe had never discussed her "Kansas sunflowers" with Edmund or anybody else at Sotheby's, but she saw this as an opportunity to pick her boss's brain. "Do you know anything about his Van Gogh still life?"

"I've only seen photos. The consensus is that it's the fabled mystery Faucauld from the Arles series. If so, it's quite a coup."

"And he won't say where he got it."

"I certainly haven't heard any rumors," Edmond said.

"Do you think it could be stolen?"

"Only in the sense that he probably got it from an unsuspecting seller for a fraction of its value. One day it'll probably go down as the steal of the century."

Zoe shook her head at the bitter irony in that. She wanted

so badly to expose the bastard, to shout the truth from the rooftops of New York, but that would have to come later. First, she'd have to find out who'd actually put the painting in Van Biers's hands. And just as importantly—did Van Biers know it had been obtained through fraud and extortion? To her, it had to be obvious that it had been. If the seller had had a rightful claim to the painting, the asking price would have been in the tens of millions, even assuming the deal was done several years earlier.

Zoe sighed. "Well, I've got a long day ahead of me tomorrow. If you don't mind, Edmund, I'll be leaving now."

"Not at all."

Zoe gave him a brief, collegial hug. "You've been a prince from the day I first came to work here," she said. "I'll always be grateful."

"Do be careful down there in the exotic, dangerous Caribbean, though," Grey said, lowering his voice to a confidential level. "They still haven't turned up any trace of Raymond Pearson, you know, and the speculation is turning to foul play."

"The streets can be dangerous anywhere."

Edmund Grey hesitated.

"Or are you suggesting something other than a random act?" she asked.

"No, no," he replied. "It's just that Pearson's disappearance has been bothering me."

"He's not a friend, is he, Edmund?"

"No, I knew him, but not really well."

"What sort of man is he?" Zoe asked.

"Raymond struck me as someone who tended to live on the edge. And don't ask me why. I can't give you a reason. Some people just seem to live in the shadows and he's one. Let's hope whatever happened to him was an aberration."

"I can't let it bother me," Zoe said.

"And you shouldn't. I didn't mean to be alarmist. Just take good care of yourself."

Zoe didn't say anything about her conversation with the

FBI, of course. She wanted to learn everything she could, though. The last few days she'd been getting an ominous feeling. Maybe it was because Win had been so concerned.

After circulating about the room and saying her goodbyes, giving and getting her farewell hugs, Zoe got her purse and left the lounge. Minutes later, she stepped out onto York Avenue, her eyes shimmering. She sensed an era of her life had come to an end. Hailing a taxi, she gave the driver her address, then, staring out at the streets of New York, she wondered if and when she'd be back.

Once she was home Zoe warmed up the last of the leftovers in the refrigerator, then cleaned everything out except what she needed for breakfast. After eating, she started packing for her trip.

By nine o'clock she pretty well had her personal things that she wouldn't be taking to the Caribbean packed in boxes. She'd decided to sublet the apartment furnished, which meant furniture, dishes, linen and the like didn't need to be packed. Everything else would go into storage. All that remained was to get to JFK in the morning.

Zoe had just sealed the last box with masking tape when the phone rang.

"How's it going, kid? You doing okay?" It was Winifred.

"I'm a little nervous and excited."

"How many women can say they went to the Caribbean in pursuit of a multi-million-dollar painting?"

"Then you've changed your mind? You think it's a good idea now?"

"No, I'm just trying to be supportive."

"Thanks, I guess."

Win laughed. "It's got to be an improvement over life with Ahmed," she said, "no matter what happens. Speaking of which, guess who I saw in a bar on East Sixty-fifth this evening."

"Not my beloved husband, obviously."

"It was indeed. With a ninety-pound model on his arm. But

fear not, she wasn't going to blow away. Ahmed had pretty good hold of her.''

"I'm not surprised."

"I took it to be good news," Win said. "I'd like to think he's found other distractions."

"Or, maybe he's trying to convince himself that I'm not irreplaceable after all."

"Sounds to me like you're okay. Had to call one more time before you go, just to make sure. Send me a postcard?"

"Count on it."

They said goodbye, and Zoe, feeling melancholy, got ready for bed. If they weren't already packed, she'd have played some of her father's old dance records. They always made her feel sad, but it was a good kind of sad. Instead, she tuned in one of the radio stations that played music from the fifties and sixties, then got in bed to think about her life. How could she pass up an opportunity for nostalgia?

It was at times like this that Zoe would think back to the years when she was growing up in the Midwest. In some ways she'd had a fairly normal childhood, and in others it was full of eccentricity. Her people, her extended family, were essentially farm folk. Supposedly her mother and grandfather were from the sophisticated branch of the Gill family. But she had to wonder at that, considering they were the people who'd had a Van Gogh original oil painting hanging on the walls of the family home for the better part of seventy-five years and hadn't had a clue.

Zoe's grandfather, Carson Gill, had been a young doctor serving with the American Expeditionary Force in France during the First World War and had found the painting in the studio of an artist in a village outside Arles. Gill, who had little or no knowledge of painting, liked it because of the subject matter—sunflowers were the state flower of Kansas. So, he bought it to hang on his wall at home. The price he paid for the Van Gogh, Zoe later learned, was five hundred dollars, a princely sum at the time, but the painter, somebody named

Vincent, was supposed to be collectible. The doctor hadn't
cared about any of that, though. He liked sunflowers.

Carson Gill spent the postwar years quietly practicing med-
icine in Holton, a small town in northeastern Kansas. He remained a bachelor for many years, finally marrying in his forties. His much younger wife was a country girl, who found
her husband's sunflowers garish and banished them to his
study. The Gills had a child late in life, Zoe's mother, Elizabeth, who inherited the painting when her own mother died.
This was late in the 1970s, several years after Zoe had been
born. She recalled, as a child, visiting her grandmother's home
on Nebraska Street in Holton and sneaking into the study of
her long-since deceased grandfather to look at his "Kansas
sunflowers."

Zoe and her parents lived in ignorance of the fact that
Carson Gill's painting, which had since been moved into their
attic in Kansas City, was incredibly valuable. It wasn't until
Zoe was attending Stephens College, taking a course in art
history, that she first made a connection between the work of
Vincent Van Gogh and her grandfather's painting. That was
about the same time that Zoe's mother became seriously ill,
having been in very poor health for years.

The Van Gogh hadn't been high on Zoe's list of concerns,
given her mother's condition, though she often wondered
about the accuracy of her childhood recollections. The summer
after her mother's passing, before Zoe's junior year of college,
she decided to get a firsthand look at the painting she hadn't
seen since she was eight years old. But she searched the attic
in vain. When Zoe questioned her father, Laszlo Marton told
her he thought Elizabeth had sold the thing at a garage sale
sometime earlier.

Zoe knew that was a lie, though, because her mother had
told her before she died that Carson Gill's sunflowers were to
go to her. When Zoe confronted her father with the information, he finally confessed to have "given it to a friend," not
realizing Zoe cared so much about the painting. But she didn't
buy that story. Upon her insistent questioning, Laszlo finally

admitted he'd been swindled out of the painting by a woman with whom he'd had an illicit relationship. The woman, Zoe eventually discovered, had been working a con on unsuspecting adulterous husbands for years. Needless to say, Zoe was furious.

Though she loved her father, she'd long been aware of Laszlo Marton's philandering ways. Her parents had fought about it and had nearly divorced a couple of times while she was growing up. "I'm Hungarian," she remembered her father declare in the course of one late-night fight. "I have the soul of a Gypsy." He was Hungarian by birth, true, but essentially Laszlo Marton was a bon vivant, an automobile salesman who loved his wine, his women and his song—though his singing ability was suspect.

The week after Zoe graduated from college, Laszlo had a heart attack and died in the arms of a widow with a palatial home in Shawnee Mission. The timing was fortunate in that it forced Zoe to go through her parents' things. In the process, she happened upon a box of documents that had belonged to her grandfather. It was then that she discovered the extent of the tragedy in the loss of the Kansas sunflowers. Among Carson Gill's mementos from the war was a receipt from the artist, Roger Faucauld, for an original oil painting of sunflowers in a vase by the Dutch painter, Vincent Van Gogh, dated July 1888.

Seeing the yellowing, ancient paper, Zoe's heart had nearly stopped. It was at that moment she realized the depth of the tragic irony. The necessary clues had been there all along. In all probability her grandfather had never looked at the receipt after receiving it, assuming that the surname of the artist was Vincent. Though Zoe hadn't laid eyes on the painting since childhood, she did find photographs of it among her mother's things. At that time she wasn't yet an expert on impressionist and postimpressionist art, but she knew enough to recognize if something was in the style of Vincent Van Gogh. The Carson Gill "Kansas sunflowers" definitely qualified.

Her desire to learn more fueled by her loss, Zoe used some

of the money she'd inherited to take the Sotheby's course on appraisal in New York. Making late-nineteenth and early-twentieth-century European art her specialty, she learned everything there was to know about Vincent Van Gogh and his sunflower series.

Among other things, she discovered that a reclusive French artist by the name of Roger Faucauld was reputed to have owned an eighth and previously unknown sunflower painting from Van Gogh's Arles period. No one but Faucauld himself ever claimed to have seen the painting and he died in 1946, making it impossible to verify some version of the conflicting rumors concerning the painting's fate. The dominant theory was that it had been lost or stolen during either the First or Second World Wars, but tangible proof of its existence was lacking until fairly recently, when Simon Van Biers introduced a previously undocumented sunflower painting by Van Gogh. As Edmund Grey had said, experts theorized that it was the Faucauld painting. When queried about its origins, Van Biers would only say that he'd obtained the painting from a private collector with the assistance of an intermediary.

Throughout these events Zoe had kept her silence, even though she had documentary proof that an original Van Gogh in the sunflower series had in fact once been in the possession of Roger Faucauld and in turn had been sold to her grandfather. She was not interested in verifying the painting's authenticity, though. Her objective was to prove that it rightfully belonged to her and that Van Biers had come into possession of it illicitly. Proof of that would not be easy to come by. That was the challenge she faced.

Even though she was tired and knew she had a still more difficult day ahead tomorrow, Zoe had trouble getting to sleep. She kept picturing Simon Van Biers, dignified and gentlemanly with his shock of white hair and his expensive clothes; Simon Van Biers, his voice faintly tinged with the charm of the South, smiling and telling her about his sunflowers, painted by Vincent Van Gogh. It was an image that obsessed her. And it made her all the more determined to reclaim the sunflowers for herself.

Saturday
August 12th

JFK, New York

Zoe had overslept and had to rush to the airport to make her flight. Fortunately the traffic in Queens wasn't bad and the lines at the check-in counter were tolerable. She'd make it to the gate with enough time to get her boarding pass and pay a visit to the ladies' room before boarding.

As she came out the door of the rest room, Zoe got a start. Who should pass by but Ahmed. He was with two other men, also Arabs, though nobody Zoe knew, and they were walking in the direction of her gate. She froze as a panicky feeling came over her. God, this was the last thing she needed. It would be like Ahmed to have an emotional confrontation in front of half of New York.

That story about his cousin in Jordan raping his wife hadn't been far from her mind, as well. Normally, she wouldn't expect such a thing from the man she'd been married to, but these were not normal times. God only knew what her husband was capable of. Nor did it surprise her that only the night before he'd been with that model. Ahmed wouldn't see the least bit of inconsistency in that.

The question was, should she tough it out, or ask for airport security? Mostly she wanted to avoid a confrontation, whether Ahmed was dangerous or not. But how?

She spotted a passenger agent working at a gate that wasn't in use. There was no one else around, so she went over to talk to the woman.

"Excuse me," Zoe said, "but I've got a terrible problem. I'm on that flight to San Juan over there and I just spotted my estranged husband and a couple of other men. I can't swear to it, but since we're in the middle of a messy divorce, I suspect they're up to no good. Do you have any idea how I can get on the plane without having to deal with them?"

"Let me see your ticket."

Zoe showed both her ticket and boarding pass to the woman. The agent reflected for a moment. "The only way to board that plane is through the gate," she said. "Even the crew goes aboard that way. There's access to the telescopic corridor from the ground, but I'm sure they wouldn't let a passenger go down there. Let me call security. That's probably the easiest way to deal with the problem. If someone's harassing you…"

"I'd rather avoid a confrontation if at all possible," Zoe said. "Only as a last resort."

The woman thought some more. "I've got an idea." She picked up the phone and called the gate for the San Juan flight, explaining the problem to the agent there. After a brief conversation, she said to Zoe, "We can arrange special boarding, using a skycap with a wheelchair. If there was a way you could disguise yourself a little…"

"I've got a beach hat in my carry-on. And sunglasses."

"Maybe if you slouched and pulled the hat down over your eyes we could slip you by. Chances are they won't be looking for you in a wheelchair."

"Perfect," Zoe said, beaming.

The agent called for a skycap and Zoe dug her hat out of

her carry-on. In ten minutes she was ready to make a stealth entrance onto the plane. The skycap pushed the chair to the gate. Ahmed and the two men were standing near the counter, surveying the crowd and watching the concourse. Zoe slouched still lower, dropping her chin to her chest.

When they reached the counter, the passenger agent was talking to a cowboy. "I'll see what I can do," the agent told him, "but the flight is full. The only thing I can suggest is that you see if you can get somebody with an aisle seat to trade with you."

"With this back problem I can't sit for long without standing and stretching, and if I'm in the middle seat I'll be driving everybody nuts getting up and down."

"I understand, sir."

"Thing is, the lady that sold me the ticket said I'd be getting an aisle seat for sure."

"Apparently there was a mix-up, but we'll work something out, Mr. Blue."

"Thank you, ma'am. I'm much obliged."

"Now, if you'll excuse me, I've got a special-boarding passenger to take care of."

The cowboy turned, bumping into the wheelchair in the process. "Pardon me, ma'am, didn't see you there. You all right?"

"Yes, I'm fine," Zoe mumbled under her breath.

The last thing she wanted was somebody drawing attention to her, and the cowboy was doing just that. She waved her hand, shooing him away. Fortunately he backed off without another word.

As Zoe sat in the chair waiting, she glanced at the cowboy through her sunglasses. He was good-looking, tawny-headed, if a trifle bit shaggy, and exuded a certain native charm, but just then Zoe could have cared less if he was Brad Pitt. She just wanted on that plane without any hassle.

It seemed like ten minutes—though it was probably only one—that she sat there, facing the cowboy who leaned insouciantly on the ticket counter, his hips cocked, his hat tilted

back on his head, his lean body having that hard look of a
man who worked with his hands. She didn't dare look at Ahmed, but she felt his presence. With each passing second her
heart seemed to pound harder and harder.

Mercifully, the passenger agent finally came around the
counter and took her boarding pass. "This way, please," she
said, unfastening the link of chain from the stanchion.

As the skycap started to push her toward the door leading
to the telescopic corridor, she heard what she'd been dread-
ing—Ahmed's voice. "Zoe? Is that you?"

"Let's go!" she cried.

Before the skycap could push her through the door, Ahmed
shoved his way through the crowd. Seeing him coming, Zoe
stood and started to run, but Ahmed grabbed her wrist. The
other men were right behind him.

"Zoe," Ahmed said, "you can't leave until we talk."

"I don't want to talk to you, Ahmed. I have nothing to say
to you."

He gave her arm a jerk. "But you must listen to me."

Zoe swung her carry-on bag at him, but he deflected the
blow.

"Hold on there, mister. The lady clearly said she didn't
want to talk to you." It was the cowboy.

"Get lost," Ahmed snarled. "This is none of your business."

"There's no call for manhandling her. Now let her go."

The other men grabbed the cowboy, but not before he jerked
Ahmed's hand from her arm. Zoe took off down the telescopic
corridor, glancing back in time to see Ahmed start after her,
only to be tripped by the cowboy. A scuffle ensued. She could
hear the shouting as she boarded the plane, pushing past the
startled flight attendant and running to the nearest toilet, where
she locked herself inside.

Several minutes later there was knocking on the door. "Airport security," came the voice on the other side. "Are you all
right in there?"

Zoe opened the door. An armed officer waited for her. With

several airline people standing by, Zoe explained the situation. "My husband's very emotional and unpredictable. I want nothing to do with him."

"Technically, he assaulted you," the officer said. "You have the right to bring charges."

"Frankly, I just want to get the hell out of here. Can you just take him away until we're gone?"

"We're holding all three of them at the gate. The one gentleman, Ahmed, I believe, said talking to you is a matter of life and death."

"Not talking to him is a matter of life and death, too. The last thing I want to do is get off this plane."

"What about the cowboy?"

"I don't even know him. He's just a good Samaritan who tried to help."

"He got knocked around pretty good."

Zoe was horrified. "Not hurt, I hope."

"Doesn't appear to be. Said his pain was from an old injury."

"I'd feel terrible if he was inconvenienced by this."

"We're holding everybody out there until we talk to you, just to make sure."

"Well, Ahmed and his friends are the bad guys, the cowboy is the good guy."

The officer grinned. "The guy in the white hat."

Zoe chuckled. "Yeah, I guess."

"Okay," he said. "We'll take care of it. You might as well stay aboard. Have a nice flight."

"Thank you."

The flight attendant helped her find her aisle seat and stow her carry-on in the compartment overhead. Zoe thanked her and plopped heavily in the seat. Now all she had to do was wait until boarding was complete and the plane had left the gate. Only then would she be absolutely sure she was safe.

Before long the rest of the passengers filed into the cabin, including the cowboy, her champion. Zoe wanted to thank him, but the aisles were crowded and he was still six rows or so forward. As the other people took their seats, Zoe saw that the cowboy and the flight attendant were trying to get one of the passengers with an aisle seat to trade with him, but were being singularly unsuccessful.

Zoe saw that she had an opportunity to return the kindness. She got up and went to where they stood in the aisle. The cowboy's back was to her; she tapped him on the shoulder.

"Hi," she said. "I want to thank you for what you did at the gate. That was very gallant."

The cowboy was really pleased. He gave her a broad grin. "My pleasure, ma'am."

"I hope you weren't hurt."

"No, there was just a little shoving, that's all. No big deal."

"I gather you're in need of an aisle seat."

"I've got a back problem that makes it tough to sit for too long at a stretch," he explained. "If I have an outside seat I won't be constantly climbing over folks."

"If no one else will give up theirs," Zoe said, "you're welcome to mine."

"That's mighty kind of you," he said, tucking his head in a friendly way that smacked of sincerity.

"Nothing compared to what you did."

"Don't mention it," he said. "Glad to be of help."

They exchanged smiles.

"My name's Billy Blue, by the way," he said.

Zoe offered him her hand. "Zoe Marton."

"Pleasure, Zoe."

She turned. "That's my seat right back there. You're welcome to it."

"I'm sure this fella sitting on the aisle will be just as grateful as me, if he isn't already."

Zoe decided to leave her carry-on bag back where it was, and when the man on the aisle got up, she slipped into the middle seat. Billy Blue tipped his hat and went back to Zoe's old seat.

Zoe took the flight magazine from the back of the seat in front of her, chuckling to herself. It was the first time she could recall ever being "rescued." And by a cowboy, no less. She'd have to put that on a postcard to Win.

Ten endless minutes passed before they finally pulled away from the gate. It wasn't until then that Zoe finally felt free. She felt better still when they were airborne. What Ahmed had been intending, she had no idea. The fact that he'd brought a couple of friends with him was the most ominous part. Surely he hadn't planned on abducting her from a crowded airport. In any case, it was disconcerting that he knew when she was leaving and where she was headed. He must have followed her to the airport. The question was, would he try again?

Newquay Bay, St. Margaret

It was late afternoon by the time Charles reached the house where Mooky Blade and his wife were staying. Leaving the Porsche in the driveway, he strolled toward the dwelling, not feeling altogether comfortable about Blade. The guy had an independent streak that Charles didn't like. He was also pretty damned disdainful. Charles liked that even less.

Nearing the house he saw the woman, Dani, stretched out on a lounge chair in the shade of the palms. For a moment he thought she was stark naked, but then he saw she had on a bikini bottom. No top, though. She seemed to be asleep.

Charles approached quietly, taking pleasure in the sight. She had a great set and they looked real. No silicone here. Glancing toward the house, he saw no sign of Blade, nor did he hear anything. Their vehicle was gone. Could she be alone?

This was no woman for him to be fooling with, Charles knew, but if she was going to nap outdoors half-naked, he could hardly be blamed for taking a good look. Slipping into one of the nearby wooden lawn chairs, he savored Dani Blade's luscious body. It was enough to give him a hard-on. Naturally he pondered a way he might take advantage of the situation.

After a couple of minutes Dani moaned in her sleep. Her

eyes fluttered open and she squinted up at the palm fronds. She must have sensed his presence then because she lifted her head and, seeing him sitting across from her, gave a cry of surprise.

"Jesus," she said, grabbing the beach cover-up lying on the ground next to her. "You scared the shit out of me. What are you doing sneaking up on me?"

"I didn't sneak up," he said as she sat upright, hastily covering herself with the wrap. "I came from my car and sat down."

"You could have said something, coughed or made a noise," she said angrily. "You might have a gentleman's name, but you're no gentleman, Van Biers." She glared.

"So, I'm sorry, all right? I mean, this is the Caribbean. Every other beach is topless."

"This isn't the beach."

"Okay, okay. I apologize. Where's your husband?"

"Mooky went for a swim."

"What's he doing, swimming around the island?" he said dryly.

She gave him a dirty look, seeming not to appreciate the sarcasm. Charles didn't care.

"So, when's he going to be back?"

"I don't know, Mooky does things in his own way and at his own speed. What do you want?"

"I'd like to know what's going on with the two women. After all, I am paying the bills around here."

"You want a report, in other words."

"Yeah."

"I can update you."

"Fine," Charles said, looking her over through his sunglasses, wishing he could do a little more than listen to her talk. "You update me, sweetheart."

"I wouldn't get in the habit of calling me that, Van Biers. Do it around Mooky and he's likely to deck you."

"He's the jealous type?"

"Respect is important to him."

Charles smiled. "More to the point, is it important to you?"

The look she gave him was halfway between a smirk and a smile. "What guys call me doesn't matter one way or the other, but if you touch me, I'm liable to break your hands."

"Tough as Mooky, are you?"

"More dangerous, probably."

Charles lifted a brow. "Why's that?"

"Mooky has a soft spot in his heart. I don't."

"I like a hard woman."

"Forget it, Van Biers. Now, do you want to talk business or jerk off?"

Charles smiled. "What has my twenty-five thousand gotten me?"

"We figure the voodoo lady is one of your witnesses. The other one we don't know yet, but we're narrowing it down."

"That doesn't sound like much for twenty-five grand."

"Mooky wants to finesse it."

"Finesse it? He should be bashing heads."

"The old lady won't give up the information lightly. We put enough pressure on her, she'd go to the cops. It's still a mystery why she hasn't already."

"Fine, so kill her."

"What are you saying, that you want to scare the shit out of the other one so that she goes running to the police? She sees her friend dead, Mr. Van Biers, she has no reason to keep silent."

"All right, so kill them both."

"First we have to find out who the second one is."

"When you going to do that?"

"We're working on it. Mooky's got an angle, we've been talking to people. There's maybe a hundred possibles on the list."

"Hell, I could have told you that a week ago."

"The trick, Mr. Van Biers, is finding the right one. We're surgeons not a slaughterhouse."

"With all due respect, Mrs. Blade, up until now it's been a lot of talk and not much do. My ass is on the line and I don't have the luxury of farting around. A little less swimming and a little more pounding the pavement would be appreciated.''

''You don't like the way we work, we can leave.''

''Just get it done, will you?''

Charles got up. Dani did, as well. The wind billowed her cover-up, affording a nice view of her breasts before she smoothed down the fabric.

''In you, Blade's got himself a real nice piece,'' Charles said. ''Frankly, I envy the man.''

''Don't push it, Van Biers.''

Her defiance and her nakedness were a deadly combination. They stoked his fires. Charles gave in to the temptation. Grabbing her, he crushed her body hard up against him, half lifting her off the ground with a hand under her ass, so that her pubis rode up his bulge.

''This better, sweetheart?'' he said through his teeth.

Her response was quick and violent. She clamped her hand on his balls with such force that the pain shot right through the top of his head. Simultaneously she kicked the back of his knees with her heel, dropping him to the ground. Then she hit him square on the chin with her fist, sending him flying backward and flat on his back. The blow all but knocked him out. The goddamn palm trees were spinning above him and so was her angry face.

''I think I told you if you touch me, I get pissed.''

Charles rubbed his jaw, tasting blood. ''Jesus Christ,'' he mumbled. ''I was just playing around.''

She pointed a finger straight at his face. ''You don't play around with me, asshole. Ever! Understand?''

He felt a deep rage building, but he knew there wasn't a damn thing he could do, not unless he was willing to tell her to take a hike. He sure as hell wasn't going to duke it out with her. The fucking bitch was lethal. Maybe she didn't like grab ass, but he didn't appreciate getting his balls crushed and his face smashed, either. Now he had a score to settle. And he would. After he got what he wanted out of the Blades.

Without a word, Charles struggled to his feet. Then, dusting himself off as she glared, he staggered off toward his Porsche. The cunt may have won round one, he told himself, but it was only round one.

Biloxi Plantation

Mayte Van Biers luxuriated in her tub, feeling loose and mellow. It had been two hours since she'd had her legs wrapped around the president of the republic, two hours since he'd given her his all, and she was still warm and tingly. But she'd had to warn Jerome not to get too carried away. "I don't want any more whisker burns. Last time Charles noticed. I don't want Simon to know."

"Can he see that well?"

"Simon sees what he needs to see and what he wants to see."

"I presume your stepson didn't betray you."

"Charles considers me essential to his future, Jerome. Therein lies my power over him."

"But the feeling's not mutual."

"He's an idiot, to be blunt. A boy. He thinks with his gonads."

"Is he a danger?"

"I hope not. I wish now I'd been more circumspect. But Charles is his father's heir. My insurance policy."

Jerome had caressed her, arousing her powerfully. "So, how are things going at the bank?"

Mayte had been taken aback by the question. They rarely discussed bank business, both of them finding it easier if they didn't. Their alliance was implicit. Should the occasion arise, their unspoken understanding was that their first loyalty was to each other. That had been her goal from the very beginning. Jerome's commitment was to her above all else. He was madly in love with her and that was the way she wanted it. But like all men, he didn't compromise his ability to survive.

"In what way, Jerome?" she'd said in response to his question.

"The American government is schooling me on the evils of Victoria International. I wanted another opinion."

"For the purpose of…"

"Mayte," he'd said, lightly dusting her muff with his fingertips, "you know you can trust me."

"But we both agreed that the less you know, the better."

"Yes, but your countrymen are making sure I know plenty. How much truth there is in it is in doubt."

Mayte could see she had to level with him…or, give the appearance of leveling with him. "We're having a cash-flow problem. Simon is concerned. He's working on raising more capital. That should tide us over until the funds start coming in on the new offerings."

"You're using new investment funds to pay off old investors, aren't you?"

"Jerome, do you really want to discuss this?"

"The SEC insists Simon is running a Ponzi scheme. If it should blow up, Mayte, it could reflect badly on St. Margaret and me. I don't mind playing things loose, but I want to avoid a catastrophe at all cost."

"Have you discussed this with Simon?"

"I thought I'd discuss it with you first."

Mayte could see she was stuck between a rock and a hard place and that the pressure on her was likely to get worse before it would get better. She didn't want Victoria International to collapse, and losing Jerome Hurst's confidence could lead precisely to that. On the other hand, if she were to take full control, eventually she'd have to force her husband out. That called for finesse—she had to undermine Simon without destroying him.

"Naturally I'm keeping a close eye on things," she'd said. "At the moment you have nothing to fear. But, if and when the time comes to take action, you'll be the first person I come to, Jerome. You know that."

"Yes, I know that," he'd said, caressing her cheek. "But I'm very much in the hot seat. I trust you appreciate that."

"I *do* appreciate your dilemma. But I also know you're man enough," Mayte had said, "as few are."

And so, Mayte judged, she'd bought herself a bit more time, trusting love to keep Jerome Hurst on board a while longer.

"My, but isn't that a lovely sight."

Mayte jumped at the sound of his voice. It was Simon. She discreetly moved her hands from where they'd been resting between her legs, lifting a foot from the water and resting it on the edge of the huge tub. "I didn't see you come in."

"Sorry if I startled you, sugar."

"You didn't. I was daydreaming and you caught me unaware, that's all."

"Daydreaming," Simon said wistfully. "What a lovely thought." He shook his head as if recalling some long-ago pleasure. "Mind if I sit and talk a spell, or would I be intruding on your privacy?"

"Of course you can sit."

Simon went over to the small vanity chair where Mayte would sit to put on her makeup, and folded his creaky body, lowering it until he landed on the cushion with something of a thud. He smiled, perhaps to mask his pain. Simon suffered from arthritis, which was another reason he enjoyed the tropical climate so.

"I went by the office this afternoon, thinking I would find you there," Simon said, his tone so natural as to be ominous.

Mayte felt her heart quicken. "I was there for a while, Simon, but I wasn't very productive, so I went for a drive to clear my head."

"Oh, that would explain it," he said.

"Why? Did you need something?"

Simon closed his eyes, scratching his forehead. "I've been giving the situation at the bank a good deal of thought, sugar. As you know, I've been thinking about running up to New York."

"To discuss borrowing against your painting."

"Yes, but I've developed another strategy and I wanted to confer with you about it."

"Oh?"

"Tomorrow Miss Marton will be arriving. I thought I'd discuss the sunflowers with her, see what she thinks the painting would appraise at. If her figure is encouraging, I thought I'd have her put together a proposal, bring in whatever outside experts she feels are necessary to document the case, then I'd go to New York with the package."

"You've already decided you can trust her?"

"I have a pretty good nose for people, Mayte. I know who I can trust and who I can't."

She felt the heat rise in her cheeks, hoping Simon wouldn't notice. "It's one of your greatest strengths, dear."

"Hmm."

Mayte took a sponge and squeezed some of the tepid water onto her chest. Simon watched her push a strand of damp hair behind her ear.

"Do you see any reason not to press ahead with my plan?" he asked.

"I suppose Ms. Marton doesn't have to know all the whys and wherefores," she replied. "I go to great lengths to keep all but my chief bookkeeper in the dark about the overall picture."

"I see no reason to share more with Miss Marton than the particulars about the painting. She can think what she will about the uses of the money."

"I defer to your judgment on that, Simon. The art is your business."

"Hmm," he said again.

They were both silent for a time. Mayte was ready to get out of the tub, but she was inclined to wait until he left. It wasn't modesty—she could care less. But in the evenings, after she'd been with Jerome, she always felt uncomfortable around Simon. It wasn't guilt—at least she liked to think it wasn't—but a better explanation was hard to find. If she found consolation, it was in knowing that she and Simon used each other and had from the beginning.

"I hope you don't mind, Mayte, but I've asked Charles to dine with us this evening."

"He's your son, why would I object?"

"I thought maybe the three of us could discuss broader strategy and evaluate our immediate concerns. It's been a while."

Mayte knew what he was referring to—Raymond Pearson. Jerome gave Simon regular updates on the investigation, which was ironic because he never mentioned the matter to her, perhaps hoping she had nothing to do with it. As to Simon, Jerome had to have his suspicions. And, with the FBI involved and the federal government hounding them, they all knew the danger was considerable. Fortunately, Charles was the one with his neck in the noose and she had little doubt Simon would let his son hang, if it came to that.

"Whatever you wish, Simon."

He got to his feet, though not without noticeable effort. Her husband seemed to be aging before her eyes. Embarrassed, perhaps, he never complained and did his best to affect a cheerful demeanor.

"You look like you might be wanting to get out of that water," he said, again showing his uncanny ability to read what was in people's minds.

Taking a huge bath sheet from the vanity, he stepped to the tub and put it on the edge next to her hand. Mayte rose from the water, wrapping herself in the towel. Simon had not walked away as she might have expected. Instead, he stood there, looking at her rather intensely, his eyes surprisingly hard.

"Sugar, these Saturday-afternoon drives you favor, the ones to clear your head... I do hope you're being discreet. This is such a very small island."

He turned then and walked from the bath. It was a kindness not to stay and watch her squirm, even though she was capable of putting up an icy-cool front. It was not a terribly great shock that her husband knew, but the communication of the fact was still unnerving.

Mayte stepped from the tub, wondering if there would be consequences. Though everyone involved was fully capable of soldiering on, her instincts told her that some sort of denouement was in the offing. Pretense was very trying, even on the most resolute of psyches. Her marriage, she realized, had moved into its final act.

Sunday
August 13th

Billy sat in the lobby of the hotel, waiting for the limousine to the airport. Flights to St. Margaret weren't frequent, making the layover in San Juan necessary. Even though he'd been careful with his money, avoiding all expenses but necessities, his roll was shrinking fast. The airline ticket had taken most of what he'd borrowed from the bank, leaving little for hotels and food. He'd passed on dinner the previous evening, instead taking a bus into Old San Juan where he'd spent a few bucks on a beer and snack at a kiosk in the Plaza de Armas. He figured since he'd come this far, he ought to see a few of the sights.

Dressed as he was, he'd gotten some stares, but nobody hassled him. He'd strolled alone in the balmy, breezy air, trying to convince himself that coming to the Caribbean was the right thing to do. In his mind, he kept going back to conversations he'd had with his grandmother, those last weeks as she lay dying.

"Funny how one day your whole life can get turned on its

head without any warning," he'd said. "Damned well taught me I wasn't prepared."

"Most young men aren't," Sophie'd replied. "Sometimes fate has to grab you by the nape of the neck and give you a good shake. It was like that with your granddaddy. That manhunt was what turned his life around."

Sophie was referring to the saga of the most famous outlaw in the history of Northern Nevada. Back in June of 1938 Dominico Nadal, who was known as Tony Valdez among the cattlemen, shot and killed a fellow ranch hand by the name of Justo Urrutia. The victim was a friend of Willard Blue Bear's and, when word of the murder got out, a posse was formed. Willard was among the first to volunteer.

The posse tracked Valdez for twenty-three days, finally cornering him in O'Neil Basin where he was eventually captured, brought to trial and sentenced to death. Billy's grandfather had attended the execution, which closed the chapter. But seeing what happened to Tony Valdez changed him. Willard learned how empty a pointless life could be, when a man went through the motions, lacking a worthwhile dream.

Billy wondered if chasing after this painting was something that would change him forever, or if it would turn out to be a complete waste of time and money. Natalie Stern, who'd met Irwin Pettigrew and who knew a little of how the world of finance worked, hadn't given him much hope, which led him to fear he just might be naive and a fool. But Billy also had a stubborn streak in him, a stubborn streak that had kept him climbing onto the backs of bulls for the better part of fifteen years. No, he'd see this thing through, but if he didn't succeed, the disappointment wouldn't be so much for himself as for his grandmother and her dream.

Billy just wasn't used to taking responsibility for much of anything, except getting his ass to an arena in time for his event. Beyond that, his major preoccupation had been satisfying his whims and desires. A beer, a woman, a good steak, a movie or a book now and then had pretty much been his life apart from bull riding. But with his father and Van Gogh added to the mix, a simple life had become a lot more complicated.

Billy was pondering his fate and thinking wistfully of Shelly, when the doorman signaled the limo had arrived. Grabbing his carry-on bag, Billy got to his feet, pausing a moment to straighten the kink in his back. Then he ambled for the door. Once outside, he made sure his suitcase went into the trunk of the limo, then he climbed into the empty seat in the middle. A man, a woman and a little girl occupied the rear seat. Billy heard the little girl whispering something about a cowboy to her parents and it sparked recollections of some of the joys he'd known of being a rodeo cowboy. Who but a fella with a strong heart and taste for danger would climb on the back of a ton of beef just to see if he could stay on? Billy would miss that life. Hell, he already did.

The limo left the hotel grounds and they drove along palm-lined Ashford Avenue a quarter of a mile to the next stop, a beachfront high-rise hotel that was a step or two up the food chain from where Billy had stayed. He was staring vacantly at the entrance when an attractive woman came out of the hotel. She was in shorts, a blouse, sunglasses and strappy sandals. A travel bag was slung over her shoulder. She walked purposefully toward the limo.

The fact that she was attractive would have been reason enough for him to take notice, but she was also familiar. Then he placed her. It was the woman who'd given him her seat on the plane, the one he'd helped get away from those guys at the gate in New York. Zoe was her name.

What a coincidence, he thought. During the flight to Puerto Rico he'd caught her eye a few times as he'd walked up and down the aisle. They'd exchanged smiles and nods, but hadn't spoken again. Billy had been curious what the hell that drama at the gate had been all about, but hadn't had an opportunity to ask her about it.

When they'd arrived at San Juan, she'd gotten off the plane well ahead of him. And by the time he'd made it to baggage claim, she was already on her way out the door. Billy figured it was one of those encounters between a man and a woman that shows promise but quickly turns to nothing. The fact that she was so pretty had made it a particular shame. But here she was again. Fate, it seemed, was smiling on him.

The driver opened the door, and when Zoe saw him, she looked surprised.

"Good morning, Zoe," he said.

"Hi." She climbed into the limo. "Didn't expect to see you again."

"Well, I figured I'd better be at the gate in case you ran into trouble again."

She laughed. "You've decided to become my guardian angel, have you?"

"It was so much fun, I thought I'd try it again."

"I hope you don't have the opportunity," she replied, "selfish though that might be."

He stared at her pretty mouth, her eyes shielded as they were by the sunglasses. "Don't mean to get personal or anything, but what did those fellas want?"

"I'm involved in a very acrimonious legal action," she said cryptically.

"Seems like they decided to take the law in their own hands."

She smiled at the remark. "That's as good a way to describe it as any."

Billy gathered she didn't want to talk about it, or considered it none of his business. Which was her right. Since she'd already thanked him for what he'd done, there was nothing left to say about the incident. But it wasn't in his nature to be sitting next to an attractive woman and ignore her. Billy had enjoyed women his whole life; he liked talking with them, being friendly, having a laugh and a good time. They didn't have to be beautiful for him to take pleasure in their company, but it did add a little extra spice. And maybe some incentive.

After loading her luggage in the trunk, the driver climbed back in the limo and they took off. Billy decided to try again.

"If you're headed for the airport, you must have laid over, same as me," he said.

"Yes," she replied. "I've got a flight to catch."

Again, she was brief and to the point. Not unfriendly exactly, but not what a fella would call encouraging, either. He'd checked. She didn't wear a ring. That wasn't conclusive proof of anything, though most married gals tended to wear their rings when they were out in public. Whatever her situation was, Zoe was circumspect and didn't seem eager to turn their acquaintance into a friendship. He could respect that. But still, tenacity was in his blood.

"On vacation?" he asked.

"No. Business."

"Me, too."

She didn't ask what business a cowboy would have in the Caribbean, or where he was from, or any of the obvious things. Her unwillingness to make conversation pretty much told the story. A lot of women had a belief that ordinary friendliness with a man they didn't know could backfire on them and become a pain—probably not without good cause. Billy was gentleman enough not to make her uncomfortable. He let her have the silence she wanted.

Even so, he couldn't ignore her. He was acutely aware of her scent. It never ceased to amaze him how fragrant and sweet a woman could smell. She had long slender hands and shapely legs, he noted. In her case, the shorts were a very good idea. An excellent idea.

After staring out the window for a while, he glanced her way for another look. Her glossy jaw-length dark hair was so dark it was nearly black. He tried to remember the color of her eyes. He'd seen them on the plane. His recollection was that they were pale blue. But it was her mouth that intrigued him most. It was pretty, yes, but it was also "smart." She hadn't said much, but he knew the woman had bite. It radiated from her. He figured she was probably pretty intelligent. College educated in all likelihood, classy, probably a career girl. Billy took a deep breath, filling his lungs with Zoe's scent, savoring it the way he would one of Granny's fresh-baked pies.

The limo arrived at Luis Muñoz Marin International Airport. The family in the seat behind them got off at the first stop. Billy sat quietly as the limo continued, wondering if he or Zoe would be getting off first. Now that they were alone he could have tried another conversational gambit, but there probably wasn't any point. They were about to part for good. Maybe Zoe, in her wisdom, had realized that and that explained her reserve.

The next stop was the terminal for the smaller carriers serving the intra-Caribbean routes, including his airline, Inter-Carib. "This is my stop," he said, warning her he'd be getting out.

"It's mine, too."

"Oh, really?"

After clambering out of the limo, they waited on the sidewalk for their luggage to be unloaded from the trunk. Billy stood behind her, noticing the way the sun shone on her hair, bringing out errant strands of red in the black.

Zoe signaled a porter to take her bag, then handed the limo driver a couple of bucks. She glanced at Billy. "Goodbye, Mr. Blue. And thank you again for your gallantry."

The comment pleased him. Billy touched the brim of his hat. "Glad to be of help, ma'am."

She smiled farewell and led the porter into the terminal building. "Have a nice life," he said under his breath, admiring her derriere. That was what the classy woman with the invalid husband down in Arizona had said to him at their parting. "Billy, have a nice life."

Though he was out of ones, Billy wasn't the sort to stiff anybody, so he gave the limo driver a five, figuring he could skip lunch. He also waved off a porter. He'd carry his own bag, whether his back appreciated it or not.

Inside the terminal, he was surprised to find his lady friend standing in line at the InterCarib ticket counter. Stopping by the door, he wondered whether she could possibly be going to St. Margaret. That would be too much luck for a fella like him who'd been on a losing roll. Of course, there were many islands and many destinations. On the other hand, it was time something good came his way.

Billy hung back, admiring her legs as he tried to decide whether to find out now, or wait and see if she was at the gate. If she wasn't, it hardly mattered where she was going. He decided to wait for fate to give him the answer.

Once she was at the head of the line, with only one person behind her, Billy sauntered over. Even two places back he caught a whiff of her perfume, liking it. Soon she was at the counter. Billy observed the way she stood and used her hands, the flick of her hair behind her ear, the way she tilted her head.

Once she'd checked in, she headed for her gate, not noticing him in line. In just a couple of minutes Billy was at the counter himself. The agent, a slender young man with a nameplate on his shirt that said "Hector," took his ticket. "You're going to St. Margaret this morning, Mr. Blue."

"I am unless you put me on the wrong airplane."

The man chuckled. "The only other possibility would be Belize…or Jamaica in an hour and a half."

"No, let's stick with St. Margaret."

"Sounds like a plan," the agent said as he started tearing copies from the packet.

"Has Zoe Marton checked in yet?" Billy asked.

"Just a few minutes ago. Are you traveling with her?"

"We came down from New York together. I told her to save me a seat. Did she remember?"

"No, she didn't mention a friend."

"Out of sight, out of mind," Billy said with a laugh.

"It's a very small aircraft, but the seat adjoining hers is available. Want me to seat you there?"

"Sure, why not?"

Billy had a good feeling, smiling with satisfaction as the agent completed the check-in process. The fact that fate kept bringing them together had to mean something. His grand-

mother would have said it did. He could picture Sophie Blue
Bear tuck her head in that distinctive way of hers and say
"Billy, nothing happens by accident."

Zoe sat yawning in the small waiting area at the gate. The
day had only begun and already she was tired from worrying
about Simon Van Biers, her Kansas sunflowers, the FBI and
Ahmed. When she'd called Victoria International from New
York to confirm her travel plans, they'd said someone would
meet her at the airport. "I believe Mr. Van Biers plans on
being there," the girl had said in her sweet Caribbean accent.

"Simon Van Biers?"

"No, Ms. Marton, Charles Van Biers."

In her meeting with the Van Biers in New York, Zoe had
focused on Simon and hadn't paid much attention to the son.
Charles was good-looking, but also full of himself. Though
she'd hardly interacted with him, she recalled thinking he was
arrogant. He'd made some suggestive remark that annoyed her
at the time, but she'd dismissed it because her focus was on
Simon and the job. She didn't remember what it was—something about bringing several bikinis with her, though considering it was the Caribbean, she could leave the tops at home
if she wanted. Something like that. Zoe expected that he'd be
hitting on her at some point, and that she'd have to put him
in his place diplomatically. No small challenge, considering
he was the boss's son.

Charles Van Biers was the primary reason she hadn't made
much of her pending divorce during the interview. Simon had
asked her how the separation from her husband would set with
her. "We lead rather independent lives," she'd said. "Ahmed
travels a great deal and I'm busy with my career. We get
together when we feel we need to. It won't be a problem." It
was hard to say whether that would deter Charles or egg him
on, but if nothing else, Ahmed was good for that—an excuse
not to get involved.

Zoe found a copy of the Saturday edition of the *Washington
Post* on a nearby seat and paged through it idly. It had been

days since she'd read a newspaper. She'd been so preoccupied with her own troubles that the world could be coming apart and she wouldn't have known the difference.

She was reading an article about The Smithsonian when she happened to glance up and catch sight of a man coming down the concourse in a wheelchair. What was remarkable was: first he was wheeling himself—there being no skycap in sight—and second, it was Billy Blue. He had his hat tilted back on his head, his carry-on bag on his lap and a big grin on his face.

He didn't look at her until he was almost beside her. Stopping, he gave her a phony surprised look.

"Lordy, if it isn't you again, Zoe. My, but it is a small world!" Then he laughed.

"Don't tell me you're going to St. Margaret," she said.

"Yes, and I can't help but wonder, are you following me, or am I following you?"

Zoe decided it wasn't a bad question. She hadn't given the man all that much thought, except when he seemed to pop up at every turn. Was it possible this wasn't a coincidence? What could he be up to, though? Surely he wasn't with the FBI. Or with Simon Van Biers? But that seemed unlikely. She couldn't imagine what Simon could hope to achieve by sending someone to spy on her. And it couldn't be Ahmed who was behind it because Billy had thwarted him at JFK...unless that scene had been staged, a way for the cowboy to win her trust. But then she realized how ridiculous that idea was. Ahmed had nothing to gain. The divorce would be final within a few weeks. The problem was she was paranoid. That's what it was.

"I'm definitely not following you," she said.

"And I'm not following you."

"Must be a coincidence, then."

"Must be." Billy grinned.

He was a good-looking devil. Disarming. That's what made him dangerous, she decided. "If you don't mind a personal question," Zoe said. "Why are you going to St. Margaret?"

"Actually, to see my old man."

"Your father?"

"Right. Never have laid eyes on the S.O.B., pardon my French, so I've come calling."

"You told me you were in the Caribbean on business."

"I am. I've got business to conduct with my old man."

"Really?"

"Yes, ma'am."

She had no idea whether it was a story or not, though it seemed just odd enough to be true.

"How about you?" he said. "What sort of business have you got in St. Margaret?"

She wasn't sure how candid she wanted to be. "I've taken a job."

"Yeah? Doing what?"

"Advising an investor."

"You're an investment adviser."

"Yes, in a manner of speaking."

"Hmm. You from New York?"

"For the past several years."

"Before that?"

"Kansas City."

"No kidding."

"No kidding." She figured a little innocent conversation may be the best way to proceed. "How about you? Where are you from and what do you do?"

"Until recently I was a rodeo cowboy. Busted up my back so I guess you could say I'm retired now."

"You really were in the rodeo?"

"Professional circuit. Bull rider, mostly."

"I never would have thought."

"Why? Don't I look the part?"

Zoe laughed. "Well, I guess you do. I just never met anybody in the rodeo before."

Billy reached into his hip pocket and pulled out his wallet. "I can prove it, if you doubt me." He began removing cards, handing them to her. "Nevada driver's license," he said. "See, there's my name, Billy Blue Bear. Medical insurance card...but that's no longer valid, since I lost my job. Membership card for the American Association of Rodeo Cowboys. See, Billy Blue," he said, pointing. He examined the next card. "What's this? Oh, library card, Elko Branch. That doesn't prove much, except that I'm literate, I guess." He looked at it closely. "Hmm. Expired. Well, I'm not home much. Guess that makes me semiliterate," he said with a grin.

Zoe chuckled. "You really don't have to continue. I believe you."

"No, let's do this right. A man's whole life is in his wallet, you know." He handed her a business card. "My grandmother's banker in Elko, Ed Carlsen. And..." He examined the next item. "The business card of the lady I had dinner with in New York two nights ago. See how honest I am?"

"Very convincing," she teased.

"If I had a signed affidavit from the president of the United States declaring I'm an honorable man and safe to befriend, I'd show you that, too, but unfortunately, I don't know the guy."

She shook her head, handing back the cards. "Okay, you've convinced me."

"I'd say we keep ending up on the same plane because fate intends it, Zoe."

"Either that or we happen to be going to the same place."

He shook his head, his expression sober. "That's not nearly so romantic a notion."

"You're right, but I'm not a romantic," she said.

"No? Pretty lady like you?"

She studied him as he put his cards back in his wallet. He was pretty cute, she had to admit, but he was also so far removed from anyone she'd ever had the slightest interest in that it was laughable. A cowboy was about as far from her type as you could get.

"How'd you get hurt?" she asked. "Did a horse or a cow kick you?"

He gave her another grin. "More like a bull moose."

Her look was questioning.

"Let's just say I got involved in an altercation and came out on the short end."

"You got into a fight, in other words."

"Yes. A very painful experience, and not just because of the bumps and bruises. But we aren't well enough acquainted for me to go into detail."

Zoe repressed a smile. "I see."

He ran his fingers back through his rumpled tawny hair, squinting at her as though he was staring into the sun, sizing her up maybe, managing to look terribly sexy as only a man who was very physical could. Zoe realized then he was a womanizer. The disarming, aw-shucks charm, the easy self-confidence was the giveaway. This guy had ridden as many cowgirls as he had bulls. Zoe would bet her life on it. Her instinctive impulse was to retreat.

"Sounds like you'll be staying on St. Margaret for a while," he said.

"It's quite likely."

"I don't expect to be there all that long myself," he said, sounding disappointed. "Unless I can get my old man to foot the bill for a little vacation. Travel's not cheap."

"No, it's not."

Billy appraised her again. "That said, a fella's still got to take advantage of the travel opportunities he's got. To be honest, I don't know thing one about St. Margaret, but I intend to make the most of my visit. I'm the adventurous type."

"I imagine somebody who rides bulls for a living would have to be adventurous."

The comment seemed to please him. "Do you know anything about the food on St. Margaret?"

"Not really."

"Well, how'd you like to have dinner with me and we'll discover it together?"

"I'd really like to, Billy, but I've got plans. I'll be dining with my new employer."

"Could we make it another night, then?"

"You're a very nice man," she said, "and you did me a

good turn at the airport in New York, but you've got the wrong idea about me. I'm not available. I'm married.''

"You're married?" he said, his eyes going to her left hand.

"I don't wear my ring in the tropics because it gives me a rash." She opened her purse, fished in the zippered side pocket until she found her wedding band. She slipped it on her finger and held it up for him to see.

"This is a very great disappointment," he said, looking completely sincere.

"I hope I didn't give you the wrong impression or send the wrong signal."

"Nope. I reckon the fault lies with the wishful thinking on my part. I certainly meant no offense."

"None taken."

Billy studied her, shaking his head. "It's a shame," he said. "A crying shame."

"I'll take that as a compliment."

"By all means."

Zoe felt a touch guilty because Billy Blue was very nice, but she wasn't in the Caribbean for romance. She had terribly important business to tend to. Even the most casual fling was not in the cards. Besides, cute or not, the guy wasn't the type she'd get involved with.

"I expect I'd better go talk to the passenger agent to make sure I'm all checked out," he said. "Will you please excuse me?"

"Sure."

Billy got out of the wheelchair, pushed it to the side, then started to walk toward the desk. But after a few steps, he stopped and said, "I arranged for us to sit together...not re-alizing...well, you know. Would you like me to change that?"

"It doesn't matter," she said. "I'll be sleeping or reading most of the flight."

He nodded. Then, wagging his finger, he said, "You being a married lady comes as one of the ten greatest disappoint-ments of my life."

She smiled. He smiled back, but sadly. As he went off, Zoe

decided he had to be one of the ten most disarmingly charming men in America—of the down-home variety. And he was probably one of the most devious, as well. Billy Blue would recover from his disappointment, she was certain. Probably when the next miniskirt happened along.

Queenstown, St. Margaret

"Wouldn't you know it," Elise Hurst said as she watched her husband adjusting his tie. "I finally get you home for a day and we have to entertain."

"It's only for the afternoon, Elise. A few hours."

She came up behind him and put her arms around his waist. "Yes, I know, but I hunger for time alone with you, dear. Do you have any idea how long it's been since we've spent a leisurely day together, taking breakfast in bed, lounging about...making love." She placed the flat of her hand on his abdomen, then moved it a few inches lower, enough to suggest what she had in mind.

Jerome Hurst, feeling a stab of guilt, turned around and took her by the shoulders. "I know it seems I neglect you, love, but you're in my heart as you've always been. I won't be in this job forever. After it's over we'll have a more normal life."

"By then you'll be too tired."

"Nonsense."

He gathered her to him so that he wouldn't have to look into her eyes any longer. He was certain his perfidy must be written on his face. Jerome Hurst did love his wife, but he was madly, dizzily, helplessly in love with Mayte Van Biers. He'd fallen for her so hard he couldn't help himself. Every opportunity he had, he wanted to be with her.

"Jerome, have you any idea how long it's been since we've made love?" his wife asked.

"A week?"

"Three. I recall the days when it was you who kept track."

"Elise, I'm preoccupied with so many concerns…it's not you. It has nothing to do with you."

She pulled back so she could look directly in his eyes. "Is there someone else, Jerome?"

Summoning all the strength within him, he managed somehow to appear incredulous. "Darling, of course not."

"There's no 'of course not' about it. You're a man of influence and power and God knows you're attractive. There is no shortage of women who'd be more than happy to…"

"Like who? Elise, a person can't sneeze on this island without everyone knowing about it, much less someone in my position."

"There are ways."

"Darling, this is beginning to annoy me. Truly. There's no basis."

"There's got to be some reason why you neglect me."

"Neglect? We sleep in the same bed every night and dine together nearly every evening."

"That isn't what it means to be husband and wife."

He gave her one of his most sincere looks, the sort he'd perfected after years in politics. "I promise to make more time for you, dear. You're right, you deserve better."

It was his conscience speaking. Not that there wasn't genuine feeling in what he said, but it was hard to pretend Mayte Van Biers didn't exist. For the time being, though, Mayte could only be his lover. He had appearances to consider, and an affair with a married woman would not endear him to the voters. But no matter what the future held, he was certain he'd never let Mayte go. She would be in his life, he was convinced, perhaps forever. Yet, for now, it was crucial that he keep peace with his wife.

"This evening, after our guests have gone, we'll spend time together," Jerome assured her. "Just the two of us."

"How?" she said, brightening.

"Any way you like. We can go for a swim or sail or just lounge about the house. You decide."

The happiness he saw on the face of his wife of eighteen

years tore at his soul. He did not want to hurt Elise, but when a man loved with a burning, uncontrollable passion...he became helpless, a child. Yet, he owed his wife his best effort, not just for her sake, but for his own. He could ill afford to alienate her, not with the election only two months away.

"I think I should like to stay home," she said. "Have a nice bottle of wine, perhaps."

She smiled in a suggestive way that was so familiar. Ironically, it saddened him. Her innocence was terribly hard to bear. Sometimes he felt a desperate need to throw off his blanket of sins, but then he would think of Mayte. All it took was the mental image of her long, lean naked body, her sleek, elegant beauty, her defiant smile, her wit, her razor-sharp mind, for his resolve to melt. She had utter and absolute control of his heart and she could make him hard merely with a touch of her fingertip. And yet, Elise was his wife.

"That's what we'll do then," he said. "We'll stay home, just the two of us."

Elise looked over at the clock on the dresser. "I'd better get downstairs and make sure Rogers and the girls have everything arranged properly. I do so want this to be a nice party."

"That's the only kind you know how to give."

"Yes, but this one's special because of Poppy Tuttlebee. I know how badly she wants this baby and I'm so very happy for her."

"It's nice that we can celebrate with them," Jerome said.

"You all work so very hard. I imagine some of the other wives feel a bit neglected, as well. This afternoon shall be good for everyone."

Elise kissed him lightly on the lips, then left their bedroom to go complete the preparations for their party. Jerome thought of the implicit promise he'd just made to make love with her after their guests had departed. He worried that he would be able to do it convincingly. The tragic and bitter truth was that Mayte was the one he wanted to be with, only Mayte.

* * *

Over the Caribbean

They had the back row of the small, eight-or-nine-passenger commuter plane. Zoe sat next to him, an elderly retired French schoolteacher named Claudette, on the other side of her. Zoe had spent the twenty minutes they'd been airborne talking to the Frenchwoman. Not that Billy felt neglected or had a right to expect anything different. Still, he was almost sorry they were sitting together. Zoe had piqued his curiosity—no, it was more than that, she'd gotten to him, touched that place in his gut where yearning was born. Truth be known, he was still smarting from the surprise she'd dropped on him. She was married and therefore "unavailable," as she'd put it.

There was a time when Billy would have considered that not only okay, but even preferable. If a woman said she was married but continued to flirt or otherwise show interest, he took it as a challenge, a red flag being waved in front of his nose. There were times when a woman claimed to be happily married and really meant she had no desire to become involved. Often things would end right there. But there were other times when a woman didn't really mean it, wanting one thing with her mind, perhaps, another with her heart. He'd seen his share of them vacillate back and forth before finally inviting him to their bed.

The secret was helping the gal find a way to rationalize her misgivings, making it easy for her to give in to her desire. That was probably Billy's greatest skill as a lover. He knew how to make women feel good about themselves, and about being with him.

With Zoe Marton he was at that critical juncture, the point in time where he either backed off or went for the jugular and found out what she really wanted. One thing he knew with certainty was that she was not as happily married as she'd have him believe. What husband in his right mind would let a gem like her go off alone to a tropical island? Unless, of course, he had no choice in the matter. And what loving wife would want to go? Zoe might be married, but it was a crazy marriage.

So, what did that mean? Which way did he go?

The situation was not without complications. Billy reminded himself that this wasn't just about her. It was also about him. He'd come to the Caribbean for a very serious purpose, which didn't leave a lot of time and energy for fun and games. Plus, his experience in Cheyenne was supposed to have taught him a lesson. Screwing around with married women wasn't a game. There were consequences. And just because Zoe rang his chimes didn't mean he could set his principles aside. Either he'd reformed, or he hadn't.

When he stopped to think about it, maybe the temptation of a Zoe Marton was exactly what he needed. If he could walk away from her, he could walk away from anyone. Maybe this was a test of his resolve, something he should welcome. The pretty face, the great legs, the quick mind and spunky personality—all things he had to learn to ignore.

Closing his eyes and lying back in the seat, Billy tried to put her from his mind, but the luscious scent of her was right there, filling his lungs. Damn. This wasn't going to be easy. He was determined to succeed, though. All he had to do was keep his mouth shut and his hands to himself.

Queenstown, St. Margaret

Jerome Hurst sat at the umbrella table with his chief aide, Basil Tuttlebee, surveying the scene before them. They were each smoking a cigar and Basil had a glass of beer in his hand, which he turned absently between his fingers as he watched his wife playing croquet out on the rolling lawn. Beyond the grassy area and partway down the slope was a wall, and beyond that the rooftops of the town and beyond that the blue-green Caribbean. Jerome could see a cruise ship several miles out to sea and thought how he'd love to have the freedom to get away, to indulge himself with several days of leisure, preferably in the arms of Mayte Van Biers. But he knew that if their time did come, it wouldn't be soon.

Focusing once again on the croquet players, Jerome considered the irony of the fact that as president he was in effect the island's chief prisoner. Holding on to power required tremendous sacrifice, a point driven home in his earlier conversation with Elise. He could not look at her now without feeling guilty. Perhaps that was the price he had to pay for his precious minutes with Mayte.

Elise, a proud and serious woman who understood duty, was among the croquet players out on the lawn. Poppy was with her, as was Lenore Smythe, the director of social services, and Reginald Goodson's very British and very pinched and proper wife, Mildred. Reginald was himself at the other end of the terrace, speaking with his chief lieutenant on the force, Ellis Toliver, who had arrived a few minutes earlier and who happened to be, coincidentally, Elise's cousin. This island nation was practically one large extended family. There were advantages to that, but also disadvantages. As far as Jerome was concerned, the latter usually outweighed the former.

Though entertaining had never been one of his greatest joys, he'd usually endured events like this with a certain amount of grace and patience. These people were, after all, his colleagues and friends. Many of them were instrumental in putting him in office. And yet, Jerome found himself longing to leave, to get in his car and go find Mayte. It would be a week, in all probability, before they would be together again. It seemed an eternity. Basil, who among Jerome's staffers was probably his closest confidant, sat quietly, letting him enjoy the silence. They understood one another well enough that they could do that without growing uncomfortable. Jerome was taken to more and more silences of late. If Basil wondered about it, he said nothing.

"I've never seen Poppy so radiant," Jerome said, figuring the time had come for some sort of comment.

"The thought of being childless really wore on her, Mr. President. This baby is a godsend."

Jerome puffed on his cigar. "So it seems."

Out on the lawn, Poppy knocked Mildred Goodson's ball out of bounds and instantly apologized. "Isn't that typical of women?" Basil said, drawing on his cigar and pointing with it. "The object of the game is to win, yet they feel badly, knowing it's at someone else's expense."

Jerome considered the point, thinking it might well apply to Elise, but certainly not Mayte. She had a killer instinct. He wondered if that was one of the things he found so alluring about her. A tiger, yet a woman. He brought his mind back to Basil. "Your Poppy does seem changed."

"She's still a worrier, though," Basil said. "Agonizes about losing the baby, which I guess is normal enough, considering how difficult it was for her to get pregnant. But everything seems to bother her, not just that."

"What do you mean?"

Basil shrugged. "The oddest things. She's constantly asking about Raymond Pearson and the investigation, for example. Afraid there's a killer loose on the island, I suppose."

Jerome puffed on his cigar. "A number of people have been unnerved by it, Basil. Fear of the unknown, I would surmise. I just wish there'd be some resolution so that we could put it behind us."

"I expect Mr. Goodson is unlikely to admit it, but Ellis tells me the FBI agent has been very helpful."

"Reginald hasn't said a thing to me as yet, other than the investigation is continuing. As best I can tell, they're no closer to finding Pearson than they were the day he disappeared."

"Ellis thinks they're making progress."

"Maybe I should have Ellis brief me instead of Reginald."

"Here's your chance to say so, Mr. President. Sir Reginald is approaching now." With the last, Basil rolled his tongue in his cheek.

Jerome turned to see the head of the national police making his way across the terrace. As always, Chief Inspector Reginald Goodson was in his proper tie and too-tight shirt collar, somehow managing to look crisp, despite the heat. Perhaps it was the military bearing with which he carried himself. He was a large man, ruddy-faced, always perspiring and with thinning gray hair and a rather large, drooping mustache that gave him a dated look.

Behind his back Goodson was called "Sir Reginald" because he was so painfully British in speech and manner. The only holdover from the colonial government, Goodson had made himself an institution for two reasons—he was a good policeman and he understood the art of politics. Already past retirement age, Goodson had proven useful, if not essential, to Jerome's predecessors, as he'd proven himself useful to Jerome. The man knew where all the bodies were buried and, like his American counterpart of days gone by, J. Edgar Hoover, Reginald Goodson made it his business to know as much about the country's leaders as possible. The more sensitive the intelligence, the better. Goodson was so skilled in that regard, that if there was only one person alive who knew about Jerome and Mayte, it would have to be the man at the head of the national police.

"Hello, Reginald," Jerome said as he approached the table.

"Mr. President. Good afternoon." Coming to a stop, he effected a subtle movement with his upper body that was half nod and half bow. "Delightful party, if I may say so, sir."

"It is a nice day, isn't it?" Jerome said, staring out to sea. He puffed on his cigar, then motioned with it for Goodson to sit down. "Join us, old man. How about a cigar?"

"Thank you, Mr. President, but I shan't." He touched his neck. "Throat polyps, you know."

"Ah, yes. Have a beer, then."

"I've had a pint already, sir, thank you very much indeed. If I may, we've just had an interesting bit of intelligence from the American, the FBI agent."

"Oh?"

"Ellis has just had a word with Special Agent Tsu, who's waiting in the entry."

"He's here now?"

"She, Mr. President. Special Agent Joyce Tsu, spelled, T-S-U."

"Joyce Tsu. Unusual name."

"I believe she's Chinese-American, sir."

"What does she have to say?"

"Several days ago we noted a pair of unusual visitors in our midst, Mr. President. The Americans have identified them for us and given us some interesting background information. As chance would have it, we've been able to connect the pair with certain prominent citizens. I'm concerned enough, Mr. President, that I thought you should be informed immediately, with the thought that perhaps you'd like to speak with Special Agent Tsu yourself."

Jerome flicked the ash from his cigar into the ashtray. Goodson had a flair for the dramatic and always enjoyed bearing news, whether good or bad. But Jerome sensed something ominous in his tone.

"Why not?" he said. "I expect my guests can get along without me for a few minutes."

Jerome got up from his chair. His aide stood, as well.

"Basil, why don't you come along?"

"Yes, sir."

The three of them trooped across the terrace toward the French doors accessing the executive mansion where Ellis Toliver, a thin, dark-skinned man, the second-highest-ranking police officer in the country, waited.

"Mr. President," he said respectfully.

"Ellis, good to see you." Jerome touched Toliver's arm, then led the way into the house.

He found a slight, rather short but solid-looking Asian woman waiting in the entry. She rose from where she had been seated on a straight chair next to the grandfather clock. Jerome would have said her background was likely military, considering the way she came to attention.

"Good afternoon, sir," she said.

Goodson made the introductions. Tsu, dressed in khaki pants, leather walking shoes and a white cotton blouse, shook

Jerome's hand firmly, then assumed the at-ease position. She had a short, nondescript haircut, a rather flat face and flat chest. There was a sturdiness about her, and she gave the impression of being quick and wiry. Something about her suggested she might be a worthy adversary in hand-to-hand combat.

"Let's go into my study," Jerome said. He led the way, inviting the others to sit, and took a seat himself behind his large mahogany desk. Special Agent Tsu was in the visitor's chair directly opposite him. "I understand you've turned up something of interest," he said. "Why don't you fill me in."

"Yes, sir. I'd be happy to, sir. This morning we were able to confirm through Washington the identity of a suspicious individual first spotted on the island Wednesday of last week. The subject's name is Marvin Blade, also known as Mooky Blade, a citizen of Jamaica. His wife, Danielle, French-Canadian by birth but raised in the States, is with him. The Blades are thought to be contract killers, sir, active throughout the Caribbean and possibly in South America and the States. They are suspected of as many as ten hits, though charges have not been filed in any of the homicides in question. Interpol has a lengthy rap sheet on them, sir, but neither subject has a criminal record of consequence. As a young man, Blade did time in Jamaica for assault. He has a special aptitude with munitions. Both individuals are skilled in martial arts. Beyond that, little is known."

The report, given in a clipped, businesslike tone, gave Jerome an ominous feeling. Contract killers? He swallowed hard. "Do we have any idea what they're doing on St. Margaret?"

"That's the interesting part, Mr. President," Reginald Goodson said. "Continue with your account, Special Agent Tsu."

"Gladly, sir. The Blades are staying in a villa on the south-western side of the island, on Newquay Bay," she said. "The lease was signed by an associate of Charles Van Biers. Van Biers himself was seen in the vicinity of the villa on at least one occasion. Naturally, we suspect that he has retained the services of the couple, but there's no hard evidence of that."

"We've got them under surveillance," Reginald Goodson added.

Jerome cleared his throat. "Who are the people they're thought to have killed? Are they political assassins?"

"No, sir," Tsu replied. "We think their work mostly involves the criminal elements, organized crime, drug traffickers and so forth."

Jerome looked at the others. "Could they be in any way connected with Raymond Pearson's disappearance?"

"We've discussed that, Mr. President," Goodson said. "We think it unlikely. If Pearson is dead and the Blades are responsible, it's unlikely they'd return to St. Margaret, even for an undertaking that's unrelated."

"Then they've only recently arrived."

"We think so. Immigration has no documentation. They most likely arrived by boat."

"Then they're here illegally," Jerome said.

"Yes," Goodson replied, mopping his brow with his handkerchief.

"Why don't we deport them?"

"We can, sir, we have that option. But I would advise against it," Goodson said, returning his handkerchief to his pocket.

"Why?"

"This may be our only chance to discover what they're up to, sir."

"If they're assassins, it may be better not to know."

"There is another consideration, Mr. President."

"What's that?"

Chief Inspector Reginald Goodson turned to his subordinate. "Ellis?"

Ellis Toliver leaned forward on the sofa where he was seated next to Basil. "Mr. President, you may recall the old Haitian woman we questioned, the voodoo priestess…"

"Yes, what about her?"

"We've had her under surveillance. Not around the clock, but whenever we can spare the manpower. The other evening we got lucky. While we had a man on stakeout, she had visitors."

"Who?"

"The Blades, sir."

Reginald Goodson had a knowing smile. Jerome wasn't sure he understood.

"What's the significance of that?"

"We can't be certain, Mr. President, but one possibility is that Blade is looking for the same thing we are."

"A murder suspect?"

"No, sir, that's unlikely."

"Then what?"

"A witness."

Ogden Bertrum International Airport,
St. Margaret

Billy looked out the window as the plane taxied toward the small cinder-block terminal building with the Quonset-hut annex. There was no way this place could be mistaken for JFK, or O'Hare, DFW, or any of the other big airports he'd seen along the way. In fact, the bus station in Elko was a cut above OB International.

"I've been in gas stations with fifty miles of desert in all directions that didn't seem as isolated as this," Billy said as much to himself as to Zoe. He did turn to her, though. "Maybe it's all that water. I've never been on an island before. How about you?"

"My husband and I honeymooned in the Virgin Islands."

"I guess that's appropriate."

She smiled faintly. He could see it was hopeless.

They lurched to a stop at the gate.

"Well, here at last," he said, knowing they'd come to the

end of the line in more ways than one. "It's been nice traveling with you, Zoe." He offered her his hand.

She was a bit surprised, but shook his hand.

"Good luck with your job, I hope everything works out great."

"Thanks," she said. "I hope things go well with your father."

"It ought to be interesting."

The door to the plane was open and the passengers in the first rows disembarked. The old Frenchwoman and Zoe followed. Billy was the last one off the plane. When he stepped down on the ground, he took a moment to stretch his back. That was the longest he'd sat at one time without being able to stand and unkink.

Zoe and the Frenchwoman, walking side by side, went into the Quonset-hut portion of the terminal building with the others. The structure was open on one side and appeared to house both the baggage claim and customs. The air didn't seem all that hot, but it was quite humid. Billy ambled toward the terminal, already feeling the perspiration forming under his collar and the band of his hat. Workers sitting on a baggage wagon, smoking, watched him stroll by in his boots, jeans and hat. They wore shorts, tank tops and sandals. He had to admit they looked a lot more comfortable.

Once inside the building Billy stood off by himself, trying to get a mental grip on the fact that he'd soon be seeing the father he'd never met. He'd been repressing that part of it to some degree, keeping Irwin Pettigrew in that mental box of forbidden notions—things hated, things dangerous, things obscene. Pettigrew was all that and more, even in his new persona as Simon Van Biers.

Although he couldn't pretend to know her, Billy felt a bit nostalgic about saying goodbye to Zoe Marton. He wasn't sure why that was. Hell, he couldn't come up with the name of a single woman—other than Shelly, of course—who'd meant more to him than sex and maybe a few laughs and companionship. Connie Meeks had been his friend and sexual partner for a lot longer than most, but there wasn't anybody he could remotely associate with the term *love*. Probably not Zoe either, though she stirred feelings in him that certainly felt different. He imagined that when you fell in love with somebody it started out something like this.

But he could only speculate about that. The point was, he needed to distance himself from her, the way he did with all the other women he'd bumped up against and then left behind. Billy had the technique honed to perfection. God knew, he'd had lots of practice. He had to do it yet again. "So long, Zoe," he said silently. "Have a nice life."

It didn't take long for the bags to arrive. There were nine or ten of them on one wagon along with two baggage handlers. Billy didn't muscle up to the trough, instead letting the others get their cases and move across the room to customs. Then he snatched his worn imitation-leather bag and got in line. Zoe was a couple of places ahead of him. As a light breeze moved through the room, he caught what he thought might be a whiff of her scent. It made him very sad.

The passengers who seemed to be locals had their baggage searched a bit more thoroughly. The inspector didn't look inside Zoe's bag or the French schoolteacher's either. Their passports were stamped and they were ushered outside. When Billy got to the counter, the inspector, a small bald man with bad teeth, asked for his passport.

"Don't have one," Billy said, glancing toward the exit as Zoe disappeared from sight, "but I reckon this will do." He pulled his driver's license and birth certificate out of his shirt pocket. "At least, that's what the airline said."

The inspector studied the documents closely. "Have you lost your passport, sir?"

"Never had one. Don't need one for Canada or Mexico, and that's about as far as I've strayed from home till now. This is sort of an emergency trip, last-minute thing."

"How long will you be staying in St. Margaret, Mr.... Blue?" the inspector said, consulting the driver's license again.

"A day or two, I reckon. As brief as possible…. Not that I wouldn't like to stay longer, but I've got to get back to my cattle."

He gave the inspector a wink. The man did not seem amused.

"Are you here for business or pleasure?"

"Business."

"What sort of business, sir?"

"Family business. I'm retrieving an heirloom that's been out on loan."

"You don't represent a commercial enterprise?"

"No, sir. Just myself and the estate of my late grand-mother."

"I'll put down pleasure, Mr. Blue," the inspector said, completing the form. He stamped the paper. "Please keep this form with your identification papers and be prepared to surrender it when you leave the country. If you plan to stay more than thirty days, a visa will be required. You can obtain the forms at the constabulary in town."

"I'm sure that won't be necessary."

"In any case… Now, will you be good enough to open your bag, Mr. Blue?"

Billy opened the suitcase. The inspector gave the contents a cursory glance, lifting the items in the corners.

"I'm not much of a packer, as you can see," Billy said, sort of embarrassed.

The man did not comment.

"Thank you, Mr. Blue. Enjoy your stay in St. Margaret."

"That wasn't so bad," Billy said, closing the bag.

The inspector acknowledged the comment with a nod.

"Can you recommend a good hotel?" Billy asked. "Nothing too fancy. Clean's all I care about."

"I suggest you apply at the tourist office in town. It's or the main square. You'll find it easily enough, sir."

To Billy it seemed awfully strange to hear a British accent As best he could recall, he'd never spoken with a Brit face-to-face. But he himself was a bit of an oddity. The only guys east of Nebraska that dressed like him were mostly on bill-boards.

"Much obliged," Billy said to the man as he hoisted his suitcase. "Adios."

"Good day, sir."

In front of the terminal building there was none of the usual bustle you found outside airports. At the far end of the little circular drive a family group was moving off with one of the passengers from Billy's flight. At the other end the French schoolteacher was climbing into a taxi. Standing on the curb next to the taxi was Zoe Marton. She waved goodbye to the Frenchwoman, then stepped back into the shade of a palm tree.

Billy lingered under the overhang of the entrance to the terminal, trying to decide whether to join Zoe or wait until she was gone. They'd already said goodbye. Why undo the nice bow? On the other hand, she was at the taxi stand and he had as much a reason and right to be there as anybody else.

Shifting his case to the other hand, Billy sauntered over to a point fifteen feet from where she stood waiting and put down his bag. Zoe had watched him approach, acknowledging him with a nod. He perfunctorily touched the brim of his hat.

"The French lady get the last taxi?" he asked.

"The driver said another would be arriving soon."

"Must mean there's two on the island," he said, chuckling. It would have been a perfect opportunity to suggest they share a ride into town, but she'd almost certainly take it wrong, so he didn't bother. He tilted his hat back on his head. "Doesn't look like a guy could drive very far without running into water, so I reckon we won't have long to wait."

"The next taxi is yours," she replied. "I've got a ride."

"Oh?" He rubbed his jaw. Damn if he didn't feel the sting of disappointment, having thought fate might have yet another surprise in mind. She was so pretty it took a guy's breath away. Not that she was the most gorgeous creature on earth maybe, but she certainly had a special effect on him. There was something about her, something in her nature that seemed made just for him.

Billy was determined to stick to his guns, though. He had two things working for him, a carrot and a stick—his promise to his grandmother was the carrot, and that trailer in Cheyenne, Luther and the boys lyin' in wait, was the stick. So he hung tough, not letting himself look at Zoe, showing the same forbearance he would if she were on her husband's arm. Instead, he gazed at the funny cone-shaped mountain across the valley, covered with deep green vegetation. He inhaled the unfamiliar smell of the sea air, tinged with the scent of tropical blossoms, and tried to think of other things, like his dear old dad. The sonovabitch.

His reverie was soon broken by the sound of a vehicle coming down the road. The distinctive whine of a high-performance engine told Billy it was likely a fancy sports car, and sure enough a moment later a silver Porsche Carrera flashed into view. Whipping around the circle drive, its tires squealing, the car zipped past Billy, screeching to a halt right in front of Zoe.

The driver's door of the Porsche flew open and a dark-headed young man in a white polo shirt, khaki pants and trendy sunglasses emerged. He had a bouquet of flowers in his hand. Purposefully striding around the vehicle, he walked up to Zoe.

"Sorry I'm late, Zoe," he said, reaching out and touching her upper arm. "Believe it or not, traffic. Some jackass dumped a load of lumber across the road and I couldn't get past."

"No problem, Charles. My flight just got in a few minutes ago."

"I planned to be here early to give you a proper welcome. Here," he said, extending the bouquet. "These are for you. Welcome to St. Margaret."

"How sweet, thank you so much."

She glanced Billy's way as she said it. She looked embarrassed, probably because she'd told him she was married...assuming it was the truth, which was beginning to look doubtful. Of course, she could be married and came to St.

Margaret to fool around with the Porsche jockey. In either case, Billy was annoyed. Not that she owed him anything—including the truth—but he hated being made the fool, even if it was only in his own mind.

When she glanced his way again, Charles turned to see what she was looking at. He took Billy in with one long, slow glance, his expression indicating incredulity first, then amusement. He turned his attention back to Zoe.

"So, how was your flight?"

"Fine. It was good."

"Well, I'm glad you're here. I've been looking forward to your arrival for weeks."

She sniffed her flowers, sneaking a peek at Billy, who remained annoyed. So, she'd come to St. Margaret on business, huh? Yeah, sure. And he didn't like this guy Charles one whit. Not that either of them was likely to give a damn what he thought. But he was entitled to be disgusted.

Charles touched Zoe's cheek, which seemed to surprise her. Her surprise didn't appear to bother him though. Billy heard the guy laugh as he reached down for her suitcase. Taking her arm with his other hand, he said, "Shall we go?"

As they moved toward the car, Charles again looked in Billy's direction. Their eyes met and Charles frowned. He was no longer amused.

"What are you looking at, cowboy? You got a problem?"

"Just waiting for a taxi."

Charles, who still had a hold of Zoe's arm, stopped. He put down the suitcase and said to her, "Was this bozo bothering you before I arrived?"

"No, not at all."

Her response didn't seem to matter. He said to Billy, "Why don't you go on up to the other end and wait? The lady and I don't need an audience."

"I'm real comfortable here, mister."

"Yeah? Well, I'm not comfortable with you standing there, so scram."

Billy could see the guy's blood was rising, but his was, too.

He didn't cotton to assholes. "Maybe I missed something. Is your name St. Margaret?"

"You trying to be funny?"

"You act like you own the island. I thought maybe you're Mr. St. Margaret and the whole damn thing was yours."

Charles started for Billy with blood in his eye. Billy saw a fight coming and the adrenaline in his blood surged. Zoe ran after Charles, grabbing him by the arm, stopping him.

"Don't," she cried. "He hasn't done anything. He was on the plane with me."

"I don't care if he landed in a spaceship," Charles said, red-faced. "I don't take lip from some hick cowboy. Not on my turf."

Breaking free, he came at Billy, who braced himself, bad back and all. Charles gave him a shove in the chest and Billy went flying backward, landing on the pavement, a terrible pain surging through him. His every instinct was to leap to his feet and charge the sonovabitch, but he couldn't even sit upright without first rolling onto his side. He was doing just that when Charles kicked him in the ass.

"Get your butt up to the other end like I told you, Tex."

He turned, and Billy, still on the ground, watched him stride back to where Zoe stood waiting, her hands on her hips. She looked angrier than hell.

"That was completely uncalled for," she said. "That man is recovering from a serious injury. I'm appalled you could do such a thing."

"You heard what he said, Zoe," he said defensively. "The guy's got a smart mouth."

"Well, you're out of line. And I don't care who your father is."

"For crissakes, it's not that big a deal."

While they argued, Billy picked up his hat from the sidewalk and put it on. Then he got to his knees, and finally his feet.

"I'm not riding with you, Charles," she said. "I'm taking a taxi."

''No, please don't,'' he said. ''It was a misunderstanding.''

''It was no misunderstanding, you were completely out of line.''

The pain in his back notwithstanding, Billy was sort of amused, listening to them. It wasn't often that he'd had a woman rush to his defense that way. Of course, it wasn't so much him as the way the Porsche jockey had behaved that set her off. Or, maybe she felt she owed him a good turn after what happened at JFK.

''All right,'' Charles said to her. ''I'm sorry. I made a mistake.''

''Don't apologize to me. It's Mr. Blue you owe the apology to.''

Charles glanced in Billy's direction. ''Hey man, I'm sorry.''

Billy, dusting his rear end, waved him off, not really looking at the guy. Then Zoe came over to him. ''I'm sorry, Billy,'' she said in an intimate tone. ''You didn't do a thing to deserve that.''

''I got a little cheeky, but thanks for sticking up for me.''

''I feel terrible.''

''Don't.''

Charles came over then, a contrite expression on his face. ''Here,'' he said, taking several twenty-dollar bills out of his wallet and extending them to Billy. ''Buy yourself a couple of beers on me.''

''Keep it,'' Billy said, shaking his head. ''I don't want your money.''

Charles looked at Zoe helplessly, as if to say, ''Well, I tried.'' She took the money from his hand and stuffed it in Billy's shirt pocket. ''No, I think you deserve a nice dinner tonight. Charles and I are both sorry.'' Then, to Billy's surprise and Charles's too, she handed Billy the flowers. ''Come on,'' she said to her companion. ''Let's go.''

Billy flexed his back as he watched Charles stick Zoe's bag in the space behind the seat, then help her into the car. After that, Charles walked around to the driver's side. Before getting in he held his hand over the roof and flipped Billy off.

Smiling, Billy called to him, "Have a nice day, partner."

Charles mouthed the words "Fuck you" and got into the car. Moments later the Carrera roared away. Billy chuckled, thinking Zoe Marton was proving harder to put behind him than he'd expected. Something kept bringing them together at every turn. And maybe it wasn't over yet. Considering the Porsche jockey was an asshole, it was possible she might be needing a friend. The question for Billy was, could he handle the temptation?

Biloxi Plantation

Charles drove a little too fast for her taste, but Zoe didn't say anything. She was sorry she hadn't taken a taxi after all, but once he'd apologized to Billy Blue, she couldn't very well punish him anymore. So, she'd given Charles the benefit of the doubt. An enemy was the last thing she needed, especially not Simon Van Biers's son. There was only one thing that mattered at the moment and that was to get the day behind her.

Charles had told her his father was eagerly awaiting her arrival, which was encouraging. "The sooner we get to work on the collection, the better it'll be," he'd quoted Simon as saying. Zoe just wanted to get on the inside and find out what she could about how Simon had got his hands on the Kansas sunflowers.

The plan, Charles told her, was for her to stay at the Van Biers' plantation, at least initially. He said it was nicer than any hotel on the island, so she should be pleased. "Mayte's got a big welcome planned, including dinner," he said. "So you'll be able to meet her, get acquainted with everyone and become part of our happy little family."

The way he'd said it, with a suggestive lilt in his voice, reinforced her suspicion that he had designs on her, which was an annoyance. She did not like the man—even less now than in New York. Attacking Billy Blue that way had told her everything she needed to know about Charles Van Biers.

With the sun now very low over the water to the west, they roared through the gated entrance and Zoe got a glimpse of the plantation house up on the hill. "What a gorgeous setting," she said.

"Yeah, it's the nicest place on the island, bar none."

"Your father has done very well in a short time."

"He's a sharp old dude, all right. But this will all be mine before long. I guess you could say I'm sort of waiting in the wings."

Zoe thought that was a rather tasteless thing for somebody to say about their own father, but it didn't surprise her, not coming from Charles. "Is Mr. Van Biers in poor health?" she asked.

"Not particularly, but he's over seventy. He was already pretty old when I was born."

"Is your mother still living?"

"Yeah, but I hardly ever see her. She and the old man got divorced when I was in high school and she went back to live in England, and remarried. Her husband's a university professor. Funny thing is, Van Biers is her family name. My old man adopted it."

"You mean, he took her name instead of the other way around?"

"Yeah, she wanted me to be Charles Van Biers, and the old man didn't care. For a while he used both Van Biers and Pettigrew, depending on who he was dealing with. But when he started the bank, he dropped Pettigrew for good."

"That's unusual."

"Don't say anything, but he's from a pretty modest background. Grew up in the South. In marrying my mother, he married up and decided to capitalize on the name when it suited his purposes. I've got to admit, though, he's done pretty damned well. From Mother's side I got aristocratic blood in my veins—some great-great-grandfather was a German prince or duke or something—not that it means all that much on this side of the Atlantic, but what the hey, something to talk about at a cocktail party, right?'' He chuckled with self-satisfaction. ''The way I see it, I got the best of both worlds—the old man's cunning and moxie and my mother's breeding.''

Charles Van Biers obviously had no shortage of self-esteem and he definitely had a full-blown sense of his own importance. He was also a first-class jerk.

They'd reached the top of the hill, entering a big circular drive that ran past the entrance to the huge manor house. Zoe had to admit, it was impressive. She was glad to have arrived, if only because Charles was a terrible bore, a rude, violent, self-centered ass and she wanted badly to be free of him. He stopped the Porsche in front of the entrance.

''Zoe,'' he said, reaching over and taking her hand. ''I've got to ask you something. What was the deal back there with that cowboy? Was something going on between you and him?''

She was appalled by the rudeness of the question, but decided it was easier and wiser to ignore that than make an issue of it. ''No, there was nothing going on, absolutely not.''

''How come you gave him the flowers?''

She thought she'd better not say because they were from him and therefore she didn't want them, so she said, ''Because I felt sorry for him. He was badly hurt in a riding accident or something at the rodeo. Getting knocked down must have hurt.''

''Riding accident?'' Charles said, almost laughing. ''More likely he got the shit kicked out of him by somebody who didn't appreciate his lip.''

''It doesn't matter what happened, Charles, he was clearly in pain.''

''You must be the type that takes in stray cats.'' He gave her hand a firm squeeze. ''Too softhearted for your own good, maybe.''

Not too softhearted to tell him to get lost, though she'd restrain herself until she absolutely had to do it. Even so, she felt very uncomfortable with him holding her hand. Gently pulling it free of his grasp, she said, "I believe in common courtesy, that's all."

"I figured he wasn't anybody, but I wanted to hear you say it."

She half smiled, not knowing what else to do.

"The reason is, I've been thinking an awful lot about you since New York, really looking forward to your arrival." He gave her a smug grin. "But I couldn't remember what you told me. Are you and your husband separated or getting a divorce?"

Zoe wanted to say she'd planned to reconcile with Ahmed, but she didn't want to get caught in an out-and-out lie. She could be equivocal, though, and said, "It's pending."

"A divorce?"

"Yes."

"Well, that's good."

"I must say, however, the experience is proving more traumatic than I expected. Obviously I still have feelings for Ahmed."

"Maybe I can help you get past that," he said.

Zoe wanted to tell him to mind his own business, but she knew diplomacy was called for. There was no point in adding to her problems. She had a tough enough row to hoe as it was. "I think I'll put my personal problems from my mind and concentrate on business," she said.

"But you've got to have a little fun, though," he said, stroking her cheek.

Zoe recoiled. "Please, Charles, I don't think that sort of familiarity is appropriate."

"Zoe," he said, shaking his head, "you've got to learn to relax. Don't be so uptight. Trust me."

Oh, God, she thought, this is going to be hell. She just knew Charles was going to make her life miserable.

"But don't worry," he said, perhaps realizing she needed reassurance. "We'll take care of business first. I told the old man I'd be glad to help you get adjusted. So, if you need anything, anything at all, you just let me know."

"Thank you, Charles."

"Well, looky there," he said, peering past her toward the front door. "It's Mummy and Daddy."

Zoe turned to see a rather elegant couple standing in the doorway. It was Simon Van Biers, tall, patrician, with a shock of white hair. He had on a white suit and black tie. But the woman was truly striking. She was black, very light-skinned, also tall, and wearing a sleek, strapless, satiny black hostess gown and large gold hoop earrings. The effect was of a fashion model. Considering she was still in her travel garb, Zoe felt like a frump.

Charles got out and came around to open her door. Zoe looked up at the striking pair on the steps, reminding herself who they were and what they'd been involved in. These were the people the FBI suspected of some kind of wrongdoing, and Simon Van Biers had the Van Gogh sunflowers that rightfully belonged to her.

"Zoe," Simon said, stepping forward, "it's good to see you again. Welcome to Biloxi Plantation. We're so happy you've arrived. I hope you had a pleasant flight."

His hand was extended. Zoe took it. He was surprisingly strong, practically lifting her up the final step. "Very nice, thank you."

"May I present my wife, Mayte, the light of my life and my personal brain trust..."

Zoe shook hands with the gorgeous woman.

"So glad you're here," Mayte said in a tone that was more polite than genuinely warm. "I imagine you'd like to freshen up, perhaps change before we have cocktails and dinner."

"That sounds fabulous," Zoe said, truly grateful.

"The men are eager to talk business, I know," Mayte said, "but I'll keep them at bay until you've had a chance to regroup."

The remark struck Zoe as considerate.

"Shucks, sugar," Simon said, lapsing into a Southern drawl. "You know I'm more of a gentleman than that. I respect a proper lady's needs. Zoe can have all the time in the

world. But what on earth are we doin' standing out in the
heat? By all means, let's go inside.''

Zoe sensed that Simon Van Biers and his wife were a prac-
ticed pair, a one-two punch of charm and guile. They were
probably every bit as insidious as Charles, only more subtle.
Even so, they were a welcome relief from the son.

As she stepped through the door and into the cool air of the
huge plantation house, Zoe Marton took a deep breath. Mayte
was right, she did need to regroup. And she also had to keep
a clear head at all times. One false step and everything could
be lost.

Queenstown

Billy had decided there was no point in procrastinating. This
island nation was like a village, and Pettigrew would be hearing about a cowboy hitting town and might start putting things
together. A guy couldn't be a successful con and miss many
tricks. So, Billy figured he'd strike while the iron was hot.

The cheapest accommodations turned out to be the Queen's
Inn, the small hotel right in town. Ninety bucks a night—a
bargain according to anybody's account but his. The more
resortish places ran a couple hundred a night and up, so maybe
he was getting a deal. Even so, three days and he'd be out of
money. And no idea where he'd get more. The irony was he
had a cashier's check for fifty-five thousand on him, but every
penny of it was needed to get Granny's sunflowers out of
hock.

Billy had a shower first thing, dressed in the fanciest western shirt he had with him, and gabardine western-style pants.
At his request the desk had sent a kid to fetch his boots and
take them to get polished. Billy brushed his hat and polished
up his bull-riding championship belt buckle. When the kid
brought back the boots, Billy put them on and went downstairs
to the desk. The clerk, a chubby black girl in a pink T-shirt

dress that made her look a little sausagey, asked if he wanted recommendations for a restaurant.

"Thank you kindly, but I'm going to make a social call before I have dinner. Would you happen to be acquainted with a gentleman by the name of Simon Van Biers?"

"Most certainly, sir," she said with a big full-tooth smile. "Everybody knows Mr. Van Biers. He owns the bank, or as some say, he *is* the bank."

"That would be him," Billy said. "Could you direct me to his house?"

"He lives clear on the other end of the island, sir, on Biloxi Plantation—at least he calls it that. To most people it's still the Queen's Head Plantation."

"How do I get there, by taxi?"

"Unless you choose to walk. That would take most of an hour. Bicycle would be twenty minutes, perhaps."

"I think I'll take a taxi."

"Shall I ring up Able for you, sir? He's the most reliable."

"I'd be much obliged."

"Unless he's having tea, he should be here in five minutes. Perhaps you'd be more comfortable waiting in the lounge. I'll tell you when he arrives."

"If it's all the same to you, ma'am, I'll sit out front, get a breath of air."

"As you wish, sir."

Billy stepped out into the balmy air and took a seat on the wooden bench next to the entrance. The temperature had gone down since he'd arrived, the sea breeze having become quite pleasant. Now that evening had arrived, people—both the locals and tourists—filled the streets of the small commercial district. It was only three blocks long on a single street, one block from the tiny harbor. Billy had seen most of it when he'd walked from the tourist office to the hotel, pausing a couple of times to look in shop windows or to check a menu posted outside a restaurant.

Inside one shop he'd heard a woman with an Italian accent saying, "Why shouldn't you bargain the price of something so expensive? It's no longer a British island, no?" Then, when he reached the hotel, two Frenchmen were at the desk trying to explain something to the clerk, but were obviously having trouble expressing themselves in English. They'd stopped long enough to look him over, mostly with haughty disdain. *"Est-ce-que vous parlez français, monsieur?"* one had asked him. When he'd given a shrug, the man tossed his head and said, "Of course not. What am I thinking, *alors?"*

To Billy, foreign travel was a totally new experience, a whole lot more like a visit to the U.N. than anything he'd encountered on the rodeo circuit, including a cosmopolitan city like San Francisco where there was plenty of diversity. St. Margaret wasn't a glitzy place, maybe even sleepy in its way, but it was most definitely foreign territory to his way of thinking.

Billy's dress had to be the main reason he'd garnered attention, but now that the street was full, lots of eyes were turned his way. Everyone who passed by gave him a long look. Even the tourists found him a curiosity. An older couple, obviously American, glanced his way, their brows rising with surprise. The man, bald and heavyset with knobby knees protruding from his shorts, said to his wife in a voice indicating he was probably hard of hearing, "I thought Disneyland was in California, or do they have a Frontier Land here, too?" The woman shushed him, making Billy smile.

The local children passing by stopped and gawked, until a parent took them by the hand and dragged them along. One little boy with huge round eyes and very dark skin, who looked to be about five, peeked at Billy from behind a column at the end of the hotel overhang. Billy grinned and the boy continued to stare.

"Howdy, partner," he called to the kid.

The boy did not reply. Instead, he drew back behind the column so as not to be seen. Billy waited and, after a minute, one eye appeared. Billy pointed his finger at the youngster as though it was a six-shooter.

"Bang, bang! Got you, amigo."

"No, you didn't!" came the reply from behind the column.

"Sure did. Saw you fall down."

"Couldn't. I'm still here."

"Naw, that's your ghost talking."

The boy stepped out from his hiding place. "See, it's me!"

"Oh, it is you. Guess I'm not shootin' as straight as I used to."

The boy giggled, tucking his head shyly.

"What's your name, son?"

"Henry."

"Come over here, Henry, and shake my hand."

The boy hesitated, but screwed up his courage and went over to the bench where Billy sat. Henry was in shorts, a scruffy T-shirt and dusty sandals. Billy offered his hand. Henry put his in it and they shook.

"I'm Billy Blue. Pleased to meet you."

"Are you a cowboy or only pretend?" Henry asked.

"I'm a little cowboy and a little Indian, but no pretend at all."

If Henry understood Billy's meaning, he gave no indication. "Is that hat real?"

"It's the real McCoy, all right. Here, have a look."

Billy took off his hat and dropped it on Henry's head, completely covering his eyes. The boy giggled. After a moment he took off the hat and inspected it. Then he put it back on his head and beamed.

"Henry, what are you doing?" It was a woman's voice, coming from up the walk.

Billy and Henry both looked in her direction. She was tall and painfully gaunt, an impression magnified by the fact that she wore a bright red turban that sat tall on her head. Her yellow cotton blouse was faded, her skirt a length of green cloth wrapped about her and tied at the waist.

"Don't bother the gentleman, child," she said. "Give him back his hat and come here."

"It's no problem, ma'am," Billy said. "We're just gettin' acquainted."

"Thank you for your courtesy, sir, but it's time we go home."

Henry lifted the hat off his head and deposited it in Billy's hands, beaming at him. Billy held out his hand again.

"It was a pleasure meeting you, Henry. Maybe our trails will cross again."

The boy smiled, then scampered to his mother, who nodded appreciatively. Billy got to his feet.

"Fine young man you've got there."

"Thank you."

"Evenin', ma'am."

The woman and boy headed off and Billy put his hat back on, then sat down again. Seemed like maybe he'd made a friend. Probably could use a few more, maybe a lot more, before this adventure was over.

Whenever he'd stopped to ponder this quest he was on, he mostly thought about his grandmother and her dream. That pleading look in her eyes haunted him. But, until today, his father only came to mind in passing. Irwin Pettigrew had never been particularly real to him—more an idea than a man—but the old boy was about to become very real. There was little doubt Billy would not be a welcome presence, especially after he explained his purpose in being there. Most likely Pettigrew had been treating the painting as his own. Hell, you ride a horse a few years and it seems like it belongs to you, even if you don't have papers. But the law was the law and right was right. That's why Billy had come—that, and because Granny had made him promise.

Just then a vehicle pulled up in front of the hotel. The driver, an elderly man with a fringe of gray around his skull, stepped out. "You Mr. Blue, sir?" he called to Billy over the top of the car.

"Yes, that's me."

"You wish to go to Queen's Head Plantation, if I'm not mistaken, sir."

"The Van Biers' place. Biloxi, isn't it?"

"Right you are, sir. I meant to say Biloxi Plantation."

Billy stepped down to the vehicle, looking at the man over the top of the car. "This going to cost me an arm and a leg or just an arm?"

The driver scratched his head. "How long will you be there?"

"Say an hour."

"Twenty dollars U.S., and you can take up to two hours."

"You've got a deal, amigo."

Billy opened the front passenger door.

"Won't you ride in back, sir?"

"Only if you make me. The back seat's mostly for women and aristocrats to my way of thinking. I like to see the road."

"As you wish, sir."

"You're Able?"

The man grinned broadly. "As I like to tell the tourists, sir, I'm more than Able."

"Hey, that's pretty good. Your own slogan. I'm Billy, by the way. And any slogan pinned on me isn't suitable for polite company."

Able chuckled. "You from Texas, sir?"

"Nevada. But I reckon from your point of view there isn't a hell of a lot of difference."

"Las Vegas?"

"North of there a piece. A little over four hundred miles, to be exact."

Able nodded. "America's a big country."

"Big and open, my friend." Billy felt a twinge of homesickness. The Caribbean was a pretty place, but about then he could have used a whiff of sage blowing in off the high desert.

They hadn't driven a minute before they reached the edge of town. It being dusk, Able had put on the headlights. Emerging from the obscurity were a woman and a boy walking at the side of the road. Billy recognized them to be Henry and his mom.

"Able, those folks going our way for long?"

"To the Queen's Head Plantation, as well, sir."

They zipped past.

"Whoa, stop, partner."

Able put on the breaks and looked over at Billy.

"No harm in giving 'em a lift, is there? She's a woman, and the kid looks like an aristocrat to me. Back seat's empty, as best I can tell."

The man grinned broadly. "As you like, governor." He extended his arm out the open window and signaled for Henry and the woman to come. Billy glanced back and saw the pair running up the road to the taxi. When the woman reached the vehicle, she saw Billy and gave the driver an inquiring look.

"I'm taking the gentleman up to the big house, Esther. He's offered you and the lad a lift."

Beaming, she opened the door, ushered Henry into the back seat and slid in after him. "That's very kind, sir."

"My pleasure, ma'am." Billy turned to look at her over his shoulder. "We haven't properly met. My name's Billy Blue."

"I'm Esther Tye. This is my son, Henry."

"Yeah, Henry and I are old friends." He glanced back at the boy. "You see, son, I told you our trails would cross again." Removing his hat, he reached over and stuck it on Henry's noggin, eliciting gleeful laughter from the child. Billy glanced over at Able. "Nothing quite like seeing a child smile, is there?"

"Right you are, sir."

They rode for a while in silence then Billy said, "So, what do they grow on this Biloxi Plantation, Able?"

"Many years ago it was sugarcane, sir. Now they don't grow a thing."

"Money," Esther Tye said from the back seat.

"Aye, money. You're right about that. Money's what they grow at the plantation these days, Mr. Blue."

"That good?"

"It's good for Mr. Van Biers and many would say it's good for St. Margaret. Since the bank's come to the island we've got a new hospital, a new runway at the airport. Jobs."

"You work at the plantation, Esther?" Billy asked.

"Yes, sir. I clean, do wash and serve meals."

"You're the housekeeper."

"I'm a maid, sir. One of three."

"Henry must be the butler," Billy said, glancing back and giving the boy a wink.

"No, I'm a cowboy!" the boy exclaimed.

"Henry!" his mother said.

"With that ten-gallon hat on, I don't know what else you could be, son."

The child grinned shyly.

"You a friend of Mr. Van Biers, sir?" Esther asked.

"Not rightly. Haven't met the gentleman, but I've got business with him. That's the main reason I've come."

"Hope you have better luck than Mr. Pearson," she said.

Billy saw Able glance quickly into the rearview mirror, suggesting he was surprised by the comment. "Mr. Pearson?" Billy said. "Who's he?"

"An American gentleman who came to St. Margaret to do business with Mr. Van Biers, sir," Able said.

"What happened to him?"

"Nobody knows for certain. He disappeared several weeks ago. Some say he drowned in the sea, some say he's running from an unhappy wife at home, some say he was murdered. First time he went to Queen's Head Plantation it was in this taxi, Mr. Blue. Sat there where Henry is now."

"Hmm," Billy said. "Sounds like maybe I made the right decision sitting in front."

Able laughed and grinned his wide grin. "You better than most we see, sir, I'll tell you that."

"Thank you."

"Wouldn't you say, Esther?" the driver said into the mirror.

"I wish him better luck than Mr. Pearson, that's for sure."

"So, what was this guy Pearson doing here?" Billy asked.

"According to the paper, sir, he came to St. Margaret to advise Mr. Van Biers on his art collection."

"Oh, really?"

"Yes, sir."

"The old boy has a lot of pictures, does he?"

"Esther'd know better than me, sir."

"There's art all over the plantation house," the woman said. "Old paintings?"

"I don't know much about art, sir, but seems like there's every sort."

"Ever seen a picture of some sunflowers in a vase?"

"You mean the famous one," she said.

"Yes, ma'am. A Van Gogh."

"Mr. Van Biers keeps that at the bank offices where there are guards and a security system."

"Is that right."

"Yes, sir."

"And where might that be?" Billy asked, glancing back at Esther Tye.

"We'll be going by it in a minute, sir," Able said. "It's on a hill nearby."

"What's that over there?" Billy asked, pointing to a group of buildings surrounded by palms and a great open field next to the sea.

"The polo club, Mr. Blue. Mr. Van Biers built that, as well."

"For the rich to play tennis and ride their polo ponies," Esther piped up from the back seat.

"That's true, but there's jobs there, too," Able said.

"Am I mistaken, Mrs. Tye," Billy said, "or do you have a low opinion of Mr. Van Biers?"

"Oh, he's been good enough to me, sir. I can't complain about the way I've been treated. Not by him. Can't say the same about his wife or his son, especially not the son."

"Van Biers has a son?" Billy said, shocked.

"Don't get me started on him," Esther said. "The devil's own."

"The less said, the better," Able interjected.

"Be glad you're not a woman, sir," she said. "And that's all I'll say on the subject. But it's true, as Able says, that Mr. Van Biers brought money and jobs to St. Margaret...it's just that not everybody thinks that makes it a better place. It's been a poor island since independence, but until recently it belonged to the people."

"Still does, Esther," Able said. "And there are more who are pleased than not about all the changes. Didn't Mr. Jerome Hurst get reelected because of bringing progress to the island?"

"Sounds to me like I've got myself in the middle of a family squabble," Billy said.

"There's an election coming," Able explained. "That always brings out the passions. Esther doesn't mean to be critical of Mr. Van Biers."

"Oh no, sir," she agreed. "If you talk to him about this, I hope you won't say I had bad words."

"Don't worry," Billy said. "Simon Van Biers is no friend of mine."

"Forgive me, sir," she said, "but I'm happy to hear that. Speaks well of you."

"There," Able said, pointing to a nearby hilltop. "That's the headquarters of Victoria International Bank."

"Same spot as used to be a beautiful little house," Esther said dryly.

"Funny place to put a bank," Billy said.

"That's not a bank for the people," Able said. "It's a bank for investors. I can't say I've been inside the building, but people say it's got all the modern technology you can find in any major city. Mr. Van Biers controls investments all over the world from right there on that hilltop."

Billy stared up at the building until it was lost from view. That's where his grandmother's sunflowers were, in Irwin Pettigrew's private fortress. For the first time since he'd begun his quest, Billy had a sense of the magnitude of what he was facing. Maybe this wasn't going to be quite as easy as he'd hoped.

Everybody seemed to be silently reflecting on what had been said. Billy had learned a tremendous amount in the course of this short ride. If Irwin Pettigrew had a son, that meant Billy had a brother. That was even more bizarre than the notion of having a father. The situation was getting weirder by the minute. And the closer they got to this Biloxi Plantation, the more ominous the coming encounter seemed.

It was practically dark now, with only a faint glow in the western sky. The sea was as beautiful as the desert could be at this time of day, and the rich, lush vegetation of the island made it seem as though they were driving through a jungle, the headlights cutting through the gloom.

As they rounded a sharp curve, a creature suddenly loomed up in the middle of the road, its brightly colored wings and arms and feathers flailing. Able slammed on the breaks and the taxi screeched to a halt before striking the critter, which toppled backward, falling to the pavement. Esther gave a shriek of surprise.

"Blimey!" Able exclaimed.

Billy leaned forward to see the creature, only then fully realizing it was a woman in brightly colored garments layered over her body like feathers. She was writhing on the ground. Able and Billy opened their doors at the same time and hurried to the front of the car.

The woman was quite old and wrinkled, her skin so black the whites of her eyes shone like reflectors in the headlights of the taxi. Her body shook and she made a weird sound that seemed much like chanting.

"Ko lo jee mo," she muttered. "Ko lo jee mo."

"It's the old Haitian," Able said. "The voodoo woman."

"Voodoo?"

"Yes, sir. I believe her name's Marie."

As nearly as Billy could tell, she wasn't hurt. In fact, she seemed to be looking at him with rounded eyes, not so much terrified as shocked. But even so, she did continue chanting.

"Ko lo jee mo. Ko lo jee mo. Ko lo jee mo."

Billy glanced at Able, who seemed at even more of a loss. This was completely out of his range of experience, but he didn't feel he could just stand there, so he gingerly knelt down beside her.

"Ma'am? Are you all right?"

Her eyes rounded a little more. "*A l'Esprit partout. Roy-aume de Bon Dieu. Aidez-moi,*" she muttered.

"Ma'am?"

"She's praying." It was Esther. She'd come from the taxi with Henry in tow.

Completely ignoring the others, Marie looked at Billy as though he was an apparition. Then, her mouth opening wide, she cried, "Ayza!"

"Pardon?"

"Ayza!"

Billy started getting the feeling she'd mistaken him for somebody named Ayza. "No, ma'am, the name's Billy. Billy Blue. Billy Blue Bear, if you want to get technical."

"Ayza," she said more softly. For the first time she smiled. Then, to his surprise, she reached up and ran her boney fingers over his cheek. "*C'est vous! Ayza.*"

Billy glanced up at Able, who seemed as bewildered as he. "I can't tell you a thing, governor. I'm afraid her mumbo jumbo means nothing to me."

He looked at Esther and the boy, who stood holding his mother's hand, his eyes as round as Marie's.

"I think Ayza is a spirit," Esther said.

"A what?"

"A god, sir."

Billy turned his attention back to the old woman. She again touched his cheek.

"No, ma'am, you got the wrong fella. In fact, you're off by a country mile. I'm a bull rider from Elko, Nevada, by the name of Billy Blue. You ever heard of the rodeo?"

The old woman stared at him, mesmerized, probably not having understood a word. He looked up the dark road, then said to Able, "We probably ought to get her off the road. Somebody could come along."

"It's possible, but not likely, sir. There's no traffic to speak of on the island, especially this road. That's probably why the old bird was walking down the middle."

"Well, we can't leave her here," Billy said. "Marie, are you hurt? Do you need to see a doctor?"

"You have come," she mumbled.

"Yes, but I didn't rightly mean for it to be such a shock. Can you tell us if you're hurt?"

She shook her head. "No, I am not hurt."

"Well, that's good news," he said, glancing up at his friends.

Marie tried to sit up then and Billy helped her. The old woman seemed a bit more coherent, like maybe she'd just woke up.

"I think she was in a trance," Esther said. "I've heard sometimes she walks about in the dark, chanting."

Marie tried to get to her feet. Again Billy helped her.

"You don't seem to be hurt, but you might find a bruise or two tomorrow."

She looked into his eyes. *"Merci, monsieur."*

"I'm sorry we gave you a fright."

She gazed at him in a curious way, then turned and hobbled away into the darkness. Billy, Able, Esther and Henry looked after her.

"Mum," the boy said, "where's she going?"

"Probably home."

"Her house is up that little side road we passed just before the curve," Able said. "It's the only dwelling on this end of the island, except for the plantation house."

Billy rubbed his chin. "Do you suppose she'll be all right?"

"Nobody's killed her yet, including the police," Esther said. "I don't know if it's the voodoo or she's lucky."

"Why are the police bothering her?" Billy asked.

"It's something to do with Mr. Pearson," she replied. "Nobody knows just what."

Billy could see there were all kinds of things going on in this sleepy little island. Things were not as simple and innocent as they appeared and he probably hadn't heard the half of it yet. Hell, he hadn't yet laid eyes on his old man.

* * *

Biloxi Plantation

Simon liked the girl. She was bright, she knew her stuff and she seemed eager. Perfect for the job. If there was a downside, it was that she was too attractive for her own good. Charles was all over her. At the moment Simon's errant progeny had her cornered by the bar, sweet-talking her. This was going to be a problem. Simon was trying to run a business, not a dating service.

But Zoe also struck him as resourceful. She wasn't as tough as Mayte, perhaps, and almost certainly lacked the killer instinct of his wife, but he judged that she could take care of herself. That had been his impression in New York, it was his impression now. He saw it in her deft handling of Charles, thus far—keeping him at bay without offending. It was a quality worthy of a well-bred Southern gentlewoman, the kind he'd so much admired in his youth. From afar.

Judging by the looks Mayte was throwing his way, Simon could tell his wife was also troubled by Charles's attentions to Ms. Marton. He concluded she wanted him to intervene, which as the head of the family he would be expected to do. Simon walked over to the bar.

For dinner Zoe had changed into a simple sleeveless white cotton dress with black trim. With her black hair she looked rather stunning. Beautiful legs, Simon thought as he approached.

"Charles, you've got to let Zoe come up for air every once in a while," he said to his son.

"I was telling her about the polo club and the great swimming on the island. If she's going to be here, she should take advantage of what we've got to offer."

"You're right. But I suspect Zoe is also interested in her new job. Why don't you fix her another drink while I show her a bit of my collection? We'll be dining in fifteen minutes."

"Thank you," Zoe said, "but I don't care for another cocktail. One's my limit."

"One?" Charles said.

"She's a lady, son. Of the sort I knew in my callow youth. Your roots aren't in the South by any chance, are they, Zoe?"

"Kansas."

"Ah, the sunflower state."

"Yes, Mr. Van Biers, the sunflower state."

"Call me Simon, my dear. This is the modern age." He took Zoe's arm. "Now, if you'll excuse us, son, Zoe and I must talk awhile."

They went off, leaving Charles. Simon could tell she was relieved.

"You'll have to forgive Charles if his attentions are excessive, my dear. The island is not exactly overflowing with eligible young ladies. One as attractive as you is like a cool glass of water on a sweltering day."

"Thank you."

"As regards Charles, be firm as you have been. In his heart he's a gentleman, if impetuous on the surface."

"I appreciate the advice."

They went into what Simon Van Biers called the gallery room, which was devoted to his paintings. They were mostly contemporary works, a few that were notable. Simon had a Hockney and a couple of Warhols, which immediately got her attention. The rest were less impressive and less valuable—art he'd selected for aesthetic value rather than collectability. Simon watched Zoe studying the paintings as he sipped his vodka tonic.

"You mentioned sunflowers," she said. "Where do you keep the Van Gogh?"

"Under lock and key at the office. It's well displayed, but quite secure. I'm sure you'll want to see it."

"I'm more than eager. Van Gogh is a personal favorite, as you know."

"What is it that appeals to you about his work, apart from the value?"

"The same things that appeal to everyone, I suppose. But the sunflowers for a particular reason."

"And what might that be?" Simon asked.

She hesitated a moment then said, "Van Gogh expressed it best when he wrote that his pictures were almost a cry of anguish, an attempt to renew himself. To him, the rustic sunflower was a symbol of gratitude."

"Hmm," Simon said, studying her. "Interesting. I haven't heard that before."

"Van Gogh's craziness reminds us of the craziness in us all."

"I would like to agree with you, Zoe, but what appeals to me is the simple beauty of his work. And the value. Not necessarily in that order."

She laughed. "Sounds like you're more an investor than a connoisseur."

"Maybe."

"Well, the sunflowers call to me," she said.

"Must be the Kansas soil."

"I'm sure it is."

He drained the last of his vodka tonic. "How many paintings in the sunflower series have you actually seen?"

"Among the four in the Paris group, only the one in the Metropolitan in New York. But I've seen several in the Arles group, including the one in Philadelphia, the one in London at the National Gallery and the one at the Van Gogh Museum in Amsterdam."

"Do you have a favorite?"

"Yours, Simon."

"Which you've only seen by photograph."

She smiled pleasantly.

"That'll change tomorrow, my dear. I'll take you to the office first thing in the morning."

"I can hardly wait."

Simon liked Zoe Marton. He liked her energy and her confidence. And he would probably like her artistic sensibilities, though of that part of her he'd only had a glimpse. And she was a lady. He liked that about her, too.

Mayte, on the other hand, was a tigress, a sleek, elegant tigress capable of having most businessmen for lunch. Mayte lacked an artistic soul, but she had the passion of a predator and that very much appealed, as well. Danger called to him as much as beauty.

"Simon, dear." It was his wife at the door.

"Yes, Mayte?"

"I'm sorry to disturb you, but there's a gentleman at the door who'd like to see you."

Simon glanced at his watch. "A visitor at this hour? Who is it?"

"I don't know. Charlotte only said he'd come from the States and had urgent business to discuss with you."

"Find out who he is, will you, sugar? And if it seems legitimate, have him come to the office tomorrow. But not if he's a reporter. I won't talk to any reporter who's not a recognized business journalist."

"I'll speak with the man," Mayte said. "Oh, and dinner will be served in just a few minutes."

"Perhaps I'll freshen up," Zoe said. "Please excuse me." She followed Mayte out the door, leaving Simon alone with his paintings.

He went over to the window that offered a perspective of the moonlit sea. He could smell the fragrant scent of tropical blossoms, which momentarily took him back to Biloxi and the summertime parties at the gracious homes of the well-to-do. During his high-school years he'd attended a goodly number, though never as a guest. Simon had worked for a caterer and found himself cheek and jowl with the elite of Biloxi because of his ice punches and his supervisory skills with the "nigra help."

Simon had been a favorite of the hostesses, especially some of the younger ones. It was toward the end of the war when he entered polite society in his white caterer's coat, at a time when most of the young men were overseas defending liberty. In those days there were a lot of lonely women languishing at home, which meant the burdens of sexual congress fell on the very old and the very young among the male population. That was how Simon had lost his virginity. It was on the satin pillows of a twenty-eight-year-old matron whose husband was repelling Hitler in the Battle of the Bulge. War, Simon discovered, created benefits and obligations of the most ironic sort.

"Simon."

He turned at the sound of Mayte's voice. His wife had a surprisingly distressed expression on her face.

"What's the matter?"

"There's a cowboy on our porch. He says his name is Billy Blue and he claims he's your son."

Billy stood at the top of the stairs and looked out across the lawn that sloped toward the cliff above the Caribbean Sea. He'd never seen such a grand sight before...in any case, not from the perspective of somebody's front door. To think it belonged to his old man was not surprising, but the notion still didn't fit into his own personal universe. Off to the edge of the panorama, in the direction of some outbuildings, Billy saw a flicker of movement in the trees. There was just enough light for him to make out a small figure hiding behind a tree trunk. When the little face appeared, Billy realized it was Henry.

Billy moved over behind one of the porch columns then, peeking around, lifted his hand, pointed his imaginary six-shooter in the boy's direction and pulled off a couple of make-believe rounds, complete with sound effects. "Pow, pow."

Henry's small "bang, bang," echoed back across the lawn.

"You missed me by a mile, Henry," he called. "I'm going to have to teach you to shoot."

The boy laughed and went running off. Billy smiled. He liked the kid. Maybe he identified with him, as well. Esther said Henry had never seen his father. "That makes two of us," he'd told the boy.

Billy turned then to find a tall, slightly hunched man with a head of thick white hair standing in the doorway. With the light behind him, the man's features were lost in the obscurity, but Billy knew who it was.

"Billy?"

"Sir?"

"I'm Simon Van Biers," he said, stepping out onto the porch.

Billy waited where he stood, taking a deep breath to gather himself. His heart had been thumping nicely ever since they'd rolled through the gate, but now it was really rocking. He cleared his throat.

"A man by the name of Irwin Pettigrew is my natural father, Mr. Van Biers. Never seen the gentleman in my life. Would that be you, sir?"

"Yes, Billy, it is me."

Van Biers moved closer, extending his hand, the features of his face emerging from the gloom like a photograph in a pan of development solution. His nose and ears showed the prominence of age, along with wrinkles and sagging skin, but Billy saw hints of the familiar in the man's face. He saw glimmers of himself.

"This is a most unexpected surprise, indeed," Van Biers said as their hands joined firmly, two large hands filled with the same blood, but touching for the first time ever.

"I know I'm dropping in unannounced," Billy said, "and I do apologize for that, sir, but I have important business to discuss with you, if I might have a few minutes of your time."

"Actually, the timing is a bit awkward. We have a guest and were about to sit down to supper. But I'm sure we can find time to talk while you're here. You're staying on the island, I take it."

"Yes, sir."

Simon Van Biers thought, stroking his chin. Billy noticed the gesture. It was something he himself was inclined to do when reflecting. A shiver went through him. Van Biers drew a slow breath.

"Perhaps, if you gave me some indication of the nature of the business you wish to discuss…"

"It's regarding my grandmother's painting, sir, the sunflowers by Mr. Van Gogh."

Even in the fading light Billy could see his father blanch.

"It turns out the painting now belongs to me," he continued. "Granny passed away a few weeks back and I inherited all her possessions, including the painting. I know it was put up as collateral and that you're owed a good deal of money. I'm prepared, sir, to repay the loan plus interest and reclaim the painting. I have a check for you in the amount of fifty-five thousand dollars. That's what brings me here."

Van Biers seemed stunned. For a long moment he said nothing. Then finally he muttered, "This is all coming as a very great surprise."

"I'm sure it is. And I do apologize for that. If there was any other way, I'd have done it. But, since I've never had the pleasure of meeting you, I thought I owed you the courtesy of asking for my painting in person."

"That's most considerate of you, son." Van Biers reflected for a moment, then said, "As you might imagine—or maybe not—the situation with the painting is very complicated. There have been developments over the years of which you would have no knowledge. Naturally, I intend to bring you abreast of all that and we'll discuss it in good time, I promise you."

"When?"

Simon thought some more. "Perhaps tomorrow."

"All right. What time do you want me to be here?"

More chin stroking. "You know, as I think about it, son, maybe you should join us this evening so we can get better acquainted. I must tell you in all honesty, Billy, for many years I've been pained by the fact that we've never had a relationship, never been acquainted. Naturally, I take responsibility for that. Whether it was wise or correct or fair to keep my distance, I cannot say, but it was my judgment that you were best served being with your mother's people. Being aware of your grandparents' dislike of me, I elected to keep a wide berth. I know you had no part in that decision, but I hope you understand that my intentions were, and have been, the very best."

"With all due respect, sir, I didn't come to discuss that. As far as I'm concerned you don't owe me an explanation. The past is over and done with. I'm here to pay you the money you're owed, take my painting and head for home.''

"I understand your intentions, but the better acquainted people are, the easier it is to talk business.''

"What do you have in mind, Mr. Van Biers?''

"You probably aren't aware that you've got a younger brother. Charles is twenty-seven and works with me at the bank.''

Charles? Billy thought. Charles was the name of the guy who'd picked up Zoe Marton at the airport. Surely that jerk wasn't his brother!

"The two of you deserve to get to know each other,'' Simon went on. "Why don't you come in and meet the family and join us and our guest for dinner?''

Could the guest be Zoe Marton? Billy wondered. If it's the same Charles, then it had to be. "Are you sure, sir?'' Billy said. "I wouldn't want to impose.''

"It's no imposition, Billy. Not at all. I would be honored if you were to join us.''

Somehow Pettigrew's cordiality didn't ring true. He was buying time, maybe intending to do a little soft-soaping. Billy had no burning desire for a relationship with his father or the old boy's family. The thought that the Porsche jockey might be his own flesh and blood was enough to turn his stomach. But he would gain nothing by offending people. Why foul his own nest?

Billy removed his hat and followed his father into the house, feeling as if he was entering an enemy camp under a truce flag. He didn't buy Pettigrew's hospitality for a minute. This was a diversionary tactic. He could also see this business with the painting wasn't going to be resolved quickly or easily. But Billy had already decided to do what he had to do. If this was the first step, then so be it.

As they entered the main salon, Billy's worst fears were realized. The Porsche jockey was there and so was Zoe, although her back was to him and, unlike Charles, she couldn't react to his presence. Charles was shocked at the sight of him.

His chin might have fallen to the floor if it wasn't attached to his jaw.

Zoe, realizing something had happened, also turned, her eyes rounding at the sight of him. Billy smiled at them both and nodded. Mayte, the wife who had first come to the door, gravitated toward him and Simon.

"Ladies and gentlemen," Simon said in oratorical fashion, "I have a great and pleasant surprise for y'all. We have an unexpected visitor and it's none other than my...well, let me put it bluntly...my long-lost son, Billy Blue, who's come calling all the way from the state of Nevada. He's here to claim his Van Gogh sunflowers."

There was a loud thud as Zoe's empty glass dropped to the floor. Fortunately, it landed on an Oriental carpet and didn't break. She bent down and snatched it up.

"The cowboy's your son?" Charles said.

Simon took Billy by the arm and led him toward the others. "Charles, I told you I had a full life before I met your mother. And you were aware I spent a number of years in Nevada. Well, if I may be so indelicate as to put it this way, Billy was the product of one of my...shall we say, Nevada adventures."

Charles said, "Jesus Christ, I can't believe this."

"Mayte, sugar," Simon said, turning to his wife, "you met this young man earlier. But may I formally present your other stepson—and I promise you, darlin', the last stepson you're ever going to meet—Billy Blue Bear."

Billy reached out to take her hand. "Pleasure, ma'am."

"My, my, Simon," she said, "you never fail to surprise me."

She shook Billy's hand. "Hello, Billy, and welcome."

Taking his arm, Simon turned Billy the other way again. "Now allow me to introduce a very special guest, Billy. This lovely young lady is Zoe Marton just in from New York City."

"We met on the plane coming down here, Simon," Zoe said.

"We just didn't realize we were coming to see the same man," Billy added.

"Well, isn't it a small world," Simon said. "But if you didn't discuss me, I guess you didn't discuss my Van Goghs, either."

Zoe blinked. "Simon, did you say Van Goghs? As in plural?"

"That's right, my dear. Didn't I mention I had two identical sunflower paintings? Two virtually indistinguishable works from the Arles period. Of course, only one is a genuine original. The other is a fake."

Again Zoe's drink glass slipped from her fingers. Only this time it hit the floor and shattered.

Zoe had felt flushed for the past hour and had eaten only half her meal at best when the maid finally cleared their plates. She was sure the color still hadn't returned to her face, though no one seemed to notice. Simon had realized he couldn't very well drop his bombshell on them without further explanation, so he'd promised to give them the details after supper, while they had their coffee. "No point in spoiling a good meal," he'd said.

Zoe couldn't say what had surprised her more—Billy's claim to the Van Gogh sunflowers or Simon's announcement that he had two identical paintings. But it struck her as unconscionable that he would keep them in suspense as to which was real and which was fake. Would the authentic Van Gogh be the one from Kansas or the one from Nevada? Was the rightful owner Billy or was it her?

There was no telling what Simon might say, but Zoe herself was absolutely convinced that the painting Carson Gill had brought back from France was the authentic Van Gogh. That meant any painting Simon had gotten from Billy's family was the fake. Of course, this was not the time to advance a claim. First, she'd let Simon dispense with Billy.

Not that she would revel in his loss. The poor thing had been completely stunned by his father's announcement. She felt sorry for him. But she'd been no less surprised than he. The thing was, no one had any idea she had a personal stake in the matter. As a specialist in impressionist and postimpressionist paintings, she could be expected to have an intellectual interest in the news of a fake Van Gogh, but only she knew that millions of dollars were hanging in the balance for her personally.

Zoe had been seated next to a taciturn Charles Van Biers. Billy was across from them. Simon's shocking news seemed not to have adversely effected Billy's appetite, but she could tell he'd been blindsided and still hadn't recovered. She couldn't say he was distraught or angry, but he was not the happy-go-lucky cowboy he'd been when they'd first met. This was a different Billy Blue.

The conversation during dinner had been carried mostly by Simon and Mayte, who skipped among a variety of subjects. They discussed the history of the plantation, the flora and fauna of the island, its cultural and political background. Simon did talk some about his native Mississippi and the bank. Charles hadn't said a word, having brooded throughout the meal. Zoe couldn't begin to fathom what was in his mind, unless he was fearful his inheritance had been diluted. Of course, she had no way of knowing what provisions Simon had made for his heirs. That was the least of her concerns, though.

With all the other surprises that evening, she hadn't yet given much thought to the fact that Billy had turned out to be Simon Van Biers's son, and Charles's half brother. She studied the faces of all three men, trying to find similarities. Charles probably favored his father more, though she saw something of Simon in Billy, as well, especially around the chin and jaw. They also had the same broad forehead. Billy evidently favored his mother's family in the eyes and mouth, which were gentle by comparison. Billy was the more attractive of the two sons, though perhaps the judgment was based more on his likable personality and his playful manner. Charles was certainly good-looking—ruthlessly handsome might be a better way of putting it. His arrogance and the cruelty she'd seen in him were his death knell.

As for Billy, she no longer knew what to make of him. He was still a rodeo cowboy at heart, but now he was also her competitor for the Van Gogh. It made her wonder if she'd missed something, underestimated him, perhaps.

A different maid served the coffee, a tall, painfully thin woman with a pretty face. Zoe noticed her paying special attention to Billy and she also caught him giving her a subtle wink. What was with this guy? Sure he was cute, but my God, his smile seemed to work like an aphrodisiac. Maybe she had reason to be grateful she was experienced in the ways of irresistibly beautiful men. Thanks to Ahmed, she was immune. An attractive man had no special magic as far as she was concerned.

Simon cleared his throat to get everyone's attention. "Now that we have our coffee we can discuss the paintings, if you like, Billy. But I'll leave it up to you. If you prefer, we can discuss it in private tomorrow."

Zoe's breath wedged in her throat and she silently screamed, "No, not tomorrow!" But Billy Blue showed mercy by saying he had no problem with hearing Simon out now. She could have kissed him.

"All right, fine. I won't keep you in suspense, son," Simon said. "That painting I got from your grandmother is the copy, the fake."

Zoe was so relieved that she sighed audibly, though everyone was so focused on Simon that no one seemed to notice.

Simon continued. "About the time I founded the bank I was contacted by an appraiser and dealer I'd worked with in the past. He was familiar with your grandmother's painting and told me he'd come across an identical one in a private collection. I was stunned. Obviously, one painting had been copied from the other. The question was whether I was in possession of the original or the copy. I immediately negotiated to purchase the other painting and, then having both paintings in my possession, I knew I had the original. All that remained was to determine which one it was."

"What makes you so sure the one you bought is the real one?" Billy asked.

"I had my appraiser examine both paintings. There was a complete consensus of opinion, Billy. Though the copy was remarkable—absolutely remarkable—there were discernable differences, mostly having to do with physical, rather than artistic qualities. The painting I bought was done in the late 1880s, which is consistent with what we know of Van Gogh's Arles sunflower series. The other painting dates from approximately the turn of the century. It was a copy produced between ten and fifteen years subsequent to the authentic piece, and long after Van Gogh's death."

All eyes shifted to Billy. He wiped his mouth with his napkin and tossed it down next to his coffee cup. "Well, sir, I don't know squat about art, I'll be the first to admit that. I take your word about one being copied from the other, but how do we know which one is which? The appraiser could have switched the paintings and the documentation. Or, with all due respect, sir, you might have."

"But I didn't, Billy. The painting I bought was clearly marked and identified before it came into my possession."

"Who was the fella that handled the deal for you, if you don't mind me asking?"

For the first time, Simon showed a flicker of annoyance. "His name is Raymond Pearson."

"Raymond Pearson," Billy said. "Isn't that the fella that disappeared down here a while back? Seems to me I heard he drowned by accident or was murdered."

"Yes," Simon said. "Ray disappeared several weeks ago here in St. Margaret. He'd come to consult on an art syndication Victoria International is organizing."

"Well, that's a real shame," Billy said. "It means we won't be talking with him, doesn't it?"

"Look, Billy," Mayte said, "I can understand how deeply disappointed you must be. I would be, in your shoes. But I want to assure you, Raymond Pearson's work has been thoroughly documented and is available for examination. Professionally speaking, there's no one who could be more disappointed in his disappearance than we are. If he were alive we'd have his direct testimony. He was like insurance to us. Now that's lost."

"Just at the time I show up asking questions."

"I think we'll be able to convince you of the accuracy of our position," she replied.

"Pearson found the original, is that right?"

"Yes," Simon said.

"Who did Pearson get it from?"

"We don't know," Mayte said. "It's very common that transactions like this are done anonymously and discreetly."

"There's no need to tippy-toe around it, sugar," Simon interjected. "The boy deserves the unvarnished truth. Son, the seller didn't know what he had. He thought he had a copy, because that was what he was told when he obtained it."

"But he was wrong," Billy said, obviously skeptical.

"I know that seems odd, but there's more. Ray didn't share the details, but we know the people he was dealing with weren't terribly sophisticated when it came to art. And after the transaction was completed, Ray confided that there may have been some criminal activity in the seller's background, as well."

"What do you mean by that?"

"The painting may have been a payment in lieu of cash for contraband. The seller wanted to turn a quick profit and convert the painting to cash. I came along at the right time, oblivious to what had been going on."

Zoe felt the air rush right out of her. If Simon's story was true, he could have gotten the Kansas sunflowers from the people who'd defrauded her father, unless perhaps they'd sold the painting to a drug dealer or the like, who in turn sold it to Simon. Either way, if he'd come into possession of it innocently, he could be a purchaser in good faith, which, as Win had explained, could make him the rightful owner of the painting.

Zoe felt just awful, the euphoria of moments ago already dashed.

"Pardon me," Billy said, "but let me get this straight. You bought the painting from somebody, some sort of criminal, who thought he had a fake, but it was actually authentic and the only one who can attest to that fact is this fella Raymond Pearson, who's probably dead."

"In a nutshell, Billy, that's correct."

Billy shook his head. "If I was a lawyer, which I'm not, I'd say all that comes across as pretty damned convenient."

"I can see how you'd say that, son."

Zoe saw the color rising in Billy's face. He leaned forward, his two hands clenched into a large fist. "What kind of money are we talking here, anyway, if you don't mind me asking?" He turned to Zoe. "You're the expert, ma'am. What's the value of an original Van Gogh painting in today's market?"

It took an effort for her to summon the energy to answer. "One from the sunflower series could be worth seventy to a hundred million dollars."

Billy looked back and forth between Simon and Mayte. "I may be a hick cowboy, folks, but I'd say that's enough to justify looking a mite deeper than the words of a dead man. But since we're asking questions, there's something else bothering me. Van Gogh's a pretty famous guy, right? So, why is it nobody's ever heard about this deal with Pearson until now? How come the word didn't get out? Zoe, have you heard about this before tonight?"

She glanced at Simon. "No, I haven't, but Mrs. Van Biers is right, these things are often handled discreetly."

"You mean art appraisers don't talk to their buddies?"

"I told Ray I didn't want publicity, and he respected that," Simon said. "Besides him, my bankers were the only ones aware the Van Gogh was in my collection."

"Why your bankers?" Billy asked.

"Because I capitalized Victoria International with a bank

loan. The Van Gogh was the security. It wasn't a large loan. Several million dollars. It's since been paid off.''

"Did your bankers know there were two paintings?'' Billy asked.

"No, I saw no point in saying anything. All they saw was the original, the one I bought through Raymond.''

"Didn't they have it appraised?''

"I gave them an appraisal.''

"Who did it?''

Simon again seemed annoyed. "It was Raymond.''

"So, this guy Pearson is the only expert who's seen the two sunflower paintings side by side.''

"There's been no reason to have anyone else involved. All my bankers cared about was that they had adequate security and they were satisfied with Raymond's appraisal. The world doesn't need to know there was a copy. The only reason it's come up at all is because you've come to claim it.''

Billy scratched his head. "You're asking me to accept an awful lot on faith.''

They waited.

Billy started to rub his chin, but caught himself. "Look, folks, I don't mean to insult a soul in this room, but before I accept what you're telling me, I'd want it proven to my satisfaction. My granddaddy taught me that if you buy a horse, you best look him in the mouth. That way you got nobody to blame but yourself if he's got a few extra years more on him than was represented. A horse worth a hundred million is definitely one that's got to show his teeth.''

"I can't blame you for that, Billy,'' Simon said. "I'd feel the same if I were you. But incidently, the copy your grandmother had isn't exactly chopped liver. As Zoe can tell you, a good copy of the era can be worth a great deal of money.''

"How much is a great deal?''

"Could reach into six figures.''

"More than you've ever had in your jeans, bro,'' Charles added dryly.

It was the first he'd spoken up. Simon did not look pleased with him. Zoe was disgusted.

But Charles, having finally opened his mouth, wasn't through. "Where did your grandmother get the painting, anyway?"

"Bought it from the estate of a rancher who collected western art. It happened to be in the lot. The fella brought it back from Europe after World War II, not knowing what he had."

"So, she didn't pay much for it, right?"

"That's right."

"So, what are you complaining about? It's pure profit. The problem is you're greedy."

"Charles," Simon said, his tone admonishing.

"No, really," Charles said, his choler rising. "How many boots and hats and beers can you buy with a couple hundred thousand dollars? A lifetime supply, I'd say."

Everybody looked embarrassed.

"Let me ask you something," Billy said. "You're your father's heir, aren't you?"

"Yes."

"Did you pay anything to the drug dealer for the original Van Gogh sunflowers?"

"No, but what does that have to do with anything?"

"But you're going to inherit it."

"So?"

"Did your dad pay ninety or a hundred million for it?"

"No."

"Well, brother, seems to me you stand to make a little windfall profit yourself."

Simon cleared his throat loudly. "The point is, everybody wants maximum value for what's rightfully theirs. Billy's entitled to what's his, Charles, the same as you."

Mayte rolled her eyes. Charles turned bright red. Billy had led him down the garden path. Zoe was glad. Charles was a fool and he deserved it.

But instead of cutting his losses by keeping his mouth shut, Charles trumped himself. "I don't have time for this bullshit," he said angrily. Then, throwing down his napkin, he got up and strode from the room.

When he was gone, Simon said, "A young man raised in affluence sometimes has more trouble learning the ways of the world than those less fortunate. I apologize to y'all on my son's behalf."

After an extended silence, Billy said, "Anybody who does much riding is bound to fall off his horse eventually."

"I see your grandparents raised you well," Simon said.

"They were good people, sir."

After another silence, Mayte said, "Who would like an after-dinner drink?"

"Much obliged, ma'am," Billy said, "but I best be on my way. I know it's not polite to get up from the table and leave, but it's been a long day."

"Where are you staying?" Simon asked.

"In town."

"At the Queen's Inn?"

"Yes, sir."

"That's a nice quaint little place, but there's no need for a hotel when you've got family here. You'd be much more comfortable at the Biloxi Plantation, son. We've got half a dozen guest rooms, a private beach and scores of acres to wander on. Be our guest."

They all turned at the sound of an automobile engine outside. It was the high whine of the Porsche as it roared off into the night, kicking up gravel, some of which pinged against the side of the house. Mayte groaned with obvious disgust.

"I appreciate the invitation," Billy said to Simon, "but I've paid for the night. And there's a taxi waiting for me down the road. I think it best if I go back into town."

"All right, but I insist you come back in the morning. I'm taking Zoe to see the sunflowers and you might as well come with us. In fact, join us for breakfast. And bring your suitcase so you can stay. We're not letting you leave St. Margaret until you're satisfied justice has been done."

"I appreciate that, Mr. Van Biers."

"Simon," his father said.

"Right."

They all rose and made their way out of the dining room, walking past the maid, Esther, who waited to clear the table. She gave Billy a smile and Zoe marveled once again.

In the entry they said their goodbyes. Simon clasped Billy's hand in both of his.

"We've got a lot more to talk about than this painting, son. I look forward to spending some time with you."

"Thanks, Simon."

Billy shook hands with Mayte, then turned to Zoe. "Would you mind walking down the drive with me a piece?" he asked.

She glanced at Simon. "No, I suppose not."

"If it turns out all I'm getting out of this deal is a copy, I'd like to get your expert opinion on whether an idea I've got is feasible." He turned to Simon. "Could I borrow your guest for just a minute?"

"St. Margaret is a free country."

Billy said good-night and he and Zoe walked out onto the porch, the door closing behind them. The moon had come up and so had a light breeze off the sea. Billy stared out at the water and stretched his back. It had stiffened up after sitting through the long meal. They went down the steps and along the drive.

"So, what's your idea?" she asked.

"I don't have any ideas. It was just an excuse to talk to you in private."

"About what?"

"Bullshit aside, Zoe, were those folks feeding me a crock?"

The question, stated so directly, surprised her. "I really don't know."

"Well, I think they must take me for a fool. Of course the one they bought is the real Van Gogh and the one they're holding for me is the fake. With a hundred million dollars at stake, what else would they say?"

"It is possible," Zoe said.

"But I've got to take the word of a guy who's probably

dead." He started to rub his jaw and caught himself. "Do you have any idea how we can prove whether Simon bought the real one or bought the fake?"

Zoe shifted uncomfortably. "I may not be the right person to ask, Billy. I work for Simon. My interests aren't exactly hostile to his like yours are."

"Well, you're honest, aren't you?"

"Yes, of course."

"That's all I'm asking for, Zoe. The truth."

He had absolutely no idea what a dilemma she was in. The last thing she wanted was for Billy to be the rightful owner of the authentic painting, because that would mean she wasn't. But at the same time, she had much more sympathy for him than for Simon Van Biers.

"The best way to get at the truth is probably to trace the history of the painting Simon bought," she said.

"How am I going to do that?"

"Find the seller of the painting Pearson located for him, and the owner before that, and so on. Somebody along the line will have convincing proof."

"I doubt Simon would cooperate in that, unless he knew for sure Granny's painting is the fake. Personally, I think the man's a liar and a cheat which, considering you work for him, I'm sure you don't want to hear."

Zoe could hardly tell him what her real motives were in coming to St. Margaret, but she was tempted to tell him about her conversation with the FBI, if only to put his mind at ease and lay to rest any doubts he might have about her. But there was risk in that, too. She didn't know Billy Blue from the man in the moon, and, though she wanted to trust him, she knew she couldn't. Not yet. Not so long as they had opposing interests.

"Maybe you need to hire an investigator," she said. "That's off the record, by the way."

"I understand. You're in a difficult position."

Zoe thought, if he only knew.

"To be honest, Zoe, I don't have that kind of money. Coming down here for a few days has pretty much busted the budget.''

They walked for a while in silence. Then Billy stopped.

"I won't ask you to come any farther. You best head back up to the house.''

She nodded. "I know how disappointed you must be," she said. "I'm really sorry for your sake.''

He shrugged. "A horse race goes a full lap, don't forget, and we're just entering the first turn. Besides, I've got an ace or two up my sleeve.''

"Oh?''

"My grandmother may not have been a high-priced New York art dealer, but she was no fool. She marked that painting before she gave it to Simon, with a mark known only to me.'' Smiling, he gave her a wink and went sauntering on down toward the gate.

Zoe stood frozen, amazed once more. Why had he told her? she wondered. To win her confidence, or to put the fear of God in Simon Van Biers? Then she smiled, realizing Billy Blue was not as simple as he seemed.

Queenstown

Charles had gone by the Blades' place, but nobody was home. They'd either gone for a walk on the beach or were out for the evening. Apart from restaurant bars, there weren't many places on St. Margaret to party. The most popular club was the Speak Easy on the edge of town. It was patronized by the locals, but younger tourists looking for a party showed up, too. Charles would drop in when he was on the prowl for a woman.

Before heading for the Speak Easy, he swung by the two restaurants that were closest to the Blades' villa. They weren't at either place, nor had anyone seen them, so he drove to the Speak Easy, where he found their vehicle parked in the gravel lot along with half a dozen others. Charles was glad to have tracked them down. He needed to talk to Mooky and he wouldn't mind ogling the wife while he was at it, even if she was a bitch queen.

The Speak Easy was as vanilla as could be—booths with vinyl seats on the perimeter, a worn dance floor surrounded by small Formica cocktail tables with ordinary straight wooden chairs. The only nod to decor was the string of colored lights across the top of the mirror behind the bar. But the place was really jumping. Mooky and Dani Blade were on the dance floor and had drawn a crowd. They were gyrating to the rhythms of The Rum Runners, a local group Charles had heard many times before.

Blade, in a black muscle shirt and black pants, had a couple of lusty mamas on each leg, and Dani, in a white miniskirt and skimpy top, was dancing with a couple of black studs. Charles only had to watch them a minute to pick up that what they were doing was turning each other on. The rest of the crowd might not have been there, for all it mattered to them. It sure didn't take much of Dani Blade for Charles to get a hard-on right along with every other guy in the place.

As he watched Dani twist and thrust her ass, those ripe tits of hers looking as if they were going to pop out of her top at any moment, he realized there was a remarkable similarity in looks between her and Zoe Marton. Dani was real buff by comparison, her features not so refined, her tits bigger, but the two women were of the same general type. The similarity of the color and style of their hairdos was especially remarkable.

Taking a place at the bar and ordering a rum and Coke, Charles thought how shitty it was that the two women he'd like most to fuck were unavailable. Blade had a chastity belt on Dani and Zoe had on one of her own. And, as best he could tell, Zoe's disinterest had nothing to do with being married. The bitch didn't like him. And though she'd probably deny it, if anybody interested her, it was the fucking cowboy.

It still knocked him out to think that some hick cowboy was his half brother—though he wasn't surprised that his old man had left a few loose ends along the way. Hell, Simon had previously alluded to the fact that he'd had a child out of wedlock before he'd married Charles's mother. But the impression he'd given was that his bastard was completely out of the picture, maybe even oblivious to his father's identity. Billy actually showing up at their door was the shocker. And the business about him having a claim to the Van Gogh, Charles didn't get at all. Obviously the bastard wasn't blowing smoke out his ass because Simon didn't dispute the claim.

Charles wasn't sure what the truth really was—which painting was the fake and which was the original. When the problem with Raymond Pearson came up, Simon had been vague. Pearson must have known, but he was dead now. And at the moment, it suited Simon to claim Billy's painting was the fake. But Charles wouldn't bet the change in his pocket that was the truth.

Watching Dani Blade swing her ass was really making him horny. God, she had a body. He'd never laid a broad who could break his arm, yet looked sexy as hell, having all the right moves. The woman could probably bench-press a hundred and fifty pounds, but she was no Russian shot-putter. No way. Incredible piece of ass was what she was. Watching Blade, Charles could tell the sonovabitch knew it, too.

The music stopped then and the band announced they were taking a short break. As everyone retreated from the dance floor, Blade and his wife embraced. The behemoth took her by the waist and lifted her over his head, eliciting a cry of delight. Charles took a slug of rum and Coke, thinking how badly he wanted to screw Dani Blade.

The couple made their way toward the bar, Blade not noticing Charles until he was only a few steps away. "Well, if it isn't Mr. Van Biers himself," he said cheerily. "What you doin' here, man?"

"This is my home away from home," Charles said coolly.

"What was that?" Blade said loudly.

Charles repeated his remark as Blade watched his lips. Then Blade grinned.

"All the black ass a turn-on?"

"Black, white," he said, shifting his gaze to Dani, "it's all the same to me. I'm equal opportunity."

"Considering Dani's the only white chick in the house, it ain't equal opportunity tonight, man."

Charles chuckled dutifully. Blade ordered a couple of drinks from the bartender. Charles put a large bill on the bar.

"Take it out of this," he told the bartender.

"Why, thank you, Chuck," Blade said.

Charles hated the name Chuck, and figured Blade probably knew that. "My pleasure."

Mooky Blade, his brow, neck and shoulders glistening with perspiration, studied Charles. "Man, you have one of those I've-got-something-important-to-say looks on your mug. What's up?"

"I've got some business to discuss."

"Hey, it's Sunday, my man," Blade said loudly over the general din. "Never on Sunday, okay?"

"I could make it well worth your while, Mooky."

Blade glanced at his wife and groaned. "Hey, man, we're having a good time here. What you want to go fuck it up for?"

"Really worth your while."

Dani turned Blade's face to her so he could see her lips. "The band's on a break, babe. Go talk, and when you come back, we'll dance."

The bartender delivered the two drinks. Blade gulped down half of his, then handed the glass to his wife. Tossing his head toward the door, he said to Charles, "Let's go outside."

The outdoor air was light, in stark contrast to the air inside, which was thick with the smell of warm bodies. Blade looked up at the starry sky like a lover as he ambled over to a low wall by the edge of the road. Sitting, he clasped his hands at his groin and waited for Charles to join him. Charles dropped down next to the huge mountain of a man.

"You've got a beautiful wife, Mooky," Charles said in a clear, loud tone. "You ever rent her out?"

Blade's head whipped in his direction. "What kind of a dumb-ass question is that?"

Charles shrugged. "Some people like to swing. Looked to me she was having fun riding a couple of hard-ons on the dance floor."

"Well, that was on the dance floor with me ten feet away, man. That what you brought me out here to talk about?"

"No. I just thought I'd start with a compliment. Not everybody's got a woman like that, Mooky."

"Thanks. Now, say what you've got to say so I can go back inside."

Charles lowered his voice to a discreet level. "Blade, I want you to kill somebody for me," he said, carefully enunciating his words.

"Oh, shit," Mooky Blade said too loudly by half, rolling his eyes. "Somebody else? You shitting me?"

"No, I'm dead serious." He was practically whispering now but Blade read his lips without trouble.

"Who now?"

"A cowboy named Billy Blue."

"Cowboy?" The word echoed in the night air.

"Shh!" Charles said, glancing around.

"I don't do the Wild West," Blade said, modulating his voice.

"The sonovabitch is right here on St. Margaret."

"A cowboy here? What you smoking, man?"

"The bastard's staying at the Queen's Inn in town, Mooky. I'm not joking. He arrived this afternoon, and I want him dead as soon as you can do it."

"What'd he do to you, man, that you want him whacked?"

"Does it matter?"

"Hell, yes, it matters. I always got to know why."

"The sonovabitch is trying to steal my inheritance. Is that good enough?"

"Say again."

Charles repeated his remark.

"Who is this guy that he's stealing your inheritance?"

Charles didn't want to say out of fear of Blade's reaction, but neither did he want to appear a coward. "My half brother."

"The cowboy's your brother."

"Yeah, that's right."

"Jesus, Chuck, you're a sick fuck."

Charles flushed. "What are you, Mr. Morality all of a sudden?"

But Blade had turned away and didn't hear. Charles realized it was just as well. Mooky Blade annoyed the hell out of him, but he was also the only act in town.

Blade reflected for a minute, then turned back to him, pursed his large lips ponderously. "It'll cost you fifty K, U.S."

"Fifty? That's what I'm paying for the other two combined."

"This dude's white, isn't he?" Mooky said.

"Yeah, but what's that got to do with it?"

"I'm prejudiced, man."

"Thirty."

"Forty-nine, nine ninety-nine."

"All right," Charles said, furious. "Fifty thousand, but do it quick."

"Quick is fine," Blade said, "but safe is better. If I fuck up, you swing, too."

Charles hated the sonovabitch. "Okay, okay."

"Bring me twenty-five in cash, same as before. I start to work as soon as I got the down payment."

"Fine."

Blade groaned. "Since you already fucked up my evening, we might as well discuss the business I got."

"What's that?"

"Dani and me think we got your other girl."

"The second woman?"

"Yeah. It's only ninety, ninety-five percent sure, so we got a little more work to do. But I think it's the one."

"Who is she?"

"Lady named Poppy Tuttlebee."

"Tuttlebee? The wife of the guy who works for the president?"

"Don't know about that. But she's pregnant and we're pretty sure she's hiding the medical details."

"How do you know that?"

"Gotta spend your money on something, man. Why you think this work is so expensive? Besides, we pretty much eliminated everybody else who is a possible. I figure if I put her and the mambo together in a room it won't take long to get to the bottom of things. But assuming I'm right and they've got you by the balls, you still want them whacked?"

"Damn right."

Mooky Blade said, "At the rate you're goin', brother, you're going to need the Russian army. I'm already overextended, considering the size of this place. You sure you want all three?"

"Yes, all three, Blade. For a hundred thousand you should be able to figure out how to do it."

"It could take a little time, man. I gotta check out this dude, Billy Blue."

"He won't be hard to find. All you have to do is listen for the jingle of spurs." Charles got to his feet and offered his hand. "It's a pleasure doing business with you, Mooky."

Charles was in no way a small man. To the contrary, he was muscular and well above average in size, but his hand seemed to be swallowed by Blade's.

"You coming back inside?" Blade asked.

"No, I think I'll go. My compliments to your wife."

Blade said nothing to that. He just turned and walked away.

Joyce Tsu and Ellis Toliver ducked as the headlights of the Porsche swept over their vehicle and they rose again after Van Biers roared past them and headed down the road. Toliver, who was behind the wheel, adjusted the rearview mirror as he peered into it.

"I don't think they were exchanging stock tips," he said.

"No, but it sure would be nice to know what they were discussing."

"You didn't get any of it?" Toliver asked, indicating the field glasses resting in her lap.

"Quite a few expletives and I think maybe the word *cowboy*."

"Cowboy? What's that? Code?"

"Who knows? And I might have gotten it wrong. It's pretty dark and I'm not the best at lipreading. You definitely need to modernize your technology, Inspector Toliver."

"Our entire national budget is probably smaller than what the FBI pays for ammunition."

"I'll get on the horn to Washington and see if I can get some equipment down here," Tsu said.

"Meanwhile, our mate Blade seems to be partying on."

"I swear the guy is a hard one to figure. All he did yesterday was swim and lie on the beach. And the same this morning."

"The bloke acts as though he's on holiday," Toliver agreed.

"He's awfully blatant about it too," she said, "which leads me to believe he wants us to watch him."

"That would make sense if it's the wife doing the dirty tricks. We lost her again this morning, you know. She was unaccounted for for five hours."

"That could explain a lot."

"Just keeping track of these two requires all the manpower available on any given shift," Toliver said. "For the weekend I had to pick between them."

"It seems you picked wrong."

"I quite agree."

"We may have to rely on the citizenry," Tsu said. "Somebody had to see her. I mean, how many places can she go?"

"Tomorrow, I'll make inquiries," Toliver said.

"It might be worth having another chat with the voodoo lady. Maybe Mrs. Blade called on her while she was unaccounted for."

"I don't see any harm in it."

Joyce Tsu gestured toward the Speak Easy. "So, how long we going to stay at the party?"

"I don't know about you, but my feet are aching from all the dancing."

Tsu nodded solemnly. "I think it's time to go home. It's unlikely Blade will be killing anybody tonight."

Mooky Blade sipped his drink as he sat watching the dancers, but his mind was on Charles Van Biers. Not liking the sonovabitch was one thing, feeling he was bad news was another. Every instinct Mooky had told him to pack up and go home. A hundred thousand was nothing if it cost a lifetime in jail. The vibrations just weren't good. And yet, it was against his nature to be scared off a job by anyone or anything.

He glanced toward the back of the club. There was still no sign of Dani. A busty woman with big, sensuous hips, one who'd been eyeing him all evening, came off the dance floor, headed his way. As she passed by, she dragged her fingers across his shoulders.

"Your lady leave you, honey?"

"No," Mooky said, looking up at the woman. "She'll be back."

"If I was her, I wouldn't let you out of my sight. Not for one minute." Then she went off.

Mooky drained the last of his drink, then put the glass down on the table. He was about to go outside and look for his wife, when she appeared in back, making her way across the room. She sat on the chair next to him, facing him squarely.

"Well?" he said.

"They're gone."

"So, no more baby-sitters."

"Looks like it's just you and me free to do anything we want," Dani said.

"Well then, you want to go check out a cowboy, or do you want to go home and fuck?"

Dani held up her hand, indicating she wanted to do paper, scissors, rock.

"One, two, three," they said in unison.

She had a rock and he had scissors.

"What'll it be?" he asked.

"Let's fuck," she said.

The busty woman passed by just then. "I would, too, honey, if he was mine."

Biloxi Plantation

As Mayte Van Biers walked across the lawn from the garage she glanced up at the only lighted window in the guest wing of the big house. Through the cracks in the plantation shutters she was able to see a figure moving and knew that Zoe Marton was getting ready for bed.

Simon and Charles were both taken by the woman, though for very different reasons. Mayte herself wasn't so sure about her. There was something about Zoe that made her uncomfortable, but she couldn't say what, other than a false note of some kind. On the surface Zoe's reasons for coming made some sense—a woman in the midst of a divorce, going to a tropical island to lick her wounds and keep her career going at the same time. And there was also the handsome rich playboy plying her with attention. But that was before she'd seen them together. It was obvious Zoe wanted no part of Charles, despite her overweening politeness. And she'd had a hell of a good job in New York. St. Margaret was a pretty place, but after a few weeks of swimming and sun, boredom would set in. Zoe must appreciate that fact.

The greater worry, though, was Charles. He seemed to be getting more and more out of control. Simon was worried about him, too, Mayte could tell. Charles was under a lot of strain because of the Raymond Pearson business, though he acted confident, even blasé. Having a half brother walk in and upset his applecart hadn't set very well, either.

Mayte was more than a little surprised by Billy Blue's sudden appearance. Simon handled it remarkably well, though.

There was no question her husband had a knack for landing on his feet. It must come from a lifetime of living by his wits, the bobbing and weaving and posturing that goes with making something out of nothing, of profiting at other people's expense. Simon was dumb like a fox. She was more convinced of that every day.

Recently she'd been wondering if he'd been a hundred percent straight with her. It was paranoia on her part, to be sure, but could her beloved husband be preparing to abscond in the night and leave her holding the bag? He knew she was having an affair, though he almost certainly didn't know with whom. Yet the way Simon had reacted confounded her. She hadn't sensed deep hurt. Sure, he'd long since resigned himself to the fact that she was young and had needs he might not be able to fulfill, but this was different.

Rubbing her bare arms against the light chill in the air as she mounted the steps, Mayte knew she was becoming more and more insecure. She no longer trusted Charles to hold himself together and she was beginning to think her husband was thinking of abandoning her, just as she was preparing to abandon him. And even Jerome, obsessed over her though he was, had feelings of uncertainty about the situation.

Mayte could see the problem clearly now—things were slipping out of control. Ostensibly she was in the driver's seat—she ran the day-to-day operations of the bank, Simon giving her practically free rein; his son had a pact with her to snatch control of the bank should Simon falter, and she was literally in bed with the man who gave their operation legitimacy and the political protection it needed to survive. All three looked to her for guidance, yet any of them could stab her in the back at the drop of a hat.

Once inside the front door, Mayte locked it behind her and fell heavily against it, shivering as she rubbed her arms again. It was not like her to cry, but she certainly felt like it. That damn cowboy showing up had thrown a wrench into the works, making an already delicate situation even more fragile. Mayte wondered if it was time to start looking for a safe exit.

Once their ship started going down, the rats would be climbing over one another to escape. She knew death when she smelled it and this patient had definitely taken a turn for the worse.

In the morning she'd take a good hard look at their financial situation before deciding what to do. But meanwhile she had to get a clearer idea of what Simon was thinking. She'd doubted him in the past and he'd managed to pull a rabbit out of his hat. The guy was a survivor.

Making her way upstairs to the master suite, Mayte found Simon sitting on her bed with his head in his hands. Not a good sign.

He'd taken off his jacket, shirt and tie, though he still wore his suit pants and one of his old-man sleeveless undershirts, immodestly covering his pale, spongy skin. A profusion of white chest hairs blossomed from the scoop neck of the undershirt. Mayte hated seeing him that way. He actually looked better naked.

Simon glanced up a moment after she entered. He seemed tired and old, his thick white hair mussed from the intrusion of his fingers. "Is he back?"

"No," she said. "He's not in his room and the Porsche isn't in the garage. My guess is he's either out on the town or he crashed at the club."

"He sleeps there more than he does here."

"Naturally, Simon. You won't let him bring his whores here."

"Do you blame me?"

"No, I was simply explaining."

He sighed wearily. "I'm sorry, sugar, if I was short. I've got a blazing headache."

"Prodigal sons will do that to you."

He smiled wearily.

Mayte went and sat beside him on the bed, feeling exhausted and headachy herself. Not wanting to hug him as he probably would have liked, she put her hand on his knee. "What do you think? How much trouble are we in?"

"Billy showing up has certainly put a spanner in the works.

Given enough resources, he could give us a run for our money. But I'm banking on the fact he won't have the resources or the will. When the time is right, I'll make him a good offer and hope he takes it and leaves.''

"And if he doesn't?''

"I'm not giving him a hundred-million-dollar masterpiece, even if it's his.''

"Is it?''

"I said, 'if.'''

She sighed wearily. "We can beat him eventually, I have no doubt about that,'' she said, "but he could raise enough of a stink that the bank might get nervous and balk. I don't have to tell you we need that infusion of capital pretty badly.''

"How much time we got, Mayte?''

"Not long. Soon the Band-Aids will start coming off and once people see the open wounds, the whole thing'll come down like a house of cards.''

"Weeks or days?''

"A couple of weeks...maybe.''

He gave her a sad smile. "Ever the optimist, aren't you, sugar?''

"I'm a realist, Simon.''

"Hell, what's real? If I lived my life by what other people said was realistic and possible, I'd be livin' in my daddy's house, sellin' insurance to poor black folk.''

"So, what do we do?'' she asked.

"I'm going to spend some more time with Billy, and see if I can get a better read on him. He's got some of me in him, so it's likely he's more clever than he lets on.''

"I agree.''

"What do you think his game plan is?'' Simon asked.

"He's going to try to make you prove the original is rightfully yours. And that won't be easy...of course, you would know better than I.''

"It all comes down to whether he'll buy the documentation Pearson did for us,'' Simon said. "And poor Ray is in no position to say which is the one I got from the old lady and which is the one I bought.''

"Do you know which is which, Simon?"

He glanced her way, giving her a crooked smile. "Of course.''

"The original is the one you got from Pearson, isn't it?"

"Lord knows, if it isn't, my elder son will be a hundred million richer and we'll be a hundred million poorer.''

Mayte could see Simon wouldn't give her a straight answer. He just wasn't capable. She had an idea why. He'd once explained his view of life in a few succinct words—"There are no absolutes, Mayte," he'd said. "There is only necessity. That's why right and wrong are the fictions of sick minds. Right and wrong for what purpose and for whom, that's what I want to know.'' He was probably correct. She'd lived pretty much according to the same dictum herself. But such a philosophy made true friendship impossible. There could be no trust because necessity was unpredictable.

"Don't get upset by me saying this," she said, "but I'm wondering if maybe it's time to pull the plug.''

He turned his head, looking at her out of the corner of his eye. "You want to quit, sugar, is that what you're saying?"

"If we picked up our marbles and went home we'd have quite a lot of booty.''

"You'd have to be prepared to spend the rest of your life in Rio de Janeiro," he said.

"I can think of worse fates.''

"Thing is, Mayte, I don't want to go out a loser.''

"Loser? Simon, you've built an empire with nothing but smoke and glass, chewing gum and baling wire.''

"And a hundred-million-dollar Van Gogh.'' He stared off vacantly. "You know, I was actually hoping to make some honest money this time around, pay off the investors and still have a profit.''

"I know," she said. "Me too.''

Simon took her hand and, pulling it to his mouth, he kissed

it. "Say one of these days I climbed on an airplane headed for Rio. Would you want to be aboard?"

"What else am I going to do, Simon?"

He gave her a half smile, "Besides mop the brow of a tired old man? I think you've got options, sugar."

"I admit I'm not the nurse type," she said. "I'd need to have a life. But you and I are partners."

"That we are, sugar. That we are." He gave her hand a real firm squeeze. "But this ball game is far from over. We've had a little setback this evening, that's all. By morning things will look much brighter, I'm sure of it. And, who knows, we might even find a solution to our little predicament. Now, if you'll excuse me, my dear, I believe I'll have myself a shower before I retire." Simon stood. "Oh, I need to have a word with Charles. He's all ablaze and needs to be doused. When you see him, send him my way, will you?"

"I'll be getting an early start in the morning. If he isn't here by the time I leave, I'll go by the club."

"Thank you, sugar."

Mayte watched him go. Not surprisingly, she'd learned very little, except that her husband was concerned about both Billy and Charles. It was also apparent he didn't fully trust her. Even his escape plan was shrouded in mystery. And one thing remained unchanged. She had a great deal of influence, but no real control. Simon had the purse strings firmly in his hands. She had a nice salary and seventy-five thousand in the bank, but for the big bucks, she'd have to keep kissing his ass. It was no accident things had worked out that way. Simon and half a dozen grandfathers before him had lived by making others beholden to them.

Maybe it was time, she decided, to have a very serious conversation with Jerome Hurst.

Monday
August 14th

It was still dark when Mooky Blade went back inside. He'd been crawling around the undergrowth for fifteen minutes. Dani was sitting at the table, dressed and waiting.

"I guess the boys and girls are still snuggled in their cozy beds," he said. "No sign of cops anywhere."

"You know, this is really a pain," she said, rising. "How we going to take out three people with the cops watching our every move?"

"With great difficulty, I grant you, babe. But we've got a big advantage."

"What's that?"

"We nearly outnumber them."

Dani laughed. "Mooky, you're something else."

"Besides, I like a challenge."

"I'm not liking this job, though," she said. "It feels funny."

"Chucky's an idiot."

"Besides that."

Mooky Blade had learned to listen to his wife. Not that she had all the answers or that he let her call the shots, but sometimes women had a better feel for a situation than a man. He carefully considered everything she had to say. Always. "Like what?"

"An old lady, a politician's wife who's pregnant and a cowboy. Does that sound like people we should be whacking?"

"A hundred big ones, Dani."

"I know it's a lot of bread and that money's important, but remember what we promised each other. We'd never let money trump our judgment about a job. We were never going to force it and I think we're forcing it."

"I don't know about that, babe…"

Dani took his face and turned it to her, so he'd see her lips. "You think this is a good clean job, Mooky?"

He took several moments to think about that. "The voodoo bothers me some," he admitted. "But maybe that's why I'm inclined to do it. That's the only thing that ever scared me when I was a kid. The spirits. I'd sort of like to clean the slates on that score while I'm at it."

"As you know, I'm not into that God shit," she said, "but if it makes you think twice, maybe that's reason enough to question it."

"Help's on the way, don't forget. I've got my own voodoo guy comin'."

"I don't know, Mooky, this is getting crazy."

"All right, so what are you suggesting? That we walk?"

"I'm saying think about it."

He nodded. "So, I'll think about it after my man does his thing. And tonight we'll talk. But don't forget, we do this job and we don't have to do nothing for six months."

"Maybe that's not a good enough reason."

Mooky grabbed her by the nape of the neck and pulled her over, planting a kiss right on her mouth. "You're getting soft on me, babe."

"No, Mooky, just cautious in my old age."

He laughed, slapping her on the butt and guiding her toward the door. "The day you're old, I'll be dead."

"Don't say that!" Dani said, frowning. "You know I'm superstitious."

They went outside. Mooky locked the door. They got in their SUV and pulled out the driveway into the dark road. They drove for a while, headed for town, before Dani said anything.

"To you, what's old?" she asked.

"I don't know, like the old mambo, I guess."

"Shit, I'll never live that long. I don't even want to live that long, Mooky. When you and me are too tired to get it on, we're old. Besides, we're in a dangerous business. One of these days we're going to fuck up, no matter how careful we are."

The way his wife was talking, Mooky knew things had changed for her. She used to get off on what they did. Not that it was fun, exactly, but when they'd ace some scumbag under challenging conditions, then get paid a ton, they'd both get a rush. It wasn't that the sonovabitch necessarily had to deserve it, but their job was sort of like being a soldier in a war. It was mostly impersonal. Maybe they'd grown beyond that, maybe the thrill was gone, he didn't know, but he allowed it was something to think about.

"Whatever we do, let's don't fart around," Dani said. "Once we decide, let's jump on it."

"That's cool."

"Good," she said, resolve in her voice.

He was glad. Doubts weren't good. "Are we agreed, then?" he said to his wife as they drove, the headlights boring into the tunnel of foliage surrounding the road. "You check out the pregnant one and the cowboy and I'll fetch my man at the airport and cook up a plan for the mambo. I'll meet you at the London Bridge Café this afternoon, what say around three."

"Okay. You going to kill the old lady, Mooky?"

"I don't know. I'll play it by ear." He grinned in the dark. "Me and the bokor will see what the spirits have to say."

St. Margaret Polo Club

Charles woke up at 6:00 a.m. pissed and horny. It was a deadly combination. He decided to burn off some venom on the polo field, but Tommy Epps wouldn't be around for a couple of hours and Charles would have to saddle his ponies himself. That didn't appeal, but if he wanted to ride at this hour it was a necessity.

After going to the locker room and changing into a polo shirt, jodhpurs and riding boots, he headed for the barn. The air was still cool, the grass on the field sparkling with dew. Charles found the barn door open, which gave him pause. Had someone neglected to close it the night before? Then he saw a well-used bike leaning against the side of the barn. Maybe one of the stable hands had come in early. That would be a blessing. Maybe he wouldn't have to saddle the ponies, after all.

He went inside. There was nobody in sight, but he heard the sound of water spraying and he saw a hose running down the middle of the stable wing. Somebody was cleaning the stalls. He ambled to the far end where the work was in progress. Reaching the door to the stall being cleaned, he looked in. To his surprise and delight, it was the girl, CeCe.

Her back was to him, so she was unaware of his presence, and the noise of the hose prevented her from hearing his boots on the concrete. CeCe wore shorts, a skimpy little tank top and big, oversize rubber boots that made her seem even more slender and vulnerable than usual. For a moment he admired her sweet little ass, her bare shoulders and waspish, yet graceful, limbs. Her nappy hair was pulled up, but tendrils hung about her long neck. Charles had a terrible urge to grab her and kiss that neck, to hold her reedy body in the circle of his arms, to bite her skin. But he reminded himself she was fifteen.

Even so, he decided to have a little fun. Bending over he picked up the hose and crimped it, cutting off the flow of water. CeCe turned to see what was the trouble and, seeing him, let out a little cry of surprise.

"You frightened me, sir."

"That's the last thing I'd want to do, CeCe, scare a pretty little girl like you. What are you doing here so early, anyway?"

"Mr. Epps said if I come in early I can leave at midday. My brother's coming home from the hospital this afternoon."

"Well, that's good news, isn't it, CeCe?"

"Yes, sir."

He looked at her long slender legs, finding it especially sexy the way they protruded from the boots. He also noticed she didn't have a bra on under the tank top. He liked that. She was nubile, virginal. It made him wonder if she really was a virgin.

She seemed nervous, perhaps because he'd trapped her in the locker room the last time they'd met. Charles continued to hold the crimped hose in his fist. "Do you like cleaning out the stalls?" he asked, his eyes continuing to move over her.

"I don't mind, sir."

Charles smiled, liking her earnestness, her innocence. She was young, but he wondered if he could find a way to entice her to play around a little. She didn't seem like the grab-ass type, but maybe that was only because she was shy.

"Begging your pardon, sir, but would you be good enough to put the hose down so I can finish my work?"

"Cleaning the stalls can wait. I'm going to exercise my ponies. I need for you to saddle them. You know how, don't you?"

"Yes, sir."

Charles let the hose drop very suddenly, catching the girl unprepared. The water from the hose gushed out, splashing over the front of her and making her jump. "Oops," he said. "Sorry about that." He tossed his head. "I'll be down in the tack room. You get the horses."

CeCe, realizing her wet shirt was revealing, covered herself. "Yes, sir."

Charles went to the tack room and got out the saddle and bridles for all three ponies. He waited a few more minutes, sticking his head out the door occasionally, growing progressively more annoyed when CeCe didn't show up with the horses.

"CeCe!" he shouted, his voice echoing through the barn.

"Coming, sir," she called from the stable wing.

"Get your ass in gear, girl," he called. "I don't have all day."

He heard the clomping of the horses' hooves, then she appeared, leading all three ponies. She'd put a towel around her neck, letting it hang down, covering each breast. She was a modest little bitch, all right. Modesty was one quality that annoyed him.

"All the gear's out," he said, gesturing toward the tack room. "Saddle up Smoke first."

"Yes, sir."

He clapped his hands. "Come on. Hop to."

CeCe quickly secured the lead of each pony, then hurried into the tack room as Charles sat on a bench to watch. The girl was not exactly efficient, but she knew what she was doing. He did enjoy watching her move, especially when she'd duck under an animal to secure the girth. She'd glance at him warily from time to time, obviously uneasy about him watching her.

"You've got a nice figure," he told the girl. "You should be proud of it."

CeCe, her back to him, did not respond. Instead, she continued her work. Charles wondered what it would take to get her to interact. Maybe he had to be a little more commanding, forceful.

"Turn around," he said to her.

"Sir?"

"I said, turn around."

She turned her head and shoulders, a deep furrow in her brow as she looked at him.

"All the way."

"Why, sir?"

"Because I want to get a good look at you."

"Please, Mr. Van Biers."

"Please, what? Don't you know a man enjoys looking at an attractive girl? And if you're pretty you should like having a man look at you."

CeCe shook her head.

Charles didn't like being defied, especially not by a little black girl who was lucky to get compliments from a man like him. When he abruptly stood, CeCe flinched, backing into the side of the pony, making him neigh and toss his head. Charles, feeling the twin fires of anger and lust, strode purposely toward the girl. Her eyes rounding, she bolted, trying to run past him to the door, but he grabbed her by the arm, jerking her around.

"No!" she cried, cringing. "Please no!"

"No what?" he growled. "All I'm trying to do is talk to you."

"Let go of me!" she screamed, baring her teeth.

Charles, getting really pissed, gave her a good hard shake. "You don't talk to me that way, hear?"

Grabbing the towel, he yanked it from her neck. It was a symbol of her defiance. She shrieked as though he'd whacked her, which only made him more angry.

He had her by both arms now, holding her so firmly she couldn't move. She was like a feather in his hands. She started to cry. He looked down at the front of her tank top, the wet fabric plastered to her skin. He could see the swell of her small breasts and the hard button of each nipple. His heart pounded heavily. He wanted her.

"CeCe," he said softly, "I'm not going to hurt you. I like you. Can't you tell? Every time I try to be nice to you, you run away. You're a grown lady now. Grown-ups don't act like this."

Big wet tears bubbled from her closed eyes. She refused to look at him.

"CeCe!" he said, giving her a shake.

She shook her head violently, but wouldn't open her eyes. He stared at the little mounds under her shirt and milk-chocolate smoothness of her skin. He had a terrible hunger.

"You ever been with a man before?" he asked, pulling her closer to his body, inhaling her scent.

She stiffened.

"CeCe! Answer me! You ever been with a man before?"

"No," she sobbed.

"If you have sex with me, I'll give you five hundred dollars."

"No!" she wailed, horrified.

Charles dug his fingers into the soft flesh of her arms and pulled her up against him. CeCe began struggling, trying to twist free. When she couldn't extricate herself, she bit him on the forearm, her teeth cutting deep into his flesh. The pain was so intense he let go of her. Blood seeped from his arm.

CeCe ran for the door, but lost her footing in the clumsy rubber boots and went sprawling. That was all Charles needed.

"Fucking little bitch!" he shouted as he grabbed her by the nape of the neck and pulled her to her feet.

There were several bales of hay stacked along the wall nearby and Charles dragged her over, shoving her down on them, face first. CeCe continued to fight him, but he was able to subdue her by pressing his knee into the middle of her back.

"I'll teach you to bite me, you little cunt," he cried. Then, pressing her face into the hay, he grabbed the band of her shorts and pulled them down over her buttocks.

CeCe let out a shrill scream and he shoved her face even harder into the hay. With his other hand he ripped her panties down off her butt. Then he yanked at his belt and tore open the front of the jodhpurs, pulling off a couple of buttons in the process.

He had trouble keeping the girl pinned and getting his shorts down over his swollen cock at the same time, but he finally managed when he heard another shriek, this one coming behind him.

"Charles! You idiot!"

It was Mayte, he knew even before looking over his shoulder. She came charging at him, pausing just long enough to grab a feed bucket. Knowing what was coming, Charles tried to get his pants up and jump away, but he got his feet tangled in CeCe's rubber boots and hadn't moved a step before the bucket slammed against the side of his head and he went down like a rock.

The girl cried hysterically as Mayte helped her to her feet. She no sooner had her pants up than she was in Mayte's arms, hugging and sobbing. They both looked down at Charles, his jodhpurs halfway down his thighs, his undershorts barely covering his private parts.

Mayte picked up her purse from the floor and led the girl outside the barn. They walked toward the clubhouse, their arms around each other, stopping when they reached a big shade tree to sit on the wooden bench encircled with bedding flowers. The girl's chest heaved as she sobbed, tears streaking down her face.

"You're okay now," Mayte said, patting her hands. "Catch your breath and calm down."

After a minute or so, the girl got control.

"What's your name?" Mayte asked.

"CeCe," she replied, wiping her eyes.

"Tell me what happened, CeCe."

"Is my brother going to lose his job?" the girl implored.

"No, nobody's going to lose their job. Just tell me what Charles did."

The girl recounted the morning's events, the things that Charles had said and done. In answer to Mayte's questions, she explained her family situation and why she was working at the stables.

"How old are you?"

"Fifteen, ma'am."

Mayte rolled her eyes. "Did Mr. Van Biers know?"

"I told him."

"Is this the first time he's done anything like this to you?"

CeCe told her about last time in the locker room.

"But he didn't hurt you either time, right? I know today he pushed you around, but that's all. He didn't touch you sexually, did he?"

CeCe shook her head. "No, but he tried."

"Charles has been sick, honey. Emotionally sick. There have been lots of family problems, but that doesn't excuse what he's done. What he did was wrong. He had no right to scare you that way."

"I hate him."

Mayte smoothed back the girl's hair. "I know you do, but the question is what we're going to do about this."

CeCe looked at her for guidance.

"You can go to the police and tell them what happened," Mayte said. "That's one possibility. Charles will get in trouble, but there'll be trouble for everybody, including you, CeCe. These things are never easy. But I've got a better idea."

"What, ma'am?"

"You can go home. There's no need to stay, but I'll talk to Mr. Epps and see that you get paid for the full week or until your brother comes back to work. You won't have to see Charles again, ever. And I'm going to offer you something extra, CeCe. A thousand dollars over and above your paycheck. But you're going to have to do something for me, if you want the extra money. A big favor."

CeCe blinked her big wet lashes. "What?"

"You can't tell anybody what happened. Not Mr. Epps, not your brother, not your friends. Nobody. Do you understand? I need your solemn promise, CeCe."

"How will I explain why I'm not working, and what do I say if my brother wants to know where I got the money?"

Mayte thought for a moment. "Let's see, what can you say? I know, tell him you found my ring in the stables. See," she said, holding up her hand with her glittering five-karat diamond, "it's very valuable, so I gave you a reward, plus the week off. Is that okay?"

"Yes, I'll say whatever you want."

"Good. Now remember, CeCe, I stopped Mr. Van Biers from hurting you. So, we're friends. Special kind of friends."

"Yes, I know."

Mayte opened her purse and took out her checkbook. She wrote a check for a thousand dollars and gave it to the girl. "Remember your promise. If you break it, you'll have to give the money back and it's possible your brother will lose his job."

The girl put the check in the pocket of her shorts. "I won't say anything."

"Good. Do you think you can get home all right? Are you feeling okay?"

"Yes, but my bicycle's by the barn."

"What about your shoes?"

"My sandals are with the bike."

"Okay, we'll walk back together."

CeCe's eyes rounded in fear.

"It's all right, sweetheart. You're safe with me."

Mayte took the girl's hand and they walked back to the barn where CeCe got her sandals and her bicycle. They hugged goodbye and in moments the girl went pedaling off toward town. Mayte watched her go, feeling both compassion for the girl and fear for herself and Charles who, despite being a total moron, was still family. Their fate was tied up together, all of them.

At the visceral level she felt great compassion for the girl. She knew the terror CeCe felt. Growing up, she'd been raped once by an older neighborhood boy who'd dragged her into a musty basement in an abandoned building. She was thirteen at the time and didn't tell her mother what had happened for two weeks. But now she was on the other side. Charles was a scumbag, no doubt about it, but a major scandal was the last thing they needed, especially now when everything was so shaky.

Still, she was pissed that Charles could be so mindless and irresponsible. She could kill the bastard...if he wasn't already dead. Figuring she'd better find out what condition he was in, she went into the barn and found him sitting on the bale of hay, rubbing his head. A bloody handkerchief was wrapped around his forearm. He glanced up as she approached.

"I know, I know," he said with a groan, "I fucked up."

"Fucked up? What were you thinking? You can't go around raping children, for God's sake. That could have cost us everything, Charles. I can't tell you how stupid that was."

"The bitch bit me," he said, holding up his bleeding arm.

"Why was that, I wonder? Because she didn't have breakfast?"

"Very funny."

"Seriously, what were you thinking, that she'd enjoy it?"

"Give me a break, Mayte. I was playing around with her, teasing her. It was no big deal until she bit me."

"So, naturally you had to rape her to teach her a lesson."

"She took a chunk out of my arm and I was pissed, all right?"

"Yeah, I know, it was her fault."

"Well?"

"Charles, you're so full of shit, it's pathetic. I saw what happened."

"All right, all right. I admitted I fucked up. So give it a rest, will you? You damn near knocked my brains out as it is."

"Too bad I didn't put you in the hospital for a month. At least then we wouldn't have to worry about you raping the entire female population of St. Margaret."

"Fuck you," he grumbled.

"You should be thanking me."

He glared, rubbing his head. "Yeah, sure. So, what are you going to do, tell Simon to ground me?" He stood then. Though wobbly, he went over to one of the ponies and stroked its muzzle affectionately.

Charles's tenderness toward his animals was a constant

source of amazement to Mayte. If he treated people half as well as he treated his ponies, he'd be far more successful in life, less an object of loathing and hatred. She was no Mother Teresa herself, but she did have the sense not to make enemies unnecessarily.

"Charles, what, pray tell, are you going to tell the police when they show up to arrest you for molestation and attempted rape?"

"It didn't happen, that's what. Who they going to believe? The stable girl or me?" He patted a second pony on the neck, then combed its forelock with his fingers.

"Fortunately we won't have to find out because I've taken care of it," she said.

"How?"

"I paid her off. For the moment you're safe, but you fuck up again and I'm going to let them throw you to the dogs."

"You're really tough, Mayte. Scare the shit out of me."

"And you're an ungrateful sonovabitch."

"Oh, thank you so much. Thanks for knocking me unconscious. Thanks for saving my ass. Thanks for the lesson in morality. Have I forgotten anything?"

Mayte put her hands on her hips. "You know, maybe you ought to take a vacation, get out of here for a while, go visit your mother in England or something."

"Yeah, well, fuck you," he said, flipping her off.

Mayte, disgusted, turned on her heel and walked out of the building. She hadn't gone far before remembering she had to take care of the business that had brought her there in the first place. Stepping back inside the barn, she found Charles where she'd left him. He was leaning against one of the ponies and looking at his bloody arm.

"Charles, I forgot to give you a message from your father. Two things. First, you're to stay away from Zoe Marton. Simon doesn't even want you talking to her. We can't afford you alienating her...or raping her, for that matter. And second, stay away from Billy Blue. Simon and I will deal with him."

"Fine. I don't give a shit about the bastard. The old man can do anything he wants."

"I'm glad you understand."

"But tell me something, Mummy dear, what are you and Simon going to do about the two women, the witnesses who can send us all to the slammer?"

"I thought that was being taken care of."

"It was, but now that I've been sent to my room..."

"Can you deal with the problem without raping them, Charles?"

"Very funny."

"I'd feel much better about you if you'd grow up."

"That reminds me. I need some allowance money so that I can bury Pearson once and for all."

"I've given you twenty-five thousand already."

"I need seventy-five more, Mayte."

"Seventy-five? Charles, you're out of your mind."

"No, Mummy, I'm not. It turns out one of our girls is very prominent and taking care of her will be very risky and very expensive."

She narrowed her eyes, sensing he was bullshitting her. "I don't believe you."

"You want all the details so you can take over and arrange the hit yourself?"

"Charles!" She looked out the door. "Watch what you say, for crissakes."

"Yeah, that's what I thought. Nice to have a kid around to do all the dirty work, isn't it?" He leaned under one of the ponies to check the girth.

"I don't want to discuss this."

He glanced back at her. "Okay, fine. I won't hassle you and in turn you can stay off my butt."

Mayte had had enough. She left, not wanting to stay in her stepson's presence a moment longer. She hadn't gone far before she heard Charles's voice echoing behind her.

"Mayte, tell the old man I'll think about his request regarding Zoe. It might be tough to stay away from her, though. I really think she likes me."

Shaking her head as she headed for her car, Mayte knew that somehow, some way, Charles was going to screw things up royally. And, if he did, in all likelihood he'd take the rest of them down with him.

Biloxi Plantation

It was still early by the time Zoe started downstairs, even though she'd had a leisurely shower, taken special pains with her hair and done her nails. Despite the fatigue that comes with travel, and not having had an easy time falling asleep, she had awakened early and immediately began obsessing about Billy Blue.

Zoe couldn't decide if he was a naive braggart or a force to be reckoned with. Surely he wouldn't have claimed his grandmother had marked the painting if it wasn't true. But then, who was to say the old woman hadn't marked the fake? Of course, it might not matter, if Zoe was unable to assert her own claim successfully. Simon seemed to have had his ducks in a row, his story ready for Billy. Could she reasonably expect it to be any easier for her?

The thought had also occurred to her that she and Billy could be laying claim to the same painting, assuming his grandmother had gotten it, directly or indirectly, from the people who'd conned it out of her father. There had been no mention of how long Simon had been in possession of Billy's "fake" Van Gogh. She'd have to ask about that.

After reaching the bottom of the stairs, Zoe wandered about the public rooms, finding them deserted. The house was quiet, though there were signs of life coming from the kitchen area. Taking a peek into the dining room, she saw the table had been set, but there was no evidence that anyone had eaten. Simon hadn't set a timetable for the morning's activities, saying instead, "Folks can have breakfast when it pleases them, and once we've all eaten, we'll head for the office," so she didn't feel any particular urgency. To the contrary, she figured that unless he was one of those cowboys who got up with the sun, Billy Blue would likely be the last to show and they'd all have to wait for him.

Checking her watch, Zoe decided to see what was going on in the kitchen. As she made her way through the house, she heard humming. Entering the huge, industrial-style kitchen, she discovered it was the toothpick-thin maid who'd served the coffee at dinner the night before. The woman wore a red turban, white blouse and a red flower-print wraparound skirt.

"Morning, ma'am," she said. "You ready for your breakfast?"

"I'll wait for the others, I think. Is everybody else sleeping in?"

"Mr. Van Biers likes his bed, it's true, but Mrs. Van Biers was gone shortly after first light of day."

"Oh, really?"

"Yes, ma'am. Had a quick cup of coffee and she was gone. Would you care for some?"

"I'd like a cup, please. It certainly smells great."

"It's the best, all right. Finest coffee beans in the world. Mr. Van Biers doesn't have anything in this house if it isn't the very best." The woman smiled. "Maybe including you and me."

Zoe returned her smile. "I'd like to think you're right."

The maid poured some coffee into a mug. "Cream and sugar?"

"Splash of cream, please."

The maid added some cream and brought Zoe the mug.

"I'm Zoe Marton, by the way."

"Esther Tye, ma'am."

Zoe sat at the large wooden table and Esther returned to the counter where she'd been working. Leaning against it, she faced Zoe, who took a sip from the mug.

"Mmm. This is good."

Esther nodded.

"You been with the Van Biers long?" Zoe asked.

"Only a few months."

"Do you like it here?"

"It's good work. I mean the pay is good. I guess I'm lucky an opening came up. The girl before me quit."

"Oh? Why's that?"

Esther seemed embarrassed. "I don't know if I should say."

"Well, if it's personal…"

Esther glanced toward the door, then lowered her voice. "It's not that. I just don't want to say bad about anyone, not that he doesn't deserve it."

"Mr. Van Biers?"

The woman hesitated. "Mr. Charles Van Biers, ma'am."

"Oh, I've already found out about him, Esther. You don't have to worry about that."

"He hasn't bothered me much yet, so I'm hanging on. I won't leave unless I have to. This is such a pretty place and my Henry loves it."

"Your husband?"

"No, ma'am. My little boy. Henry's five. You'll see him running about the garden." Esther tucked strands of hair under her turban. "You a single lady, if you don't mind me asking?"

"Yes and no. My divorce will be final in a few weeks."

"Oh." Esther folded her arms over her chest. "I've never been married."

"No?"

"Henry's father was in the British navy and lives in England now. Sometimes he sends money, but that's about all we see of him."

"That must be difficult for your son."

"He's needing a man in his life, it's true." Esther cocked her head. "You don't have children?"

"No, fortunately. Not that I wouldn't want to…under the right circumstances. For the time being, anyway, it doesn't seem to be in the cards."

Since Esther Tye was friendly and willing to talk, Zoe decided to find out as much as she could. She didn't expect the

woman to know anything about the Van Biers' business dealings, but there could be other bits of information that would
be valuable.

"Do the Van Biers have many visitors?" she asked.

"Here at the plantation? Quite a few, ma'am. Sometimes
two or three at the same time."

"Are they mostly friends?"

"I'd say mostly business friends. Investors, judging by the
bits of conversation I hear." Esther glanced toward the door.
"Which is probably something I shouldn't be talking about."

"Don't worry, Esther. I'm an employee just like you."

"All due respect, ma'am, but they don't treat you like an
employee."

"It's a matter of time."

"What is it you do, exactly?" Esther asked.

"I appraise and evaluate art."

"Oh, same as Mr. Pearson. I hope your luck is much better
than his."

"You knew Ray Pearson?"

Esther shook her head. "I didn't know him, but he was a
guest here, same as you. He might have said a few words to
me when I served his morning coffee, but we didn't have a
conversation."

"So, he stayed here," Zoe said, finding that interesting
without seeing any special significance. It did make her wonder if Esther knew anything about Pearson that might have
bearing on the Kansas sunflowers. "I guess the police must
have asked a lot of questions."

"Oh, yes, ma'am. They talked to everybody on the plantation, even Henry. But nobody knew anything that could
help."

"What do you think happened to Ray?" Zoe asked, doing
her best to sound offhand.

"Ma'am, I have no idea."

"Weren't Mr. Van Biers and Mr. Pearson personal
friends?" Zoe asked.

"They acted like they knew each other pretty well. Sometimes I'd hear them talking business at the dinner table, mostly friendly conversation. But one night they had a big argument. It was in Mr. Van Biers's library. Both of them were talking quite loud.''

"Do you know what they were arguing about?''

Esther hesitated. "No, ma'am. But maybe I shouldn't be talking about this. It's not my business and I want to keep my job. Anyway, the police already asked me.''

"Did you tell them about the argument?''

Just then there was the sound of someone entering a door in back. Esther looked relieved. A moment later the older, heavier maid, a woman named Charlotte, appeared.

"Morning,'' she said.

Zoe and Esther said hello. Esther immediately got busy. Zoe couldn't help wondering about her uneasiness when the subject of Raymond Pearson had come up.

Charlotte looked around the kitchen. "How many breakfasts so far, girl?''

"Mrs. Van Biers and Ms. Marton had coffee and that's it.''

"And it's quite good,'' Zoe volunteered.

"This girl can make coffee, all right,'' Charlotte said. "Could be why Mrs. Van Biers keeps her.'' Then she laughed. "The lady sure does like her morning coffee. If she's not in a hurry, sometimes she takes her mug and strolls in the garden.''

"That sounds pleasant,'' Zoe said.

"Feel free, ma'am, if you would like to, as well,'' Charlotte said.

Zoe thought maybe that was a hint to get out of their kitchen, so she took the cue. "I think I will go for a stroll.'' She tried to catch Esther's eye, but the maid wouldn't look at her. Zoe couldn't be sure if it was because of the presence of Charlotte, or the aborted conversation about Raymond Pearson.

"Door to the back is right through that way, where I came in,'' Charlotte said. "Follow the path around.''

Zoe thanked her and went out back, following the path

through a small forest of flowering shrubs and around the huge house until she came to the big sweeping lawn that sloped toward the sea. There was a bench under a mimosa tree that looked inviting, so Zoe sat to contemplate the view. It was lovely. But she couldn't get Esther's comment about Simon and Pearson arguing out of her mind. Did it mean Simon was somehow involved in Pearson's disappearance, or did it mean nothing at all? An argument in and of itself wasn't an indication of foul play.

What could they have argued about? It could be anything. The value of a painting. A bill for services rendered. Esther had used the word *argument,* and said nothing of threats or violence. Was it because the argument was meaningless, or did she find it politic not to be specific? Or were Zoe's prejudices showing?

Suddenly she heard a "Bang! Bang!" nearby and jumped. But then, a little elf of a boy in shorts and a tiny tank top leaped from the bushes, pointed an imaginary gun at her and cried "Bang! Bang!" again before disappearing from sight. Zoe laughed. The little munchkin had to be Henry. She could hear him moving stealthily in the bushes. He was obviously engrossed in a game calling on her to be a bad guy. Zoe wasn't sure how she felt about that.

Just then she heard a vehicle down at the foot of the drive. A man with a suitcase got out and, though he was some distance from her, the cowboy hat was a giveaway. Apparently Billy Blue had decided to accept his father's offer to stay.

As the vehicle pulled away, Billy came through the gate and started the long walk up to the house. He was in jeans and boots, dressed much as he had been on the plane. He had a bit of a limp as he walked. Zoe wondered if that was from his rodeo accident or from being assaulted by Charles.

She watched him with fascination. Billy was quite an interesting guy, a curious blend of country boy and man on horseback. A charming rogue and a decent down-to-earth guy. He was earnest, disarming, yet alluring. The guy had sex appeal to spare. But underneath it all, he had a lot of common sense, a feel for people. You couldn't call him sophisticated, but he was a lot more aware than he let on.

Zoe liked him, even if he wasn't the sort of man that usually attracted her. She preferred sensitivity, class, subtlety, intelligence in a man. But there was definitely something about Billy that struck a chord—a manly quality, a magnetism—that resonated. She'd seen it, she'd felt it. Billy Blue was one of those guys who simply had a way about him.

A sweet-talking man was what her grandmother used to call men like Billy Blue. And, from the time Zoe first began to understand such things, she knew a woman became involved with that type of guy at her own risk. All she had to do was observe Billy Blue for five minutes to know he'd left a trail of broken hearts stretching from the Rockies to the Pacific.

Billy was about halfway up the drive when Zoe heard a gleeful shriek of laughter, then saw Henry dash across the lawn. Billy stopped and put down his suitcase as Henry approached. When the boy was about ten feet away, he stumbled to a halt, suddenly shy. Billy assumed the pose of a gunslinger ready to draw, but Henry appeared not to understand. When Billy drew his imaginary gun and fired, Henry laughed and fell down on the grass. Billy went over and grabbed the boy by the stomach and started tickling him, which produced gales of laughter.

Zoe noted that Billy Blue seemed to have friends everywhere, not all of them women. When Henry got to his feet, Billy put his hat on the boy's head and retrieved his suitcase. Then he took the boy's hand and the two of them began walking toward the house.

The bench where Zoe was seated was not exactly hidden, but neither was she easily seen. It wasn't until Henry pointed her out that Billy noticed. Changing course, they headed over in her direction.

"Morning, Zoe," he said, sounding chipper, not at all like a man who'd lost a hundred million dollars the evening before. Of course, Billy hadn't accepted the loss as yet.

"Looks like you have a friend," she said, feeling the boy's joy.

"Henry and I are old buddies," he said, letting his suitcase drop. "Aren't we, partner?"

"Yes, amigo!" Henry cried.

Billy lifted the hat off the boy's head, tousled his hair, then put the hat back down.

"Can I keep it?" Henry asked, lifting the brim so he could look up at Billy.

"How about if you borrow it for a few minutes instead?"

"Okay!" Henry started to dash off.

"Don't go far, okay?"

"I won't."

Billy looked at her, shaking his head. "Little rascal."

"You must be the first real live cowboy he's ever seen in his whole life."

"I reckon I am."

"When did you meet him?" she asked.

"Henry and his mom shared a taxi from town when I came last evening."

"Oh, so that's how you know Esther."

"Can't really say that I know her. I guess we talked a little." He gestured toward the mug in her hand. "Having a little java for the trail, I see."

"I stopped by the kitchen before coming out to enjoy the view. The back door is just around that way, if you want a cup. Follow that path, it'll take you right to the door."

"Thank you, but I think I'll wait until breakfast...or have I missed it?"

"No, Mayte's already gone and Simon hasn't come downstairs yet. Your father's not an early riser, apparently."

Billy shook his head. "Sounds mighty strange to hear anybody referred to as my father." He indicated the bench. "Would you mind if I sit a spell, Zoe? My back doesn't appreciate standing. Of course, it doesn't appreciate me sitting, either, but I try to keep a step ahead of its demands."

She chuckled. "No, please do."

He dropped down on the other end of the bench. It was long enough that they weren't uncomfortably close. He glanced over at her. "So, how is it, staying in the big house?"

"It's a lovely place. Comfortable. I certainly can't complain." She sipped her coffee, though it was tepid. "I see you'll be staying, too."

"I figured a clean bed and a few meals is small enough compensation for a Van Gogh."

"Have you given up, then?"

"No, but I can see I'm not going to have an easy time of it."

"When there's a lot of money involved, people get really stubborn."

"Tell me about it," he said.

Zoe figured this was as good a time as any to learn what she could about his sunflowers. "Billy, out of curiosity, when did your grandmother first get the painting?"

"I'm not exactly sure. I was still in school, I know that."

"Oh, then it's been a long time."

"Let's see. I'm nearly thirty-five and I was eighteen when Simon took it as security against the loan. What's that, seventeen years? And she had it several years before that, so I'd say twenty or more."

"A long time then."

"Not so long that she wasn't burning to get it back, right up to the day she died."

If Billy was to be believed, the painting his grandmother had was not her Kansas sunflowers. And if Simon was to be believed, Billy's was the fake and hers the real one. "You're sure your grandmother got the painting from the rancher?"

"Yes, I remember when it happened and she talked about it recently, during her final illness. Ol' Bob Halloway brought it back with him from Europe after World War II," Billy explained. "Got it off some German officer who'd pilfered it in France, as I recall."

Zoe considered that. If the story was true, Billy's painting had been in the States since the 1940s and the Kansas sunflowers since 1919. Either could be the authentic one in theory, but she did have a receipt stating that her family's painting was a genuine Van Gogh.

"I don't suppose your grandmother had any documentation on the painting."

"Not that I know of."

"Ever have it appraised?"

"Some expert looked at photographs years ago and said it could be the real McCoy, but when she tried to get formal appraisal Simon wouldn't go for it. He claimed right from the get-go that it was a copy."

Zoe brightened at the news. Billy's claim to the authentic work seemed to be based more on hope and a prayer than hard evidence. "So, this isn't something he just started saying."

"No, but that doesn't mean jack. He could have known Granny's painting was the real deal and he got the fake so he could pull a switcheroo if and when the need arose."

"Isn't it just as possible he had the copy and when the original came along he grabbed it?"

"Who's going to sell him a Van Gogh for little or nothing?"

"Your grandmother supposedly did."

"No, she gave it to him as security against a loan. There's a big difference."

"A painting worth tens of millions of dollars? Either way she handed it over to him. I don't want to say it was foolish but…"

"She didn't know it was a genuine Van Gogh at the time. It wasn't until later she became more certain. And the only reason she gave up the painting was because of a financial emergency. She was under a lot of pressure."

Zoe considered that. Billy's theory could be sound. But what intrigued and worried her was the ace he claimed to have up his sleeve—his grandmother's mark on the painting. That could very well be the whole ball game.

Zoe checked her watch. "Maybe we should go inside

Simon may have come down for breakfast. I imagine you're anxious to see the sunflowers.''

"I don't have an emotional attachment, if that's what you mean."

That was ironic, she thought. She did have an emotional attachment, which went beyond the money. After all, the painting had been in her family for years.

Billy contemplated her, his expression a touch serious. "Not to be personal or anything, but I've been curious about something. How is it your husband doesn't mind you coming down to a romantic spot like this without him?"

It was a shift in the conversation she hadn't expected, making her redirect her thoughts, from Billy, her competitor for the Van Gogh sunflowers, to Billy, the charming rogue. "He does mind," she said, knowing she was being disingenuous even as she said it. But it was easier and safer to leave him with a false impression. "These things happen in modern marriages when both people have careers."

"What does your husband do, if you don't mind me asking?"

"He's a fashion photographer, a rather prominent one, as a matter of fact."

"Are you a former model?"

She laughed. "Heavens no."

"Where did you meet?"

"At a party in New York. I was taking the Sotheby's course and he knew one of my classmates, a good friend. He was dating her, actually."

"And he saw something he liked better."

"It ruined a friendship," she confessed.

"Smart man."

"Julie was quite lovely."

"I'd take you, Zoe, even without seeing the other gal. Your husband's a smart man. Trust me."

She felt the blood in her cheeks. "Maybe we should go inside."

"I've got to find the varmint that's run off with my hat

first," he said. "Henry!" he called. "Where you hiding, son?" He stood and peered about. "Henry!"

The boy jumped out from behind a bush, firing two invisible pistols.

"Okay, partner," Billy said, "I think we've shot enough desperadoes for the day. How'd you like to loan me your hat?"

"Let's play some more."

"I would, Henry, but I've got to eat breakfast then do some business. How about you and me see each other this evening? You can show me your secret hiding place."

Henry approached them. "What secret hiding place?"

"You must have one. Every boy's got a secret hiding place."

"Do you?"

"Well, certainly I do."

"Where is it?"

"A long, long way from here, Henry. But I'll tell you about it tonight."

The boy took off Billy's hat and handed it back.

"Thank you kindly, Mr. Tye."

"Bye!" Henry exclaimed, then went romping off.

"You seem to have a way with children," Zoe observed.

"I don't know that I do. I just treat 'em like people, which is what they are."

"But why the gun business, if you don't mind me asking? Is it your western heritage that makes you reach for a gun, or is shooting people a guy thing?" The words were out before she'd given them proper reflection. Zoe realized too late she'd probably gone too far.

Billy cocked his head, a slightly pained expression on his face. "Seems like I touched a political nerve there somewhere."

"I shouldn't have said that. I'm sorry."

"Don't apologize. You wouldn't have said it if you didn't mean it. You don't like the idea of guns, I take it."

"The first thing Henry did when he saw me was shoot me

with pretend guns. I wonder if somewhere along the line he got the wrong message, like maybe the way to relate to people is by shooting at them, whether it's pretend or not."

"Yep, we're definitely into politics."

"I don't mean to start an argument," she said, somehow allowing herself to get sucked into it just the same. She had to stop. "What you do is none of my business. He's not even my kid. I was out of line. Please forget it."

"Obviously your comment was aimed at me, since I'm the only gunslinger in town."

"Billy, I'm sorry. I withdraw the comment."

"I don't reckon there's much to be gained by arguing it, but just so there's no misunderstanding, I'm not some kind of gun fanatic, Zoe. For the record, I've never shot anybody. In fact, I don't even own a gun."

"Really? A cowboy without a gun?"

He grinned. "The object of bull riding is to stay on the critter's back, not shoot him between the eyes."

"I just assumed…"

"Maybe there's something in the culture that shouldn't be, I grant you. Maybe it's so ingrained a fella doesn't even notice what he does when he's horsing around, I don't know. And as to whether playing Cowboys and Indians is bad for kids…well, you'd have to ask somebody smarter than me. All I can say for sure is my experience with guns, whether real of pretend, never made me want to shoot anybody. I don't know if that proves anything, but it's a fact."

"The effect is probably subtle."

"I don't rightly know about that. I can tell you this, though, child or adult, the gun you're mostly likely to encounter out West is a hunting rifle, not a Saturday-night special."

"Are you saying it's just fine to teach children to kill animals?" Zoe closed her eyes and groaned, realizing she'd done it again. Why did she feel compelled to spar with the man? She was liberal-minded, true, but it was not as if she was a gun-control fanatic or anything.

Billy, for his part, didn't seem particularly eager to let the matter drop. "The fact is that as a kid I used to hunt with my grandfather," he rejoined. "We didn't do it for sport, but for food. He was an Indian, after all."

"Billy, I didn't mean to pick a fight…"

"No, let me tell you a story about my hunting experiences. When I was fifteen my granddaddy and I went hunting up in the Ruby Mountains. I shot a doe, but it wasn't a clean hit and she limped off, leaving a trail of blood. We tracked her for a mile and when we finally found her she'd dropped from loss of blood, but wasn't quite dead. I looked at her big brown eyes and damn near cried. My granddad had to finish her off. That was the last animal I ever shot."

Zoe could hear the emotion in his voice. She felt badly for criticizing him.

"I didn't tell you that to sound politically correct," Billy said. "If I was politically correct, I guess I wouldn't have a pretend gunfight with a five-year-old. But I didn't want you making the wrong assumptions about me. You really can't judge a book by its cover, Zoe."

She felt duly chastened. "You're right. And I don't imagine political correctness with children is nearly as important as being a good friend and a good person."

"Thank you for saying that."

"I really mean it. It's not so important what we do with children as the spirit in which it's done. Which is to say, I'm withdrawing my criticism and extending an apology."

Billy grinned at her, then went over and got his case. "Could be we've got a chance after all, Zoe," he said as they started along the path.

"A chance?"

"Yes, ma'am. A chance to be friends."

Queenstown

Poppy Tuttlebee scrubbed the kitchen sink with uncommon determination. She had been anxious for days, afraid to leave the house, hardly daring to see her friends. She expended her energy cleaning and doing laundry. And worrying. She couldn't read or watch television—her mind wouldn't allow her to concentrate. All she could think about were the stories about the police, the FBI, the gangsters, the man who was missing, Mr. Pearson, and the Bon Mambo Marie Vincente de la Croix.

Poppy especially worried about the mambo because she worried about her baby. So many times she'd wanted to tell Basil everything, then she'd recall the solemn promise she'd made to Marie. How could she not keep her word? Hadn't the Bon Mambo given her the one thing she'd wanted more than any other?

And though she'd wanted to see Marie to get the reassurance she so badly needed, Poppy dared not make the trip out to where the mambo lived. She was sure people were watching—including the police—and she couldn't take the chance. There was talk of a white woman asking questions, and nobody was sure why. That made Poppy even more nervous. How badly she wanted to confide in Basil, but she knew if she did, that would be the end of it. She would be defying Marie and the spirits. And if she tried to explain the problem to her husband, he would scoff. Basil didn't believe in God, much less the spirit world that had brought them their baby. No, for the first time in her life she was completely alone.

Poppy rinsed the sink and stared at the soapy water as it swirled down the drain. She was sorry when the last of it was gone because it meant the job was done. Should she scrub the floor? She looked around her tidy kitchen, trying to decide what to do next, when there was a knock at the door.

Who could it be? Sara? Her friend had already called that morning to see if she wanted to go with her to the market. "No," Poppy had said, "I'm feeling a little nauseous this morning. I'll send Basil later." It wasn't true, but it avoided the problem. Sara was unhappy with her and told her she was becoming a recluse. "Hasn't the doctor told you exercise is good for you?"

Now Poppy wondered if perhaps her friend had dropped by on the way home from the market to check on her. She went to the front room and peered out the window, but whoever was at the door was standing too close to it for her to see. She considered ignoring the knocking, but decided her failure to answer might cause concern. Already people were talking about her strange behavior. About the only time she ventured out was in the evening with Basil. Holding his arm, she felt safe.

Poppy decided it would be best if she talked to Sara or whoever it was for a minute or two. She opened the door. But it wasn't Sara. It was a white woman. She was pretty, but the sight of her almost made Poppy's heart stop. Poppy started to close the door, but the woman, dressed like a tourist in shorts and a tank top, reached out, gently stopping the door from closing.

"Poppy?"

She was shocked the white woman knew her name. "Yes?"

"Can we talk?"

Poppy's lip trembled. "Who are you?"

"I want to talk about your baby," the woman said, ignoring the question.

Again Poppy tried to close the door, though not forcefully. With equal gentleness the woman prevented her from doing so, using only her hand. She seemed very strong.

"I think you should talk to me, Poppy."

"I don't know you."

"No, but I know you."

There was something about the woman's tone that frightened her, something that said she knew more than Poppy would like. There was no direct threat, though, nothing that suggested she should go running into the street, crying for help.

"My husband will be home in a few minutes," she said, hoping that might scare the woman off.

"I don't think so, Poppy. There's no reason to be afraid. I want to help you."

"Help?"

"Can I come in?" She said it like a question, but she didn't mean to ask for permission because she came right in without waiting for a reply.

Poppy was incensed that a perfect stranger should come barging in that way, but the woman seemed not to care about anything. She glanced around Poppy's cozy little sitting room with the chintz sofa, Basil's chair, the TV and a few other small pieces of furniture. Poppy had lots of knickknacks, things she'd gotten from her mother and her aunt. It was a homey room.

"Nice," the woman said.

Judging by her accent, she was American. A British woman wouldn't be so rude...at least that was Poppy's experience. "Thank you," she said, showing civility the other hadn't.

"Let's sit down," the woman said.

Poppy, who'd stayed at the door, gathering her resolve, was not going to make it easy. "I think you should tell me who you are first."

"It doesn't matter who I am, Poppy," the woman said, sitting in Basil's chair.

Poppy wanted to tell her not to sit there, but it was too late. The woman waited. Poppy didn't leave the door.

"You want the whole neighborhood to know you were at the beach that evening with the mambo?"

Poppy was stunned. Who was this person? And how did she know? Marie must have told her. That was the only explanation. Poppy closed the door and took a few steps into the room where she paused before finding her courage and continuing to the sofa where she sat, her hands folded on her knees. "Okay, what do you want?"

"I want to talk about your baby and the mambo, Poppy. You really want this baby, don't you?"

Poppy bit her lip. What was this woman threatening? It was evil, that much she knew. If she had any intention of harming... Her eyes filled with tears. Why was this happening?

"I want you to have this baby," the woman said. "I want

everything to be just fine. But it won't be unless I get your cooperation.''

''What?'' Poppy said, stifling a sob.

''All I want to know is what happened that night on the beach, when you and Marie were in the water. What did you see, Poppy?''

''Did you talk to the Bon Mambo?''

''Never mind that. Just tell me what you saw.''

Poppy sniffled, chewing on her lip. ''Nothing. I didn't really see anything.''

''You expect me to believe that?''

''Nothing important,'' Poppy insisted. ''I saw the white man come out of the bushes and I saw the other men chase him on the beach. But the Bon Mambo turned me toward the sea so that I couldn't see anymore. She said Yemalla was vanquishing the evil spirits and it was bad luck if I watched. We went under the water and when we came up, they were gone. I swear it,'' Poppy said, pleading. ''I swear on the life of my baby. That's all I saw. And Marie told me not to speak of what happened, even to my husband. And I haven't. I've kept my word. I swear it is so.''

The woman studied her. There were questions in her eyes. Doubt.

''Don't you believe me?''

The woman didn't answer.

''Why don't you speak?'' Poppy pleaded. She was so afraid. Afraid she'd made a terrible mistake. Was she right to tell the truth or had she betrayed Bon Mambo Marie and angered the spirits?

''There is something you aren't telling me?'' the woman said.

''No,'' Poppy said desperately. ''No, nothing.''

''Who was the white man on the beach?''

''I don't know.''

''You don't know?'' the woman said, her tone incredulous.

''He did not look familiar and it was getting dark. We were not close.''

"You have no idea?"

"I think I know, but I'm not sure."

"Who do you think it was?"

Poppy froze. She had painted herself into a corner. She had tried so hard to be sincere that she'd spoken of something she hadn't even spoken of with the Bon Mambo Marie.

"Poppy, who do you think it was?"

Poppy closed her eyes and prayed to God. The truth or a lie? This woman seemed to know everything and Poppy had been truthful until now. She couldn't lie.

"I think it was the man who disappeared," she said in a small voice. "I think it was Mr. Pearson."

"Why do you think it was Mr. Pearson?"

Poppy bit her lip again. "Because it was about then he disappeared."

"What do you think happened to him?"

Poppy shook her head. "I don't know. I've told you everything. Everything!"

The woman contemplated her again.

Poppy didn't know what to think. But she was afraid. Tears again filled her eyes. "What are you going to do?"

The woman took a long, slow breath. "Nothing for now. I am going to leave. But it is very important that you say nothing of this to anyone. If you obey, it will be as if I never came. Our conversation will be your secret and mine," she said. "Do you understand, Poppy?"

"Yes."

The woman stood. Poppy got to her feet, as well. But she was not satisfied. It was not enough that the woman went away.

"What about my b-baby?" she stammered.

The woman seemed surprised by the question. "Your baby?"

"Yes... Marie said I should never speak of...the evening of my immersion, the things I saw. The evil spirits..."

"You don't have to worry," the woman said. "Your baby

will be fine, but only if you keep our secret. Never speak of it to anyone. Okay?"

Poppy nodded. "Yes, I promise."

The woman went to the door, where she stopped and looked back at her. Then, without a word, she left. Poppy sat in a daze, uncertain what had just happened, whether she'd doomed her child or saved it. How could the woman have known everything, if she wasn't filled with the spirit herself? Shivering, Poppy rubbed her arms. She no longer had one terrible secret, she had two.

Basil Tuttlebee handed Jerome the file. "This is what the SEC gave us on Victoria International," he said. "My memo's on top."

Jerome looked at it without opening the cover. "I'm beginning to feel like King Midas," he said.

"In a way, Simon Van Biers is too good to be true," Basil said. "Maybe the time has come to pay the piper."

Jerome Hurst had been thinking the same thing. It was beginning to have the feel of a scandal in the making. And it couldn't come at a worse time, considering the election was only months away.

The telephone on his desk rang. It was his private line. Jerome reached for the receiver. "Yes?"

"Jerome," she said. "It's me."

The sound of Mayte's voice sent the usual tremor through his heart.

"Just a moment," he said, putting his hand over the mouthpiece. "Basil, could you give me a minute?"

"Yes, Mr. President."

The aide got up from his chair and left the office. When the door was shut, Jerome said, "Darling, what's up?"

"I need to see you," she said.

"Is something wrong?"

"I'd rather talk in person. Can you get away?"

"I have a full calendar, but I might be able to find an hour or two late in the afternoon. Say, five?"

"The usual place?"

"Yes."

She hung up. Jerome did as well. There was something different in her voice. Fear.

World Headquarters,
Victoria International Bank

The Mercedes limousine pulled up in front of the glass-and-stone building perched on the tropical hilltop. Billy glanced out the window, impressed, which was Irwin Pettigrew's obvious intent when he built the place.

"Well, here we are," Simon said.

The portly chauffeur, Andrew, got out and came around to open the rear passenger door. Simon, who was closest, got out first. Zoe, morning fresh and smelling sweet as ever, climbed out next. Simon helped her out with gentlemanly excess. Billy, fighting the pain in his back, followed. As he moved past Andrew he handed him the New York subway token he'd found in his jeans pocket that morning, and gave the man a wink. Andrew grinned a wide grin, shaking his head with amusement.

Simon, meanwhile, had mounted the steps with Zoe, and the two of them stopped to take in the view. As Billy climbed up after them, he peered at his father's face, still not having fully accepted the fact that he was in the presence of the man who'd given him life, the man he'd disdained all these years, the man who now treated him like the prodigal son returned, a man of sweetness and light, good cheer and bonhomie. In Billy's judgment, Simon was still the guy who'd cheated him out of a fortune and was therefore a scoundrel. But he did have a soothing, pleasant manner, the sort that made you smile while he put it to you. It took a real con to make a person feel good about getting screwed. His pappy had a talent, all right.

Simon, looking genteel in another of his white suits and

pale blue Italian-silk ties, said, "I picked this spot for the view, obviously." He gestured grandly toward the sweep of sea stretching to the horizon. "But beyond the raw splendor is a certain majesty of setting reminiscent of a Mayan temple I visited some years ago." He turned and looked back at the building. "And, as you can see, the architect captured something of the spirit of the pre-Columbian period. I think it gives it a timeless quality," he added. "What do you think?"

"Well, it's magnificent," Zoe said. "Both the setting and the building."

Billy, standing next to Zoe, enjoyed both her scent and the view. "Not a lot in Elko to compare this with," he added amiably.

"I like to think of this as my monument," Simon went on. "A man hungers for tangible proof of his achievements in life, I've found. But if your origins are humble, as are mine, you can look back with an even more poignant sense of accomplishment." He glanced past Zoe over at Billy. "You may appreciate this, son. When I was a boy living in Biloxi, the grand homes of the day were located along the water overlooking the Mississippi Sound. In the days before air-conditioning was common, rich folks would build shooflies, which were raised platforms out on the green, often around a big oak or whatever. The purpose was to have a place to go to escape the pesky flies and capture those soft gulf breezes. I recall walking along the road seeing the gentlemen and ladies relaxing on their platforms, high above the rest of us, sippin' iced tea or lemonade without a care in the world, and me thinking, 'Someday I'm going to have the biggest, fanciest shoofly a body ever did see.' Well, sir, this is not exactly a shoofly, but I like to think of it as such. Symbolically speakin', of course."

Billy couldn't deny his father's achievement, though the manner in which he'd gotten there was certainly suspect. To say it was on the backs of other people would be a gross understatement—he had to look no further than the example of Sophie Blue Bear. Reconciling himself to the fact that it was this man's blood running in his veins was a tougher task than he would have imagined. But Billy had also been thinking of the old adage that when you had lemons, you might as well make lemonade. The thought brought a secret smile. Maybe he was more his father's son than he realized.

"You have a dream, Billy?" Simon asked.

Billy reflected a moment, then said, "One that's come to me secondhand."

"Any dream will do, son. The important thing is to have one."

"I want to build a trade school for Native American kids in honor of my grandfather," Billy said. "A place where they can go to learn honest work that builds up rather than tears down."

There was a long silence before Simon said, "That's commendable." After another silence, he said, "Now, who would like to see my master work by Vincent Van Gogh?"

Billy chuckled to himself and, catching Zoe's eye, he winked, eliciting a little smile from her, one indicating that maybe they'd shared an insight, if not a cause.

The world headquarters of Victoria International Bank was not huge but, to Billy's way of thinking, it was certainly gold-plated. The marble entry was expansive and naturally lit with a cascading water feature, a forest of palms and other tropical plants with wide stone steps leading to the upper level where the executive offices were located. The administrative staff was on the two lower levels, which stepped down the mountainside in pyramid fashion. As they'd driven up the twisting road, the design effect could be seen. The entry level, interestingly enough, was just below the apex of the building with most of the floor space actually located below.

"We only have forty-two employees," Simon said as the three of them moved up the steps abreast. "But they manage a portfolio of several hundred million, with millions more coming in every week. I don't keep up with the details on a day-to-day basis. Mayte handles that."

At the upper level, glass doors led to the inner sanctum of

the Victoria International executive brain trust. But because a large number of the walls were glass, the impression was one of openness rather than secrecy, the space seemingly alight with tropical sunshine, some filtered down through the atrium above, the rest through floor-to-ceiling glass on the outer walls.

The spacious reception area had a mood that was serene, from the potted ferns and palms to the huge gold bank logo behind the elegantly dressed receptionist, a poised black woman with elaborately braided hair, a woman who seemed more a living statue than a working employee. But she did greet them with a warm smile.

"Good morning, Mr. Van Biers."

"Good morning, Charis."

Simon introduced them as his art adviser and his son. They proceeded through the suite, first coming to Mayte's glass-enclosed office. She was at her desk, speaking on the phone as they passed by. She waved. Next to it was the largest office, one seemingly occupying a third of the floor itself. Billy had seen more than one bulldogger wrestle a steer to the ground in less distance from the chute than the span from one side of Simon's office to the other.

It was on a stone wall behind a desk bigger than a pool table that Billy saw the Van Gogh. Zoe saw it at the same moment and gasped. The three of them gazed at a canvas painted by an eccentric Dutch artist in the South of France when Grover Cleveland was president. The sunflowers were in a glass case, dramatically lit against a dark backdrop.

Billy had seen the painting a number of times as a teenager, though he'd had only the vaguest recollection of it, probably because it had meant nothing to him. For a long time they hadn't even suspected it might be famous and valuable. His grandmother had kept it on a wall in the smaller back room of her shop, The Blue Bear, along with what she thought was her most valuable piece, a painting of a bronco rider by Charles Russell. That, Billy could relate to.

The eight sunflowers in a vase did look familiar, though,

coming back to him like a mountain peak emerging from the mists of early morning. Was this his painting? he wondered. And just as importantly, was it the real McCoy?

Billy glanced over at Zoe, whose eyes shimmered with emotion. Her reaction surprised him. Van Gogh was her guy, he knew, but how could a painter who'd been dead for more than a hundred years affect a woman like, say, Clint Black or Garth Brooks? Simon noticed, too.

"Beautiful, isn't it, Zoe?"

She could only nod. Billy had to admit that his knowledge of art was limited, beginning and ending with random tidbits he'd picked up at his grandmother's knee. Hardly enough to know the difference between an impressionist and an illusionist. The thing about Van Gogh, Granny had said, was "he knew color." Billy, for his part, couldn't get real excited about color. He preferred the work of Charles Russell whose painting of the bronc was so realistic Billy could almost smell the critter, heaving and bucking for all it was worth.

"How do you think it compares with the other paintings in the series?" Simon asked Zoe.

"It certainly looks like it belongs in the Arles group. I've heard it most resembles the painting of the five sunflowers that was destroyed during the Second World War."

"The Yokohama painting?"

"Yes," she said.

"One in the series is still in Japan, right?"

"Yes, a vase with fourteen blossoms at the Yasuda in Tokyo." She continued to stare, slowly shaking her head. "This is just lovely," she said, wiping her eyes.

"Raymond said he believed it's the famed and mysterious Faucauld sunflowers," Simon said.

"Faucauld?" Billy said. "What's that?"

"Roger Faucauld was a reclusive painter and art dealer who lived in the South of France," Zoe explained. "For years it was rumored that he had an eighth and previously unknown canvas from the Arles sunflower series. It wasn't until Simon brought this painting to light that its existence was verified."

"You're looking at a Van Gogh that only a handful of experts have ever seen," Simon added. "According to Raymond, this painting had probably been languishing somewhere in obscurity for years and years, most likely in the hands of people who didn't know what they had."

Billy noticed the color rise in Zoe's cheeks and he wasn't sure why. "You're saying Faucauld kept it a secret? Why?"

"He apparently was as eccentric as Van Gogh, refusing to confirm the painting's existence, let alone the particulars of its history. He died shortly after the Second World War, so the details may never be known."

"And you're saying somehow the painting got into the hands of the people you bought it from," Billy said.

"Yes, somehow."

Billy and Zoe exchanged looks.

"So, what's the story on my painting?" Billy asked.

"Raymond wasn't sure. We know that it's old, probably painted ten or fifteen years after Van Gogh did the original. Most likely by Faucauld himself. Raymond determined that he was an expert copyist. As far back as the 1890s, Faucauld did copies of the French impressionists. Having reproductions was the fad back then. There's some evidence that he knew Van Gogh. Beyond that, it's pretty much speculation."

"Where's the copy?" Billy asked.

"Downstairs in a storage vault," Simon replied.

"Any chance of seeing it?"

"If you like."

"Can we take a few more minutes here first?" Zoe asked as she went over for a closer look at the painting.

"Sure, take all the time you like."

Zoe was very close to the case. She seemed to be studying the brush strokes, the signature in the corner. She stepped back a few steps then closer again, as Billy and Simon waited.

"Beauty admiring beauty," Simon said appreciatively from the corner of his mouth.

Billy couldn't tell if Zoe heard or not. He certainly shared the sentiment with his old man, though. Zoe was definitely growing on him. He couldn't say why. She was attractive, sure. She had more class than most women he'd known…at least known well. She indulged him, maybe liked him a little, but mostly she kept an emotional distance. Maybe it was because of her husband, but somehow he didn't think so. Her comments about the guy seemed stock, without warmth. She had the air of a woman alone…alone, but preoccupied.

After a while she turned away from the painting, joining them. Simon led the way to an elevator that they took to the lowest level, a basement carved into the mountainside. He unlocked a steel door leading to a good-size vaultlike storage room.

"This is where the investment pieces are stored," he explained, "with space for hundreds more. It's climate controlled. There's a studio–workroom through there for your use, Zoe. You'll also have an office on the executive level." He went to one of the large cabinets. "The copy of the Van Gogh sunflowers—your painting, Billy—is in here. If you'll give me a hand, we can take it out. Zoe, perhaps you could grab the easel over there in the corner." Simon opened the cabinet door and pulled out a sliding rack holding a package the size and shape of a painting, wrapped in protective material. "Let's put it on the worktable."

Billy helped him carry the package to the nearby table. It was heavy, but not too heavy between the two of them. Simon loosened the cord and peeled back the wrapping material, exposing the back of the canvas and frame. They lifted the painting off the table and set it on the easel.

Zoe, standing several feet back, saw it first. "My God," she said. "Incredible."

Billy and Simon joined her. Billy was as surprised as she. It was the same painting they'd just seen upstairs in Simon's office, at least to his untrained eye.

Zoe moved up close to the canvas, examining some of the detail and the signature as she had before. "Slightly different frame," she noted. "What about the dimensions, Simon?"

"Within a centimeter."

"I'd like to see them side by side," she said, "but the achievement is remarkable. These are Van Gogh's brush strokes."

"Could he have done both paintings?" Billy asked.

"No," Zoe said. "He would have no incentive. Artists frequently repeat their subject—Van Gogh certainly did—but they don't copy themselves, not in detail."

"Why not?"

"Because it would be practically as hard for them to do an exact duplication as it would for anyone else. Painting is an expressive, creative process. The reproductive mentality is different. When you write your signature you never do it exactly the same twice. But a forger will duplicate your signature almost exactly. It's a different state of mind. What's remarkable about this is that the copyist did such a good job with a painting style that is so free and expressive. Imagine Van Gogh freely applying paint, almost with abandon, then imagine Faucauld or whoever carefully and meticulously trying to duplicate each stroke. To emulate style is one thing, but to capture a particular painting exactly is another."

"How do you tell the fake one from the real one?"

"In a case like this, where the copy was made almost contemporaneously with the original, we have to rely on technique rather than the age and nature of the materials—in other words, on art rather than technology. An expert who knows Van Gogh, for example, can look at brush strokes closely and see the artist's fingerprints, so to speak."

"You're an expert, what do you think?" Billy asked.

"I'd not only like to see the two paintings side by side, but I'd like to see them both next to the sunflower still life at the Museum of Art in Philadelphia, say. It's best to compare a painter with himself, not a skillful copyist. I'll tell you this, though, this is no small achievement. If only the copy existed, there could be a spirited debate as to whether it was authentic."

Billy glanced a Simon, who seemed to be taking it all in with equanimity. But then, what did he have to worry about?

He had control not only of both paintings but also of the documentation. Billy found Zoe looking at him questioningly.

"Do you need a closer look at this?" she asked. "The back, perhaps?"

She was referring to the identifying mark his grandmother had made, obviously. She was giving him the opportunity to spring it on Simon, which told him she probably hadn't said anything to Simon herself. Maybe that was a good sign. But Billy also knew it was important to pick his moment and this wasn't it.

"No," he said, shaking his head. "The whole time my grandmother had the painting I never paid much attention to it. And, to tell you the truth, it only looks vaguely familiar."

Zoe nodded.

Simon cleared his throat. They seemed to have arrived at a dramatic moment. "Let's talk value for a moment, Zoe," he said, his tone shifting to serious. "What figure would you put on an expert copy like this, one of the era and practically indistinguishable from the original?"

"It's rarity alone makes it quite valuable. Even experts familiar with Van Gogh couldn't dismiss it as a fake summarily."

"A hundred thousand?" Simon said. "Two hundred? Half a million?"

"I really couldn't say. I suppose it's worth what somebody would be willing to pay. For the right person, the novelty value alone might put it in the millions. But you'd have to find the right person."

Simon sat on the corner of the worktable. "Billy, I'm prepared to offer you a quarter of a million right here and now for the copy. But, if you want to take it to the market and see if you can get more, that's your right."

"My plan has always been to take my painting home with me," Billy said. "Seems to me the only question is which painting I take, this one or the one upstairs."

"Son, this is the one your grandmother gave me seventeen years ago."

"Unless somewhere along the line they got mixed up."

"In other words, you plan on disputing the fact."

"I wouldn't want a mistake, even an innocent mistake, to stand between me and a painting that's rightfully mine. This painting hasn't been under your bed the whole time you've had it. No telling what's happened along the way."

"How do you propose to resolve the dispute, son?"

"I've got something in mind. All that's left is to figure out the best way to play out my hand. Standing here, I can't tell you which of these Van Goghs is mine and which is yours. But there is a surefire way of distinguishing them, good enough for any impartial judge. I can assure you of that."

"And you'll make the fact known in due course."

"Yes, sir, I will." He gave Zoe a wink. "Now would you like some help wrapping this up again?"

"No, that's all right. I can take care of it later."

An awkward silence hung in the air.

"Well," Simon said after a few moments, "why don't we take a little tour of the building? Then I thought maybe we could drive down to the club. A little later Mayte will join us there for lunch. How does that sound?"

"Fine," Zoe said with a shrug. She glanced at Billy.

"Am I right they play polo down there?" he asked.

"Yes," Simon replied. "Perhaps you'd like to have a look at the stock. Charles has three ponies. If we can find him, maybe he'll give you a little demonstration."

"I'd enjoy that," Billy said. "It's been a while since I've had my hand on horseflesh. Once a man is accustomed to it, he's not easily weaned, you know." He made no mention of it, of course, but he might have added that the same could be said of being weaned from women.

The Countryside

The Bon Mambo Marie Vincente de la Croix had spent her nights and much of her days in her secret hiding place under the altar, coming out only to tend to necessities and to perform ceremonies to serve the spirits. In the darkness of night she was tormented by the great black bull and the white woman. Marie knew her only protection against the evil was in the loa. She performed ceremonies for Ayza, the protector god, but she also turned to the patroness of abused women, the spirit Erzulie Dantor, the black woman who was much feared and whose love of knives and aggressiveness seemed the perfect defense against the bull.

Marie spent many hours singing songs to the mistress of the house, whose spells were stronger than the evil. Erzulie Dantor and the seven stabs of the dagger. Erzulie Dantor vomiting blood, stronger than the evil, strong and not so easily destroyed. When Erzulie Dantor possessed her, Marie sang and danced her praises. She sang in Haitian Creole. She sang in English. "Erzulie Dantor, kill the bull!"

It was after an hours-long ceremony as she lay exhausted on the dusty floor of the hounfour that Marie felt the evil Baka approaching. She lifted her head and heard the sound of a vehicle coming down the road. It was the bull, Marie was certain. Crawling to the altar, she summoned the last of her strength to lift the door so she could hide in her secret place, protected by the spirits.

Marie peered through the narrow crack and waited for the bull. In the yard, between the hounfour and the house, she could see two chickens pecking at the dust. She could hear birds cawing in the woods. She could hear the vehicle stopping out front in the road. Dripping with sweat, Marie waited, her birdlike heart pounding. "Erzulie Dantor," she murmured, "kill the bull."

Then she saw him come around the house, his black shoulders as wide as a door, his bald head gleaming in the midday sun. The earth seemed to rumble under his feet. "Erzulie Dantor, kill the bull."

Another figure appeared behind the bull, but it wasn't the white witch. It was a black man, small compared to the bull, thin with dangling arms that swung loosely from his shoulders.

He had a long neck and a smallish head and smallish eyes. He looked familiar. Terribly familiar. Then she realized it was Jean Bien Dumont, a discredited houngan Marie had known in Haiti. Jean Bien had served the loa with both hands. In other words, he was a bokor, a practitioner of black magic.

During the Duvalier regime Jean Bien had led a corrupt Sanpwel secret society and he had done much evil, using the sanctions inappropriately, using black magic to frighten and intimidate the people. Jean Bien's name had become synonymous with the darkness. All the good houngans and mambos had renounced Jean Bien, but all it did was drive him into deeper secrecy. His potions and poisons for evil were legendary. Like a mercenary, Jean Bien sold his services to anyone willing to pay for evil. Often he himself became possessed by the loa, almost always Damballah, the spirit of snakes. But in Jean Bien's person, Damballah was not only a source of virility and power, he was a source of cunning and evil. People all over the Caribbean feared Jean Bien. He was the priest of death.

Summoning her courage, Marie peeked out again. Jean Bien had knelt on the ground in the center of the hounfour where he'd begun arranging bowls and vials of potions and poisons in preparation for a possession. She understood what was happening. Jean Bien would become the hated snake, Damballah, and he would try to kill her.

Bon Mambo Marie Vincente de la Croix began to tremble. "A l'Esprit partout. Royaume de Bon Dieu. Aidez-moi. Erzulie Dantor, kill the bull. Kill the snake!"

St. Margaret Polo Club

The four of them—Billy, Zoe, Mayte and Simon—sat at a window table, having a leisurely lunch. Outwardly Simon was his usual serene, amiable self, but his insides were in turmoil. Billy was a time bomb ready to explode in his face, and Simon couldn't tell if the bastard was going to fight him to the death for the Van Gogh or if he was merely posturing in hopes of squeezing as much out of him as he could.

The trouble was Simon didn't have the luxury of time to finesse things. He needed an infusion of capital—that credit line—and he needed it fast. What it meant, of course, was that he couldn't take precautions or prepare as carefully as he'd like. He had to strike a deal with Billy, and he had to strike it soon.

At the bank, before they'd left for lunch, Simon had managed to take Zoe aside for a few words in private. She would be key, so he wanted to get the ball rolling with her.

"The first thing I'd like you to do is to sit down with Mayte to discuss valuation of the Van Gogh," he'd told her.

"Do you plan to sell it?"

Simon had noticed a touch of urgency in her voice, which struck him as odd. But he could see no particular reason why she should care—other than the fact that it might affect her job, of course—so he ignored it. "No," he said. "I plan to use it for collateral to raise additional working capital. Until the new syndications are online and the money flows in, we're going to need additional cash. I'll be using the painting as security for a credit line. The question is how much we can get."

"I don't know anything about banking practices," she'd said.

"That's Mayte's and my job. We need to establish the value of the asset. That's where you come in, Zoe. What I need is a document of the value."

"What you feel it's worth?" she'd asked. "Or, maybe I should say, what you want it to be worth?"

"Can we make a case for a hundred million?"

She'd hesitated before answering. "Possibly. Some time has passed since the *Irises* sold for $53.9 million. But that was at auction. As you know, anything unique is worth what somebody's willing to pay for it."

"Well, we'll have to do the best we can," he'd said. "I'll

probably be going to New York sometime in the next several days. I may want you to go with me.''

Although it seemed fine with her, he didn't like dragging her into the middle of things so quickly. It was damned risky because he had no way to gauge her loyalty. Of course, he wouldn't be telling her any more than was absolutely necessary, but even the most casual remark could signal to Billy that he had leverage. Simon had decided to guard against that by telling her his concern straight out.

''There's one other thing, Zoe,'' he'd said. ''Please be careful what you say around Billy. He's my son, but at the same time my business competitor. It's fine to be friendly with him, I encourage it. But please be discreet. Don't mention anything of a business nature that we've discussed.''

Something had momentarily passed over her eyes, but she'd said, ''Certainly. I understand.''

He hadn't mentioned he was the one who would be signing her paycheck because it was self-evident, the point not lost on her. Zoe was no fool.

As the four of them had dessert, he again observed the by-play between Billy and Zoe. Simon was long past his prime, but not too old to recognize chemistry when he saw it. Billy liked the girl and she was...well, intrigued. That would be the most polite way to put it. But there was enough going on that Simon was concerned he may have miscalculated. It was something he had to keep his eye on.

But he also knew the importance of appearances. The last thing you wanted to signal was self-doubt or insecurity. Even at the brink of disaster, a man had to exude confidence.

''Ah, there's Charles,'' he said, pointing out the window.

The others turned and looked out at the polo field where a lone horseman was trotting his pony back and forth, a polo mallet resting on his shoulder like a lance.

''What's he doing?'' Zoe asked.

''Exercising his ponies and knocking a ball around. He does it a few times a week. Says it's important to keep both himself and the ponies sharp. I don't know a great deal about polo myself. I get it all secondhand from Charles.''

"How'd he get involved in polo?" Billy asked.

"Originally because of his mother. Bronwyn's sole ambition for the boy was to make him a gentleman. When he eschewed—her word, not mine—the Eton and Oxbridge routine, she looked for other trappings of class and came up with polo. Gave him lessons and damn if he didn't take to it, much to Bronwyn's delight. All three of his ponies were a gift from his mother. He adores those animals like nothing else in the world. The club was a gift from me."

"Charles gets the benefit of the club, dear," Mayte said, "but it's not his."

"That's true. If it belongs to anybody, it's me. There haven't been enough memberships sold to sustain it," Simon explained. "I still hold over fifty percent of the units." He drained the last of his vodka tonic—his third—and put down the empty glass. "You're a man who knows horses, Billy. Ever had a yearning to try your hand at polo?"

"Afraid not, sir."

"Too pretentious?"

"I'd have trouble with the cute pants," he replied drolly.

"I wouldn't mention that in Charles's presence," Mayte said, arching a brow. "He doesn't have a sense of humor about some things."

"No, ma'am, I expect he wouldn't appreciate that." Billy gave Zoe a sly smile, which Simon noted.

That subtle little spark again. Zoe was fighting it, but Billy was getting to her. She herself didn't know how badly just yet. But Simon had an inkling. He realized he needed to find a way to turn this budding love to his advantage if possible. Nothing was as vulnerable as a man in love.

"You know," Mayte said after taking her last bite of cheesecake and putting down her fork, "I hate to be a party pooper, but I do need to get back to the office."

"I understand," Simon said, giving her a lethargic smile. Mayte was another concern. He sensed a subtle shift in her

attitude. It was barely perceptible, but it was real. Their cash-
flow problems had been weighing on her for some time, but
Billy showing up and laying claim to the Van Gogh had
shaken her. From the beginning, owning the painting had been
Simon's ace in the hole, his reserve. Without it the house of
cards could come tumbling down very quickly, and his dear
wife knew it. That had definitely set her on her heels. Mayte
wasn't one to make something out of nothing, of spinning
words into fine cloth. She was too much of a capitalist for
that, even if her ethics were relative.

And then there were the complications of their personal
problems—the state of their marriage and the state of her outside interests. Simon was the captain of a ship that was growing less seaworthy by the hour. Thank God he'd planned for
the worst.

"Will I see you back at the office?" his wife asked.

"I expect you will, yes."

She started to get up from her chair when Simon spotted an
ominous presence across the sparsely populated room. Reaching out, he touched her arm. "Hold on, sugar. It appears Chief
Inspector Reginald Goodson has just arrived and, unless I'm
mistaken, it's us he wants to speak with." Simon gave Billy
and Zoe a playful smile. "Never a good sign when a policeman shows up when it's time for coffee."

Goodson promptly made his way to the table. He was in a
jacket, tie and heavily starched shirt. His face was red, his
forehead beaded with perspiration, his mustache drooping a
bit more precipitously on one side. The grave expression he
wore telegraphed his concern.

"Good afternoon, Mr. Van Biers," he said stiffly. "Please
forgive the intrusion, but I have urgent news. May I have a
word with you?"

"Is it personal, Goodson?"

"It concerns the Pearson case, sir."

"Oh. Well, I'm among family and friends, no need for formality. Why don't you join us?" Simon signaled for the waiter
to bring another chair. "Let me introduce everyone." He made

the introductions and, after shaking hands all around, Reginald Goodson sat at the end of the table, mopping his brow with his handkerchief. "Will you have coffee?"

"No, thank you very much, indeed."

"What's your news, Chief Inspector?" Simon said.

"Mr. Pearson's body was found a few hours ago, sir."

Simon felt a deep stab in his gut, but his only outward reaction was a slight elevation of his brows. "His body. Do you mean by that he was dead?"

"Very dead indeed, sir."

"What were the circumstances?"

"The body was found by a French marine-exploration boat a mile off our northern coast. They were looking for ancient shipwrecks and happened across the body in fifty meters of water. Pearson's leg was chained to an oil drum filled with cement. Despite the decomposition, there is evidence of serious trauma. It appears the poor man was bludgeoned to death."

"Dear God," Simon said, sounding shaken. "You're saying he was murdered."

"Indeed I am, sir. In light of your friendship with Mr. Pearson, President Hurst thought you'd like to know."

"I'm stunned," Simon said. He glanced around the table. "I think we all are."

"A tragedy," Mayte agreed.

"The family has been notified," Goodson said. "I believe his wife is on her way down to claim the body."

"Be sure and let us know when Eunice arrives," Simon said. "We'll want to express our condolences."

"I shall indeed, Mr. Van Biers." He solemnly glanced about the table. "Sorry to bring such unfortunate news, but as I said, the president thought you'd want to be apprised posthaste."

"That's very considerate. Thank Jerome for me, Goodson."

"Yes, sir, I shall. I'll be leaving then. Goodbye, all."

They watched Reginald Goodson make his way back across the dining room and disappear out the door. For several moments more no one spoke. Finally, Simon took it upon himself to break the ice. "Well," he said, "on top of everything else, a murder."

Everyone looked uncomfortable, but no one—with the possible exception of Mayte—could possibly be half so shaken as he. Whether there was any immediate danger, he had no idea. Goodson gave no indication of suspicion. Even so, this was another dangerous development. Simon's hopes for a breathing spell had been dashed by his fool son who seemed incapable of hiding a body successfully. Now they were all in jeopardy.

Simon was no longer in the mood for niceties, and pretense was beyond even him. He needed to retreat and gather himself. "If you're headed back to the office, sugar," he said, "maybe I'll catch a ride with you. That way the young folks can take the limo and make their way home at their own pace. Have a closer look at Charles's horses, if you have a mind, Billy. And Zoe, if you feel like a tour of the island, just tell Andrew. He knows every square inch of the place. Point is, I want y'all to feel right at home."

"Thank you," Zoe said.

Billy got to his feet, along with Simon and Mayte. Simon clasped him on the shoulder. "Sit down, son. Have a cup of coffee with the young lady."

Simon followed Mayte. They'd no sooner left the dining room when she said, "Well, is this it, Simon? Do we run for the hills?"

"Not just yet," he said from the corner of his mouth. "Finding a body is one thing. Connecting us to a murder is quite another. We'll survive this to fight another day."

He'd said it with conviction, as he said most everything with conviction. But he couldn't deny they were sprouting leaks as fast or faster than they could plug them. Once again he was glad he'd had the foresight to make Mayte comfortable financially, yet still beholden to him. If she wished to spend the rest of life living in exile in South America, she'd be far better off with him and his millions than with the hundred thousand she'd socked away. His dear wife, for all her brilliance, didn't have a better friend than him.

Billy leaned back in his chair, slowly circling his thumbs, thinking. Zoe was mute for a time. Then she said, "The plot thickens."

"Yep, it sure does. Seems somebody didn't like Mr. Pearson. Or didn't like what he knew."

"You think they had something to do with it?" she asked, inclining her head toward the door where Simon and Mayte had disappeared.

"I don't rightly know, Zoe, but somebody wanted him dead. That's pretty clear."

"And went to great lengths to see that the body wasn't found."

Billy dipped his head in assent. He stared out the window at the polo field where Charles rode furiously, mud flying as he swung his mallet, knocking a polo ball from one end to the other. "I wonder how he'll react to the news of Pearson's body being found?"

"You don't plan to tell him, do you?"

He gave her an artful smile. "I wouldn't mind having a look at those horses of his."

"Is that why? Surely you don't want to see him squirm?"

"Not everybody loves his brother, and I probably love mine less than most. But, to be honest, yeah, seeing him uncomfortable would bring me pleasure. Hope that doesn't make you think any less of me."

"I certainly can't blame you, Billy, but let's not go down there." Her anxiety was plain to see and he wondered why. Was she afraid for him? Maybe she was and didn't want him to know, because in an offhand way, she added, "Unless you're a glutton for punishment."

"Honey, there's three things I can't stand in a man. One who mistreats people. One who lies. And one who's selfish. Charles qualifies on every score. And if I should offend the sonovabitch, what's he going to do? Knock me on my butt?"

She gave him a weary look. "It wouldn't be the first time."

Billy leaned on the rail fence, watching Charles put his pony through its paces, patting the animal with what seemed like genuine affection. It struck Billy as incongruous, but even the most evil and dishonorable man had to have some redeeming feature. Zoe stood silently beside him. She was clearly uncomfortable. He glanced over at her.

"You know, I can't hate the guy for his horsemanship and regard for his animals. He seems to know what he's doing and he does it well."

"Maybe around horses he doesn't feel inadequate."

"Think that's his problem with people?"

"He's a bully, isn't he?"

"You've got a point," Billy said.

A small, older man who seemed to be tending Charles's horses came walking by, leading the third polo pony. "Excuse me, partner," Billy called to him.

The man turned. "Sir?"

"Van Biers seems to know what he's doing out there. How's he regarded by his friends?"

"If you mean by the players, he's considered one of the best."

"Then he's well liked."

The man hesitated. "That wasn't my point, sir. He's regarded as a fine horseman and a jolly good polo player. Mr. Van Biers is thought to be aggressive, but most would agree the object of a match is to win."

"He seems to like his horses."

"He's very fond of his ponies, indeed, sir."

"But he rides them hard."

"Mr. Van Biers believes a pony won't be prepared for the rough-and-tumble of a match if his workouts are soft. Polo's a rigorous sport for man and beast. Mr. Van Biers thinks it cruel to drive a pony in the rough-and-tumble of a match without conditioning him properly."

"What's your job, if you don't mind me asking?"

"Trainer, sir. Name's Tommy Epps."

"You approve of his philosophy, Mr. Epps?" Billy asked.

"His philosophy regarding the ponies, yes."

Billy and Zoe exchanged looks. It was what Epps had left unsaid that was significant.

The man seemed uncomfortable with the conversation. "If you'll excuse me, sir, Mr. Van Biers will be wanting to change ponies soon. I don't want to keep him waiting." Epps led the horse off to the edge of the field and stood waiting for Charles to arrive.

Billy watched Charles, rubbing his chin. "When you see him full of love like that, you've got to wonder how he got so screwed up when it comes to his own species. You suppose anybody's ever asked him?"

"Let's go, Billy," Zoe said, taking his arm in a surprisingly firm way.

Billy knew the smart thing was to avoid confrontation. But every fiber of his being implored him to regain his honor. His back was all that was standing between him and action. More than ever he hated the fact he was incapacitated—only half a man. When he'd gotten knocked to the ground at the airport the hurt pride he'd suffered had been a lot worse than any physical pain. He hadn't been able to walk away then. He couldn't walk away now.

"I want to watch a little longer," he said.

"Why are men so stupid?"

"It's hormones. Can't do a thing about it, Zoe."

"You could. You aren't brave enough, that's all."

He looked her way. "Not brave enough?"

"That's right. It takes courage to do the smart thing rather than what feels good to your pride."

"You admire a coward, is that what you're saying?"

"I admire a man who has the sense to control events instead of letting them control him."

"Walking away is controlling events? Sounds like cowardly retreat to me."

Zoe threw up her hands. "I give up."

"Calm down," he said. "I'm not going to pick a fight. I just don't like that guy."

"I don't either, but I get no pleasure standing around staring daggers at him." She turned her back, folding her arms over her chest as she leaned against the fence.

Billy didn't mean to upset her, but anger made him stubborn.

A hundred feet away Charles came riding up to the spot where Tommy Epps waited with the fresh mount. He hopped off his horse, showing little fatigue despite the hard riding. Taking the bottle of water Tommy handed him, Charles guzzled some down and handed it back.

Billy saw a large bandage on Charles's forearm. A love bite from one of his horses?

About then Charles noticed them standing at the fence, probably for the first time. He mounted a fresh horse, but instead of returning to the field, he guided the pony over to the fence where Billy and Zoe stood.

"Well, if it isn't the dynamic duo," he said sarcastically.

Zoe, having turned around, spoke first. "Hello, Charles."

He gave her a passing smile, but seemed more interested in engaging Billy. "Smelled the horse sweat and had to come for a look, huh, cowboy?"

"Yeah, glad to see you have a regard for your animals, Charles. It'd be a crying shame if you treated them the way you do people."

Charles laughed derisively, almost as though he didn't consider Billy's words an insult. "This is a man's sport, bro. We ride in real saddles, not sedan chairs. None of this throwing ropes around the necks of little calves. Ever try to hit a little ball with a club on a long stick while riding full tilt into a half-a-ton wall of man and horse?"

"No, but it sure sounds like fun."

"Happy to give you a lesson anytime you like, Billy-boy."

"If I ever get the urge to beat up anyone, I'll take you up on that, Charles."

Charles Van Biers smirked.

"By the way," Billy said, "have you heard the news?"

"What news?"

"They found Pearson's body."

"What?"

"Fished him out of the drink. Somebody clubbed him to death."

Charles seemed shocked, but managed a tepid smile. "You're shitting me."

"No. The cop, what's-his-name, the British guy, drove out and told the old man while we were having lunch."

Charles gave him a hard glare that lasted a while. Then, without another word, he lifted himself in the saddle, expanded his chest, wheeled his horse and went galloping off, kicking a spray of mud back at them in the process.

Zoe said, "Feel better?"

"I probably shouldn't, but I do." He watched his half brother race up the field. "Charles must not have been too fond of Pearson. Didn't seem terribly upset to hear he'd been confirmed dead, did he?"

"No."

"I wonder why."

"Could be because he's an insensitive, uncaring human being."

Billy nodded. "Yeah, but one who loves his horses."

"I'm glad he didn't take more offense at your comments than he did. I was afraid he rode over here to prove his balls are bigger."

"Do you think they are?"

"Oh, for God's sake, Billy, the least you can do is show more maturity than he does."

"I told you I wouldn't pick a fight, and I didn't."

"No thanks to your tact, however." She glanced toward the field. "Come on, let's go."

They strolled back toward the club where Andrew and the limo waited.

"You feel like taking a tour?" he asked.

"I don't think so. I'm not in much of a holiday mood."

"Because of Pearson?"

"Maybe." She glanced over at him. "What do you think will happen?"

"I think the shit's about to hit the fan, pardon my French."

She sighed. "I think you might be right."

They walked a bit farther, then Billy said, "If you don't feel like playing tourist, how'd you like to go with me to pay a visit on an old friend?"

"An old friend? Here on St. Margaret?"

"Yep."

"Who?"

"Lady named Marie."

"An airline stewardess?"

"No," he said with a laugh. "Voodoo priestess."

Zoe gave him an incredulous look. "You've got to be kidding."

"No, ma'am."

"Where did you meet a voodoo priestess?" she asked. "If that's not too personal a question."

He shrugged. "What can I say, Zoe? I'm a friendly guy."

The Countryside

Mooky Blade had watched Jean Bien Dumont doing his thing for the better part of an hour now and he had to admit the cat put on quite a show—writhing on the ground like a snake, hissing and cursing and spewing venom, all for the benefit of the old witch hiding in the hole under the altar.

Jean Bien had pulled out all the stops. After drinking his potion, he'd struggled with the spirit, staggering about the temple, finally overcome by spasms. As Jean Bien had explained, once Dumballah had taken full possession of him, he'd become the snake.

"The mambo will fight against this," Jean Bien had said in his heavy French accent, "but she cannot win. My powers, they are too great."

Jean Bien Dumont might be the feared death priest, but his black magic sure wasn't greased lightning. After the first twenty minutes, Mooky had gotten bored and he'd retreated to the hammock at the edge of the clearing to wait for the spirits to fight it out. He'd even dozed a bit, but then he'd awakened, sat up in the hammock only to see old Jean Bien slithering and slobbering and making a god-awful noise. Mooky figured the old lady had either died of fright or was laughing her guts out. Either way, Mooky had had enough.

He swung his legs out of the hammock and sauntered over to the edge of the temple. Jean Bien's skin had turned powdery white from the dust, his eyes rolled back in his head and he was jabbering away in Haitian Creole. It sounded like gibberish. Mooky went over to the black magician turned snake and picked him up by the shoulders. Jean Bien's eyes rolled back in his head again and he coughed and wheezed a few times. Mooky gave the man a gentle shake.

"Okay, man, I think you've done enough for one day. You go on outside and calm yourself down. I'll take over now."

Jean Bien continued to babble, though more coherently. He seemed to be coming out of his trance. Even so, he was unable to stand, so Mooky half dragged, half carried him out of the hounfour, depositing him in an old wooden lawn chair next to the house. Then he returned to the temple.

Standing before the altar, he said in a loud voice, "Okay, mama, time to come out and talk business." He waited. "I know you're in there. Come on out. I don't got all day."

Still getting no response, Mooky took the rough-hewn altar and tilted it back, exposing the large hole. The old mambo was cowering, her eyes shining like animal eyes in a cave.

"Come on," he said impatiently. "You and me got to talk. I'm not going to hurt you, if you cooperate."

The old lady refused to budge, so Mooky reached down, got a hold of her bony arm and lifted her out of the hole as though he was pulling an opossum from its den. Marie didn't really struggle, though her body stiffened. When he deposited her on the ground, she sank to her knees at his feet, her head bowed.

"I want you to listen to me now," he said. "And you listen good, mama. I took the snake man away before he killed you and that makes me your friend. I expect a good turn from you now, so if you don't cooperate I'm going to have to bring the snake god back here to finish you off."

The old mambo was muttering something, but Mooky couldn't hear because her face was hidden. He reached down and turned her face up so he could see it.

"What you saying, mama?"

"Ko lo jee mo! Ko lo jee mo!"

"No, I don't want to hear no more of that shit. You speak English. You hear? And speak nice and loud so I can hear you. I'm going to ask you a question and you damned well better answer or I'm throwing you and the snake man back in the hole together. Understand?"

The old lady's eyes narrowed with hatred, but she didn't respond.

"When you were on the beach with Poppy that day, what did you see? Tell me everything and don't give me no stories, mama, or I'm going to throw your ass right back in that hole."

"Ko lo jee mo. Ko lo jee mo. Ko lo jee mo."

Mooky could see she wasn't taking him seriously, so he slapped her up against the side of the head. "You ain't listening, mama. Tell me what you saw."

The limo pulled up behind a black SUV and stopped. Andrew looked back at them.

"The old lady lives in a little house back through those trees," he said.

Billy peered in the direction the chauffeur pointed, then at the vehicle in front of them. "Looks like she has company."

"That's a rental. There are three on the island."

Billy glanced at Zoe, who seemed wary. "Feel like crashing a party?"

"You weren't kidding, then. We're coming to see a voodoo priestess?"

"Andrew?" he said to the driver.

"Her name's Marie Vincente de la Croix, Miss Marton, and she's a voodoo priestess all right."

Zoe shrugged. "How often do you get to visit a voodoo priestess with a rodeo cowboy?"

They got out of the limo, Billy taking her hand. As she brushed past him, he got a lungful of her compelling scent. "Have I mentioned how good you smell?" he asked, closing the door.

"No, and I don't think you should, either."

"In that case, I guess I won't." He leaned in the car window and told Andrew they'd probably only be a few minutes.

"Take your time, Mr. Blue, I'll have myself a little nap."

Billy slapped the door in acknowledgment, giving the man a wink. He turned to Zoe. The two of them began walking along the path. The house wasn't far. He could see the roofline through the trees.

He wasn't exactly sure what had prompted him to suggest a visit to the old woman except that it seemed like something different to do, something out of the ordinary. Plus, he'd felt badly about them almost running down the poor old dear the other evening. He'd been thinking about her, wondering if she was all right.

"Billy, do you hear that?" she said, stopping.

He did. It sounded like somebody having a terrible argument. A woman shrieking. A man's booming voice.

Zoe seemed reluctant to proceed.

"I think I'd better investigate," he said. "Wait here."

"No, I want to come."

The house was just ahead and Billy continued, with Zoe following.

"Are you sure we're not intruding?" she said. "Maybe it's some voodoo ritual."

"And maybe not."

They came to the house, but the altercation was coming

from somewhere in back. A woman shrieked with terror. Billy jogged around the house, despite the pain in his back. He came to a stop when he spotted three people under a large open-sided shed, essentially a rusty metal roof supported by poles, built right on the bare ground.

An older skinny guy was half sitting, half lying in the dust. Standing over him, holding on to the old voodoo lady, Marie, was a huge black guy in a black muscle shirt. The man on the ground seemed to be bleeding. The big man was clearly angry, he had the look of a pit bull with a snappish little lapdog in his teeth.

Zoe came up next to Billy. Seeing the trio, she said, "My God..."

About then Marie spotted them and began flailing her arms. "Ayza! Ayza!"

The man on the ground turned to see what she was looking at and, noticing Billy, grabbed a hold of the big man's leg to get his attention. Then he pointed.

The drama in the shed suddenly came to a halt. All three participants' attention was on Billy. Marie, still in the jaws of the pit bull, continued her lament, though softer now. "Ayza. Ayza. Ayza."

Billy, who'd been in more than his share of barroom brawls, sauntered toward them.

"Billy..." Zoe said.

"You stay back, sweetheart." Traversing the short distance to the shed, he stopped as he stepped from the sunshine into the shadow. "What's going on? What's the ruckus about?"

The huge man, his black skin gleaming, looked even more imposing close up. He stared at Billy incredulously.

"*Ayza*," Marie implored, "*aidez-moi!*"

The older guy tugged on the pant leg of the mountainous man, babbling something incoherent. He looked as if he was seeing a ghost. The big guy let go of Marie, who almost fell to the ground before catching her balance. She staggered toward Billy, falling at his feet and wrapping her arms around his leg.

"Bon Dieu! Bon Dieu, merci," she muttered.

Billy stared hard at the big guy, who stared hard at him. Being a former bull rider, Billy knew what it was like to face down a mountain of muscle, but he was also used to having the assistance of a couple of rodeo clowns and a fence he could leap over. Yet, despite being a near cripple, Billy fell back on old habits of taking the offense.

"What are you doing abusing this lady?" he asked.

"I'm not abusing nobody, man. I'm saving this poor old dude's ass. The old lady attacked him with a knife. Look at him. The mambo just pulled this blade out of her skirts and slashed the sorry bastard."

Billy peered down at Marie, who stared up, seemingly oblivious to what was being said. He wasn't going to get much help there. He turned his attention back to the behemoth. "This is Marie's place. What are you folks doing here?"

"The old dude came to do a ritual. I gave him a lift. Next thing I know, they're having this screaming fight and she attacks him. I stopped her from killing him, man. Wasn't for me, this could be a murder."

Again Billy looked at Marie.

"The bull and the snake," she muttered. "Erzulie Dantor, she save me with her knives."

"Huh?"

"Don't you know? The bull, he wants to kill me and you, too, Ayza."

Zoe came walking up. When Marie spotted her, she let out a yelp, cowering and clinging even closer to Billy's leg. But then she blinked up at Zoe.

"Oh, you not her." Then to Billy, "I thought it was the white witch who ride the bull."

Billy gave Zoe a woebegone look. "I think my friend's having a bad day."

"That's my impression, too," Zoe said. "It's been a while since I've been mistaken for a witch."

Marie pointed a bony finger at the two men. "They want to kill me, *monsieur*."

"Seems to me you fellas aren't accomplishing much here. I'll be damned if I know what's going on, but talk's not going to make it any better. How bad's your partner hurt?"

"Huh? What'd you say, man? I've got this hearing problem, so unless I see your lips, you've gotta speak real loud."

"I said, how bad's your partner hurt?" Billy said, raising his voice.

"Nothing serious, man. He's just slashed up a little. A few Band-Aids and he be fine. But it could have been worse. I'll take him to get fixed up."

"Yeah, I think that'd be a good idea."

The big man reached down and lifted his friend to his feet like he was a rag doll. The guy was wobbly, but managed to stand.

"That woman's a raving maniac," the big man said, pointing at Marie.

Then, holding his friend by the arm, he came toward them. Marie crawled around Billy's legs, keeping him between herself and the two men. As they neared, the behemoth stopped. "What's your name, man?"

"Billy Blue."

The big guy nodded, glancing over at Zoe. "That's what I thought." Then he trudged on, practically carrying his bloody sidekick.

"What's your name?" Billy called after the guy.

The man ignored him, continuing without so much as glancing back.

"That's got to be the biggest, most scary-looking man I've ever seen in my life," Zoe said under her breath.

"Looked ornery enough," Billy replied. He glanced down at Marie who, though calmer, hadn't quite found the courage to let go of him. "Ma'am? You all right?"

"Ayza," she said, smiling.

"No, ma'am, you got me confused with this Ayza last time, too," he said, bending over so he could look her in the face. "The name's Billy Blue and I'm from Elko, Nevada. We almost ran you down in the road. Remember?"

She nodded.

"And this is my friend Zoe. We called on you to see how you were doing."

"They tried to kill me."

"Looks like you did a pretty good number on the little guy, but the big fella looked like he was about to tear you limb from limb, I grant you."

"The bull wants to kill us both. You, *monsieur,* and me."

"Kill us? Now, why would they want to do something like that? I don't even know those folks."

"Billy," Zoe said, "don't you think she'd be more comfortable inside? The poor thing looks like she's been through hell."

"Yeah, I expect you're right." He leaned over again. "Marie, can you stand up? You aren't hurt, are you?"

She shook her head. Billy took her arm and helped her to her feet. Then the three of them made their way to the little house, entering the back door. The place was dark and cluttered like a junk store, every surface piled high with pots and bowls and jars and boxes. It was not dirty, but it was messy. And it was filled with exotic smells. Billy pulled a chair from the table and sat the old woman down in it. She looked up at him, her shoulders slumping.

Billy squatted beside her. "Is what happened out there something the police need to know about, Marie?" he asked.

Her eyes rounded. "Oh, no, *monsieur. Jamais. Je vous en pris!*"

"Sorry, ma'am, but I'm not too conversant with your voo-doo lingo."

"I think she was begging you not to involve the police," Zoe said.

"You speak her lingo?"

"It was French."

"Oh. Well, that's what I get for taking Spanish in high school."

Marie took his hand, gazing at him with imploring eyes. "You don't understand, I know, but it is true, *monsieur.* We

are in danger. The bull brought Jean Bien to kill me with black
magic. He serves the loa with both hands. Very evil.''

''Who's Jean Bien? The snake?''

''*Oui, monsieur*. The bull and the white witch want to kill
me. And you, Ayza.''

''Marie, I'm afraid you're a bit confused. Maybe somebody's after Ayza, but not me, not Billy Blue. And my friend
Zoe's anything but a witch.''

''No, not this one, the one who looks the same as her.''

Billy and Zoe exchanged glances.

He shook his head. ''I think all the excitement has gotten
you a little confused. Between that and the heat.''

''She looks thirsty,'' Zoe said. ''She'd probably like something to drink.''

''That's a thought. You want something to drink, Marie?''

The old woman pointed toward the small refrigerator sitting
on a heavy wooden crate against the wall. Zoe went over and
opened the door. She found an old glass juice bottle without
a label that appeared to contain tea. She held it up for Marie
to see. The old woman nodded and Zoe brought it to her.
Taking off the lid, Marie guzzled a healthy portion of the
contents. She seemed content.

''You reckon you'll be okay now?'' Billy asked her.

She tipped her head in assent.

''Maybe Zoe and I will be moving on, then. I'm real sorry
about your ordeal, but glad we came along when we did.''

Marie reached out and took his hand. ''I know you think I
am crazy, but it is not true. I saw the white man die. The son
did it, then he sends the bull to kill me and the bull brings the
snake. And Ayza sends you, Monsieur Billy. But I have this
terrible dream. You are in great danger. Very great danger.
You must believe me.''

''Well, I'll keep an eye out for the bull, if that'll make you
feel better.''

''Death comes, *monsieur*. On his horse. The same as when
I was in the sea with Poppy. The man in the white suit.''

Again Billy and Zoe exchanged looks.

He patted Marie's shoulder. "Everything'll work out. I think you need a good rest and you'll be right as rain."

The mambo said, "I know the future. It is a gift of the spirits."

"Usually my fortune is a little more hopeful than what you've been touting," he said.

"You must believe me, *monsieur*."

"It'd be a whole lot easier if you had a dream about a painting worth a hundred million. Or me meeting a beautiful lady on an exotic island."

The old woman shook her head sadly.

"That's a shame. How about Zoe, then? See anything interesting in the cards for her?"

The mambo extended her hand to Zoe, taking her fingers. She ran her gnarled thumb over them, then turned over Zoe's hand. After running her finger over the lines in Zoe's palm, she looked up at Billy and said, "This one has a great secret."

"That so?" he said, glancing at Zoe. "What kind of secret?"

"I do not know. But wait for the truth, *monsieur*. It is very important. Wait for the truth."

"That it?"

"She is afraid and it is hard to read her heart."

"You may be onto something there, Marie. I've been thinking the very same thing." He gave Zoe a wink, but she seemed not to see the humor in it.

"I'm glad you're having so much fun with this," she said dryly.

"You're right, we may have worn out our welcome." Billy stood, struggling a little as he stretched his back. "Anything you need before we go?" he asked the old woman.

Marie shook her head.

Billy glanced around. "How about food? You got enough on hand?"

"You already saved my life, Monsieur Billy Blue."

"That's a bit of an exaggeration, but if it was true, it'd be a terrible shame if you should turn around and starve to

death." He removed his wallet from his hip pocket and too
out a twenty-dollar bill. "I expect there's a market where yo
can stock up." He took out another twenty, then handed he
both bills. "Here, take this."

The old woman shook her head, refusing the money.

"It's okay, Marie. Consider it a little gift from Ayza."

He put the two bills down on the table. Then, patting Mari
on the shoulder, he took Zoe's arm and they headed for th
door. Once they were out in the sunlight, they made their wa
back through the trees toward the waiting limo.

"So," he said, slipping his arm around her waist and play
fully bumping his hip against hers, "what's your secret?"

"Billy, the poor old woman was half-delirious."

"Yeah, but some people have a gift, Zoe. My grandmothe
was a firm believer in fortune-telling and some of it rubbe
off on me. I think the mambo is onto something. I know
you've got a secret. So, give."

Zoe smiled. "It would hardly be a secret if I told you, now
would it?"

Queenstown

"Isn't that ironic?" Dani said as she glanced out the ope
window of the London Bridge Café. "You had two of th
three right in your hands, I had the third and we didn't do
one of them."

"I also had two witnesses," Mooky said. "Three, countin
the chauffeur out in the road."

"Aren't you concerned about what they saw you doing t
the old lady?"

"They didn't see much and she's obviously crazy as a loo
Besides, I'm not going to do the cowboy without the dow
payment. If Chucky wants him dead, he's going to have t
come up with the money first."

Dani sighed. "What's this about a broad who looks lik
me? You said she was with the cowboy?"

"Yeah and it was crazy. I look up, I see her behind him and I thought it was you, bringing the lamb to the slaughter, but then I saw it wasn't you. Up close I could see the difference easy, but at a distance, fuck, babe, it was you."

"Was she prettier than me?"

"No, you're the better woman, no contest."

"You're just saying that, Mooky."

"I saw her, Dani, and she was definitely good-looking. She'd have to be if she looked like you. But don't you think I'd take my own wife?"

"Not necessarily."

"Dani…"

"Never mind, I'm just checking."

"I ever two-time you, even once?"

"No, and you damned well better not or I'll cut off your black balls."

Mooky shook his head. "Somehow we got off on the wrong track."

Dani slowly nodded. "It's my fault. I got jealous. Never mind. Let's get back to business. So, the witch doctor was a bust."

"Big bust. But at least I've got the sonovabitch on a plane and out of here. That was one of the dumbest ideas I ever had. I don't know what I was thinking."

She took his hand. "This whole thing is dumb, Mook. Let's blow this place. Seriously."

"You afraid?"

"Afraid, my ass. It's too squirrely. Everybody and everything about it. Christ, the cops are on to us, even if they don't know what they're doing."

"They spot you?"

"After I'd been in town for a while. I think they're outside now."

Mooky stared out the window, thinking. He took a good long while. "I'll tell you what, we have one more conversation with Chucky and if it don't pan out, then we split. If he comes up with the bread, we do the job and go."

"All three of them? Why Poppy? She doesn't know shit."

"I don't think Van Biers is going to buy that the politician'
wife doesn't know anything, just because you say so."

"She doesn't, I'd bet anything on it."

"It's not because she's pregnant, is it?"

"Fuck you, Mooky," she snapped. "I ever go soft on a jol
for sentimental reasons? Even once?"

"No, you're hard as nails. If either of us has a weak stom
ach at times, it's me."

"So, you know where I'm coming from, then. I just don'
like this job."

"Yeah." Mooky reflected. Then, after a minute, he said
"All I ask is one more conversation with Chucky. That don'
work out, we do it your way."

"We split?"

"We split."

The Countryside

Charles roared up the mountain, cutting corners at th
curves as usual, when Mayte's BMW came out of nowher
and they nearly collided. He half spun out, his Porsche coming
to a stop against the embankment. Mayte continued down th
mountain, probably cussing him out.

"Damn bitch," he said. It didn't matter that he'd been o
the wrong side of the road.

Charles sat for a moment trying to decide what to do. H
had been on his way to the office to get the twenty-five gran
he needed to pay Mooky Blade. But if Mayte was heade
home, he could talk to her there. Turning the Porsche aroun
on the narrow road, Charles went roaring back down the hill
He wouldn't be able to catch her before she reached the gate
of the estate, no matter how fast he drove, so he didn't pres
it.

As he came to a horseshoe curve a quarter of a mile fron
the bottom of the mountain, he saw the BMW head towar

town rather than back toward the plantation. Charles wondered where the hell she could be going.

Moments later he came to the crossroads and decided to follow Mayte. But, rather than try to catch her, he hung back to see where she was going. His curiosity was aroused when she didn't go into town, instead taking the bypass road leading to the southern portion of the island. Could his beloved stepmother be headed for some secret rendezvous? he wondered.

Charles was surprised when she parked in a lot at a public beach, especially considering the way she was dressed, in work clothes. He pulled down a side track across the road and left his car hidden in the trees. Then he took off down the beach in pursuit of Mayte, keeping to the edge of the palms so that she wouldn't spot him.

Charles couldn't believe his stroke of luck. It certainly would be handy to find out who was giving the bitch those whisker burns.

Biloxi Plantation

The one bad thing about being a cowboy was the god-awful farmer tan that went with it. Billy stood out on the lawn in the swimsuit he'd borrowed from the visitors wardrobe along with the flip-flops that were a size too small. With one of his western shirts worn as a cover-up, he felt and looked like a geek. Damned if a cowboy wasn't at a terrible disadvantage in civilian duds.

Not that Billy was such a hick that he couldn't wear regular clothes. He'd worn a tuxedo on a couple of occasions and more than one woman had told him he looked pretty hunky. Shelly had said she'd been in love with him from the first time he'd spoken to her, but seeing him in a white dinner jacket the night of the junior prom had sealed the deal. But standing on his old man's lawn in the Caribbean, his feet and legs and torso as white as bread dough, Billy didn't feel like Mr. Cool. He almost hoped Zoe had some white flesh to hide, as well.

It was sad when a fella was this vain, but Billy Blue always prided himself on his physical appeal and there was little chance of changing his attitude now.

Naturally, when he'd asked Zoe if she wanted to check out the beach, he'd been thinking more about her in a swimsuit than himself in one. Maybe that was the price of lust. It also highlighted the fact that he'd been unsuccessful in keeping his mind off her and on business. There was something about the woman, though, something he couldn't resist. Was it the same old thing? he wondered. Keeping after a pretty girl until she couldn't say no any longer? Taking satisfaction in the final conquest?

Somehow he didn't think so. This thing with Zoe felt different. He actually hated it that she was married. He wanted her to be available, though what for, exactly, was hard to say. Being with her was the thing. He wanted to hear her voice and see her smile. It almost didn't matter what they talked about or what they did, as long as they were together.

She must have sensed that something like that was churning inside him because of the way she'd questioned his motives. When he'd asked if she felt safe enough around him to go for a swim, she'd been pretty direct in her reply.

"What do you have in mind?"

"In mind? A swim."

"No, besides that."

"Nothing besides that."

"Really?"

He'd rubbed his chin, until he remembered his old man had the same mannerism. "Isn't it good enough that I sort of like you and there aren't all that many trustworthy folks in the neighborhood I can be friends with?"

"Sounds like a line to me. A rather bad one, actually. Besides, you're forgetting, I work for the enemy."

"Except for that, you seem trustworthy."

Zoe had laughed. "All right, Billy Blue, I'll go to the beach with you, as long as you don't misunderstand my motives in accepting your invitation."

"Which are?"

"Friendship, same as yours."

Zoe had a bit of an edge, which he liked. He couldn't call her sweet-tempered, though there was a softness about her under the surface. And there was also something going on in her head he hadn't been able to figure out. Maybe she did have a secret. Maybe the mambo was right.

Just then Esther Tye came out of the servants' quarters on her way to the main house. She made a detour from the path in order to say hello.

"Looks like you're going for a swim, Mr. Blue," she said.

"Yes, Zoe and I are going to check out the beach."

"She's a nice lady, Ms. Marton is."

"That she is. Very nice."

Esther smiled. "You mean nice the way I think you mean nice? If I'm not asking something too personal."

Billy shrugged. "Zoe's a married woman."

"Yes, but she's getting a divorce."

"She is?"

"That's what she told me. Said in a week's time it'll be official, if I remember right. Maybe a fortnight."

"Well, I'll be…"

"Didn't you know?"

Billy shook his head. "She said she was married, but didn't mention anything about a divorce."

Again Esther smiled. "Maybe she thought she didn't know you well enough to tell you she'd be available soon."

Billy rubbed his jaw. "Maybe not."

"Guess I let the cat out of the bag."

He smiled back at her. "It's always nice to know a person's secrets, isn't it?"

"Depends what you do with the information, now, doesn't it, Mr. Blue?" She tossed her head toward the house. "I got to get inside and go to work. Enjoy your swim."

Billy thanked her. He figured he would. He'd enjoy it a lot more than he would have thought only minutes ago. Filled with a curious joy, he wondered if that was Zoe's secret. She might be married at the moment, but not for long. As far as Billy was concerned, that seemed real fine.

Bristol Beach

Mayte sat on the bed, her shoes off, her legs crossed. Jerome, in shirtsleeves, leaned against the doorframe leading to the bath, appraising her, his arms folded over his chest. Though he hadn't yet said much of anything, she felt distance. And distance from a man was frightening when you needed him, counted on him. Jerome had been her reserve, her fallback position, her rock. She'd believed she could count on him...until now. Uncertainty had begun to creep in and it really, really scared her.

"Why don't you just level with me, Mayte?" he finally said. "We've been dancing around the subject for weeks."

"I'd love to, Jerome. I'd love to more than anything. But don't you see what an awkward position I'm in? I'm stuck between a rock and a hard place."

"Why did you ask to see me?"

She lowered her eyes and sighed deeply. "I suppose I feel the need for reassurance."

"What kind of reassurance? Immunity from prosecution?"

She looked up at him, her eyes flashing. "That was certainly kind."

"Well, what do you expect? I'm in a bit of a corner myself. You've been vague from the beginning. I don't know what your intentions are...really are...and everything around us seems to be crumbling."

"I thought you loved me, Jerome."

"I do love you, but sometimes I think you simply use that as a form of bloody insurance."

She got to her feet, shaking with anger, frustration, fear. "What do you want from me?"

Jerome stared at her for a long while before he walked over and took her in his arms. Once her face was buried in his shoulder, the tears began to flow, but she didn't cry. She couldn't surrender completely, not until she was sure she could trust him.

Her lover stroked her head. "Maybe it's time for the truth," he said. "Once everything is on the table, then we'll be able to figure out what to do."

Mayte knew that was easy for him to say, even if he was well-meaning. She was the one with the most at risk. And it involved a lot more than just financial security and happiness. In a very real sense, her life was at stake.

"Things are getting very shaky at the bank," she said, modulating her voice to sound calm and businesslike. "Simon has done things that are questionable, some of which I'm aware of, others I was out of the loop. There's a chance everything will crash, and if that happens, Simon will disappear. He thinks he can hold things together because of the Van Gogh, but now there are problems even with that."

"Good Lord," Jerome said.

"Naturally I feel a certain loyalty to my husband," she continued, stepping back so she could look into his eyes. "And of course to the bank. I want to do what's right, but I've been squeezed into a difficult position, Jerome, a position where I'm forced to choose. I guess what's kept me going is the long-term view. I've seen myself coming out of this mess and ending up with you. That's what I really want."

"Is it, Mayte?" he asked, taking her face in his hands.

"Yes."

"And you have doubts about that?"

"Being a mistress is a very precarious existence," she replied. "So much more so when your lover is the president of a country and he's up for reelection."

"My feelings for you go far beyond that."

"Do they, Jerome?"

He looked her dead in the eye in that sincere manner that every politician worth his salt could affect without half trying. "What is it you want, darling? Tell me what you want to happen."

"If the bank goes under and Simon takes off, the people of St. Margaret will be left holding the bag. You'll have to put the operation in somebody's hands. I'd like that somebody to be me."

"Can you come out of it with clean hands?" he asked. "I'd have to make a case that you're the person for the job."

"It depends on how honorable Simon chooses to be. It's always possible that he and Charles will try to gang up on me, say I'm involved in their shenanigans when I'm not."

"What shenanigans are we talking about, Mayte? Financial irregularities, or something else?"

Mayte lowered her eyes. She knew she'd reached the moment of truth, so did she duck the question or did she meet it head-on? "That's what scares me," she replied. "I'm not sure. I'm not sure what they might have done."

For the first time she saw coldness in Jerome Hurst's eyes, as well as uncertainty. "Are we talking about Raymond Pearson?" he asked, his voice trembling slightly.

She did all she could possibly do, she shrugged.

Jerome closed his eyes.

"I don't know anything for certain," she quickly added. "But I'm...well, I'm afraid."

"Murder? Simon?"

"I honestly don't know."

"But why?"

"Simon and Pearson were at odds over some business issue. It probably had to do with the painting, but that's speculation. Jerome, it really scared me when I heard Pearson's body was found and that he'd been murdered."

Jerome Hurst stared off. He was clearly shaken. Mayte knew she'd taken a terrible risk opening this particular can of worms, but she also knew that if things were to blow up, she'd be in the middle of the rubble. This way she had a chance of cutting her losses, maybe even coming out of the mess unscathed. It all depended on Jerome. How much he really loved her.

"If that turns out to be the case—Simon and Pearson, I mean—then it's a very different kettle of fish, Mayte."

Her heart sank. "What do you mean?"

"It would be very hard for me to get in your corner. Guilt by association, I mean."

"Are you saying I'm branded by my husband's sins?"

"Don't you think it would look odd to the world if I were to put you in charge?"

"Never mind how it would look to the world. I want to know how it would look to you."

"You know my feelings for you."

"I'm not so sure I do."

"You've got to trust me," he said.

"Tell me what I want to hear, what I need to hear."

"I love you, Mayte."

"And we'll be together?"

"Yes, we'll be together."

"When?"

"Right after the election."

"Thank you," she said. "And you know what? I love you, too."

He kissed her. "Now I've got to run." Jerome touched her cheek. "Don't worry, love. Everything will work out all right."

"Do you promise?"

"I promise."

Jerome Hurst left then. After she'd heard the front door open and close, she sat on the bed and picked up her purse. Opening it, she turned off the mini tape recorder inside. Pressing the rewind button, she waited. When the tape was at the beginning, she pushed the play button. The first sounds were of a door opening, then footsteps, then Jerome Hurst's voice. "Mayte, darling, you beat me here for once."

* * *

Biloxi Plantation

"I promise you," Zoe said, "you'll be red as a lobster if you don't put on sunscreen."

Billy lay on his beach towel, propped up on his elbows, ostensibly looking at the gentle breakers rolling in, though in fact he'd been giving her sideward glances, subtly watching her applying lotion to her own shoulders, arms and legs. Zoe was in a hot-pink bikini that made him feel weak in the stomach. God, he liked what he saw. But more than that, he liked the person he was getting to know, even if she was holding back.

It had given him a lift when he learned that she was getting a divorce. He felt like a new man. Maybe he had a chance, after all. Of course, it wasn't a good sign that she'd wanted him to believe she was married. For some reason, she'd been trying to keep her distance from him. Just why, he wasn't sure. Maybe it was because of him, or maybe it was something else. Whatever was going on, it had put her at war with herself and at odds with him.

But Billy also sensed a softening in her attitude. Was she lowering her guard? Knowing women as he did, he was hopeful.

"All right," he said, relenting, "I'll put some on."

Zoe grinned sardonically, handing him the tube. "Getting smart in your old age, are you?"

"Just never mention this to the boys on the circuit."

"Billy, I'd never destroy your manly image on purpose."

"Now you're making fun of me," he said, smearing lotion over his pale skin.

"Don't take it personally. I have fun chiding guys about their macho bullshit."

"Your husband must love that."

"Oh, I rub him the wrong way at times. It's inevitable."

He grinned with secret knowledge and finished putting lotion everywhere he could reach. "How about our backs? I'll do you, if you do me."

Billy could see her trying to decide whether to reject the offer outright or accept it without comment. These baby steps toward intimacy couldn't be lost on her. The question in her mind had to be whether her position was stronger if she ignored them or took a stand.

"Okay," she said, signaling her decision.

For Billy the only question was whether she chose to secretly enjoy being touched or genuinely believed in her own indifference. He bet it was a little of both. "You first?"

"Fine," she said.

Zoe rolled onto her stomach, reached back and unfastened her top. It was amazing how much more naked a woman could look if just a half an inch of fabric was removed from her skin. Billy, dutifully giving her butt an admiring glance, knelt beside her and proceeded to squeeze lotion onto her back. She purred at the cool sensation. He began rubbing the cream into her skin, carefully working her shoulders and the small of her back, running his thumbs firmly up her spine.

"Billy, you're supposed to be putting on sunscreen, not giving me a massage."

"You don't like it?"

"No."

"All right," he said, giving her butt a slap.

"Hey!" she protested, glaring back at him. "You're out of line."

"Sorry, it was too inviting a target. I'll try to get control."

She reached back to fasten her strap. "I didn't come with you for fun and games, you know. I took you at your word on the friendship thing."

"I apologize."

He lay facedown on his towel and Zoe got up. She applied some lotion to his back in a businesslike fashion, with the dispassion of an army nurse.

"Not to prolong your agony or anything," he said, "but I haven't been able to get any therapy on my back for several days. I couldn't talk you into rubbing it a little extra, could I?"

"Is this a ploy?"

"No, swear to God, Zoe. Can't you see the scars?"

She relented, rubbing his back with greater care, perhaps even tenderness, though he was sure she wouldn't have framed it that way. He groaned, doing his best not to make it sound like a sigh of pleasure, though her touch did feel damned good.

"What happened to you, exactly? Did a bull step on you or something?"

"You put me in a difficult position," he said. "Would you feel better about me if I was politic, or would you prefer the cold hard truth?"

When she didn't answer his question he glanced back at her and saw that she was in a quandary. He could almost hear her asking herself whether it was smarter to play or not play his game.

"Let's have the truth," she said bravely.

"Okay, the truth it is. I was having an affair with my boss's wife. Good ol' Luther got wind of it and he and a bunch of ruffians waylaid me and damned near beat me to death. Considering the inconvenience to the lady, I'd have rather been stepped on by a bull, but that wasn't what happened. I ended up paying for my sins with a stint in the hospital."

"You're kidding."

"No, ma'am. Connie was cheating and I was helping her cheat. Some would say I got what I deserved."

Zoe sat back on her own towel. Billy turned his head to confirm the surprise on her face.

"I can see I've disillusioned you."

"No," she said. "I just wasn't prepared for such a frank admission."

"You asked for the truth."

"I guess I did, didn't I?"

"You weren't under any illusions that I was a saint, I hope."

She smiled at that. "No, not at all."

"Let me tell you my philosophy, Zoe. I've found over the years that if you pretend to be something you aren't, you end up getting bit in the ass anyway, so you might as well be what you are and let the chips fall where they may."

"An honest lech is better than a dishonest one, I guess."

"I won't try to defend the life I've lived," he said, "but I am a single fella."

"But she was married."

"She propositioned me, not the other way around...not that it makes a difference, I suppose. But I make it a policy to avoid situations where somebody might get hurt, if I possibly can."

"Looks like you failed. Did she get beat up, too?"

"I miscalculated. It was a bad mistake."

"I guess it's admirable that you can admit it."

"I'd like to think you can see the good in me as well as the bad."

"Well, I don't think you deserve a medal, Billy."

"I don't want a medal, I just want to be able to live with the truth, not feel I've got to lie to win a person's respect. I mean, I could have given you a song and dance, maybe even tricked you into believing I'm a thirty-four-year-old virgin. And, Zoe, despite any suspicions you might have on our wedding night, eventually—after our third kid, maybe—you'd figure me out, divorce me and I'd end up back here in the Caribbean, giving some other pretty girl the same song and dance, except that I'd be stuck with alimony and child-support payments on top of everything else. This way there's an outside chance you'll love me for who I am, saving us both a lot of trouble."

Zoe laughed, really laughed, shaking her head. "Billy, you are one of a kind."

"The logic's sound, isn't it?"

"No, actually it's badly flawed."

"How so?"

"You're forgetting. I'm married."

"Oh, yeah. Your husband. I keep putting him out of my mind."

"Husbands can get in the way of a man's plans, can't they?" she said, lying down and staring up at the blue sky.

Billy rolled onto his side, propping up his head on his elbow. He took in the length of her body, from her pink toenails to the tiny beads of perspiration forming on her brow, savoring the curves in between. He wanted nothing more than to kiss her, but that was old news. He was in a battle for her mind and her heart. Probably in that order.

"Let me ask you a hypothetical question," he said. "Let's say your poor husband got hit by a truck or something, heaven forbid. And let's say the grieving passed and you and I met on a tropical beach and we traded the kindness of applying sunscreen to each other's backs."

"You're really into fiction, aren't you?"

"Let me finish. So, we talk a little and you know everything about me that you presently know. Say further that I say to you, 'Zoe, I can't recall ever meeting a woman I was more attracted to. Would you do me the honor of having dinner with me tonight?' What would be your response?"

"Thanks, but no thanks."

"Really?"

"Really."

"Why?"

After he was silent for several moments, she rolled her head toward him. She gave him a pretty smile, the sensuousness of her lips accentuated by the fact that her eyes were masked by sunglasses.

She drew a deep breath, her chest rising slightly, her stomach flattening. "Billy," she said, "you aren't my type."

He blinked. "That's all?"

"Isn't that enough?"

He considered that. "Maybe you don't know me."

"Well enough."

"You don't like cowboys."

"That's not exactly it."

"I'm too stupid?"

"No, you're a lot more clever than I first thought."

"You think I'm a womanizer."

"Well, that doesn't help."

"I'll bet I'm no more of a womanizer than your husband, and you put up with him, don't you?"

"That doesn't mean I like it," she snapped.

He grinned.

Zoe rolled her head away in frustration. "Enough games, Billy, okay?"

"One last question. Say, hypothetically, I turn out to be the proud owner of a hundred-million-dollar Van Gogh..."

"Would you be my type then?"

"Something like that."

"You want to know if I'm mercenary in other words."

"Women tend to call it practical, but I'll go with your definition."

Zoe thought for several moments. "You know, in your way, you're kind of a bastard."

"And a womanizer. But right now we're trying to figure out what you are."

"You won't like my answer," she said.

"What is it?"

"I'm inscrutable, Billy." With that she got up and walked off toward the water, swinging her ass just enough to make him groan in agony.

He didn't know if he had her number, but she definitely had his.

World Headquarters,
Victoria International Bank

Mayte Van Biers was alone in the building, sitting at her desk, staring through the glass wall at the ingenious work of a crazy, penniless Dutch painter—a hundred-and-twelve-year-old chunk of canvas, oil and pigment that could and had made or broken lives and fortunes, including, perhaps, her own. How bizarre to think that the key to the puzzle could very well lie in the hands of a rodeo cowboy.

And because of Billy Blue, she was now standing on the

brink of destruction, unsure who to trust or which way to leap. As she so often did when facing a major life decision, Mayte tried to envision different scenarios. She saw herself in a palatial home in Rio, overlooking the Bay of Guanabara, controlling a portfolio worth tens of millions with a laptop computer. She also saw herself as the president of Victoria International Bank and the first lady of St. Margaret, adored by a husband who flattered her with whispered promises that she would succeed him in office. And of course, if neither scenario worked out, she still had ten years to make it on Wall Street, knocking heads and gaining enough clout to earn a golden parachute before she hit fifty.

There were other possible scenarios—unfortunately, some disastrous. The one she wouldn't accept was to spend her remaining years in jail with some redneck slob who'd killed her mother or her child for a hundred thousand dollars of insurance money. Mayte was no killer, but she'd kill almost anybody before she'd endure that.

"Well, Mummy dearest, aren't you the picture of contemplation?" Charles stood at the door to her office, a grin that spelled trouble on his face. "Sex or money or both?"

"Fuck you, Charles."

"Well, Mum, if you insist…"

"Cut the crap. What do you want?"

"That seventy-five we talked about this morning."

"Charles, there is no way on earth I can get you that kind of money."

"Have you tried?"

"It's not possible."

His expression darkened and he came over to the desk, leaning across it so his face was close to hers. "Listen, bitch, there are two witnesses to Pearson's murder who have to be eliminated, and a fucking cowboy who'll bring down the goddamn bank if he isn't whacked. I've made it my responsibility to see that these problems are solved, but you've got to come through with the bucks."

"You're paying somebody to kill your brother, too?

Charles, your father's taking care of Billy. He doesn't want you to—''

"Fuck that, Mayte. By the time my old man gets out of his rocker, it'll be too late. The only way to solve this problem is to get rid of him."

"Well, count me out."

"Isn't it a little late for that? You're in this the same as me, right up to your sweet tits. Blade won't do a thing without getting paid and we don't have the luxury of time, not with Pearson's body having been found."

"You certainly fucked that up by the way."

"Yeah, well, it was a chance thing. The point is we've got to move and move fast or we're all going to the gallows."

"There's nothing I can do, Charles. I'm out of the loop. You'll have to talk to your father."

"And what am I supposed to say? That Mayte's too busy fucking Jerome Hurst to tend to company business?"

Her insides froze. "What are you talking about?"

"Oh, come on, Mums, you think you can fuck the president of the country without me knowing? I've got my finger in everything. All those trips to Bristol Beach—are you saying they were to confer about affairs of state? I don't think so. Now, if adultery turns you and the prez on, fine. No skin off my teeth. Hell, you've got my blessing. But if I'm going to save our collective ass, I need a little cooperation from the lady with the purse strings. If you can't find seventy-five measly grand, maybe I should go ask for a loan from Jerome."

"Are you threatening me, Charles?"

"What do you think?"

"I think you're insane."

"I think you're a hot piece of ass, but seeing as I'm not into incest—though I could be persuaded, maybe—I'll settle for the seventy-five thou. Get me the money, get it now, so I can take care of business. We can discuss your sex life later."

"There's not that much cash in the building."

"How much can you come up with?"

"I don't know. Twenty, twenty-five, maybe."

"Simon's got some at home, doesn't he?"

"I believe so," she replied, "but I have no idea how much."

"Get me everything you have here, and I'll go make a down payment on Tex's ass. You get the rest from Pops, so I'll have it to pay off Blade as soon as he does the deed."

Mayte's head was spinning, but it wouldn't land on a clear, logical thought. All she knew for sure was that she needed to buy time, to sort this out. "Okay, I'll give you what we've got."

"I knew logic would prevail." He smiled. "If you don't mind me asking, how is Jerome in the sack, anyway? He's black and he's a politician. The sucker must hang all the way to his knees."

"Charles, you are absolutely disgusting."

He grinned. "Don't you know that's what makes me so popular with the ladies?"

She rose and moved around the desk, headed for the safe. As she went by, Charles reached out and grabbed her ass. Mayte spun and slapped his face. His fist shot back and hit her square on the jaw, decking her. She lay sprawled on the floor, her head spinning as she stared up at him, incredulous.

"I think we're even now, Mum. After you clobbered me with that bucket this morning, I've had a fucking headache all day long."

He offered her his hand, which she ignored. As she stood weaving, trying to clear her head, Charles moved behind her, encircling her with his arms, cupping her breasts and kissing her neck. Mayte peeled his hands off her, swallowed her gorge and staggered off to get the money.

Biloxi Plantation

Zoe swam until she was thoroughly exhausted. With the sun sinking toward the horizon, she waded to the shore. Billy, still on his towel and propped on his elbows, watched her emerge from the water, his eyes on her like a duck on a june bug, as his grandmother used to say.

Damned if the guy wasn't full of surprises. It seemed as if every time she was with him he did or said something to make her take a little more notice. She was beginning to see that the guy had some substance, though he was clearly what he confessed to be—a good-time Joe. It was not surprising that she found him attractive, though. With a guy like Billy, it was practically a given. What did surprise, though, was that she was beginning to enjoy the game. She felt a compulsion to play with him, a niggling the-hell-with-it impulse. Whenever she got that feeling, she knew she was in for trouble.

It had been like that with Ahmed. Every rational fiber of her being had told her that a torrid affair with the man was plenty and that marriage was lunacy. Yet she'd put her finger in the fire. There had to be a reason why a woman who was otherwise sensible would willingly put herself in emotional danger. But what was it?

All Billy Blue could offer her was a good time. Zoe was long past the raging-hormone stage. She had enough life experience that she didn't obsess over the notion of sex with an attractive man. She was fully capable of walking away. So, why didn't she?

Zoe recalled a conversation she'd had with her father when she was leaving for college. "There are only two ways to live," Laszlo Marton had said. "Safely and dangerously. The trick is not to choose one over the other, it is to find the right balance. To live too safely is not to live at all. To live too dangerously can cost you your life." Ironically, her father never could find the right balance, but he had been a good teacher. He'd helped her to understand the forces tugging at her soul. Zoe knew that a guy like Billy Blue who was both safe and dangerous made a woman want to listen to her heart. Who didn't want to be loved? The Billy Blues of the world made it a little too easy.

"I thought maybe you'd decided to swim to Mexico," he said as she approached.

"You can't get rid of me quite that easily," she said, picking up her towel and drying her face.

"Now, why would I want to do that, when I've gone to so much trouble to be your friend?"

Zoe spread the towel back out again and dropped down beside him. "You know," she said, looking out at the water "euphemisms about sex are the worst euphemisms of all."

"What euphemism?"

"Friendship. You're an admitted womanizer, Billy."

"So naturally everything I do and say has to be seen in that light."

"Seems logical."

"This is going to seem self-serving, I know, but I have to correct a faulty impression. I have a reputation as a womanizer and, in all fairness, I probably have been one since I was eighteen. But my recent experiences have changed me."

"Oh, you're a reformed womanizer."

"Basically."

Zoe couldn't help smiling.

"You don't believe me."

"I always thought a leopard didn't change its spots."

"Ever heard of Saul?"

"Oh, you've found religion, too?"

He didn't look pleased. "You know what your problem is Zoe? You talk out of both sides of your mouth."

"Meaning?"

"Meaning you're trying to drive me away so that I'm the one to decide and you don't have to wrestle with the problem."

The accusation offended her. "You flatter yourself, Billy."

"No, I just can tell when somebody's trying to go in two different directions at the same time."

Again, his insight surprised her. Safe and dangerous. It went back to what her father had said. But it wasn't easy to surrender to your own desires, not when so much was at stake. "You forget, I'm unavailable."

"Are you?"

She wasn't sure whether he was alluding to her divorce or her lack of commitment to Ahmed. Either was possible, assuming he'd somehow found out about the state of her marriage. "Am I that important a conquest?" she asked.

"Do we have to put it in those terms?"

"You tell me what you want, Billy, if it isn't sex."

He studied her for a long minute, then he said, "You know, sometimes things just aren't meant to work out, are they?" Another long pause, then he continued. "Maybe the timing's wrong. Or maybe the chemistry's off. I don't know why we aren't clicking."

"Every woman's not going to fall in love with you. It's unrealistic to expect that they will."

"Shoot, I know that. What bothers me about us is it doesn't have to be this way. I can tell I'm a problem for you, so, out of respect, I'll back off. I apologize for any unhappiness I may have caused. If we're to be friends, seems to me we're going to have to do it from afar."

Zoe could tell he was speaking from the heart. Or seemed to be. And everything he said was true. Yes, she had forced him to make the decision, and it was just as well. She said, "I appreciate your consideration."

"Would it be ungentlemanly of me if I were to leave you now?"

"No, not at all."

"If you'll excuse me then."

Billy got up and began trudging across the small beach to the base of the cliff. She watched him make his way up the wooden stairway rising thirty feet to the lawn above. He did not look back. Once he was out of sight, Zoe lay back down in the sand and stared at the variegated clouds overhead, tinged with color from the setting sun.

What had just happened was for the best, she decided, even as she felt twinges of regret. There was enough danger in her life without risking her emotions on Billy Blue.

* * *

Newquay Bay

Charles Van Biers opened the case and gestured matter-of-factly toward the bundles of cash. "The down payment on the cowboy."

Mooky Blade looked into the man's cold blue eyes. "You mean on your brother, don't you?"

When Charles ignored the comment, Mooky picked up a bundle and idly riffled through it, glancing over at Dani as he did. She did not look happy. That didn't please him. He and his wife had always been of one mind on their work. Always.

"Let's talk about this, man," he said to Charles.

"What's to talk about?"

"The two women."

"Yeah?"

"The pregnant one, Poppy, don't know shit. The old lady is so dingy, it don't matter what she saw."

"Easy for you to say, Blade. Your neck isn't on the block."

"So you say kill them, just in case."

"You have a problem with that? It's what I've paid you to do."

"How about we do the mambo and the cowboy? After we do the hit you only owe twenty-five more."

"And when Poppy suddenly remembers everything and goes to the police, then what?"

"I do her for free, so she can't testify."

"You'll come waltzing back to St. Margaret to do a hit, just like that, take the risk for free. And I'm supposed to believe you."

"Look, man, what choice you got? Me and Dani could pick up and go home right now, take your money with us. But instead, I'm being straight with you. I know my business. The pregnant one don't know shit."

"It's true she was there at the beach," Dani interjected, "but the old lady was trying to protect her from the evil spirits and wouldn't let her look at the shore. All she saw was Pearson before he was killed."

Charles raked his eyes up and down her in a manner Mooky didn't much appreciate. "All right then," he said, "I'll trust you. The old lady and the cowboy. Twenty-five more when the job's done. What's the plan?''

''The plan is our business,'' Mooky said. ''Arranging the money is yours.''

''Can you do it soon?''

''Pretty soon.''

''How about tomorrow?''

''We'll let you know when, man. Just be ready. Dani will contact you. Have twenty-five grand ready.''

''I'm ready right now, Blade.''

''That's good, Chucky. All you got to do is sit tight and leave everything else to us. Now, we got any more business to discuss?''

''Yeah. How about we head over to the Speak Easy? Drinks tonight on me.'' He looked at Dani as he said it.

''Thanks,'' Mooky said, ''but we've got work to do, seeing that you're in such a big hurry. You're going to have to party on your own.''

Van Biers's eyes were still on Dani. ''That's a shame. I like the way you two dance.''

''Maybe next trip,'' Mooky said, getting to his feet.

Charles reluctantly stood as well. ''Next trip.'' He looked back and forth between them, but mostly at Dani, grinning the whole time. ''Well, I'll be going then. Don't make me wait too long for that call.''

''Just have the money ready.''

Charles Van Biers left. Mooky glanced over at his brooding wife. She did not speak.

''I know you don't like this, babe. Me neither. But I'm a professional. I got a reputation to maintain.''

''Is that why you didn't kill the sonovabitch when he was mentally undressing me? There was a time, Mooky, when you'd have slit a man's throat for less.''

Dani was goading him. He didn't like it but he understood it was because she was pissed. She wanted to split, probably with the money. But when Mooky Blade made a deal, he kept his word. Tossing his head toward the door, he said, "I'm going for a walk on the beach."

"So, walk on the beach. I don't give a fuck."

"You're pushing it, Dani."

"Just get out of here and leave me alone, will you?"

Biloxi Plantation

Zoe took extra care with her makeup and wore her favorite summer dress, a white linen with a halter top and open back— it was sexy in a refined, oh-so-ladylike way. She always wore it with strappy sandals that had high heels. So she was feeling more than just a little confident when she descended the stairs for dinner, hopeful of an opportunity to make peace with Billy. She felt badly, knowing she'd been more heavy-handed than he deserved.

Zoe entered the dining room to find she was the first to arrive. The heavyset maid, Charlotte, and Esther were at the buffet, talking quietly.

"Well, if it isn't Miss Zoe," Charlotte said. She checked out the dress. "Looking pretty as a flower, I might add."

"Thank you." She glanced around as if to say, "Where is everybody?"

"I'm afraid you may be having a lonely meal tonight, honey," Charlotte said. "Mr. Van Biers has been feeling poorly all afternoon and Mrs. Van Biers came home with a terrible headache. They're having a light supper in their rooms. We don't know about Mr. Charles. With that man, you never know."

"What about Billy?"

"He's out for the evening."

"Out?"

"He got all dressed up and called a taxi, ma'am," Esther explained. "Said he'd have dinner in town."

"I see."

"But Charlotte's cooked a very fine meal, so you'll be eating well, even if it's a bit lonely."

Zoe forced a smile. "It won't be the first time I've eaten alone. But what about you two? You have to eat, don't you? Why don't you join me?"

"We've already eaten, ma'am."

"Well then, I'll just have to pretend I'm home in New York."

"Sit down, if you please," Charlotte said, "and Esther will bring you your salad."

Zoe did, repressing her disappointment. Maybe she'd put on her favorite dress for nothing.

Queenstown

"That's definitely the best baked fish I ever had," Billy said to the proprietor of the tiny café. Her name was Josie and she was also the cook and maître d'.

"Thank you, sir. People say there's no finer food on the island, for five times the money. Will you have coffee?"

"No, thank you, I'm fine."

The woman, probably older than she seemed, beamed. "Will there be anything else?" she asked, signaling the girl to clear the table.

"Maybe you could tell me if there's a place in town where I could tip a few beers, maybe someplace with a little music."

Josie chuckled. "You're asking where to go to meet women."

"Not necessarily." Still, he colored. "I was thinking folks must gather someplace."

"On a Monday night there won't be many people out, but your best bet would be the Speak Easy on the edge of town."

"Sounds like maybe it's a roadhouse?"

"If that's anything like a disco, the answer is yes."

"Could you point the way?"

"Straight up the road, through town and up the hill. If you can hear music, you won't be able to miss it."

After Billy paid for his meal he stepped out into the light tropical air. The street was nearly empty, the few people in sight mostly sitting on their stoops or chairs by their doors. There was no traffic. He walked up the street, not bothering with the sidewalk. Tipping his hat to a couple of elderly women, he elicited white toothy smiles.

Billy was doing his best to maintain an upbeat attitude. Zoe's rejection had hurt more than usual. In the past, he'd always dealt with rejection from one woman by finding another—and the sooner, the better. It was habit and habit had brought him to town in search of comfort for his bruised ego. But if he was a hundred percent honest, his heart wasn't in the exercise. He'd fallen for Zoe Marton a lot harder than was either wise or healthy, and he was beyond the point of denying it.

Biloxi Plantation

Zoe stepped onto the front porch as the moon rose from the dark Caribbean Sea. What a lovely, lovely sight. And the air was perfumed with the fragrance of blossoms. If not magical, it was certainly romantic. And wouldn't you know, it was Billy Blue who came to mind.

Zoe figured he wanted her to feel guilty. Men did when a woman was less than fully cooperative. The annoying thing was she did feel badly about snubbing him. But the real problem was she liked him.

Feeling restless and frustrated, Zoe went for a stroll in the garden. The moonlight was bright enough that she could see the color of the flowers and the various shades of green in the foliage. And the wonderful smell!

The truth was she felt wistful. And lonely. She'd have enjoyed Billy's company just then, even knowing what she knew. Funny how you could be strong and determined about someone, then, when a little crack formed and desire seeped in, everything seemed to crumble at once—all resolve and good intentions. It was probably a good thing he wasn't there.

Just then she heard a woman's voice coming from the other end of the house. It wasn't exactly a shriek, but the tone was sharp. Stopping to listen, she heard the voice again. Could it be Mayte?

Curious, she walked back in the direction of the sound. Upstairs, at the far end of the building, she could see light behind the shutters. There were two voices, the other a man's. She couldn't make out what was being said, but she was certain it was Simon and Mayte.

Eavesdropping on a marital conversation wasn't Zoe's style, but the anguish in Mayte's tone aroused her curiosity. "Who's in charge?" she heard Mayte say. "Your crazy son?" Simon's response was not intelligible, but Mayte's next words were— "How do you know he wouldn't...us, too? How many... before...to me enough's enough." As Zoe listened, slack-jawed, she heard the names "Pearson" and "Billy," but Mayte's voice was fading in and out. A few more words filtered down to where she stood at the edge of the lawn. Zoe heard "...thousand dollars," "I wash my hands" and "we'll lose everything." For the first time she heard Simon clearly. "What do you want me to do, Mayte? Go to the police? He's my son!" Her response was, "They both are." Then the voices became muffled. A door inside closed and she could hear nothing more.

Shaken, Zoe retreated along the front of the house to the entrance. The suddenly cool air sent a shiver through her and she rubbed her arms. There was no way to be certain, but she surmised Charles Van Biers was involved in something illicit that Mayte found distressing and it involved Billy. Just as troubling was the mention of Raymond Pearson's name.

Naturally Zoe imagined the worst, and she was scared. She already knew Charles was violent. Could he intend to harm Billy? And why would Simon and Mayte be arguing about it? Her imagination ran wild. She couldn't say with certainty what

she'd heard. But neither could she ignore it. She'd been looking for an excuse to contact the FBI, but until now she'd really
had nothing to say. Until now.

Zoe went back inside, glancing up the stairway leading to
the second floor. She saw nothing but she had a strong sense
of danger in the house, of evil lurking. The phone number of
the FBI agent that Special Agent Harris had given her was
upstairs in her purse. So she climbed the stairs, stopping at the
top to listen for voices coming from the direction of the master
suite, but she heard nothing. She went to her room and retrieved the phone number, then went back downstairs. Esther
was in the kitchen cleaning up.

"Something I can help you with, ma'am?"

"I need to make a personal call. Is there a room that's
private where I can use the phone?"

"You can use the one in Mr. Van Biers's study, I suppose.
Don't think he would mind. Let me show you."

Zoe knew the way, but she was just as glad to have one of
Simon's servants show her. They walked through the quiet
house to the door to Simon's study. Esther opened it and
turned on the light.

"Telephone's right there on the desk, ma'am."

"Are there extensions?"

"No, ma'am, Mr. Van Biers has a private line. Nobody will
be listening in."

Zoe smiled at the directness of the comment and thanked
her.

Esther withdrew and Zoe stepped into the study, closing the
door behind her. She went directly to the telephone and dialed.
The phone rang and rang, but there was no answer. She
groaned. What did this mean? That she could only reach the
agent during business hours? She hung up, frustrated.
"Damn."

Glancing around the office, she recalled the remark Esther
had made earlier about Simon and Ray Pearson having had an
argument, an argument that had taken place in this very office.
After having overheard Mayte and Simon, Zoe's mind was

naturally full of suspicion and dark thoughts. Pearson had been murdered. Could that mention of the poor man's name mean that his death was in any way connected to the Van Biers family?

There were a couple of file folders on the desk. Zoe lifted the cover. The first contained some sort of bank financial reports. A cursory glance told her she'd never be able to figure out what they meant—numbers had never been her thing. She checked out the other folder. Marketing materials, as best she could tell.

Having violated Simon's privacy already, she was prone to continue her snooping. There wasn't anything in particular she expected to find, but there was no shortage of issues—her Kansas sunflowers, Ray Pearson, bank matters that might be of interest to the FBI. The large drawers on either side contained file folders. Zoe ran her finger along the tabs, looking for something of interest. Most labels were hand-written in pencil, indicating they were most likely Simon's personal files. The majority of the abbreviations meant nothing to her. But then she came across one labeled V.G./R.P. It had to be Van Gogh/Raymond Pearson.

Zoe felt her heart begin to lope. As she started to pull the file folder from the drawer, she heard a sound in the hall. She quickly closed the drawer and frantically looked around for something to justify her presence. Spotting the phone as the door began to open, she quickly snatched up the receiver.

"Zoe!"

It was Simon, his face registering surprise.

"Oh, hi," she said. "I hope you don't mind, but Esther said I could use your office to make a credit-card call."

"Not at all."

Zoe put the receiver back in the cradle. "I was hoping to reach my lawyer in New York. Divorce details, you know."

"Were you able to get through?"

"No, Win wasn't home."

"Ah."

He stepped inside and gently closed the door behind him.

Simon wore a light silk robe over his pajamas. A tangle of white chest hairs blossomed from the opening in the pajama top. The light from the desk lamp cast deep shadows on his face, exaggerating his strong features.

Simon seemed large to her and there were echos of his son, Charles, in his countenance, echos she hadn't fully noted before. She also saw suspicion, or perhaps only imagined it because of her guilty feelings.

"I came down for some files," he said.

"I'll get out of your way then," she said, starting to get up.

"No, no, don't leave." He motioned for her to stay seated, then dropped heavily into a leather armchair. "I also wanted to get some cash from the safe." Then he grinned. "Isn't that just like a banker, to keep his own money under the mattress?"

Zoe was relieved by his lighthearted tone. Either he didn't suspect she'd been snooping or he was lulling her into a sense of false security with affability.

"Let me ask you, Zoe, has Billy given you any indication of his intentions?"

"Regarding your offer?"

"Yes."

"No, he hasn't. We haven't discussed the matter."

"Hmm. I see."

She waited.

"I note the two of you have become pretty friendly," Simon said, appraising her.

Zoe wondered where this was leading. She hoped not to an inquisition. "I guess we're both the new kids in town."

"Hmm." He stroked his chin. "Let me be blunt, Zoe. There have been some more developments," he said somberly. "Developments that add urgency to the matter of resolving things with Billy. I was wondering if I might prevail upon you to feel him out a bit on his thinking...and, well, if you were so inclined, give him a nudge toward settling."

"I'll be happy to do what I can," she said, "but I don't believe I have any particular influence."

"To the contrary, I expect the young man would take special heed of anything a bright young lady like yourself would have to say on a subject in which she has special expertise. All the more if he was especially fond of you."

"Mr. Van Biers, I'm sure you're overestimating my influence," she said, knowing what she said was quite true.

"This is extremely important to me and to the bank," he said. "If you can convince Billy to settle our outstanding differences and be on his way, I'll give you a bonus of twenty-five thousand dollars. But it must be done immediately."

She wondered if Simon's offer was a result of the conversation he'd been having with Mayte. Or, worse—a diversion.

"That's very generous," she said, "but I certainly don't want to create false hope. As I say, I'll do what I can, but I can't make any promises."

"I'm sure anything you say to him will be useful."

They contemplated each other. Zoe could feel the distrust, the uncertainty, flowing both ways.

"By the way, you look lovely this evening," he said.

"Thank you."

"Much too lovely to be sitting around making calls to lawyers. Do you have plans?"

Zoe saw an opportunity. "As a matter of fact, I was thinking of going into town, just to see a little of it. My next call was going to be for a taxi."

"Oh, don't do that. Andrew can drive you."

"I'd hate to take his time."

Simon gave her a knowing smile. "Maybe you'd like a little more privacy. Tell you what, take the Jeep. It's available for your use. Didn't I already mention that?"

"No."

"You can get the key from Charlotte or whoever's in the kitchen this evening. I should have said something earlier."

"That's very kind." Zoe got to her feet. "Well, you have

things to do and the hour is moving on. If you don't mind, I will borrow the Jeep.''

"That's what it's for," he said, rising.

She moved around the desk and, as she passed by him, Simon reached out and took her arm. He wasn't brusque, but his grip was firm.

"Zoe, please have that conversation with Billy sooner rather than later. It's very important. Not only for my sake, but for his, as well."

"Yes, Mr. Van Biers, I'll talk to him as soon as I have a chance."

When he released her, she left the room, willing herself to move deliberately, not breaking into a run until she reached the stairs. It wasn't possible to fetch her purse and get out of the house fast enough.

Queenstown

Billy heard the music fifty yards before the Speak Easy came into sight. And, as he expected, it appeared to be the Caribbean version of a roadhouse, complete with a neon beer sign in the window. He strode through the doors with the same swagger he'd entered a hundred different clubs and lounges over the years.

The place was rather quiet, just as the restaurant lady had predicted. There were two couples on the dance floor and half a dozen other people scattered at tables or at the bar. Billy's first thought was that if the music had been country and western instead of stuff with a Caribbean beat, and if the complexion of the patrons a bit lighter, he could just as easily be walking into a bar in Bozeman or Rock Springs. Of course, there'd be a few more Stetsons, jeans and boots, but there was a lot that was the same.

Then he spotted her at the bar, very nearly dropping his teeth. Zoe was in a miniskirt and bandeau top he couldn't believe. Her back was to him, but her hairdo was unmistakable. He sauntered over and, coming up behind her, said, "What in the dickens are you doing here, Zoe?"

She turned and, much to his shock and dismay, it wasn't Zoe at all. The woman resembled her a great deal but the features were different. This gal was pretty, but not so refined as Zoe. "Whoa, pardon me, ma'am," he said. "I mistook you for somebody else."

The woman's initial annoyance turned to delight. "Well, howdy, cowboy!"

"Ma'am," he said, tipping his hat. It wasn't Zoe, and the clothes certainly weren't Zoe. On closer inspection the body wasn't quite Zoe's either. The woman was copiously endowed and "juicy as a filet mignon," as Cy Krebs would have said. "Sorry for the intrusion."

"No intrusion. The place is pretty dead tonight. I wouldn't mind a little conversation."

Billy heard a welcoming tone in her voice, the tone that said, "Let's explore this a little, big fella." He also noticed there were two glasses of beer on the bar—one in front of her and one in front of the bar stool next to her. Billy read the sign.

"You just blow into town?" the woman asked.

"No, I've been here a couple of days. You?"

"A few."

"Vacation?" he asked.

"Business. How about you?"

"Same."

She kind of shifted her shoulders the way women do when drawing attention to their breasts. "I'm Danielle, by the way."

"I'm Billy. Billy Blue."

Danielle extended her hand. "Nice to meet you."

"Likewise," he said, taking her hand.

She wasn't big, but her grip was firm, as firm as her breasts were ripe. Billy had always been quick to make friends, but this Danielle was almost unnaturally open. But that half-empty glass of beer next to her remained an untold story.

"Are you here to dance or drink?" she asked.

Billy shrugged. "A little of both, I guess."

"Me, too."

The way she smiled at him she might as well have said, "Kiss me, you fool."

He didn't quite know what to make of her.

"Well, look who the cat drug in," came a voice behind him.

Billy turned as a hand came down firmly on his shoulder. It was Charles.

"This is Billy Blue," Danielle said. "You know Charles Van Biers, Billy?"

Charles and Billy both grinned.

"Hell yes, little lady," Charles said in a mocking tone. "This here ol' cowhand is my brother."

"Your brother?"

"Flesh and blood."

Danielle took Billy's hand. "Then Chuck won't mind if you and me dance."

"Hell, kids," Charles drawled as they headed for the dance floor, "have fun!" Then, to Billy's annoyance, he hollered, "Yahoo!"

Once they were on the dance floor, the woman began to dance like no other gal he'd ever seen. She had moves that would earn her jail time in parts of the Bible Belt. Billy knew he was a yokel in some respects, but he also had a nose for things that were a little too good to be true, and this qualified. But as Cy used to say, "The name of the game is to stay on the bull till you can't stay on no more."

Mooky Blade jogged along the dark road. He was pissed. Dani didn't often pull this shit, but every once in a while she'd get a bug up her ass and do something crazy just for revenge. When he'd come back from the beach the SUV was gone—and so was she. He knew then she'd gone to the Speak Easy because that's where Charles had gone. And, knowing Dani, she'd fuck around with the sonovabitch just to make Mooky livid. When she was mad, she loved to provoke him.

One time after they'd had a fight, he'd caught her prick-teasing his little brother, Omar. Mooky damned near killed his own flesh and blood, even knowing his wife was to blame. Dani was so scared by his anger that she tearfully promised never to fuck around like that again.

This was different, but it still made him mad. Dani had his buttons down cold—the good ones and the bad. Mooky was confident she'd never fuck somebody like Van Biers just to piss him off, but he wouldn't put it past her to make him think she had, especially not if she was angry enough.

After jogging for fifteen minutes, Mooky had burned off enough adrenaline and testosterone to get himself calmed down. As his head cleared, it occurred to him that Dani was not only miffed, but she might be doing this to squirrel the job. If he put Van Biers in the hospital, it would be kind of hard to turn around and whack somebody for him. They couldn't exactly go to the intensive care ward to pick up their money. Which made him wonder if this wasn't one time where he might be able to outsmart his wife. If he gave her some rope, Dani might end up hanging herself.

As he came up the hill near the club, Mooky's breathing was nice and steady. He felt good, in control. The way he figured it, Dani was probably expecting him to show up because she knew how goddamn jealous he was. So, what if this time he didn't show up? What if he secretly watched her instead?

Zoe pulled up in front of the police station and went inside. The place was tiny, about the size of her boss, Edmund Grey's, office at Sotheby's, though there did appear to be a small private office in back. It was dark. The only person present was a middle-aged woman with huge hips draped in a red and yellow skirt. Incongruously, she also wore a police officer's uniform shirt.

"May I help you?"

"Yes," Zoe said, stepping to the counter. She lowered her voice to a confidential tone. "I'm an American citizen and I was given this telephone number to contact an FBI agent working on temporary assignment here on St. Margaret. I urgently need to talk to her and I'm not getting an answer. Can you tell me how I might reach her?''

The clerk gave her a wary look. ''I wouldn't know about that. You'd have to speak to Chief Inspector Goodson.''

''Is he in?''

''No, he won't be in until tomorrow morning.''

Zoe felt the wind going right out of her. ''Isn't there anyone else I could talk to?''

''I'm sorry, but there isn't. Mr. Toliver's on duty, but he's on patrol. And there's me.''

''Would it be possible to telephone the chief inspector?''

The woman looked at the clock on the wall. ''He retires early and doesn't like to be disturbed except in the case of an emergency.''

''This is an emergency.''

''What kind?''

Zoe lowered her voice still more. ''A man's life could be in danger.''

''Maybe you need the police, not the FBI.''

Zoe didn't want to create an incident, she simply wanted a confidential conversation with someone she could trust. But how did she explain that without offending? ''The agent has been briefed on the situation. She's expecting to hear from me.''

The clerk seemed unconvinced. ''Let me see your passport, please.''

Zoe took her passport from her purse and handed it to the woman, who studied it.

''Oh, your name is Marton. I thought you were the other one.''

''What other one?''

The clerk waved her off. ''Never mind. Let me check something.'' Deftly maneuvering her broad beam through the cramped office, the woman went to a radio perched on a file cabinet on the back wall. She clicked on the mike. "Ellis, this is base. You hear me? Over."

"Roger, base. I hear you. Over," came the reply.

"We've got an American lady here who wants to talk to the FBI. It's an emergency. Her name's Zoe Marton."

"Hold."

The clerk waited. Zoe waited. The clerk glanced back and shrugged. After a minute the man's voice came over the radio.

"Base, we got a situation here. Special Agent Tsu and I are tied up. We've got a suspect under surveillance. Can Ms. Marton wait?"

The clerk glanced back at Zoe, knowing she heard.

"If it won't be all night, yes."

"She'll wait," the clerk said into the microphone.

"Acknowledged."

The woman turned to Zoe. "You might as well make yourself at home. No telling how long it will be."

Charles stood at the bar watching Dani out on the dance floor working over his brother. If that woman couldn't give a guy a hard-on, the guy had to be dead. She was incredible. God knew, she sure was turning him on.

Which was ironic. When Dani showed up, acting friendly, he thought he might be in line for a piece of ass. "Don't tell me Mooky let you out to play," he'd said.

"Mooky might be my husband, but he doesn't own me," she'd replied. "Buy me a beer, Chuck."

Charles was ready to do that and more. But then Billy arrived and Dani was right on him. Charles wondered if she was going to lure the sonovabitch to some dark corner and do him in, or was she being a prick tease for the hell of it. Nor was he sure what to hope for. He wanted her himself, but he also knew how critical it was to deep-six his bastard brother.

First Mooky spotted the SUV, then Van Biers's Porsche, then the cops. He hoped to hell that Dani hadn't let down her guard. She was smart, smarter than him, but when she was pissed, his wife could get a little crazy. Now he had two reasons to check up on her—to make sure she didn't get carried away with Van Biers, and to make sure she didn't get in trouble with the law.

The problem was he hadn't seen the cops until they'd seen him, which put Mooky in a bind. Did he hang around outside waiting for his wife to come out of the bar, or did he go inside and run the risk of a public scene? He decided to split the difference. He'd slip inside and find a quiet corner to check things out.

Once in the door, though, he realized he wouldn't be losing himself in the crowds. The place was dead. Mooky lingered in the dark nook at the entrance where he could observe the action without being seen.

Not surprisingly Dani was on the dance floor with two dudes. Van Biers was no surprise, but damned if the other one wasn't the cowboy, Billy Blue.

Mooky watched, the fires of jealousy beginning to turn him white-hot. The bitch was putting on the afterburners. If she wasn't riding one guy's thigh or running her hand over his crotch, it was the other. It was all Mooky could do to keep from charging in, grabbing the honky bitch by the nape of the neck and dragging her home. If he did, he'd feel better, but they'd be at each other's throats for a week and he'd be getting venom not pussy. His personal pride was important enough to him that he'd be willing to endure a dry spell just to make his point, but his professional pride made him hold back.

Zoe sat for as long as she could, then got up and began to pace. The clerk ignored her, sitting at her desk reading a paperback novel.

"How long do you think it will be?" Zoe asked.

"I have no idea whatsoever."

Zoe paced some more. She was worried about Billy—though she knew the basis for her concern was vague. Still, one person connected with the Van Gogh sunflowers had died and there was no reason to think others weren't in danger.

"Excuse me," she said to the clerk. "If a man came to town with the intention of having a good time," Zoe asked, "where would he most likely go?"

"Pardon me?"

"There must be someplace that..."

"If you're asking what I think you're asking, Miss Marton, there's nothing legal like that on St. Margaret. I'm not saying prostitution doesn't exist, but—"

"No, no, no. I don't mean that." At least she thought that wasn't what she meant. On the other hand...but she dismissed the thought. "I meant a bar or something."

"Oh. Well, there are several on the island, but if you mean a place for dancing and the like, it would be the Speak Easy."

"Is it in town?"

The clerk told her where it was. "But, I wouldn't be going up there just now, if I was you."

"Why? Is it that unsavory?"

"No, it's just that there's something going on up there."

Zoe realized that was probably where the policeman and the FBI agent were, and that worried her even more. She continued to pace, now under the watchful eye of the clerk.

"Maybe I'll go up to the Speak Easy," Zoe said. "Please tell the agent that's where I'll be."

The woman shrugged helplessly. "Maybe you can tell her yourself. That's where she is."

Zoe knew it. She felt better. "Thank you," she said. She left the police station, fired with determination to save Billy Blue's butt.

At the end of the song, Dani Blade hooked her fingers in the waistband of Billy's and Charles's pants and led them over to a table. "Chuck, you're the rich bastard. Three more beers."

"Anything the lady wants."

Dani smiled to herself as he went off. She didn't like the

prick, but she'd come to the Speak Easy knowing he'd be the easiest way to get Mooky's goat. Come to think of it, where was her husband? She was sure he'd have shown up by now. Or was he calling her bluff by feigning indifference?

"So, where you from, Danielle?" Billy asked, wiping his brow with a handkerchief.

"Canada."

"No kidding. I didn't know they danced like that up there."

"I've traveled a lot, cowboy. Where are you staying on St. Margaret?"

"With...well, family, I guess."

"Chuck?"

"Yeah. How about you?"

"I'm sharing a place, but that can get tedious, if you know what I mean. I'm thinking of sleeping on the beach tonight. You ever done that?"

"Don't reckon I have."

She gave him her most coquettish smile. "Maybe you ought to give it a try."

"Is that an invitation, Danielle?"

She arched a brow suggestively. "Maybe."

He gave her a little smile. She smiled right back.

The guy was a charming sonovabitch, if an "ah shucks, ma'am," guy on horseback was your taste. She, of course, didn't give a shit about anybody besides Mooky, but she saw an opportunity to give her husband a much-needed jab in the ass and do a job at the same time. It wouldn't be the first time she'd used sex to lure a man to his doom. "What do you care if I fucked him?" she'd say in the morning. "I made you twenty-five grand last night. What more do you want?" She wouldn't fuck the cowboy before she did him, but she'd let Mooky think she had. Like most men, he'd been taking her for granted more and more of late. She had to put a stop to it.

"Here we are, boys and girls," Charles said, returning with the beers. He put them on the table.

"Excuse me for a minute," Billy said. "I'll be right back." He headed off in the direction of the rest rooms.

Dani and Charles looked after him.

"I hope you're thinking what I'm thinking," he said.

"What are you thinking?"

"That the lamb is ripe for slaughter."

She smiled smugly. "Why don't you run on home and get the money?"

"So, we're thinking the same thing. What can I do to help?"

"Just leave it to me, Chucky-boy."

"You know, I'd like you a whole lot better if you wouldn't call me that," he said, showing irritation.

"I don't give a shit what you like and don't like, Chucky."

"Hey. Why the hostility? Half an hour ago you acted like I was the last man on earth. You develop a sudden taste for cowboys?"

"I do whatever serves my purposes and you've outlived your usefulness."

"You know, if we weren't such good friends, I'd be tempted to teach you how to show a gentleman respect. You've spent too much time in bed with that nigger husband of yours."

"You keep talking that way, white boy, and Mooky just might cut out your heart—after he takes your money, of course."

Charles smiled. "You still owe me, Dani. I haven't forgotten."

"You threatening me?"

The bastard smiled and stood up. He took a long drink, chugging half of it before putting it back down. Then he reached out and ran his fingertip over the top of Dani's breast. She slapped his hand away. Charles chuckled. "Tell my brother I had to go. Guess I won't see him until…when? Judgment day?" Laughing, he left.

Dani Blade really didn't like the man. He disgusted her. But that was all right. She'd take care of the cowboy, then, in the

morning while she packed, Mooky could do the old mambo.
After that they'd be free to hop on the boat and head for
Jamaica.

Just then, Billy Blue came striding back to the table. He
noticed Charles's beer, but also Charles's absence.

"Where's our friend?"

"Chuck had to go. Said he'd see you later. How about you,
Billy? Ready to blow this place?" She stared at his crotch.
"I'm getting really horny."

The cowboy stroked his chin briefly before dropping his
hand. "I kind of enjoyed dancing with you. How about sticking around for a while? Wouldn't hurt to get a little better
acquainted, would it?"

Dani was surprised at his reluctance. That was a first. But
she wouldn't let it put her off her game. She shrugged. "Whatever you want. I'm easy."

The way he smiled told her he took the comment in a
slightly different way than she'd intended. Maybe he wasn't
the dumb pussy hound she thought. Okay, if she had to use a
little guile along with her tits and her ass, she would.

Billy took a big gulp of beer. "Come on, Danielle, let's
dance."

Zoe had made a wrong turn, but now she was on track.
Ahead she could see the lights of the Speak Easy. Then, as
she pulled into the small, mostly deserted parking area, she
noticed Charles's Porsche. The headlights had just come on,
but they immediately went off again.

As Zoe got out of the Jeep, Charles opened the door of his
Porsche.

"Zoe," he called, making his way over. "Fancy meeting
you here."

She groaned. Charles was the last person she wanted to see.
The very last. But there was no point in further alienating him.
She pasted on a smile. "Hi."

"Where you headed?" he asked.

"Actually, I'm looking for Billy. Have you seen him?"

He hesitated. "No, not really."

"Could he be inside?"

"No, I just came out. I'm sure I'd have seen him."

"Well, I think I'll have a look anyway."

As she started to go, Charles reached out and grabbed her arm. "You don't want to go in there," he said.

"Why not?"

"It's a dive, Zoe. All kinds of unsavory types."

"Charles, I'm from New York."

"So, let's go someplace nice. I'll buy you a drink. Something with a little umbrella in it."

"I don't want a drink," she insisted. "Now please let go of my arm."

"I'll drive you back to the house. We can send somebody for the Jeep in the morning."

She was getting angry now. "Charles, let go of me!"

"Excuse me, Mr. Van Biers. Is there a problem?"

Charles and Zoe both turned. It was a black man with a rather official demeanor. A woman accompanied him, a stocky little Asian in a beige epaulette shirt and matching pants.

"Ah, Inspector Toliver," Charles said. "Just the right person. I'm trying to convince Ms. Marton, my houseguest, that the Speak Easy is no place for a woman alone."

"Are you a police officer?" Zoe asked.

"Yes, ma'am," Toliver replied.

"I assume I'm free to go where I want."

"Quite right. You are indeed."

"Charles," she said, "thank you for your concern, but I'm going inside."

He looked stunned, but also helpless. "All right," he said with a shrug, "be stubborn." After giving her a disgusted look, he headed off toward his car.

The trio watched him drive away, the engine of the Porsche roaring. Ellis Toliver shook his head.

The Asian woman spoke up for the first time. "Ms. Marton," she said, "I'm Special Agent Joyce Tsu. I understand you wanted to see me."

"Yes," Zoe said with a glance at the police officer. "Special Agent Harris gave me your number and said I should call if I needed to talk to you." She again glanced at Toliver. "Would this be a good time?"

"Yes, Inspector Toliver and I are working the case together, so feel free to share any information you have."

Zoe explained that she was concerned something unsavory was going on and that Billy might be in danger. "I can't prove anything, but I have a very strong feeling Simon Van Biers might be involved somehow in Raymond Pearson's death. It all has to do with the Van Gogh, I'm quite sure. Billy claims it's his and that's putting Simon in a very awkward financial situation."

The agent asked Zoe a few more questions, which she answered. "It's all pretty vague," Tsu said. "There wouldn't be justification for an arrest. Would you agree, Ellis?"

"Yes, but further investigation is certainly warranted."

"Ms. Marton, given your concerns, you might want to consider leaving St. Margaret."

"Why would I do that? I have Simon's trust...at least for the moment. And I'm not in danger. Mr. Blue is the one who should be concerned."

"Would you like me to speak with him?" Joyce Tsu asked.

Zoe considered that. "No, I really think it's my place. There's no reason why I shouldn't, is there?"

Tsu and Toliver exchanged glances.

"There's an individual inside who we consider dangerous, a man who we've been keeping an eye on for several days," Ellis Toliver said. "I really can't be more specific, but there is reason for concern."

"Would it involve Billy?"

"Frankly, I couldn't say, Ms. Marton."

Zoe looked at the building, pondering her options. "It's a public place. I'm going inside."

"It's your decision," Toliver said.

Zoe thanked them and started to leave. "Ms. Marton,"

Joyce Tsu said, "you're wise to stay clear of Charles Van Biers."

Zoe smiled faintly. "I've known that from the first day I laid eyes on the man."

Mooky was growing impatient, and he was having trouble keeping his anger in check. When Van Biers had left and saw him lingering in the shadows he'd looked duly surprised, paused for a moment, then said, "Don't worry, man, she's got everything under control. The cowboy will be dead by morning, even if she has to fuck him to get the job done." He'd given him a big grin and it took all Mooky's willpower not to throttle the bastard. Then lowering his voice, Charles had added, "Do the old witch doctor as soon as you can, mate. I'm going for the money now. Once you and Dani have done your thing, you can find me in my room at the polo club."

Mooky was in a terrible quandary. Part of him wanted to go get his wife and drag her out of there. The other part of him wanted to break everybody's heads—the cowboy, the mambo, Charles Van Biers. The whole bloody lot. As he watched his wife dragging her pussy up and down the cowboy's thigh and rubbing her tits up against him, a white-hot rage flooded him. Fuck it, he thought, I'm going after Dani.

But then the door opened, very nearly hitting him in the face. He stepped back, bumping into the wall behind him.

Zoe turned at the sound of the thud. Seeing the mountainous man towering over her, she gasped, only barely managing to stifle a scream. It was the bull who'd terrorized the mambo, Marie. But when he simply glared, not moving a muscle, Zoe fairly leaped from the door and into the noisy saloon, glancing back to make sure he didn't follow her.

Her heart pounding, she glanced around the room, looking for Billy. There weren't many people there, but the music was certainly loud. Then her eyes were drawn to the spectacle taking place on the dance floor, a spectacle that seemed to be

holding the attention of every other person in the place. It was
Billy, dancing with a woman wearing one of the briefest outfits
she'd ever seen in a public place. The two of them were going
at it. It would have been copulation if they hadn't had their
clothes on. Zoe stared, dumbfounded.

Color rose in her cheeks as she watched with horror and
fascination. Her impulse was to turn on her heel and get the
hell out. Billy Blue was about as reformed from his woman-
izing ways as oil company executives were from price fixing.
Of course, what he did was no skin off her teeth. She'd come
out of simple consideration for an innocent person she believed to be in danger.

And yet, she couldn't stop watching them. The woman, who
at least had a decent haircut, was incredible, but Billy had a
few moves of his own. Obviously, his back was feeling much
better.

After another precautionary glance back at the bull, who'd
withdrawn into the shadows, Zoe moved a few steps closer to
the dance floor. Did she interrupt? Somehow she couldn't justify that, not under any circumstances. Nor did she imagine
Billy would appreciate it, whether his life was in danger or
not.

Zoe saw that there was a resemblance between herself and
Billy's partner, a remote similarity of physical types…and
there was also the haircut. Could that have somehow figured
into the equation? But then, when she realized how stupid that
line of reasoning was, she admonished herself. Why had that
even entered her mind?

After another minute of faux intercourse, the music stopped
and Billy and his lady friend retreated from the dance floor to
scattered applause. The woman sat at their table, but Billy
remained standing. He picked up his glass and knocked down
several large gulps. Then he asked the woman if she'd like
another. When she shook her head, Zoe heard him say, "I'll
get myself one, if you'll excuse me, Danielle."

Billy took two steps toward the bar, his eyes instantly falling
on Zoe. He was so startled to see her that he came to a dead

halt right in his tracks. Then he ambled over. "Zoe, what in blazes are you doing here?"

The refrain was getting familiar. She smiled pleasantly. "Oh, things were kind of quiet at the old plantation house, so I decided I'd see if I could find some excitement. Seems I came to the right place."

Billy laughed self-consciously and glanced back at Danielle. "The lady is quite a dancer, isn't she?"

"Dancer? I think the vice squad has another name for it."

He grinned with embarrassment, looking down at his booted feet. "I suppose walking in on it looked bad."

"Bad? Not necessarily. It all depends on your taste...and your morals."

He scratched his head. "It's not like I do this every night, Zoe. I just came here for a beer and happened to run into Danielle."

"And what a collision it was, too. But you don't owe me any explanations."

"But, I don't want you thinking..."

"I don't think anything different than I thought before."

"Yeah," he said, "that's what concerns me." He looked troubled.

"Billy, your personal life has nothing to do with me being here."

"Why are you here?"

Zoe realized that the feeling of urgency with which she'd arrived had completely dissipated. Her dire warning almost seemed, at this point, like an afterthought. Inching a bit closer to him, she lowered her voice to a whisper and said, "You remember the huge black man at Marie's?"

"Yeah."

"Well, he's standing at the entrance as we speak."

Billy squinted in the darkness toward the door. "I don't see anybody."

"Well, he's there in the shadows. I bumped into him—literally—when I arrived."

To her dismay he strode right over to the door, opened it,

stuck his head outside and looked around, before returning to where she waited. "Zoe, there's nobody by the door, either inside or outside."

"He must have left."

"Are you sure you aren't imagining things?"

"No, Billy," she said, her anger flaring. "He was there, I saw him."

He looked skeptical. She was so annoyed she could have swatted him.

"There's an FBI agent outside and a policeman outside watching him...or at least I think that's who they were watching. They said he's been under surveillance and that he's dangerous."

"An FBI agent? Zoe, have you been drinking?"

"No, I haven't been drinking!" she said much too loudly, enough that heads turned, including Billy's bimbo. Zoe sighed heavily with frustration. "Oh, for God's sake, never mind. That's not why I came."

"Oh?"

Suddenly Zoe felt like a total idiot. But her motives were sound and she did have reason for concern. "I overheard Simon and Mayte having a conversation this evening," she said.

"And?"

"Well, it was kind of ominous."

"How so?"

In hushed tones she recounted the gist of what she'd heard. Then she leaned close to him, her voice barely audible. "I think your life's in danger, Billy, I truly do. And...well, I think they may have had something to do with Ray Pearson's death."

He pondered that for a moment. "It wouldn't surprise me," he said. "But the evidence is pretty skimpy."

"Billy, tonight Simon offered me twenty-five thousand dollars if I could convince you to walk away with the copy of the sunflowers or to take his offer of a quarter of a million.

He's desperate, I can tell. Desperate enough to have Charles or somebody kill you.''

"Charles was just here."

"I know. I ran into him outside. He denied having seen you, which goes to show he didn't want us to talk."

"That's no surprise, he's hot for your bod."

"Charles is hot for every bod. He's a pervert. But he's also up to something."

"Hmm. When I arrived, Charles was with Danielle."

Zoe looked past him at the woman, who was staring at them with growing curiosity. "Maybe she's in on it."

"As what? The designated dancer? I don't think so. Charles was just hitting on her. No surprise there. She gave him the brush-off."

"The details aren't important," Zoe said. "The point is you've got to be careful. Maybe you ought to leave St. Margaret while you still can."

"Isn't that what Simon wanted you to convince me to do? And he was going to give you twenty-five grand if you did?"

She let out a sigh of exasperation. "Yes, but I don't mean it like that."

He had a skeptical look on his face, which really annoyed her.

"Use your head, Billy, I wouldn't have told you he wanted to pay me if that was my motive."

"It could be compulsive honesty."

"So that I can take the money with a clear conscience? You don't really believe that, do you?" Again her voice had risen. "I didn't have to come here, you know. I did it because I was concerned. And what thanks do I get? I get accused of being selfish!"

"Oh, Jesus," Billy said under his breath. "This is going from bad to worse."

"Am I wrong?"

"Zoe, I'm not accusing you of anything. I'm grateful that you cared enough to come warn me."

"Are you?"

"Yes, of course."

She didn't want to be mollified because she was angry. And she was angry because she was embarrassed. When she saw Danielle get up from the table and head their way, she felt a deep sense of dread. The woman slipped her arm right around Billy's waist, surprising him.

"Oh, hi," he said.

Danielle pushed her hair back on one side and gave Zoe a tight little smile as if to say, "He's mine. Go find your own." Instead, she spoke to Billy. "What's up, honey? Find yourself another dance partner?"

"No," Zoe said, answering for him. "We're business associates. I had a little problem I needed to discuss with him, but we're through. I'll leave you two to your...dancing."

"Danielle, this is Zoe," Billy said to the woman. "Zoe, Danielle."

Zoe looked into eyes that were more hostile than she would have expected. She gave a nod of acknowledgment. "Well, I've got to go."

"Don't run off," Danielle said more in triumph than sincerity.

Zoe gave her a tight smile. Then, looking her over a final time she said, "Great moves, by the way. Where did you learn them?"

The other shrugged. "Comes naturally, I guess."

"Yeah, I think they call it propagation of the species." Zoe did not look at Billy. She simply walked out of the club.

Billy contemplated Danielle, but what he felt was a longing for Zoe. She'd caught him at the worst possible moment. Therapy was all it was, but she wouldn't buy that in a hundred years.

Maybe the best thing about Danielle was that she proved to him how much he cared for Zoe. There really was no comparison, not in ways that mattered. Some words of Cy Krebs's came to mind—"A good quarter horse will have the right lines, the right curves, the right proportions. A great quarter horse will have the right heart.'' Billy had learned it was the same with women. Zoe and Danielle were living proof. How would he ever be able to convince Zoe of that, especially now?

Danielle put her arms around his waist and pressed her breasts up against him. ''So, cowboy, are we going to go fuck or what?''

''I'm sorely tempted,'' he said, ''but I'm afraid I've got other fish to fry.''

''Say what?''

''I'm going home with my friend.''

Danielle looked incredulous.

''I enjoyed dancing with you,'' he said. ''A lot more than you'll likely believe.'' He gave her a wink, then headed for the door.

Billy stepped out into the light tropical air, under a starlit sky, looking for Zoe. He didn't see her, but then he heard an engine in the parking lot come to life and the lights of a Jeep come on. Under the assumption it was her, he jogged over, ignoring the pain in his back. He came up on the driver's side. Zoe was shocked to see him loom up out of nowhere.

''Billy, you scared me.''

''Sorry. I wanted to catch you before you got away. How about a lift home?''

''You're leaving?''

''Sure, why not?''

''What about your girlfriend?''

''She's not my girlfriend. She's not my anything. Just somebody I danced with.''

The look Zoe gave him said it all.

''I know what you're thinking,'' he said, ''and you're wrong.''

''Billy, don't bother.''

''No, I want you to know the truth. Danielle just propositioned me but I told her I wasn't interested. And I'm not.''

''Why not?''

''Because I'd rather be questioned and distrusted by you than go to bed with her.''

"Billy, you're so full of shit."

"Are you going to give me a lift or not?"

"All right, get in," she said. "There's no point in sitting here debating your virtue or lack thereof."

He went around and got in on the passenger side. "Where'd you get the wheels?"

"Simon loaned them to me."

"So that you could find me and talk me into leaving St. Margaret and taking the fake Van Gogh with me?"

"Yeah, right. And collect my twenty-five thousand."

"That business about the big black guy and the FBI and the CIA and the Marines—all true?"

"Yes, and as you can see, they've all gone. The latter in pursuit of the former, I assume."

Billy knew she was dead serious, but her story seemed preposterous, especially the part about his life being in danger. On the other hand, he knew that Simon was a sly old dog. Still, at the moment, he was more interested in convincing Zoe he wasn't the reprobate she thought he was.

Glancing over and seeing how pretty she looked in her white dress, how refined she was beside Danielle, his heart ached. He liked the soft line of her jaw, the way the light and shadow played on her milky skin, the ironic curl at the corner of her mouth. And he hated it that she misunderstood him. "You're dead set on the fact that I'm a scoundrel, aren't you?"

She put the Jeep in reverse and backed out. "I haven't given it any thought."

"Come on, Zoe, something must have gone through your mind when you saw us on the dance floor."

She started down the road. "If you must know, I was wondering if the vice squad was going to come busting in the door."

"That's what I thought."

"Billy, I don't care what you do. It's a waste of energy even to think about it. So, let's not even talk about it, okay?"

"You're a hard woman, Zoe. You this tough on your husband?"

"Tougher."

"Oh, that must be why you're getting a divorce."

Her head whipped over. The question in her eyes also contained accusation.

"Esther told me," he explained. "Apparently you gave her a different story than you gave me."

She brooded silently, clearly miffed.

"That's okay, though," he said. "Everybody has a flaw of some sort. I'm a womanizer and you're a liar."

"I didn't want to give you any encouragement," she snapped.

"You've been very successful. Right up until coming to save my butt."

"Oh, God," she said with disgust. "This is what I get for playing the Good Samaritan. I should have minded my own business."

"What do you say we call a truce? No point in us fighting when there are so many bad guys around to keep us busy. Let's be friends instead. Doesn't that make a lot more sense?"

Zoe found herself wanting to be friends yet fighting it, fighting Billy. Maybe that was because of Ahmed. Or her father. Or a lifetime of distrust of men. Or maybe it was because Billy had leveled with her about his painting and she hadn't leveled with him about hers. Who was to say one of them was worse than the other?

Zoe felt the ache of guilt. There was only one way to put an end to that, but God, she'd be taking a tremendous risk in leveling with him. Her situation was precarious as it was. In the greater scheme of things, how important to her was Billy Blue?

And yet, as they entered the town, she found the personal considerations tugging at her mightily. Between her feelings for the guy and the guilt she felt, she was convinced now that she had to take bold action, no matter the cost. When the

Queen's Inn came into view, Zoe abruptly pulled over and stopped in front of the hotel.

"Why are you stopping?" he asked.

"There's a very good reason why you should leave St. Margaret, Billy, a reason that has nothing to do with the things we've already discussed."

"What are you talking about?"

Zoe took a deep breath for courage. "I know for a fact the real Van Gogh sunflowers is not yours. The fake is the one Simon got from your grandmother."

"How do you know that?"

"Billy, the Van Gogh sunflowers, the original that was once owned by Roger Faucauld, is actually mine. The painting rightfully belongs to me."

"Huh?"

Zoe told him how her grandfather, Carson Gill, had purchased the sunflowers during the First World War and received a hand-written receipt for the painting from Faucauld himself. But being ignorant of art, Carson Gill had no idea that the signature "Vincent," was that of Vincent Van Gogh. "The painting was in my mother's family for seventy-five years without us knowing what we had. It wasn't until I was exposed to fine art in college that I began figuring out the truth. I found the receipt among my grandfather's effects in our attic."

"How did Simon get hold of it?"

"Ironically, my father was swindled out of the painting only months before I made my discovery. I believe Simon was aware the painting had been obtained by the seller through fraud and extortion, which would invalidate his claim. The point is I've come to the Caribbean to reclaim my rightful inheritance."

"So, the job with Simon is a sham?"

"As far as I'm concerned. He has no idea what my true motives are, obviously."

Understandably, Billy seemed to be in shock. He sat mute for several moments, staring straight ahead.

"Jesus," he finally mumbled, "you really did have a hell of a secret, Marie was right."

"I about died when she said that."

"There's no deceiving a fortune-teller."

Zoe smiled faintly. "But at least now you understand why there's no point in getting into a fight with Simon. If his claim won't stand up, mine definitely will."

Billy looked skeptical.

"I know this is coming out of the blue, and I'm sure you have your suspicions, but it's the truth. And I can document everything."

He continued his silence.

"You don't believe me, do you?" she said.

Billy rubbed his chin. "No offense, Zoe, but your track record with the truth is about as pure as mine is with the fairer sex."

"What are you talking about?"

"Well, when a supposedly happily married woman is in fact in the middle of a divorce—contrary to prior representations—and further discloses suddenly that she's the owner of a hundred-million-dollar painting—contrary to prior representations—well, a fella's feelings of trust are likely to be strained."

"You're calling me a liar."

"No, I'm just telling you that I've seen no proof and that I'd be a fool to give up the fight and ride out of Dodge on the basis of this conversation."

"I've showed you my cards, but you're saying the hand's not over."

"I'm trying to do the prudent thing."

Zoe winced with frustration. Here she was, begging the guy to save himself—and putting herself at risk to do it—but all she'd succeeded in doing was making him doubt her sincerity and her motives.

"Not much fun to have your integrity questioned, is it?" he said.

"Billy, I've leveled with you at the risk of losing a valuable painting that's rightfully mine. And what do I get for trying to save your butt? You question my integrity, my honesty and my motives. How do you think that makes me feel?''

"Probably about the way I felt when I told you I'd reformed, that my feelings for you were special, and you scoffed. Scoffed, Zoe.''

"For God's sake, you were practically having intercourse on the dance floor.''

"I mean before that. Danielle didn't mean anything to me. I was thinking about you the whole time.''

She rolled her eyes. "Please…''

"But why are we discussing my character? It's you and your story that's at issue. You're telling me to turn tail and run. Why should I?''

"Because you have nothing to fight for and by staying you only put yourself in jeopardy. Simon's desperate to get a credit line secured by the painting and, as long as you're in his hair, he could have problems, serious problems.''

"What about you?''

"I can afford to lay low. The reason I came to St. Margaret is to gather the necessary proof that Simon is not a purchaser in good faith and that the Kansas sunflowers rightfully belongs to me. My lawyer says that's key. Don't you see, you've either got to take the copy and go, or accept Simon's offer to purchase it from you. But for heaven's sake, don't go back to the house. Stay at the hotel. I'll tell Simon your decision in the morning and the pressure will be off both him and you.''

Billy thought some more. "Irwin Pettigrew may have a fool for a son, but my grandparents didn't raise a coward. I'm not about to let you walk into the lion's den alone. If you can help me, then I ought to be able to help you.''

"You'll only be putting yourself in harm's way. I can take care of myself.''

"How are you going to prove Simon's not a legitimate buyer?''

"I don't know, that's been the problem all along. But earlier tonight I did happen on a file that might contain the proof I need. If I can, I'm going to check it out thoroughly when I get back to the house.''

"I'll go with you."

"Billy, there's no point."

"I beg to differ, ma'am. We're in this together. You know my secrets and I know yours. Besides, it's always good having somebody watching your back."

Dani Blade waited for Mooky to show, but when ten minutes had passed and there was still no sign of him, she decided he hadn't come looking for her after all. Either that, or he saw what she was doing and was so disgusted he split. That wasn't like him, though. It would have been more his style to wait until Van Biers and the cowboy were gone, then come storming in and slap her around a little. He had to be pissed. After all, she was his wife!

Dani asked a stud who'd been eyeing her all night for the time. When he said it was near midnight, she decided to blow the place.

She left the club and, wouldn't you know it, the stud with the watch followed her out. Dani stopped and whirled in one smooth motion to face him.

"What do you want, asshole?"

He looked surprised by the direct confrontation.

"Nothing, sister. We're just leaving at the same time. Thought maybe we could find the same place to go."

"Forget it. Go find yourself a toilet and jerk off."

She turned and, as she did, he reached out and took her by the arm. That was all Dani needed. She did a one-eighty, dropped him with a judo kick to the back of the legs, then kneed him in the chin as he was dropping to the ground. The guy was sprawled unconscious as she made her way to the SUV.

There was a note on the driver's seat. It read:

Good work, babe. Bring the cowboy to the mambo's place. We'll have our garden party there.

It was signed "M."

Dani winced at the thought of having let Blue get away. She slammed her fist against the steering wheel. For the first time in their married lives, she'd let Mooky down. What would she tell him? That she'd tried her damnedest with the cowboy, but he wasn't interested? God almighty, what was happening? Was she losing it, or what?

Her head sagged forward until it rested on the wheel. She felt awful. But then her pride and indignation kicked in. She couldn't let things end like this. She'd go find the sonovabitch and force him to go with her, if that's what it took. Opening the glove box, she checked to make sure the 9mm automatic was still there. It was.

Dani slammed the lid closed and started the engine. There was more than one way to make a guy walk off a cliff.

Tuesday
August 15th

Biloxi Plantation

Simon awoke with a start. Mayte had been screaming at him, but it was only a dream. He looked over at the bedside clock. It was just past midnight. He'd dozed for over an hour in his robe, lying outside the covers, the lights on. When he had lain down on the bed earlier, he'd felt sick to his stomach and he still felt like hell. His heart loped in an uncomfortable rhythm—maybe from the dream—and he had an ominous sense of doom. He'd finally come to the realization that everything was slipping through his fingers.

Earlier, Mayte had been upset, too. After their fight she'd gone for a walk. Then she'd locked herself in the bathroom. After an hour, she'd come out and walked over to his bed with her hands on her hips in a sign of disgust.

"I want to know where you've put the money and exactly how much we're talking about," she'd said.

"What are you saying, Mayte?"

"Most of that money you salted away was earned—or embezzled, as the case may be—during our marriage. I'm entitled to know what's going on. If I didn't keep the books, I wouldn't know that millions have been siphoned off. At least fifty million by now, and it's got to be in an offshore account. I want to know where. I want details."

The actual figure was closer to thirty-five million, but Simon saw no point in correcting her. She'd never get more than a token amount, but he wasn't going to make a point of that, either. Instead, he would mollify her, do his best to put her off. "Haven't I always taken care of you, sugar? Nothing's changed."

"Don't sugar me, you sonovabitch. I'm tired of being your nigger girl. I want my share of the money, or else."

"Or else what?"

"Just or else, Simon."

His blood pressure had shot up. He felt it in his temples. "Are you threatening me?"

"You've put my neck in a noose, and for what? I'm a goddamn salaried employee and your live-in whore. Well, that's not good enough!"

"You're my wife, Mayte. A wife I've always treated with both generosity and respect."

"By the master's standards, maybe, but not mine. I want my half and I want it as soon as it can be arranged. I've opened a numbered account in the Caymans. I want you to put twenty-five million in it tomorrow. You do, and you'll have my undying loyalty."

Simon believed that about as much as he believed she spent her Saturday afternoons at a sewing circle. He'd taken a deep, difficult breath. "Let's get through this current problem, then we can talk about an allocation of assets."

"No, it's going to be the other way around."

"And if I refuse?"

"Then we're each going to have to do what we're going to have to do."

Simon had wagged a finger at her, feeling feeble even as he did it. "I don't like the sound of that, Mayte. I don't like it a bit."

"Well, that's too fucking bad. You might as well resign yourself. Now I'm going to bed. In the morning you'll transfer the money. Once that's done, we'll concentrate on undoing the mess."

His wife had left the room, going to the other bedroom in the suite, the one where she usually slept. Simon couldn't help wondering if they'd ever sleep together again.

Surprisingly, he'd fallen asleep as he'd anguished over this latest turn of events. He'd heard nothing more from Mayte, and there were no signs of her now. Often she'd listen to soul music before she slept, but he couldn't hear a sound. The house was quiet.

Lying there, emotionally spent, he was more aware than ever of the labored beat of his heart. He wrestled with his options for several minutes, then got out of bed. Quietly making his way to the hall, he padded downstairs. Once in his office he took his little book from the middle drawer, found the number he wanted and dialed. It rang a long time before there was an answer.

"This is Simon Van Biers," he said. "I apologize for calling so late, but I'm going to need that plane first thing in the morning. As early as you can get here."

"What's your destination, Mr. Van Biers?"

"I don't know, let's make it Rio. For starters, anyway."

"How many passengers, sir?"

"Probably just one. Myself. But there could be one or two more."

"Okay, sir, we can handle that, no problem."

"But I'll have a large crate with me, for sure."

"What size, sir?"

"About four feet by five feet by one. Less than a hundred pounds."

"That's easy enough, sir."

"Give me a couple hours' notice before your arrival," Simon said.

"Yes, sir, I will."

He hung up the phone. Then he opened the file drawer and

found the folder marked V.G./R.P. and removed it. After leafing through it in a cursory manner to confirm everything he needed was there, he again picked up the telephone and dialed the security service number at the office.

"Security," the man said.

"This is Simon Van Biers. Who's in charge tonight?"

"Mr. Richmond, sir."

Simon was glad. Richmond seemed the most capable and responsible of all the people on the security staff. "Is he available?"

"Yes, sir."

"Put him on, please."

A moment passed then the familiar voice of Tony Richmond came on the line. "Yes, Mr. Van Biers."

"Tony, it's time to crate up the sunflowers. Have it down at the service entrance and ready to be loaded in the van by dawn. I want no less than three men with it at all times. When I give the word, I want it delivered to the airport. Do you understand?"

"Yes, sir."

"Okay, I'll phone in the alarm code now. As soon as you've turned things off on your end, get to work."

"Right you are, sir."

Simon depressed the flash button, then dialed the alarm access number. Once he was connected, he keyed in the disarm code, which enabled the security people to complete the disarming procedure from their end. The system reduced the chances of the painting being taken by strong-arm tactics. Any robbers would have to force his compliance from a remote location, as well as the compliance of the guards on-site.

The task completed, Simon took a deep breath, then, his arthritic knees creaking, he got to his feet and went to the wall safe behind a Miro print. For the second time that evening, he opened it, stuffed the last forty thousand dollars into the plastic shopping bag that he kept inside. He was sorry that he'd given Charles that twenty-five thousand earlier. His son had arrived and, in his usual brusque, impatient manner, said, "Mayte told you I need twenty-five thousand, I hope."

Simon had pointed to the bag containing the money, sitting on a chair. Without another word, Charles had taken it, then left. After Charles had gone, the Porsche roaring off in the night, Simon had sat in silence for a long time. He thought of the little half breed he'd screwed in Reno those many years ago, unable even to summon from memory the way she looked. The consequences of that night were still very much with him, he knew. And sadly—yes, sadly—the final chapter of Billy Blue's life, their son's life, was about to be written.

Simon did not like the way things had worked out. It was the very last scenario he would have picked. But Billy had been stubborn and left him with little choice. At every juncture somebody seemed to want to do Simon in. First Pearson, then Billy. Even Mayte was getting into the act. A man could only endure so much.

Simon recalled how his own daddy, Maximilian Pettigrew, normally a man with a healthy respect for life, had lost patience with a "nigra preacher" up in Hattiesburg who'd tried to shake him down. After the reverend ignored two or three warnings, Maximilian finally sent ol' Amos Tull up to have a word with him. Amos ended up breaking the stock of a twelve gauge over the reverend's head, which sent the Lord's servant first to the hospital, then the mortuary. Maximilian had sent an enormous flower arrangement for the funeral, saying to his son, "Nothing is more important than for a man to respect the dead—after he protects his family and his livelihood, of course."

Billy was family, of sorts, but mostly he was a threat to Simon's livelihood, and maybe his freedom, because to placate Billy everything else would have to be sacrificed. Simon had hoped to buy the boy off but, considering the way things had snowballed, he didn't have the luxury of waiting to see how that would work out. Nor had the fact that he'd decided to bail out changed anything. With Billy out of the picture, any challenge to his own claim to the sunflowers would be behind

him, once and for all. His daddy had taught him to be prepared
for any contingency and that was exactly what Simon had
done.

The bag of money and the file in hand, Simon left his office
and started back up the stairs. He only got halfway before he
felt a terrible shortness of breath. He started getting dizzy.
God, the stress was really getting to him. He needed to get
back to bed.

He made it the rest of the way to the top of the stairs and
down the hall, steadying himself by feeling his way along the
wall. Once in his room, he was overwhelmed by nausea. A
panicky feeling welled. Dear God, what was happening to
him?

"Mayte!" he croaked as he headed for the bed. He just
couldn't get enough air to cry for help. Then a terrible pain
went shooting through his chest and his left arm. He felt his
knees buckle and he finally realized what was happening. Everything went black and he was unconscious even before he
hit the floor.

The Countryside

They drove along the dark road, headed for the Biloxi Plantation. Neither of them had said much. Billy suspected that
Zoe, in her way, was as uncertain about what was coming as
he was. It wasn't that he didn't believe her story, but there
was a hell of a lot riding on this for both of them. And how
many folks would fib if a hundred million dollars was at stake?

One thing was clear, he didn't much like having doubts
about Zoe, but he didn't want to be made the fool, either.
Women, it seemed, had a distinctive way of disappointing a
fella. More than once he'd been blindsided. He'd also found
that most gals could be pretty nimble, changing directions at
the drop of a hat—like Connie Meeks deciding Luther wasn't
such a bad guy, after all.

Maybe it was simple self-preservation that was behind these

things. When Billy had remarked on Connie's eleventh-hour conversion, she'd explained that she didn't have much choice because he didn't seem all that eager to take her on the road with him. Luther, she'd decided, was her best bet.

But who was Zoe's best bet? he wondered. Probably not a crippled-up rodeo cowboy. And yet, the niggling optimism in his heart wouldn't allow him to give up on her. She claimed to care about him, but he reckoned he'd find out the way things truly were soon enough. The question was if she'd justify his faith in her or prove that love and compassion came pretty dang far down the list of things that mattered.

Meanwhile, he'd learn what he could. So, he asked, "Out of curiosity, Zoe, are you divorcing your husband, or is he divorcing you?"

"I filed."

"Mind if I ask why?"

"Ahmed was unfaithful, but that's not the real reason. The real reason was that we were from two different worlds and we had little more in common than sexual attraction. We didn't believe the same things, care about the same things or dream the same dreams. Don't ask me why I married him. Maybe it was because exotic seemed exciting or it was because I didn't truly know myself as a person. Or maybe I was just young and stupid." She glanced over at him. "Does that answer your question?"

"I reckon."

Zoe showed no inclination to continue the conversation, so again he took the initiative. "What are your dreams?" he asked.

"Now you're getting personal," she said, smiling.

Billy shrugged.

"I want my family's painting," Zoe told him. "It's worth a fortune, so that part's obvious. But more than that, it hung forever in my grandfather's study in Holton, Kansas. If it ends up in a museum, as it surely will, I want his name on it, and I'd like the art history books to refer to it as the Kansas sunflowers."

"What about the money?"

"I like the idea of being financially secure. Beyond that, I'll do something socially responsible. I'll do some things for art and some things for women."

"And if you don't get the painting?"

"I can live with that as long as I've given it my best shot. But I owe myself and my family that much. And maybe I owe it to Van Gogh, as well."

Billy thought about that. "I assume from what you said Ahmed wouldn't understand your feelings."

"He wouldn't understand how I felt sitting on the back porch snapping beans with my grandmother on a summer evening, listening to her tales about my grandfather, the country doctor I never knew. In my young mind, I always associated Carson Gill with that colorful picture of the sunflowers that hung on his wall. I still do."

She glanced over at him, her eyes lingering a second too long. A vehicle suddenly came around a curve in the narrow road ahead, its headlights momentarily blinding them. Zoe swung the wheel and the right wheels slid into the ditch. The other vehicle stopped beside them. Billy recognized the driver. It was Able, the elderly cabby.

"Mr. Blue," Able said, recognizing him. "Las Vegas, right, sir?"

"Close. What are you doing out here in the middle of the night, Able?"

"Dropped a fare out in the middle of nowhere, if you can imagine, sir. Big Jamaican gentleman, paid me five times the tariff because of the lateness of the hour. Said he found a beach he liked and was going for a midnight swim. Didn't make much sense considering there was no special beach out that way. Dropped him in the road."

Billy and Zoe looked at one another.

"Where was this, Able?"

"On up the road quarter of a mile. Near where we nearly ran down the old voodoo woman."

Billy felt a clutch in his stomach, knowing what that likely meant.

"He's after Marie," Zoe said, realizing the same thing.

"Yeah." Billy gave the taxi driver a wave. "Thanks, Able."

"You all right there, sir? Looks like you've got a wheel off the roadway."

Billy leaned out. The tire had sunk a ways into some soft soil, but not so badly they couldn't get out with four-wheel drive. "We're fine."

"Good night then," Able said. Nodding at Zoe, he drove on.

She revved the engine and pulled back onto the roadway, kicking up a bunch of mud and dirt in the process. "What do you think, Billy?"

"I think we owe it to Marie to warn her."

She nodded. "Yes, I agree."

Zoe drove on down the dark road purposefully. Billy felt a surge of adrenaline, not unlike the feeling he'd get in the moments before the beginning of an event at the rodeo. The bull riders would pace around behind the chutes or hang on a fence, looking forward to eight seconds of hell. Billy remembered all too clearly, the air of the arena filled with the smell of horse-flesh and dung, rawhide and popcorn. Hours and days of waiting for a few climactic moments on the back of an ornery ton of beef.

"The side road's along here somewhere, Zoe," he said.

She slowed. They soon came to the turn. Zoe drove slowly down the bumpy track.

"Think I should turn off the headlights?" she asked.

"I imagine he'll figure out we're coming, lights or no," Billy replied. "With luck we'll scare him off."

"What could that man be up to? And why was he at the club earlier?"

"Beats me."

"He is one scary guy. Maybe we should have asked the taxi driver to send the police."

"We can't exactly prove he's up to no good, Zoe."

"Marie said he wanted to kill you."

"I've been acquainted with a few bulls of the four-footed variety who had a similar notion. Anyway, fortune-telling's not very good proof." He pointed to a little pull-off area ahead. "That's where we stopped before."

Zoe brought the Jeep to a halt, turned off the engine and the headlights. They were suddenly plunged into the silence and darkness of the tropical night.

"Now I bet you wished you carried a gun," she said.

"I'd settle for a healthy back." He climbed out of the Jeep. "Maybe you should wait here."

"No, I want to stay with you." She got out.

"The guy might not have sociable intentions, Zoe."

"There's security in numbers," she said, coming around the Jeep.

"Three or four more bull riders wouldn't be too many."

"Nice time to think about that."

Billy took her hand and they moved through the trees on the path leading to Marie's house. Soon they were able to see flickers of light, most likely from torches and candles. When they broke out into the clearing, they were able to see that the house was dimly lit, though there was no sign of life, no sound. Most of the light was coming from the torches that surrounded the hounfour out back.

Zoe moved so close to him that her body bumped up against his when he paused at the front door. He gave her hand a reassuring squeeze. She clasped both hands around his.

"Do you think we should go in?" she asked, her voice trembling slightly.

"It's probably the best way to find out if anybody's home."

"Maybe we should just call to Marie from here."

"On the other hand, no point in waving a red flag at the bull. You stay here and I'll have a peek."

"No, that's all right," she whispered. "I'll come, too."

Billy couldn't help a smile. "Bet you didn't like scary movies when you were a kid."

Zoe's eyes narrowed. "I have a well-developed sense of self-preservation."

Billy moved to the door with Zoe right on his heels like a shadow. He peered inside. Half a dozen candles lit the main room. Nothing seemed amiss. He picked up a candle and started toward one of the back rooms.

"You aren't going back there, are you?" Zoe said.

"You know a better way?"

"Yes, as a matter of fact. Marie?" she called out. "*Êtes-vous là?* Are you here?"

Billy rolled his eyes. "What about the guy?" he said under his breath.

"He's deaf, remember?"

Billy sighed and walked into the dark room, a bedroom. The candlelight revealed that no one was there. No person, living or dead. Coming out, he went to the other back room, the kitchen. Same result.

Zoe joined him at the back door, where he peered out at the mambo's makeshift temple. Candlelight illuminated the interior within the circle of torches. It took a moment of searching the shadows, then Billy saw him. The hulking black man was seated off to the side, on a box, his muscular arms and shoulders gleaming. Zoe saw him a second later and gasped.

"Oh my God, there he is."

Billy studied the scene with care, unsure of the situation. There was no sign of Marie. The Jamaican maintained a relaxed, contemplative pose. He almost seemed to be thinking and waiting. For what? Marie?

"What is he doing?" Zoe whispered.

"I don't know."

"Where's Marie?"

"I have no idea."

"Do you suppose he's hurt her?"

"If so, you wouldn't think he'd be sitting around."

"What are we going to do?"

"That's the real question, isn't it?"

"I think we should go, Billy. We've done everything we

can. Marie doesn't seem to be around, so we can't warn her. If we do anything, we should go home and call the police.''

"Maybe that's the smart thing to do, but the big guy might have Marie in that hole again. If he does, I wouldn't want to leave, knowing she needs help.''

"But what can you do? That man's twice your size and he doesn't have a bad back.''

"You could say the same thing about most of the four-legged critters I've known, Zoe. I think I'll go have a word with him.''

"You mean walk right in there? Are you crazy?''

"The best defense is sometimes a good offense.''

"Billy, you're out of your mind.''

"I've heard that said before.''

He stepped out the back door and walked slowly toward the structure. He'd only gone a few steps before he realized Zoe was following behind. Billy continued walking, managing to get almost to the overhang before the Jamaican looked up and saw them in the glimmering light from the torches. He rose to his feet.

"Dani? Goddamn!'' he exclaimed with a grin. "So you brought the cowboy to our little party. Good for you. Come on in, Mr. Blue.''

Billy was flabbergasted. What the hell was the guy saying? Was he nuts? Then it hit him. He had mistaken Zoe for somebody else, somebody named Dani. Dani? Then he had a second insight—Danielle. The woman at the club. She and Zoe looked alike. And in the faint light...

Billy slowly lifted his hands above his shoulders. "Zoe,'' he said out of the corner of his mouth, "stay behind me. Don't let him see your face. He thinks you're somebody else.'' Then to the Jamaican, "What are you going to do, mister?''

"Say what? Speak up, man. Bring him on in here, Dani.''

Billy stumbled forward as though he'd been pushed. He kept his hands up. "I want to know what you're going to do,'' Billy shouted at him.

"Dani, didn't you tell the bastard? Save the big surprise for me, did you? What you doing hanging back, babe. Bring him on in.''

"Where's Marie?" Billy yelled.

"She's waiting in the hole. Now come on over here. Dani, what the fuck's going on? We gotta waste these sons of bitches so we can go see Chucky and get our money." As he said the last words he started toward them.

"Hang on, Zoe," Billy said under his breath. "When he gets a little closer, I'll grab him and you run like hell."

"What about you?"

"This was my bright idea. I'll take the first punch."

"Billy..." she said anxiously.

"Just run when I say."

"But..."

The closer the Jamaican got, the more perplexed his expression became. "Dani?"

"Okay, Zoe, now!"

As he said it, Billy lowered his head and charged the bull, plowing into the hulk's solar plexis with his shoulder. He knocked the guy back a couple of steps, but only because he'd caught him flat-footed. The Jamaican, though huge, was agile. Quickly regaining his balance, he took Billy by the shoulders and slammed him to the ground. A paralyzing pain shot through his back. Billy lay stunned.

The bull, his nostrils flaring, pressed his huge sandaled foot on Billy's throat, but he wasn't looking at him, he was staring at Zoe, who was fleeing into the darkness. At about the same moment he seemed to realize his mistake.

Glaring down at Billy, he increased the pressure on his neck. "What'd you do with my woman, man? Where the fuck is she?"

"What woman?" Billy croaked, tugging on the huge ankle with all his might, but unable to reduce the pressure.

"Dani! The one you was trying to fuck in the club!"

"Danielle? I left her...there, with some...other guy." Billy could hardly get the words out. He thought at any moment his windpipe would be crushed or his spine crack.

"Bullshit! Dani was bringing your ass here!"

"I don't know...what you're...talking about."

"The hell you don't!"

The bull removed his foot from Billy's neck, reached down then and, taking him by the shirt, lifted him to his feet as though Billy were a five-year-old child. His hands around Billy's neck, he banged his head sharply against Billy's and glared into his eyes.

"You tell me where she is, man, or I'll break your motherfuckin' neck!"

Billy felt a trickle of blood run down his forehead. "I wish I knew."

The bull filled with rage. "Goddamn right!" he roared, spittle flying. "Now, man, you and me don't have nothing to talk about."

The Jamaican's fingers tightened on Billy's throat. Billy pulled frantically at the huge hands, knowing he was about to die. As the pain and the darkness closed in on him he heard a horrible shriek.

"Erzulie Dantor, kill the bull!"

There was a flash of movement behind the big man. He suddenly stiffened and his eyes bulged. His huge frame shook strangely and his mouth sagged open. The pressure on Billy's throat subsided and he felt himself slip from the big man's grasp. He dropped like a stone to the dusty ground. Above him the mountainous body twisted slightly one way, then the other. He made a horrible, aspirated gasp and slowly sank to his knees. His eyes rolled back in his head and he fell forward over Billy's legs.

Himself gasping for air, Billy stared up into the frenzied eyes of the Bon Mambo Marie Vincente de la Croix.

Her jaw slack, Marie muttered, "Erzulie Dantor killed the bull!"

Billy looked down at the behemoth lying over him and saw the handle of a knife protruding from a blood-soaked muscle shirt. The bull did not move. The bull did not breathe. The bull was dead.

* * *

Zoe had just reached the main road when she saw a vehicle coming from the direction of town. "Thank God," she muttered breathlessly.

Standing in the beam of the headlights she waved her arms for the vehicle to stop and it did. Zoe heard the door open and she saw a figure climb out of the driver's side.

"I need help," she cried. "There's a man..." About then she saw who the driver was. It was Danielle, the dancer, Dani, the black man's wife. She had a gun in her hand.

Zoe spun and started running. Glancing back, she saw Dani coming after her. Zoe's skirt was an impediment until she pulled it up over her hips, but not nearly the impediment of her sandals. She nearly fell twice on the uneven gravel surface but managed to keep her feet. Dani, who wasn't exactly in running shoes herself, gained rapidly on her.

Sensing the woman was only a few feet back, Zoe abruptly swerved off the road, plunging into the undergrowth. Dani stayed in hot pursuit. They tore through the shrubs and vines, finally reaching sand. Zoe could hear the thump of Dani's feet in the sand, then a grunt as she dove, catching Zoe by the shoulders and knocking her to the ground.

They rolled around in the darkness, Zoe clawing and flailing for all she was worth. But Dani was stronger, much stronger. A violent kick caught Zoe on the side of the head and she fell to the ground. Zoe lay there stunned for a moment until Dani pulled her to her feet.

"You're lucky I didn't blow your goddamn head off," Dani said, waving the gun in her face. "Now, what the fuck's going on?"

Zoe wove back and forth, so woozy she could barely stand. Dani gave her a good hard shake.

"Didn't you hear me?"

"We went to see Marie," Zoe said, her chest heaving. "We found your husband there. I ran for help."

"Who was with you? The cowboy?"

"No..."

"Then who?"

Zoe could see she was in no condition even to lie, but she gathered her thoughts as best she could. "Charles," she said, grasping for a name. "Charles Van Biers." She recalled the bull making reference to Chucky.

"What's he doing there?"

"I don't know. He forced me to go. When they started fighting I ran away."

"Well, let's see about that."

Dani had Zoe by the arm. She gave her a shove in the direction of the road.

Zoe prayed that maybe someone else would come along, but given the hour and the fact that there was little traffic on the island, even during the day, there wasn't much hope of that. As they walked along the dark road, Zoe's mind raced in search of a strategy.

"Do you mind telling me what's going on?" she asked. "Charles wouldn't say."

"You don't want to know."

"What makes you so sure?"

"Trust me. So, where's the cowboy?" Dani asked.

"I don't know."

"You're a lying bitch," the woman said, giving her a warning shove.

Zoe searched for a ploy. "Charles hired you, didn't he? He as good as said so."

"You want a fat lip? Zip it."

Zoe could see she wouldn't be getting any cooperation, but she'd most likely touched on what was going on. How the mambo figured into things, she had no idea.

They reached Dani's vehicle, which sat in the road just as they'd left it. Dani told Zoe to get in. She kept the gun trained on her as she drove down the track in the direction of the mambo's little house.

Zoe was terrified about what they'd find when they got there. She wondered if there was any chance Billy was still alive. What they'd do with her, she had no idea. Would they kill her because of what she'd seen? How did professional killers view such things?

Dani pulled up behind the Jeep. She told Zoe to stay put until she came around. Opening the passenger door, she rudely dragged her out of the vehicle. They started down the path. Dani pressed the barrel of the gun into Zoe's back and said, "Now keep your mouth shut."

Neither of them knew what to expect.

When they came to the house, Dani gave a cursory look inside the door. "Mooky?" she called.

No answer.

Taking Zoe's arm, she led her around the house. "Mooky?" she called more loudly. "Mooky, where are you?"

As they came in sight of the temple, Zoe saw the torches had been extinguished. Still she saw two figures scurrying about in the shadows. The small, slight figure of the mambo could be clearly seen. She was extinguishing candles.

"Mooky!" Dani cried, running toward the open-sided structure, dragging Zoe behind her.

Marie had melted into the darkness by the time they reached the overhang. On the far side Billy ducked into the shadows himself.

"The cowboy!" Dani said, spotting him.

Only one faint candle continued to burn. It cast just enough light to see a mound on the floor of the temple. The mound was a body. It was Mooky. The handle of a knife protruded from his back.

"Oh my God!" Dani cried, making the gruesome discovery at the same moment. She dragged Zoe with her to the body, where she dropped to her knees. "Mooky!" she screamed at the lifeless form.

It wasn't until Zoe looked up and saw the mambo, waving frantically at her, that she realized it was her chance to escape. Turning on her heel, she began to run toward the house.

"Stop, you bitch!" Dani screamed.

She fired a shot and Zoe heard the bullet crash into the plaster of the house. Zoe continued to run. There was shrieking behind her. Another shot rang out. Zoe looked back and saw the mambo fall. Zoe stopped and watched as Dani went over and fired two more shots at the old woman.

The next thing she knew, she was being dragged by the arm into the undergrowth. They were hunkered down in the bushes before she was absolutely sure it was Billy who'd grabbed her. There was just enough light to see that his face was smeared with blood.

They could see Dani standing in the temple, the gun dangling from her hand.

"Come out and fight like a man, Blue, you fucking coward," she yelled. "I'm going to kill you!" She seemed to be sobbing between outbursts. "Goddamn you to hell!"

Billy pulled Zoe to her feet, wincing in pain, staggering as he led her deeper into the undergrowth. "We've got to get to the Jeep."

The vegetation was dense and Billy clearly was in pain.

"Are you all right?" Zoe asked.

Billy wiped the fresh blood from his forehead with his sleeve. "I've had better days."

"Blue, you fucking bastard!" Dani screamed, her voice more distant now, though the direction seemed to be changing.

Billy and Zoe fought their way through tangles of vines and low branches. Nearing the spot where the track cut through the woods, Billy slowed. They could barely make out the two vehicles in the darkness.

Billy lowered himself to one knee, his breathing labored. He again wiped the blood from his face. "Where's the key to the Jeep?"

Zoe thought.

"I think I left it in the ignition."

Billy considered that. Then, shuddering with pain, he stood. "I'll go check."

"No, Billy, I'll go."

Before he could stop her, Zoe pushed through the undergrowth and headed for the Jeep. She was maybe ten or twelve yards away from it when Dani popped up from behind the fender and opened fire.

The first shot whizzed past Zoe's head. The second thudded into a tree trunk behind her. She dropped to the ground and began scrambling on all fours back toward the woods as two more shots rang out. She made it into the dense vegetation and Billy's arms as the firing stopped. They did not wait to see what Dani would do. They tore through the undergrowth, frantically plunging deeper into the woods. After a minute, Billy stopped and, with his back propped against a tree, he painfully fought for air. Zoe didn't have to see his face to know how much he was suffering.

"What now?" she said.

"I don't think my dancing partner wants us to ride home in style," he said, gasping for breath. "So, I guess it's on to plan B."

Queenstown

Jerome Hurst was dozing, but not fully asleep when there was a light rap on the bedroom door. He lifted his head from the pillow, uncertain where dream and reality parted. Another knock.

He pulled back the covers, not convinced until that moment that there was actually someone at the door. But then he realized he was naked, as was Elise, who continued to sleep. They'd made love with more fervor than they had in years. He'd been surprised by how passionate and loving it had been. Not just for her, but for him as well.

Another knock. Elise moaned. Jerome quickly slipped on the silk robe his wife had given him for his birthday and went to the door, opening it a crack. Rogers, in pajamas and a light terry robe, stood in the lit hall. He was sleepy-eyed.

"Terribly sorry to disturb you, Mr. President, but Chief Inspector Goodson is in the hall downstairs with an urgent request to speak with you."

"Goodson's here?"

"And Mr. Tuttlebee as well, sir."

"What time is it, Rogers?"

"Half past one, sir."

Jerome did not bother with further questions, knowing he'd get the best answers downstairs.

"What it is, darling?" Elise asked, squinting into the shaft of light from the hall.

"Some urgent police matter, dear. I have to speak with Goodson. I won't be long."

Jerome took the time to get his slippers. Beyond that he didn't care how he looked. Rogers had gone on downstairs.

As Jerome made his way along the hall, he thought of Mayte, though not with the same urgent yearning as before. To the contrary, she now was a source of anxiety. His fantasies weren't so much of them being together as her fleeing the scene. Not that the thought of her couldn't be arousing, it was that the mental image of her could evoke as much anxiety as desire.

Reginald Goodson was not freshly shaved, nor was he wearing a tie, but otherwise he remained Sir Reginald through and through. He paced with his hands behind him as Jerome descended the stairs. Basil was more reasonably attired in a lightweight jogging suit. He stood closer to the door. They both looked up at the president of their small nation descending the stairs bare-legged in slippers and a robe.

"Terribly, terribly sorry for the intrusion, Mr. President," Goodson said. "I know the hour is ungodly—"

"Never mind, what's the crisis?"

"You recall the professional assassins we have under surveillance, sir?"

"The Jamaicans."

"Yes, Mr. President, Marvin Blade and his wife, Danielle."

"What about them?"

"They've been in contact with the Van Biers boy again. They've also been in contact with an American visiting on a tourist visa, a chap named Willard Blue Bear."

"Is he an assassin, too?"

"No, Mr. President. Remarkably, Mr. Blue Bear is the illegitimate son of Mr. Simon Van Biers."

"Simon has two sons cavorting with assassins?"

"Yes, indeed, sir. Toliver and the FBI agent, Miss Tsu, witnessed the encounter. But there's more. The FBI has an informant in Mr. Van Biers's household—a young woman by the name Zoe Marton. Apparently she does similar work done by the deceased Mr. Pearson."

"Don't tell me she's been killed."

"No, Mr. President, but she informed Special Agent Tsu that she has cause to believe Mr. Simon Van Biers himself may in some way be connected with the death of Mr. Pearson."

"Good God."

"Yes, very shocking indeed, sir. I'm afraid that's not all, however. Coincidentally, Tuttlebee has additional information bearing on the Pearson matter." Goodson turned to Jerome's aide. "Tuttlebee, would you be so kind?"

Basil Tuttlebee came forward, looking sheepish. "I'm embarrassed to inform you, sir, that Poppy has information that may bear on the Pearson case."

"Poppy? Good heavens. What could she possibly know?"

"It's vague but convincing. Poppy awakened me not an hour ago sobbing, certain the baby was about to die. I thought it a dream, sir, but she kept mumbling something about Marie Vincente de la Croix."

"A Haitian voodoo adherent who's been residing on St. Margaret," Goodson interjected. "She was previously questioned in the matter."

"As it turns out," Basil continued, "Poppy has been consulting the Haitian regarding our fertility problem and in the course of the consultation witnessed a white man fitting Pearson's description being pursued by a group of chaps. One was on horseback and could very well have been Charles Van Biers. This all took place at a beach near the polo club on the day of Pearson's disappearance. Poppy believes the Haitian may have witnessed the actual killing. Poppy recounted all this only after considerable prompting,'' Basil added.

Jerome shook his head in disbelief. ''I assume you propose questioning these individuals, Goodson.''

''Quite right, sir. But we should also like to question Mr. Simon Van Biers and his wife. If there is indeed a conspiracy, as we now suspect, the arrest of some of the suspects might well alert the others and jeopardize our ability to bring all responsible parties to justice. We should like to do this in an organized fashion, as you might imagine. I would like to commence immediately, tonight, if at all possible.

''May I say, sir,'' Goodson continued, ''that I'm very much aware there are political ramifications of such an undertaking. In light of the importance of the bank to the economy, I thought it prudent to bring these matters to your attention before sending my officers out to make the necessary arrests.''

''I very much appreciate that, Goodson,'' Jerome said.

''May we have your approval, Mr. President?''

Jerome frantically weighed the matter in his mind, all the while doing his best simply to appear calmly reflective. Mayte was the trip wire that could very well do him in. If there was any hope of keeping his own name out of any scandal, he would have to give his erstwhile lover a chance to escape. He reflected a minute more, then said, ''As you gentlemen very well know, I have an unshakable commitment to doing justice. However, appearances mean a great deal. I wish for you to initiate your operation, Goodson, but could we hold off with arrests of the members of the Van Biers family until tomorrow? Being dragged from one's bed in the small hours to answer to the police is a great indignity. Should our suspicions about Simon Van Biers be misplaced, the damage could be irreparable. I would hate for the citizens of St. Margaret to suffer, ultimately, over this.''

''I take your point, sir.''

''Can we make it tomorrow afternoon, say?''

''If that is your preference, Mr. President.''

"It is, Goodson. No reason why you can't pursue matters with this Haitian woman, though, is there?"

"No, indeed, sir."

"That way, if she provides damning information about the others, we have a sound basis on which to proceed."

"Quite right, sir."

"Let's get a good night's sleep then and get at this bright and early, shall we?"

"Yes, Mr. President."

Jerome bid them good-night, then mounted the stairs. He hoped Elise was asleep, because he had no desire to discuss this with her. He wouldn't be getting any sleep as it was, anyway. He had much too much to think about.

The Countryside

They'd been tearing their way through the dense vegetation for ten or fifteen minutes, having decided it was best to circle around and connect up with the road farther down. Even at that, Dani could be waiting in ambush. She knew as well as they that there were few dwellings in that part of the island which left only two choices—either the plantation or the polo club, and the plantation was enemy headquarters.

As they slogged along, Billy was in agony, but he felt responsible for getting them into the mess and therefore responsible for getting them out. The trouble was, he wasn't doing a very good job. The jungle-like terrain was very difficult to navigate in the dark.

The vegetation getting thicker and the slope steeper, their rest stops became more frequent. Billy dared not sit on the ground for fear he wouldn't be able to get up again. Instead, he leaned against a tree or sat on a rock or log.

When he called a halt for the second time in five minutes, Zoe eased down on the mossy rock next to him. "Are we lost?"

"You can't get lost on an island, Zoe. At least not for long.

Whichever direction you go, you'll eventually hit water, then you follow the shore.''

"Yep, we're lost."

"No, we're taking an indirect route."

She laughed. "For safety's sake, right?"

"I was trying to cut overland and hook up with the road down near the club."

"I bet we're going in circles."

Billy sighed wearily. "Are you saying you want me to stop and ask for directions?"

"Yeah. And make it a service station, so I can pee."

"If that's your only problem, you've got a whole jungle at your disposal."

"It's not my only problem, it's my immediate problem."

"Want me to turn my back?"

"The one time I truly and absolutely hate men is when I'm out in nature and I have to go to the bathroom."

"Now we know why you're a city girl."

"Turn your back."

Zoe went off into the darkness. He could hear her fighting the undergrowth.

"Don't go too far or I'll never see you again," he called after her.

"Just shut up and hum or something," she called back.

"I guess this isn't the best time to mention snakes."

"Not funny, Billy."

"Just trying to keep things lighthearted."

Actually, lighthearted wasn't an empty desire. The evening had been full of horror, not the least of which had been what had happened to Marie. Why Mooky and Dani wanted to kill her was completely beyond him.

He heard Zoe tromping around.

"Billy?"

"Yes?"

"Where are you?"

"Right here where you left me."

"I think I made a wrong turn."

She did sound as though she was some distance from him. "You're off to my left."

"Which way is your left?"

"Just start walking," he said. "Eventually you'll come to water."

"Shut up and come get me. And make it quick."

"Snakes?"

"Yes, you bastard."

It took a minute, but he found her. The white dress made it easier to spot her in the gloom. She took his hand.

"Remind me to kill you when we get out of here."

"Sure, why not? Everybody else seems to want to do me in."

The vegetation thinned some and they made better headway. It seemed to him they were making their way around the domed hill that was just to the south of Marie's place. But it also seemed they should have long since broken out of the heavy growth of vegetation.

Walking on such rough terrain was a challenge for him and Zoe wasn't in the best shape herself. He was about to call another halt when he heard a sound and stopped.

"What's the matter?" she asked.

"Hear that?"

She listened. "What is it?"

"Sounds like running water to me. Let's investigate."

They only went fifteen or twenty yards before coming to a small ravine and fern grotto tucked into the hillside. The forest canopy broke open, allowing in light from the moon. Seeing the mossy bank next to the rivulet, Billy's first thought was to lie down. "How about a longer break?"

"Fine."

Billy crossed the small stream first, stepping on a rock in the middle. He helped Zoe across. He made it to the mossy area, dropped down, immediately lying flat on his back. It felt better than any featherbed he'd ever been in. "Ahh..." he said.

Zoe sat close to him.

"This is heaven," he said.

"But for a little luck, that's exactly where you could be at this very moment. And that goes for me, too, as a matter of fact."

"People used to say I lived a charmed life. Until Luther took exception to my charm, anyway."

"Your girlfriend's husband."

"Yep."

"Do you have regrets about that?"

"Damned right. It screwed up my life. That's why I'm a reformed man."

She tittered.

"Your impression of me is completely distorted," he said. "And someday you'll realize that. I just hope it's while I'm still alive."

"Given the way you pick your women, it's questionable."

"I suppose your husband wouldn't take very kindly toward me."

"No."

"See. Life's unfair."

Zoe laughed. "You're a very unusual man, Billy Blue. Anybody ever tell you that?"

He looked up at her moonlit face, feeling both warmth for her and longing. She was special. And he felt the closeness of fellow survivors. On an impulse, he reached up and grazed her cheek with the backs of his fingers. "And you're a beautiful woman."

"Oh, those words," she said. "Spoken countless times, no doubt."

"Can't I even have the pleasure of the moment?"

She looked at him an extra long time. He couldn't see her features well enough to read her expression. "Sure, Billy," she finally said. "Enjoy it."

He reached for her face again. Zoe inexplicably bent down and kissed him on the cheek.

"Ooo," she said, "you need to be cleaned up. Do you have a handkerchief?"

Billy pulled one out of his pocket. Zoe took it and crawled over to the rivulet. Having moistened the cloth, she came back and used it to wash his face.

"How'd this happen, anyway?"

"Mooky gave me a head butt and split the skin. Head wounds bleed a lot. It's not a bad cut."

"But it's not very flattering. You've looked better, Billy."

After she finished, she rinsed out the handkerchief and gave it back to him. She took her place, her bare knees only inches from him. She smiled with compassion and maybe something else, as well. He stroked her cheek again, then ran his hand over her shoulder and down her arm. He took her hand, pulled it to his mouth and kissed it lightly.

Zoe glanced around, up at the trees. He could see the moonlight shining on the slender line of her neck. He could feel the softness of her silence, her need, but also her reluctance. He wondered at her thoughts.

Zoe shivered and rubbed her arms. The air in the grotto was cool. He felt it himself.

"You want my shirt?" he asked. "It's a little bloody, but it's pretty much dried now. The sleeves would warm your arms, anyway."

"Thanks, but no. I'm fine."

He reached out and rubbed her upper arm, but that only made her shiver more. "Why don't you lie down beside me and share some body warmth?"

Looking at him, not so much with reluctance as indecision, she ran her fingertip over the back of his hand. "You know, that sounds appealing...I think I'd like it."

"Well?"

"It's scary, Billy."

"Let me tell you a story. One time I was riding the high country in Montana and got caught up in a freak snowstorm. Stumbled on a fisherman camped out by a stream. He only had one sleeping bag, which we shared for the night. Thanked him in the morning and went on my way. You can't think the worst of every dollop of human kindness. Let me be a person, Zoe. It won't hurt.''

"Easy for you to say.''

"I'm really not a bad guy.''

"I never thought you were. Not from the first moment. I know you're nice. Maybe too nice.''

"You know, I'm really confused.''

She sighed. "Just pretend I'm a fisherman, okay?''

She lay down next to him then, scooting close. Billy put his arm around her and gently drew her to his body. Zoe softened, putting her head on his shoulder and melting into him. He kissed her forehead.

Billy drew in her luscious scent. Then she lifted her face and looked into his eyes, inviting a kiss. He gently pressed his lips to hers. She purred and, when their mouths parted, she snuggled closer, murmuring, "Oh, Billy, Billy…'' He couldn't have counted to ten before she was asleep.

St. Margaret Polo Club

Charles had always been a light sleeper—except after sex. Since he hadn't had any in a while, the slight rustle of the plastic bag across the room awakened him. Lifting his head ever so slightly from the pillow he saw a figure, a very shapely figure, silhouetted against the shutters. He'd know that bust and butt anywhere. He'd certainly watched it enough at the Speak Easy.

What was she doing? he wondered. Stealing his money or just picking up her paycheck without saying goodbye? And where was Blade? Charles wanted answers, but he wasn't going to ask for them without backup. Careful not to make a sound, he reached over and pushed the button attached to the phone. He'd activated an alarm in the employee quarters. Within three minutes—if everything worked as it was supposed to—Earl Gridley and at least one of his men would come storming in the door.

A tiny beam of light from a pen flashlight cut through the darkness of the room. Dani seemed to be making a rough count of the money, probably to make sure he hadn't split it up, which, of course, he had. She was looking at five grand. Smart girl. But not quite smart enough.

"Tell you what, Dani…"

He only got that far before she whirled, shining the narrow beam of light in his face.

"…if you take off that little skirt and top and climb in bed with me, I'll tell you where the rest is."

Only then did he see the gun in her other hand. It occurred to him that he should have waited another minute or so before confronting her, but it was too late. He had to stall.

"Where is it, you sonovabitch?" she demanded.

"Why, Danielle, is that the way they treat gentlemen in Canada?" Charles reached over and turned on the lamp on the bedstand, momentarily blinding them both.

"Jesus Christ," she groused. "My finger's on the goddamn trigger. I could have blown your head off."

"Sorry. I thought we were better friends than that."

"Cut the crap, Van Biers. Where's the dough?"

Charles, getting a good look at her for the first time, saw that she was red-eyed, dirty and even had blood on her skirt. "What the hell happened to you?"

"The money!" she cried, baring her teeth.

"I take it you and Mooky have done your job."

"Yes, goddamn it. I want the money and I want to get out of this hole. Move!"

"Okay, okay, I'll get it. But I've got to get out of bed."

"Do it!"

"All right, but I've got to warn you, I sleep in the buff. Think you'll be able to control yourself?"

She cocked the hammer of her automatic and aimed at his head.

"Take it easy, take it easy," he said, throwing back the covers.

Dani Blade took half a step back, but to his chagrin she

didn't so much as look at him. Was Mooky that impressive that the rest of the world paled? he wondered.

"It's in the closet."

"Yeah, well, watch how you move those hands, because if I even get a hint you're reaching for a gun, I shoot first and check second."

Charles opened the closet door, wondering where in the hell the boys were. It also occurred to him he could find himself in a cross fire unless she saw instantly that she was outgunned. He felt a knot in his stomach.

The rest of the money was in a small satchel on the floor that also contained a snub-nosed .38. His heart beginning to race, Charles leaned down to get the bag.

"Easy," she said. "At this point I've got nothing to lose."

His hand stopped. "Oh, but Mooky does."

"Mooky's dead, asshole."

Charles looked back at her with surprise. That would explain the red eyes. "Who did it?"

"The mambo. But I got her. The old bitch and the cowboy ambushed Mooky."

"What about him?"

"Dead. I got them both."

"Really?"

"Yes, come on. Is the money in the bag?"

"Yeah."

"Pull it out of the closet. Very slowly."

Charles lifted the bag and Dani reached for it just as the door flew open. She spun, catching Earl Gridley and one of his boys flat-footed and empty-handed.

"Oh Jesus," Charles moaned, seeing they weren't armed.

"Shit," Earl hissed, realizing he'd screwed up. "Sorry, boss."

"Shut up, all of you," Dani shouted. Then to the men she said, "Turn around and put your hands on the wall. Don't move or I'll blow your goddamn heads off."

Dani was distracted just long enough for Charles to reach

in the bag and take the .38. She wasn't aware it was in his hand until she heard him cock the hammer by her ear.

"Now it's your turn, sweetie," he said.

Dani's shoulders slumped.

"Bend down and put the gun on the floor," he said. "Very slowly."

She hesitated, looking as though she was weighing the possibility of opening fire anyway, but in the end she didn't. After she set the automatic on the floor, Charles gave her an affectionate slap on the butt.

"Enough playing criminal, babe," he said. "Now it's time to play cunt. Earl, take the lady down to the tack room, tie her up and make sure she'll stay quiet. I'll be down shortly. It's too early to ride the ponies, but there's no reason I can't ride Dani Blade." He reached over and tweaked her chin. "I told you that you owed me, remember?"

Charles wasn't a slob, so he showered and brushed his teeth before he set off to rape Dani Blade. Not that he thought of it as rape. Usually the women he fucked were willing, if not eager. Not Dani Blade. She'd acted like an arrogant bitch from the start and she'd clobbered him to boot. Now he was going to rub her nose in it, royally. He'd teach her about respect, the way a woman was supposed to behave.

As he made his way toward the stables, Charles heard the sound of vehicles in the road. Turning, he saw flashing lights, the lights of emergency vehicles. They were coming up from the direction of town, headed toward the plantation. What the hell could that be about? Maybe Simon had gotten drunk and fallen again. It had happened a couple of months back. Or maybe he'd found out about Mayte and Jerome Hurst and beat the shit out of her. Charles smiled at the thought. That, he'd like to see.

Whatever it was, he'd find out soon enough. Right now he wanted to think only about Dani writhing under him. It was almost too bad Mooky wouldn't be around to enjoy the show.

Thinking about Blade, Charles decided that him getting himself killed just might turn out to be a stroke of luck. If there were ramifications over the discovery of Raymond Pearson's body, maybe he could find a way to blame the murder on Blade. But he would worry about that later.

The barn door had been left open, which annoyed Charles. Sloppy, he thought. So what if it was the middle of the night? No point advertising it, was there? Goddamn lazy niggers. He entered the barn, making his way toward the tack room. Damn if they hadn't left that door open, too. Jesus Christ!

Reaching the door, he glared in, ready to kick ass. But Charles didn't find what he'd expected. Earl and the other guy were there, but they were both on the floor. Earl was moaning, the other guy was out cold, or dead. Dani Blade was nowhere to be seen.

It was obvious what had happened. She'd somehow turned the tables on them. Charles was livid with rage. ''Jesus Christ!'' he screamed, kicking the door so hard he practically broke his toe.

Earl, a smear of blood at the corner of his mouth, raised himself to his elbow and looked at him sheepishly. ''Sorry, boss, she caught us by surprise. Did this judo thing and—''

Charles stomped over and kicked Earl in the ass, eliciting a howl. ''Idiot! What am I paying you for?''

The other man rolled over, coming to. The two of them looked pathetic. Charles paced back and forth a couple of times, beside himself.

''Get your ass up, get some reinforcements and find the bitch. I don't care what it takes, do you understand?''

''Yes, boss,'' Earl said, struggling to his feet.

Charles was so pissed he could hardly think straight. Then it suddenly occurred to him. The money! Running back to his room as fast as he could, he found exactly what he expected. The money was gone.

* * *

Biloxi Plantation

The telephone on the bedside table rang, awakening her. Squinting at the clock, Mayte saw the hour and wondered who in God's name could be phoning so early. She picked up the receiver. "Hello?"

"Mayte?"

"Yes?"

"Can you talk?"

Realizing it was Jerome, she blinked into wakefulness. "There are a number of extensions, I'd better call you back on another line."

"Okay, but do it quickly. My private line."

Hanging up, she was very much aware of the urgency in his tone. Something was up. Jerome had never once called her at home before.

Grabbing a robe, she hurried downstairs to Simon's office. Entering, she saw Esther and her little boy making their way across the lawn toward the main house. She obviously had the first shift. Mayte went back and closed the office door. Then she went to the desk and picked up the phone, dialing Jerome's number. He answered on the first ring.

"I'm contacting you as a courtesy," he began. "I hope that in appreciation you'll show me the same consideration in return."

"Jerome, what's happened?"

"Reginald Goodson came to see me in the middle of the night, Mayte. He wanted to arrest you and Simon and Charles in connection with the murder of Raymond Pearson. I think his initial intent is just to question you, I don't know the extent of the evidence, if any. I asked him to wait until the afternoon before proceeding. If you feel it's in your interest to leave St. Margaret, I've given you the opportunity. Only you know whether that would be necessary and advisable."

She was stunned. This was a waking nightmare, hitting her without warning. She was so shocked, she found it hard to breathe, much less talk.

When she hadn't replied, Jerome spoke again. "I'll leave it

to you whether to inform Simon and Charles, but it's you I care about, Mayte, and I want you to know and appreciate that.''

''Yes,'' she managed to murmur. ''I do.''

''I hope and trust this will end well for you,'' he said.

He hung up even before she whispered, ''Goodbye.''

She returned the receiver to the cradle and her chin dropped to her chest. It was like a pronouncement of death. For a long moment she couldn't move, not gathering herself until big wet drops of tears began plopping on the top of Simon's desk. She sat in his chair.

They planned to arrest her. Should she tell Simon? If she wanted to enjoy his money in South America, that was the thing to do. A criminal record would foreclose any opportunities she might have back in the States. It was beginning to look as though she was tied to the master, after all. God, what had happened that everything was falling apart? Surely Jerome wouldn't have engineered this. Was it his way of getting rid of her? That seemed unlikely, considering the harm she could cause him. The point was, she didn't have much time.

Just as she stood to leave the room, the phone rang. Her first thought was that it was Jerome calling back, but then it occurred to her that he didn't know what line she'd called him on. Would Simon have given him the number? She decided to let the machine pick it up. On the third ring the machine came on.

Simon's recorded voice said, ''Please leave a message after the tone.''

''Mr. Van Biers...'' It was a man speaking, an unfamiliar voice. He seemed to be talking over a radio. ''...this is Harvey Winston of South Florida Aviation. I've got an ETA of 9:00 a.m. at Ogden Bertrum. We've got sufficient fuel for the St. Margaret–Rio de Janeiro leg, so we won't need much ground time. If you could have people to assist with the crate, sir, it will expedite things. By the way, it will have to be placed in the cargo hold rather than the cabin. I hope that's okay. See you at nine, sir.''

The recording ended. Mayte was incredulous. Simon was

planning to take off for Rio without her. He must have gotten word of the arrests himself and made plans for his own escape without so much as a word of warning for her. The dirty rotten sonovabitch! And what was that business about a crate? Passenger cabin?

Then it hit her. The Van Gogh. Simon was taking off with the Van Gogh. Fifty million in the bank and the sunflowers to boot! What a slimy pig!

It had to be because she'd demanded her cut of the money and the bastard didn't want to share. She couldn't believe this was happening to her. After all the time and energy she'd devoted, all the ass kissing. Goddamn men. First Jerome, now Simon. The rats were abandoning ship, leaving her to fend for herself. At least Jerome telephoned. Maybe love wasn't completely meaningless.

All was not lost yet, though. She had time. And Simon wasn't home free. His ship may have come in, but his plane hadn't left. Mayte decided to start by having a word with him.

She left the office and went back upstairs. Knocking on his bedroom door, she got no answer. So she opened it and was shocked to see her husband on the floor, facedown.

Mayte rushed to him and rolled him over. Even before she pressed her finger to his carotid artery, she knew he was dead. What were the chances she'd see any of the fifty million now?

The Countryside

The sun angling through the trees awakened him, and Billy discovered he was on his side, with Zoe's backside curled against him, so that they were like spoons in a drawer.

The air was quite cool. That partially accounted for her friendliness. His heart bumped pleasantly as he recalled their kiss. She'd been hesitant but willing. The thought made him happy. He couldn't ever recall a woman fighting him so long and hard before giving in. Nor could he ever recall being so pleased by the result.

Funny, but what came to mind was his first time with Shelly in the back of that old pickup in Lamoille Canyon. There was something special about making love out in nature and he found himself wanting Zoe now. But he couldn't take anything for granted. Plus, she was skittish as a mare with her first foal. This wasn't the time to take the next step.

Billy hugged her close, though. The soft skin of her arm felt icy from a night of exposure to the cool air. She purred in her sleep, definitely liking his warmth. He pressed his face into her hair at the base of her neck and drew in her scent, which was a mistake because it aroused him. He'd apparently awakened her as well, because he felt her stiffen slightly and half turn her head.

"It's not a bear, sweetheart, it's me."

Zoe rubbed her eyes and shivered. "That's a relief." She lay still for a moment, completing the transition from sleep to wakefulness. "You kissed me last night, didn't you?"

He wasn't entirely sure whether it was a question or an accusation. "Yes, and you kissed me."

"Hmm."

"I hope you aren't regretting it," he said.

"Not as long as you don't misunderstand it."

"Oh, I realize you kissed me on an impulse and that it doesn't mean a thing."

"Billy, you are a gentleman."

He wished he could laugh, but he wasn't able. "At last you know me for the man I am."

She laughed. "I think I'm going to visit the snakes."

Zoe got up and went off into the bushes. Billy rolled onto his back and stared into the pale morning sky. He had half a recollection of having heard vehicles in the night. Probably on the road. Maybe somebody had found Mooky and Marie. It pained him every time he thought of the old woman. She'd saved his life.

Which reminded him, they really did need to get to a phone and alert the authorities before Danielle escaped. They didn't have the luxury of enjoying the wilds of the island.

As Zoe made her way back to camp, Billy decided to get up and test his back. He was stiff as the dickens, but not in as bad shape as he expected.

"What?" she said, stepping into the clearing. "Breakfast isn't ready?"

"If you want to give me a few minutes I could rustle up some bugs."

"Thanks, but I believe I'll pass. What's our plan?"

There was an outcropping of rocks at the upper edge of the grotto. He decided to climb up and see if he could get a glimpse out over the trees. "I'll see if I can figure out where we are."

Zoe waited where they'd slept on the mossy bank. His back didn't appreciate the climbing, but he did it with more ease than he'd anticipated.

"We're on the hill all right," he announced, "but a little farther around than I thought. The road's below us and the polo club out on the plain. The thing to do is follow the stream down the mountainside. That should hook us up with the road. From there it should be less than half a mile to the club. We should be able to call the cops from there."

"Dani still can't be looking for us."

"Probably not," he said as he climbed down the rocks. "But if she blames us for her husband's death, revenge could be the first thing on her mind. I don't think we should be too cavalier. And we've got to report Marie's death, don't forget."

Billy looked her over as he walked back to where she waited. Her white dress was dirty, stained with vegetation and blood. Her hair was a bit tangled and she was a trifle puffy from sleep, but damn if she didn't look beautiful to him. Boy, had he ever fallen hard. Granny told him it would happen one day. "You're not immune, Billy," she'd said. "A girl will come along who'll knock your socks off, so you might as well resign yourself and be glad."

He hadn't believed her. He thought he'd go on forever, riding bulls, having a few beers with the boys and calling on his lady of the day. A life with plenty of excitement but no complications. But Granny had had the last laugh. And wouldn't you know, it would be a woman from New York, an educated woman working in the arts, a woman about as far removed from the Shelly Richards and the Connie Meeks of the world as you could get.

Coming up to Zoe, he was surprised by the expectant, open, even friendly look on her face, the little smile. Billy extended his hands and she took them. They embraced.

"When this is all over, are you going to let me buy you dinner?" he asked.

"No, I'll buy you dinner."

Billy touched her face, running the palm of his hand along her jaw, then under her hair at the nape of her neck. He leaned over and kissed her lightly. Their second kiss.

Zoe kept her eyes closed a second or two after their lips parted, opening them to find him smiling. "But if you want that dinner, you'll have to find a way to keep me alive," she said.

"So that's the reason for this friendliness."

"Among others."

"But will you love me tomorrow? That's what I want to know."

She gave him a mischievous smile. "I told you, I'm inscrutable."

He ran his hand down her arm. "Do you think it would be selfish of us to take the day off and spend it here?"

"Considering how badly I want a bath, yes."

"I see."

"So, shall we go?"

"Okay. Right after I go have a talk with the snakes."

Biloxi Plantation

Mayte had closed the door to Simon's room and left him where he lay, though she had taken the plastic bag with the forty thousand she'd found on the floor with her to her room.

He'd probably had a heart attack, and she'd let one of the maids discover the body later.

Sitting on her bed, she pondered what to do. She'd virtually torn his office apart looking for something that might help her determine where he'd stashed the fifty million, but she'd had no luck. She wondered if Charles knew, or had a way of finding out what his father had done with the money. He was, after all, Simon's heir and he might have been given the necessary information. There was also a chance Simon's lawyers had that information with instructions to pass it on in the event of Simon's death. The chances of her getting it—or any substantial portion of it—were zilch.

But it was also true that she and Charles had an understanding, even if they didn't particularly care for one another. They'd known that one day Simon would be gone and several times they'd talked in terms of partnership. What were the chances, she wondered, of that happening now?

One thing she did know was that Charles didn't suspect that he was about to be blindsided by the police. The jolly heir could be spending the rest of his life in prison—unless she saved his butt. And found a way to get a cut of the pie. A big cut. Like half.

Thanks to Simon's foresight, there was a way to fly the coop with a nice little nest egg—a hundred-million-dollar Van Gogh crated and ready to go. Although, given the circumstances, there was no guarantee they would be able to convert it to anywhere near that kind of cash. Fugitives didn't have a lot of bargaining power. But someone would be willing to pay several million to be able to hang a genuine Van Gogh on their wall, even if it was contraband.

Mayte had no way of knowing whether Simon had completed the arrangements or not, so she called the security office at the bank. Tony Richmond came on the line.

"Good morning, Mrs. Van Biers."

"Hello, Tony. My husband asked me to check on the status of the painting."

"It's crated up, Mrs. Van Biers, and ready to go. The van

is standing by. I've got three men guarding the crate, just like Mr. Van Biers wanted.''

"Fine. He'll be pleased.''

"I've got a shift change coming up," Tony said. "Any idea when the order to move might come?''

"Oh, I thought Simon told you. Our charter will be arriving at 9:00 a.m. Simon wants you to have the painting there and ready to be loaded.''

"Very good, Mrs. Van Biers. We'll have it there.''

Mayte hung up, feeling very pleased. Things seemed to be falling right into place. Now she had the biggest decision of all. Did she do this alone or include Charles? The one thing certain was that he needed her. And he was also smart enough to realize half of the money Simon had salted away was better than none. Plus, they'd each be better off if the other wasn't in jail. In an odd way, they were in the same boat. Of course, if things didn't work out, they could part company later. Mayte didn't like making bargains with the devil, but it had become a habit.

Deciding it was worth talking to Charles, as a minimum, she went to his room, only to discover he wasn't there. It appeared he hadn't spent the night, which meant he'd be at the polo club.

Returning to her room, she tried phoning him at the club, but got no answer. Chances were he was out riding. It was still too early to phone the office and she really didn't have time to go looking for him—not if she was going to meet that plane. Then she had an idea. She'd send Andrew to get Charles.

Hurrying downstairs, she found Esther in the kitchen. The maid's little boy was at the table, eating breakfast.

"Esther, will you go wake Andrew and tell him I need him for an urgent errand.''

"It's his day off, Mrs. Van Biers. He left last night.''

Mayte groaned. "I need to see Charles immediately. He's probably exercising his ponies at the club. Go down and tell him to come right away. Tell him we've only got an hour before the shit hits the fan."

"Ma'am?"

"Oh, the hell with it, tell him we need to be on a plane by nine this morning with the Van Gogh, or else it's all over. He'll understand. Take the limo. Tell him to meet me at the airport."

"What about my Henry?"

"Take him with you if you have to. Just go! Now!"

Queenstown

Jerome Hurst was strolling in the garden, deep in contemplation, a mug of coffee in his hand, when Elise came out onto the terrace.

"Darling, you have a call. Reginald Goodson has rung you up."

"Oh, blast," he said. "The buggers just won't leave me alone, will they?"

His wife, in a flowing caftan, smiled sympathetically. "It comes with being president, Jerome."

"Yes," he said, stopping next to her. "But even presidents deserve a reprieve now and then. What do you say we take a week or two and go to London? Just the two of us."

"That would be delightful. Do you really mean it, darling?"

He kissed her. "More than ever. And I love you more than ever."

She blushed like a schoolgirl and tapped his nose with her fingertip. "You'd better take your call before Sir Reginald has apoplexy."

"Right you are, old girl," Jerome said, affecting Goodson's manner of speech. He laughed.

Elise giggled and gave him a gentle shove toward the door.

Jerome went to his office and picked up the receiver. "Goodson?"

"Good morning, Mr. President. I thought you'd like an update on developments."

"By all means."

"Regretfully, there have been two more homicides, sir."

"Good Lord, who now?"

"Last night after we spoke, I dispatched officers to the residence of the elder Haitian woman. We found her shot dead, and Marvin Blade, also dead, with a knife in his back."

"How gruesome. Suspects?"

"We believe Mr. Blue was at the scene of the crime and possibly another woman or two, judging by the footprints. Other shots had been fired and we found drops of blood trailing into the forest. A Jeep belonging to Mr. Simon Van Biers was found at the residence, as well. We haven't made inquiries of Mr. Van Biers, as per your instruction, sir. We believe it likely that the vehicle was driven either by Mr. Blue or Miss Marton. In light of the circumstantial evidence at the crime scene, we'd like to bring the two in for questioning immediately."

"Yes, I suppose that's wise. Justice must be done."

"Shall we continue to wait until this afternoon before asking for statements from Mr. and Mrs. Van Biers and the son, Charles?"

"If we possibly can, Goodson."

"It's your decision, sir."

Jerome was torn, but he had to give Mayte a chance to get out of St. Margaret—and out of his life—once and forever. "Then let's wait."

"Very good, sir."

"Anything else?"

"Just one other thing, Mr. President. Blade's wife is unaccounted for. We're searching for her as we speak. But there has been an interesting development in that regard. One of our boat patrols found a cabin cruiser lying off Newquay Bay. It had been hired by Blade and his wife to take them to Jamaica. According to the crew, they were expecting the Blades presently. The craft has been brought in and the crew is being questioned further.''

"The Jamaican woman's route of escape has been closed off to her, in other words.''

"Precisely, sir. Needless to say, we're also looking for her.''

"Excellent work, Goodson. Keep right at it and we'll get to the bottom of things yet.''

"Yes indeed, sir.''

Jerome Hurst dropped the phone into the cradle, wondering if God in his mercy would flush all the others down the drain, yet allow him to remain afloat. If only, if only he hadn't succumbed to Mayte's seductive allure.

St. Margaret Polo Club

Just as Billy and Zoe emerged from the woods a quarter of a mile from the club, Simon's limo zipped by with Esther at the wheel. They yelled after her, but Esther hadn't seen them. Then, when the limo turned off the road and went through the club gates, they saw their chance and ran after her.

The pain in Billy's back was so bad that, when they reached the gate, breathless, he had to stop for a second.

"You okay?'' Zoe asked, her own chest heaving.

"Yeah. The doctor said…exercise was good…for me.''

They were about to continue when they saw the flashing lights of a police car coming up the road from the direction of town. "The cops,'' Zoe said with a grin.

"Perfect. You flag them down.'' Billy took a couple of deep breaths. "If Charles is here…they can arrest him. I'll go see what Esther is up to.''

Billy went on then, circling the clubhouse, which was locked and dark, going past other outbuildings until he saw the limo parked at the edge of the polo field. Esther stood next to it. Charles, on horseback, rode over to where she waited. Then Billy saw the passenger door of the limo open and Henry climb out. Esther appeared to be waving him back to the car, but Henry ran toward the spot where Charles's other ponies were tethered.

Billy didn't know what was going on, but he didn't like it. Biting back the pain, he jogged toward the limo. Esther spoke to Charles, who remained astride his horse, his polo mallet resting on his shoulder. He leaned down, listening to her. But then, when he saw Billy approaching, he sat back in the saddle, upright, his back and neck stiffening. He looked shocked, as if he were seeing a ghost. Esther turned.

Billy walked the last twenty yards to catch his breath. When he got to the limo, he leaned wearily against the fender. Charles glared at him.

"What are you doing here?"

"Why the surprise, Charles? Did you think maybe I was dead?"

"I should be so lucky."

"Well, you aren't lucky, bro. In fact, your luck has run out. The police have just pulled up out front. Perfect timing, eh? They can arrest you and save me the trouble of taking you in."

Charles laughed. "Arrest me for what?"

"Hiring the Jamaican to kill Marie and me. And for all I know, Pearson, too. The old woman is dead, Charles. You're going to pay for that."

"You're full of shit."

Billy heard a vehicle behind him. It was the police car rolling toward them. "I guess we'll see."

The car stopped and two officers emerged, along with Zoe. The somber expression on her face gave Billy pause.

"Mr. Blue," one of the officers, a young, lanky man, said, "you're under arrest, sir."

"Under arrest? Me?" He pointed to Charles. "That's the man you should be arresting."

"I tried to explain," Zoe said, coming up to him, "but they insist they have to take us in for questioning."

Charles laughed. "Looks like the necktie party is for you,

cowboy.'' He patted his pony's neck. The animal was dripping with sweat, obviously having had a rigorous workout.

"Officer," Billy said, "that man hired Blade to kill me and the old Haitian woman, Marie."

"That's bullshit," Charles protested.

"Everybody can make their statements in due course," the officer said. "But we have specific orders to bring you in, Mr. Blue. Mr. Van Biers can make his statement at his convenience."

"Gladly," Charles said.

"Mr. Van Biers won't be coming in later, Warren," Esther said to the cop. "He's getting on an airplane in less than half an hour."

"Esther, shut up," Charles roared. "This is none of your business and you don't know what you're talking about."

"He's lying," Esther said. "Mrs. Van Biers sent me to give him the message to go to the airport. They're leaving and taking the Van Gogh painting with them."

Billy and Zoe exchanged looks. He saw panic in her eyes.

"Officer," Zoe said, "you can't let that man leave the country."

The two cops looked at one another. "Peter," the first cop said, "call headquarters."

"This is ridiculous," Charles blustered as the second cop retreated toward the police car. "Don't you know who I am? If you value your job, you won't even think about arresting me."

"Bang! Bang!" It was Henry's little voice. He was still by Charles's ponies. He waved.

Billy waved back.

"I'm not arresting you," the officer said to Charles, "unless I get the order. But if you're leaving the country, my chief has to know about it."

"This is going to cost you your job, mister," Charles said, wheeling his horse. "Nobody arrests me, I don't care what your chief says."

"Please dismount, Mr. Van Biers, until we get the matter resolved."

Ignoring the order, Charles rode over to his other ponies, swung out of the saddle and began to untether a fresh mount. The policeman took his service revolver from his holster and began walking toward Charles.

"Henry!" Esther screamed. "Come here."

The boy was so enthralled with the horses, and so fascinated with Charles's preparations, that he was oblivious. Esther started for her son. Billy trailed along behind her.

"Mr. Van Biers, don't mount that horse," the cop commanded.

Seeing the officer coming toward him, weapon drawn, Charles stepped over and swooped Henry into his arms, holding the boy in front of him. "Back off!" he shouted.

The officer stopped. Esther, coming up next to him, cried, "No!" Billy took her arm and they watched Charles swing up into the saddle of a fresh mount, still holding the boy as a shield.

"Oh my God," Esther cried.

Billy put an arm around her shoulder.

"Release the child!" the cop commanded.

"Fuck you!" Charles kicked the pony's flanks and came charging toward them.

The officer raised his weapon, but couldn't shoot because of the boy. With Charles bearing down on them, intent on running them down, Billy threw Esther to the side and dived himself. The cop went the other way, right into the path of Charles's swerving mount and was knocked to the ground.

Billy struggled to his feet as Charles wheeled around. The officer stayed on the ground, apparently injured. Charles, urging his horse on, charged at Billy, drawing back his mallet. Billy saw Henry's terrified face and heard him cry as Charles bore down on him. At the last second Billy dived again, but the mallet caught him in the shin, sending a bolt of pain through his leg.

As he lay on the ground writhing in pain, Billy heard a

gunshot behind him. It was the other cop, weapon drawn. He'd come partway onto the field, having fired a warning shot into the air.

"Dismount!" he shouted.

Charles kicked his pony's flanks and charged the second cop, who tried to dodge, but was clubbed in the head with the swinging mallet. Charles pulled up, wheeling again. Billy was back on his feet and Charles saw him. He made another charge. As the pony roared past, turf flying, Billy leaped away, barely eluding the hissing mallet. Charles made still another pass. This time Billy jumped to the other side of the charging horse and grabbed hold of Charles's arm, his bandaged arm, managing to pull him and Henry from the saddle. The three of them ended in a heap on the ground, Billy on the bottom.

Billy, practically paralyzed, wrapped his arms around Charles's legs, holding the writhing man while Esther rushed forward and pulled her son from the melee.

Charles and Billy rolled on the turf, their hands on each other's throats. Charles got in a punch, managing to kick himself free. Now intent on escape, he ran to his mount and swung into the saddle. To Billy's surprise, he took off across the field, retreating at full tilt.

Zoe came running up to where Billy lay on the ground, bleeding from the nose. "Are you okay?"

"I've been better."

"Where do you think Charles is going?"

"My guess is the airport, but we can't be sure. Sweetheart, go bring me that fresh pony, will you?"

"Billy, you can't ride."

"Well, I can't walk, so if I'm going to sit, it might as well be in a saddle. Hurry, before I lose Charles."

While Zoe went to get the horse, Esther and Henry came over to where he lay on the ground. Billy glanced back at the cops. One was sitting up, the other, the one who'd been hit in the head, was still flat on his back.

"Esther," he said, "you better give them a hand. That one guy probably needs an ambulance."

She went off and Henry plopped down on the ground next to him. He had Billy's hat in his hand.

"Don't you want this?" the boy said.

"If I'm going to chase the bad guy, I reckon I should. You okay, partner? Didn't get hurt in that fall, did you?"

Henry shook his head.

Zoe arrived with the horse. She helped Billy to his feet. One leg hurt so bad he couldn't put any weight on it. With Zoe's help he managed to pull himself up into the saddle.

"Zoe," he said, gathering the reins, "take the limo and get over to the airport. See if you can save our Van Gogh." He reached down and caressed her cheek. "How about this? Fifty-fifty, regardless which way it turns out?"

Zoe wrinkled up her nose. "Let me think about it."

"Sweetheart, that could be your best offer."

"We'll see, cowboy."

With that he wheeled the pony around and took off in pursuit of Charles Van Biers. As he rode away, Billy heard Henry's little voice. "Bang! Bang! Bang!"

If he survived the day, Billy decided he'd have a talk with the boy about violence. It wasn't good and it wasn't a game.

Ogden Bertrum Airport

When Mayte pulled up in front of the small terminal building in her BMW, she saw no sign of Charles's Porsche or the charter jet. But the security van was sitting on the tarmac. That was one out of two.

She had a baggage handler carry her suitcases to the field side of the building and she walked over to the van where Tony Richmond and his men waited.

"Good morning, Mrs. Van Biers," Richmond said.

"Good morning. No plane yet," she said, checking her watch.

"Not unless that's it there," he replied, pointing to the sky.

Mayte turned, seeing a plane approaching the field from the

west. Considering how little traffic there was, that had to be the charter. She felt better.

Less than a minute later, the small jet touched down, making a smooth landing on the runway directly opposite them. Mayte signaled for her bags to be brought.

"Get the crate out of the van," she told Richmond. "I want it loaded the minute the plane pulls up."

"What about Mr. Van Biers?"

"He's coming soon," she replied. "He wants everything ready so that we can take off without delay."

The security man did not look pleased, but he gave the order for the crate to be unloaded. Moments later the jet taxied up to the terminal building.

As soon as the jet engine whined down, she said, "Okay, chop-chop."

The pilot, a short, barrel-chested man with a blond brush cut, disembarked from the aircraft and opened the cargo hold. Mayte took him aside.

"Mr. Winston, I'm Mayte Van Biers."

"Hello, Mrs. Van Biers."

"Simon had some last-minute business and it looks like he'll be going to New York tomorrow instead of Rio. But he wanted me to go on ahead with the cargo. Our son may be coming with me, but he also had business to tend to and may not make it. As soon as we're loaded, we can go. If Charles is here, he can come with us, but we won't wait for him."

Winston scratched his head. "My arrangement is to transport Mr. Van Biers."

"I'm well aware of that, but there's been a change of plans. Simon couldn't very well contact you while you were in the air. I'm here and so is the crate, as you can see. What do you want, Mr. Winston, a signed affidavit?"

"No, but I don't like these last-minute changes."

"When you deal with someone like Simon, you have to be flexible."

He sighed. "All right."

Winston went over to supervise the loading of the crate.

Once it was in the hold, he climbed in to strap it down securely.

"You and your men can leave now, Mr. Richmond."

"What about Mr. Van Biers?"

"He told us not to wait if he didn't make it. Give him a call if you don't believe me."

Richmond and his men backed off, but the man was clearly suspicious. Mayte had glanced up the road from time to time during the loading process, wondering where Charles was. Maybe Esther couldn't find the bastard. Or he was too stupid to get off his horse to save his own neck.

Once her bags were on board, Winston informed Mayte they were ready to go. She took a last look at the road. As she did, she heard the faint sound of sirens in the distance. She took that as a bad sign. "Okay, it appears Charles got hung up. Let's go."

Winston helped her up the steps. She'd just stepped inside the cabin when he heard some commotion behind her. Looking out she saw a woman in a bloody white miniskirt and halter top rush to the base of the steps. She had a plastic bag in one hand and a gun in the other. She thrust it into Harvey Winston's side. For a brief instant Mayte thought it was Zoe Marton, but then realized it wasn't.

"Get on board," the woman screamed at Winston.

He obediently trotted up the steps. She followed. Mayte and the pilot backed away from the door.

"I don't know where you're going," the woman said, "but I'm coming along."

Zoe turned the big limousine onto the airport road. As she made the corner, she saw several emergency vehicles coming from the direction of town. Whether they were headed for the polo club or the airport, she didn't know. All she knew for sure was that she couldn't count on them stopping Mayte from taking off with her Kansas sunflowers. It would be up to her.

Zoe floored the accelerator. It was less than half a mile to the terminal building, but it seemed like ten. As she reached the field, she saw a private jet taxiing toward the head of the runway. A van came out of the gate next to the terminal building. Seeing the lettering on the side, she realized it was a bank vehicle. She waved for the vehicle to stop and lowered her window.

"Where's the painting?" she asked the driver.

"It's on that plane."

That was what she was afraid of. Once the van had cleared the gate, Zoe drove through. From the tarmac she saw the jet aligning itself on the runway, preparing to take off. The engine began to roar and the plane began to move.

Zoe could see that it was now or never. In moments her painting would be gone for good. Again she jammed the accelerator to the floor and raced across the tarmac and taxiway toward the runway. The jet sped toward her as she slammed on the brakes and skidded to a halt in the middle of the runway. Zoe jumped out of the limo as the plane's engine died and the pilot slammed on the brakes.

"Why'd you stop?" Dani screamed.

The pilot, who'd fought mightily to stay on the runway and keep from plowing into the vehicle, looked back at her with round, disbelieving eyes. "If I'd have hit that car, we'd all be dead."

"You could have made it!"

"Maybe or maybe not. You want to take that chance?"

"Yes, goddamn it!" Dani shouted, shoving her gun into the base of the pilot's skull. "Turn this plane around and try it again. This time, if you stop, I'll blow your goddamn brains out!"

"We'll never make it."

"You either try, asshole, or you die right here."

Zoe couldn't believe it when the jet turned around, not a hundred feet from the limo and retreated down the runway. What were they going to do, try again?

Then she heard the sirens and looked over toward the terminal building. Two police cars came through the gate, stopping on the tarmac. As she started waving at them, Zoe heard the thunder of hooves and turned to see a man on horseback come shooting onto the field near the opposite end of the runway from the jet. Her worst fears were realized when she saw that it was Charles Van Biers.

Charles charged down the runway, not pulling up until he reached the limo. He was red in the face and soaked with sweat. His eyes were wide with desperation. Hardly glancing Zoe's way, he did look toward the terminal. Seeing three policemen running across the field, guns drawn, he kicked his pony in the flanks and raced toward the jet, which was once again at the head of the runway, positioning itself.

No sooner had he ridden away than another horseman appeared at the same spot where Charles had surged onto the field. Billy Blue came galloping toward her in pursuit of Charles. As he went flying by her, Zoe saw the determined grimace on his bloodied face.

"Billy!" she cried, hoping he'd stop, hoping he'd let the police handle it, but he was already gone.

Mayte saw the two horsemen galloping furiously toward the plane. She knew who they were.

"What the hell…" Dani said, seeing them coming. She was right behind the pilot, her gun still jammed into the base of his skull.

"I can't take off," he said.

"Run them down."

"Sure I can do that, but then the plane won't fly."

"Fuck!" Dani cried, banging her fist on the back of the seat.

Mayte peered out the windshield of the aircraft as Charles pulled up right in front of them, violently waving his arms. "He wants aboard," she said.

"Screw that," Dani said.

Just then Billy Blue came riding up behind Charles and

lunged, flying through the air and catching him by the shoulders. The two of them went tumbling onto the runway in a heap as the ponies trotted off.

"Now!" Dani screamed at the pilot. "Go!"

Winston shoved the throttle to full power and the jet hurtled forward, over the struggling men. The aircraft lurched as it went over a big bump, then raced toward the limousine, still sitting across the runway.

"We're never going to make it," Winston muttered as they sped along, rapidly gathering speed. "This is suicide."

Mayte wanted the jet to fly over that vehicle ahead as much as she wanted anything in her life, but she didn't want to die. Near certain death was too great a price for freedom, so moving forward, she grabbed Dani Blade by the neck and jerked her away from the pilot.

"Stop this thing!" she cried.

As the two women struggled, the gun went off.

Zoe was in the grass, well off the runway, when she realized the jet was neither going to clear the limo or stop in time. Figuring a crash and an explosion was imminent, she turned and began to run. There was a terrible screeching sound behind her. She glanced over her shoulder and saw the jet swerve violently off the runway, missing the limo, but heading right for her.

Zoe dove headlong into the grass as the aircraft rolled to a stop above her, the landing gear scarcely a foot from her head. She lay for a moment in shock. After a few more heartbeats, she heard the door of the jet open. A man leaped out of the plane and staggered through the grass toward the approaching police officers.

Dazed, her heart racing, Zoe crawled out from under the aircraft and stood. She went over to the others and listened to the pilot explain what had happened.

"They were fighting," he said breathlessly. "The gun went off and the bullet must have got them both."

Zoe tromped on back to the runway. She'd seen Billy and

Charles go down and the plane run over them, but hadn't seen the result. From the runway she was able to determine that they remained in a heap on the asphalt. Neither appeared to be moving.

"Oh my God," she cried, and began running toward them. Billy, the damned fool, had gotten himself killed, she just knew it.

She was dying by the time she reached them, her lungs burning. The two of them were entangled, Charles mostly on top. He seemed as inert as a sack of potatoes, his torso crushed, a trickle of blood oozing from the corner of his mouth.

Billy, half under him, lay with his eyes closed, motionless, his expression serene.

"Oh, Billy," she cried, dropping to her knees next to him. She touched his clammy cheek. "Don't be dead. Please," she said, lowering her face to his chest. She began to sob. "Please be alive."

Then she noticed his chest rise slightly and he gave a little cough. She looked at his face, suddenly hopeful. She waited and his eyes fluttered open. He stared at her, a faint smile forming on his lips.

"Fifty percent is my best offer," he mumbled, wincing. "Take it or leave it."

The laugh she gave was equal part sob. "Are you okay?"

"My damn leg's broken," he said with a groan. "And I think I've got a concussion. Otherwise I feel great."

"I was afraid you were dead," she said, kissing him.

Billy gritted his teeth, obviously in pain. "You better be glad I'm not, Zoe. According to my will, now that Granny is gone, everything, including the Van Gogh, would have gone to the American Association of Rodeo Cowboys."

"I don't want to disillusion you, sweetie, but those sunflowers are mine. Get over it."

Billy winced with pain.

"Do you want me to pull Charles off you?"

"No, I think we better wait. I can't feel my toes in one foot. My leg must be in two pieces."

Zoe looked back toward the terminal building and saw an ambulance enter the field. She stood up and waved. The vehicle turned toward them. She knelt down beside him. "Help is on the way, Billy."

He again gritted his teeth. "So, you're going for the whole enchilada, huh?"

"I'll guarantee you a million dollars for the copy," she said. "That's my best offer."

Billy smiled at her. "Poor Zoe." Then he passed out.

Wednesday
August 16th

Queenstown

After his surgery, they'd pumped Billy so full of pain pills that he'd slept through the night, only semi waking when a nurse came to give him a shot or fiddle with his drip or take his temperature. They'd talked to him every time they'd come into the room, probably because of the concussion. "Can't have you sleep too well and go into a coma," he recalled one saying. "Coma sounds fine to me," he'd replied numbly, only to drift back to sleep.

After breakfast the doctor came to see him and told him he was lucky his fracture was clean. "Otherwise you might have lost the leg. But you need to have your back checked again when you get to the States. There's damage to several vertebrae."

"Nothing to amputate there, I hope."

The doctor laughed. "Just stay out of fights and off horses for a while."

"I kind of like that idea, Doc."

Zoe arrived soon after the doctor left. She'd seen him when

he'd come out of recovery, the night before, but it was all pretty hazy. He'd said something like, "God, you're beautiful," and she'd rewarded him with a kiss. Beyond that, he couldn't remember a thing.

She was in a pale blue T-shirt that matched her eyes, and white cotton pants, her black hair shiny, her mouth prettier and friendlier than it had ever been. Billy had no doubt he was in love.

"I've got some bad news, Billy," she said, sitting on the edge of his bed and taking his hand. "You're an orphan. Simon died of a heart attack at the plantation house sometime yesterday morning, apparently while all the excitement was going on."

"And Charles?"

"Dead."

"I guess I am the last of the breed, then."

"I talked to the FBI agent and asked if she thought there was any chance you might inherit Simon's estate. She wasn't sure, but she said she thought there might be a number of defrauded investors who'd get a crack at whatever was salvaged before you got anything."

"That wouldn't surprise me."

"Oh, and Mayte was in surgery most of the night. They think she'll make it."

"What about the Jamaican's wife?"

"Dani Blade was pronounced dead at the airport."

"Lord, is there anybody left?"

"You and me."

"That's a hopeful sign."

"It's been a traumatic time for this little island, but I'm afraid St. Margaret's in for a few more rough months. The police found an audiotape in Mayte's purse. I don't know the details of what's on it, but it's apparently an embarrassment to the president, Mr. Hurst, and may affect the election. Stay tuned."

Billy shook his head. "To tell you the truth, Zoe, I have a

hankering for the smell of sage in the high desert. These tropical paradises definitely have their downsides.''

''You and I still have some unfinished business, you know.''

''Yeah, I guess we do. How's our Van Gogh, anyway?''

''Safe and sound. It was taken back to bank headquarters and placed in the vault. Raymond Pearson's wife, Eunice, will be arriving this evening with an FBI agent. She has information from Pearson's research files that should help us sort out the confusion over the two paintings. And they think Ray's murder has been solved. Last night a couple of the men who worked for Charles made statements to the police, confirming that he'd clubbed Pearson to death with a polo mallet on the beach. Charles may have gotten his just desserts, but it cost Marie her life,'' Zoe said.

''That's the biggest tragedy of all, as far as I'm concerned. I owe her a lot. She saved my life.''

''I know.''

''And she warned me about you,'' he added.

''Warned you about me?''

''Yeah, she said I couldn't believe a thing you said.''

''That wasn't what she told you, Billy. She said I had a secret and I did. I'm the rightful owner of the Van Gogh, but I also told you that when it really mattered, remember? I gave you the whole story in an attempt to save your butt.''

''You mean that wasn't a ploy to get rid of me so you'd have a clean shot at the sunflowers?''

''No! And I'm offended that you impugn my motives.''

''Zoe, honey, I've offered you half of a hundred-million-dollar painting for nothing. How can you possibly be upset with me? I'm generous to a fault.''

''Yeah, but I'd have to give you half if the original turns out to be mine. The only reason you want that deal is because you know that half of my Kansas sunflowers is better than all of your Nevada copy.''

''No, actually, sweetheart, I did it because I've got a crush on you. But if you're determined to hang on to a hundred percent of your Kansas fake, so be it. Winner buys dinner, how's that?''

"Now that, Mr. Blue, I can agree to.''

Billy drew her hand to his mouth and kissed her fingers. "You know what I'm wondering but will never know?''

"What?''

"I'm wondering if you would have loved me just as much if I'd been the loser instead of the winner of this competition for the Van Gogh.''

"Pardon my French, sweetie," she said, leaning close to his ear, "but you are so full of shit even the cows would be offended.''

Billy smiled broadly. "We'll see about that.''

Thursday
August 17th

World Headquarters,
Victoria International Bank

"**N**ervous?" Billy asked her.

Zoe turned from the window of the limousine as they wound their way up the mountain. "A little. How about you?"

"I've always trusted my grandmother's intuition. She was convinced her Van Gogh was the real McCoy."

"Sorry, but I feel good about that receipt my grandfather got from Roger Faucauld."

"Did it ever occur to you that your granddaddy could have been hoodwinked by the Frenchman?"

"I don't think so, Billy."

He shrugged and moved the leg with the cast slightly to ease the pressure on his hip.

"I hope it wasn't a bad idea for you to do this," Zoe said. "The doctor would have much preferred you wait for a day or two longer."

"Well, the doctor didn't have a date with Zoe Marton and Vincent Van Gogh."

"That's right, our date. I'll have to take you to dinner tonight, won't I?" she said, grinning.

"You know what I like best about this, Zoe? I'll be able to remind you of that smug little grin on your face for the next fifty years."

She laughed.

A few moments later they pulled up in front of the bank building. Andrew came around to open the rear passenger door. Zoe handed him Billy's crutches, then climbed out. The two of them helped Billy out of the limo and got him on his crutches. He felt a bit light-headed but managed to go inside under his own power.

They were shown to the conference room on the executive level where Special Agents Joyce Tsu and Mark Harris waited with Eunice Pearson, a stout, pink-skinned woman of fifty wearing a loose, full-length sundress. The introductions were made and everyone shook hands all around. They sat at the conference table.

"Billy and I are very sorry about your loss, Mrs. Pearson," Zoe said, speaking for them both. "And we appreciate your willingness to discuss the Van Gogh with us."

Eunice Pearson pushed her glasses back up on her nose. "Ray was not without fault in this whole episode and I want to do what I can to make amends. I also feel better now that we know what happened to him and that the people responsible have gotten their due."

"Zoe," Joyce Tsu said, "you and Mr. Blue probably aren't aware that we got a complete statement from Mayte Van Biers this afternoon. She confirmed that Charles Van Biers killed Mr. Pearson on the beach, as we suspected. She actually saw it happen from this building."

"Did she say why he was killed?" Zoe asked.

"Mr. Pearson was blackmailing Simon, threatening to expose information regarding the two sunflower paintings if he didn't get a substantial portion of the bank stock. Mayte did not know what, exactly, the threat was, only that it was very damning and Simon considered it potentially catastrophic."

"Ray never told me what he was up to," Eunice volunteered. "All I knew was that he had some very secretive dealings with Mr. Van Biers."

"I have a good idea what it was," Zoe said. "Simon's lawful claim to my family's painting depended on him being a buyer in good faith, meaning that he was ignorant of the fact that the seller obtained it through extortion and fraud. Ray probably threatened to go public with the fact that Simon knew he was buying contraband, a hot painting. He may even have threatened to track down the lawful owner—me, in other words—if his demands weren't met."

"That's entirely possible," Joyce agreed. "Yesterday we found documentation in a file at the Van Biers residence showing that the original Van Gogh sunflowers were purchased by Simon through Raymond Pearson for three million dollars. The documents state that the unnamed seller was the rightful owner of the painting."

"That's pretty conclusive," Zoe said. "Nobody in their right mind would sell an original Van Gogh for three million dollars unless they knew they were selling stolen property. My grandfather received a bill of sale for that painting. My mother inherited it and some woman, probably the subsequent seller, in effect stole the painting from my father. Ray must have conspired with the woman and Simon to sanitize the transaction. When Ray tried to profit from his inside knowledge, he was murdered."

Billy had been listening carefully and decided now was the time to make his case. "Isn't there another possibility?" he said. "What if Simon discovered that my grandmother's painting was an original Van Gogh? Since he didn't own the painting, but was just holding it as security for a personal loan, he was desperate to find a way to keep it. When Mr. Pearson told him about the copy he'd found—Zoe's painting—Simon bought it and had Mr. Pearson make up a phony bill of sale, showing the copy to be real. He then switched the paintings so that if and when my grandmother ever reclaimed her Van Gogh, Simon could give her the fake and she wouldn't be the wiser. In fact, when I demanded the painting, that's exactly what he tried to do."

"He tried to do that, Billy," Zoe said, "because your grandmother's painting really was the copy. Simon's problem wasn't your grandmother, it was Ray threatening to expose him. That's why Ray was killed."

"If I may comment," Mark Harris interjected, "both theories are plausible. Let me just say that Mrs. Pearson has allowed us to go through Ray's files and in doing so we found a great deal of research information. Apparently Simon had asked Ray to investigate the mysterious Faucauld sunflower painting even before he bought the second one."

"This is true," Eunice said. "As a matter of fact, I went to France with Ray. Although I didn't know the details of what he learned, I do know that he talked to Roger Faucauld's heirs and was allowed to examine Mr. Faucauld's papers. Most of what Ray learned was recorded in documents he kept on his computer. I thought the information might help the FBI determine who was responsible for his murder, so I let them examine the files. You can probably summarize it better than I can, Special Agent Harris," she said, "so why don't you do it?"

Billy hadn't expected this and wasn't sure what it meant. He noticed Zoe seemed uneasy, too, shifting in her seat. He reached over and patted her hand. She gave him a nervous smile.

Harris cleared his throat. "Let me say up front that I don't have a definitive answer to your dilemma," he said, looking at Billy and Zoe in turn, "but I can give you more to consider. As you probably know, Roger Faucauld was a recluse in the last twenty or so years of his life and kept the world in the dark about his relationship with Vincent Van Gogh and the rumored Faucauld sunflowers, the supposed eighth in the Arles series. Faucauld knew Vincent Van Gogh during his stay in Arles and somehow obtained one of his sunflower paintings. Faucauld greatly admired the painting and tried to make an exact copy. After years he felt he'd finally achieved his goal and destroyed all his previous efforts. Ten or fifteen years after Van Gogh's death, when his genius had started being recognized, Faucauld showed the copy he'd made to several prominent dealers, completely fooling them as to the authenticity. These early showings were the basis for the rumors about the Faucauld sunflowers.

"Supposedly Faucauld kept the original under lock and key, never allowing anyone to see it. At the end of the First World War, Faucauld had serious financial problems and his emotional health was troubled. According to his niece, he told the family that he sold the original Van Gogh sunflowers to an American military doctor, presumably your grandfather, Ms. Marton."

"Yes, I have a fax copy of a signed receipt made out by Faucauld himself, which I had my lawyer send yesterday," Zoe said, opening her purse. She put it on the table for everyone to see.

Billy picked up the paper and studied it, then put it down.

"This would be consistent with what Faucauld told the few family members and friends who know about the sunflowers," Harris continued. "He told them he'd sold the original."

"Why don't you consider that conclusive, Special Agent Harris?" Zoe asked, glancing at Billy to see his reaction.

"Because there's more to the story. According to correspondence from Faucauld's wife written shortly after the Second World War, Faucauld had confessed to her that he had in fact switched paintings and given the copy to the American doctor. He knew the original would become quite valuable one day, according to Mrs. Faucauld, but he didn't want the burdens of security, insurance and pressure from his family to sell. At the end of her life she claimed that unbeknownst to everybody but Faucauld himself, the original remained locked away in his studio during the interwar period."

"You're saying it's his niece's word against his wife's word," Zoe said.

"Personally, I'd be inclined to believe the wife," Billy said drolly.

Zoe gave him a playful whack on the arm.

"Mr. Pearson was initially inclined to agree," Harris said, "but it was well known that by the end of his life Roger Faucauld was emotionally unstable, which made the representations he made in his latter years unreliable."

"Did Ray find out how the second painting, the one Faucauld kept, got away from him?" Billy asked.

"Yes. The village Faucauld lived in was active in the resistance during the Second World War and, in retaliation, the Germans ransacked the place, taking the Van Gogh sunflowers in the process. After the war, Faucauld filed a claim against Germany for the loss of his painting, even hired investigators to track it down, but nobody was able to locate the missing Van Gogh. They were unaware that an American G.I. had taken the painting from the possessions of the dead German officer who'd stolen it from Faucauld. The old Frenchman's physical and mental health deteriorated and he soon died, leaving the world uncertain about the truth of the mystery sunflowers."

"That could also explain Faucauld's change of story," Zoe interjected. "Figuring the Germans would be liable for what was taken from him, he wanted his loss to be an original Van Gogh rather than a copy."

"I suppose that's possible," Harris replied. "It's certainly logical."

"We could debate this forever," Billy said. "I say we get down to brass tacks. The bottom line is that nobody can prove anything based on the evidence, the paperwork we've got. Mr. Pearson could have faked his bill of sale to Simon, and Faucauld could have faked his bill of sale to Zoe's grandfather. All we know for sure is that one of the paintings came to the States after World War I and the other after World War II. Zoe's claim is to the first and my claim is to the second. Do we agree on that?"

"Yes," Zoe said. "We can agree on that."

"Okay, here's my next question. If the two paintings were

sitting side by side, is it possible to tell which is the original and which is the copy?''

"Experts can tell, yes," Zoe said.

"Can you tell?"

"I believe I could."

"When we saw both of them the other day, could you see a difference?"

"I didn't study them carefully, Billy, but I feel fairly certain the one displayed in Simon's office was the original Van Gogh."

"Okay, ladies and gentleman," Billy said, "we can solve the mystery here and now. As Zoe knows, my grandmother marked the painting that hung in her shop, the one Simon took for security. I know where the mark is on the canvas and what it says. Zoe, if I can find the words *The Blue Bear, Elko, Nevada* on the painting that you say is the original, will you agree that it's mine?"

"Yes, but if the mark is on the copy, that would mean the original is mine."

"Both paintings are downstairs in the vault," he said. "If somebody can dig up a bottle of ammonia, we can find out just who hoodwinked who."

"Ammonia?" Harris said.

"Yes," Billy replied. "Granny labeled her Van Gogh with invisible ink. I'm going to make it visible."

Zoe had been so certain that her grandfather had brought home a Van Gogh original from France that she'd devoted her life to proving it—and to righting the wrong perpetrated against her family. She knew Billy to be well meaning, but she also thought his convictions were based on wishful thinking. After their conversation upstairs in the conference room, she could see that the odds had narrowed and she wasn't quite as confident as she had been before.

As she, Billy, Eunice Pearson and the two FBI agents watched the security men unwrapping the two paintings, Zoe wondered if there could be some basis for Billy's self-assurance that she wasn't aware of. Could Simon possibly have told him something, or was Billy bluffing?

When she caught his eye, he gave her a wink and smiled. Zoe did her best to respond in kind, but the truth was she felt like throwing up. How could a hundred million dollars be riding on this parlor game?

Once the paintings were unwrapped, the security men placed them on twin easels against the wall. Eunice gasped at the sight of them side by side.

"Incredible," she murmured.

Because of the slight difference in the frames, Zoe knew which had been the painting that had hung in Simon's office. It was the one on the left. She would have known, even if they hadn't watched as the copy, Billy's painting, had been removed from the vault.

"Okay," Billy said to her. "Which is the original Van Gogh?"

Zoe went over and examined both paintings carefully. She looked at the signature, the brush strokes, the color. There were subtle differences, but she was confident that Vincent Van Gogh had painted the canvas on the left and that Roger Faucauld had painted the one on the right. "This one," she said, pointing.

"Which one has my grandmother's mark on it, Zoe?"

"This one," she said, pointing to the painting on the right. "Do you want me to test that one first?"

She nodded. "Yes."

Billy had the security men put the painting facedown on the worktable and asked them to remove the paper backing. Then he hobbled over to the table and sat on the stool they'd brought him. Zoe swallowed hard as she watched him carefully examine the back of the canvas. Using pliers and a screwdriver, he removed three tacks from the lower left corner of the wood stretcher and bent back a flap of canvas.

"This is where the mark would be," he said. "Hand me the ammonia, please."

Zoe's hands trembled nervously as Billy saturated a sponge

with the liquid and proceeded to wave it back and forth under the flap of canvas. She craned her neck to see if some special mark or letter would appear.

"I'm not up on my stenography," Joyce Tsu said. "What's the ink?"

"Copper sulfate," Billy replied as he continued to wave the sponge under the canvas.

"And ammonia fumes are the reagent."

"This is what my grandmother told me."

"It's been a while since I studied chemistry," Tsu said, "but that sounds right to me."

Billy dabbed the sponge in the liquid again and continued to wave it under the canvas. He examined it once more and shook his head. "Nothing." He motioned for Zoe to take a close look.

He was right, there was nothing there.

"Do you want to test the other painting?" he asked.

"Of course."

Billy smiled. "I can't blame you."

He signaled for the security men to bring the other painting over. It was laid on its face on the worktable and the procedure was repeated. Once the flap of canvas was loosened, Billy lifted the sponge from the bowl, then stopped.

"I'll give you another chance, Zoe," he said. "Fifty-fifty. If my grandmother's mark is on this one, it's mine and I'll give you half the value. If there isn't a mark, it's yours and you'll have to give me half the value." He turned to the others. "You see, I'm trying to find out what the lady thinks of me."

"Billy," Zoe said, "I'd be a fool to make a deal now. For all I know, you tested the wrong part of the other painting. The mark could be in a different corner. Or your grandmother may not have marked it at all. I mean, just because you said she did doesn't mean it's true. You could have made up this whole thing in hopes that I'd fold and you'd get fifty million dollars for nothing."

He studied her, looking her square in the eye. "That's a theory," he said, "but it could be just the other way around.

What it comes down to is if you trust me. Am I a man of honor or am I a scoundrel? What do you think of me, Zoe? That's really the question, isn't it?''

She thought for a moment. "Let's say you are honest and that you're pretty confident, if not certain, that the original Van Gogh has your grandmother's mark. It makes no sense that you'd want to give away half now. Why not take the hundred million for yourself?''

"Two reasons. One is I care an awful lot about what you think of me—really think of me—and I want to know. The other is that if we're fifty-fifty partners, I figure there's a chance our relationship could stretch out, say, fifty years. At least I'd like to think you'd give me a chance.''

Zoe smiled with embarrassment, glancing at the others. Eunice Pearson actually had tears in her eyes.

"Well, sweetheart," Billy said, "we're at that point where, as my old rodeo buddy Cy Krebs used to say, the rubber hits the road. What kind of man do you think I am?''

Zoe looked into his eyes and he looked into hers. Logic told her that a man she'd known for less than a week wouldn't give her fifty million dollars because he found her kind of cute. The odds were that it was a trick. But on the other hand, fact just might be stranger than fiction. Billy was a crazy cowboy. He was an original. And he was right, it really did come down to what she thought of him, as a man and a person.

"Would you like a little time to think about it?" he asked. "It's a pretty big decision. It can wait a day.''

"No," she said. "I've made my decision.''

Billy drew a long slow breath and his eyes shimmered. "What'll it be?''

She stared at him for a long, long time, all the while her heart hammering. Then she told him. "I'll share it with you, Billy. Fifty-fifty.''

He smiled, but not so broadly as she might have expected. Actually, his eyes glistened and a tear escaped the corner of his eye. "I thank you for the vote of confidence.''

He dabbed the sponge in the ammonia again and held it

near the canvas. For at least thirty seconds nothing happened. But slowly a mark began to form, then discernible letters. Billy moved aside so she could see better. It read, "The Blue Bear, Elko, Nevada."

Zoe threw her arms around him. Billy had won, but so had she.

Biloxi Plantation

They sat on the bench in the garden, watching the sun set into the Caribbean Sea. His leg was propped up on a box and it throbbed a little, but he felt better than he had in weeks. Billy held her hand, playing with her fingers.

"I have to admit," he said, "until you said the words *fifty-fifty* I wasn't sure what you were going to do."

"Obviously I thought more of you than you did of me, Mr. Blue."

"So, you did figure I was a man of honor."

"The honest truth?"

"Yeah," he said, nodding. "Lay it on me."

"I was pretty sure there'd be a mark somewhere. When you knew the composition of the ink and reagent, and Special Agent Tsu confirmed it, it made sense, so I figured the invisible-ink business was for real."

"Because no rodeo cowboy would be smart enough to make that up—is that it?"

"I wouldn't put it quite that way, Billy."

"I could have known there was a mark, but figured it was on the copy," he said. "And I could have checked the wrong corner of the canvas intentionally."

"I thought about that. But, after hearing the story of Roger Faucauld, I realized that my conviction about the Kansas sunflowers was really prejudice—misplaced passion over the justness of my claim. When I put myself in Faucauld's shoes, I decided that giving my grandfather the copy and keeping the original made sense."

"Zoe, that meant he was giving away his own work."

"Yes, but the reason he copied the sunflowers in the first place was because he loved the painting so much. And would he have scoured Germany for a copy, even if it was one he'd made himself? By the 1940s a Van Gogh original was quite valuable, don't forget. No, I think probably not. He was after the original, Billy. He was after yours."

"You're saying your decision had nothing to do with your feelings about me," he said, genuinely disappointed.

"I didn't say that. In fact, my biggest problem was trying to figure out why, when you were about to do that second test, you stopped and offered me half the deal. At that point you had to have known the original was yours."

"I figured it probably was, yeah."

"So, why did you give me fifty million dollars?"

He reached over and brushed her cheek with the back of his fingers. "I guess I wanted you to believe in me, Zoe. But for that to happen, I had to prove I was worthy."

"But fifty million dollars..."

"Well, it worked, didn't it? You might have had other reasons for taking the deal, too, but ultimately it came down to whether you believed I was honorable or not. I mean, neither of us was absolutely positive that mark would be on the second painting. Hell, my grandmother wasn't sure the ink would work after all these years. I took a chance and so did you. Admit it, Zoe. Say the words. You trusted me."

Zoe leaned over and kissed him on the lips. "You're cute, Billy Blue, but not a very good listener. I told you from the very beginning. I'm inscrutable. Remember?"

Smiling, he continued to toy with her fingers, staring out at the sea as he did. The pinks, oranges and violets on the horizon were intensifying. It wasn't the high desert, but it was damned pretty. He wondered if Zoe would want to buy the Biloxi Plantation with him, maybe as a winter home. The name would have to be changed, of course, but she'd have ideas about that, he was sure.

"Billy, aren't you going to say anything?"

He glanced over at her, taking a moment to savor the ornery cant of her mouth. She really was an incredible woman. Just looking at her gave him enormous pleasure.

"Well?"

"Sweetheart," he said, "inscrutable I can live with. Trust me."

Author Note

All stories are a blend of fact and fiction—that is, real people, real objects and real events on the one hand, and imaginary people, imaginary objects and imaginary events on the other. Vincent Van Gogh was real, of course, and he did create a series of paintings called the "Arles Sunflowers." While there has been some debate among the experts about the authenticity of some work attributed to Van Gogh, Roger Faucauld and the "Faucauld Sunflower" painting, which is at the heart of this story, alas, are products of the author's imagination.

R.J. Kaiser

R.J. KAISER

66614	GLAMOUR PUSS	___ $6.50 U.S.	___ $7.99 CAN.
66625	FRUITCAKE	___ $5.99 U.S.	___ $6.99 CAN.
66510	JANE DOE	___ $5.99 U.S.	___ $6.99 CAN.
66460	PAYBACK	___ $5.99 U.S.	___ $6.99 CAN.

(limited quantities available)

TOTAL AMOUNT	$_____
POSTAGE & HANDLING	$_____
($1.00 for one book; 50¢ for each additional)	
APPLICABLE TAXES*	$_____
TOTAL PAYABLE	$_____

(check or money order—please do not send cash)

MIRA®